REINCARNAGE:
MAXIMUN CARNAGE

RYAN HARDING &
JASON TAVERNER

DEATH'S HEAD PRESS

an imprint of Dead Sky Publishing, LLC
Miami Beach, Florida
www.deadskypublishing.com

ISBN: 9781639510115

Second Edition

Cover Art: Alex McVey

Book Layout: Lori Michelle
www.TheAuthorsAlley.com

AUTHORS' NOTE

Reincarnage was originally published in 2015. This is an updated version, where we have made some minor additions and corrections to the text. After the novel, you will find three bonus chapters. We had discussed writing them a couple of years ago, and when Death's Head Press contacted us about a new edition, we had our opportunity.

This is *Reincarnage: Maximum Carnage.*

Ryan Harding
Jason Taverner
June 2021

I.

ADAM AWOKE FROM a pretty awesome dream. He was in line at the post office and the girl behind the counter was topless. *How are they losing so much money every year?* he wondered. She'd been blonde, but somehow faceless, as if he used up all his dream power on her absurdly endowed chest. What was that, an F cup? He had a package for her, all right, and a potentially hazardous one at that.

"Can I help the next in line?" she asked.

He shuffled forward, noting the emergence of a smile on her otherwise blank face.

"Don't miss the shuttle, Adam," she said. "You know what day it is, don't you?"

He didn't, but knew he wasn't going to miss the shuttle since there was about to be a blast-off in his pants. He awoke as the urge threatened to reach the point of no return, and found himself face-down on the carpet. A shame he never actually touched her, but it was for the best. Splooging yourself in a hotel room with your parents wasn't very baller.

What the hell was he doing on the floor, though?

The carpet was thick and green, and might have been new when atomic bomb drills were in vogue. His mom would have one word for it—*tacky*—but Pamela Kirshoff hadn't seen it yet, and until now neither had he. This wasn't their room at the Coral Beach Inn.

Adam lifted his head from the carpet, wincing at the sharp pain in his skull. He wiped a generous helping of drool from the corner of his mouth as he surveyed the room.

No, definitely not the right room. There was only one bed, upon which his parents lay fully clothed. Adam remembered dressing for bed last night, but not in an orange shirt and red shorts, which he wouldn't have worn together in the first place. They wouldn't pass his mother's inspection if he tried.

"Mom?" he said. His voice sounded weak.

A painting hung above the bed, a mountain range with a blanket of pine trees. The décor did not suggest the ocean. The Coral Beach Inn had a sailboat painting and seashell knick knacks. This room looked like the kind of place a traveling salesman would eat a gun.

Adam had been stoked for this family outing, and two days in he wasn't disappointed in the least. He'd never seen so many girls in bikinis. It had been a solid forty-eight hours of voyeuristic splendor. He wore the darkest sunglasses he could find and watched the skin show with a sense of awe and desperate longing. In his mind he approached the hottest ones, told them a bunch of absurd lies about himself ("I'm the most popular guy at school and I'm already being recruited by Duke"), then slipped away with them under the pier and brought them all to orgasm two or three times in about as many minutes. In reality, he'd yet to strike up a conversation with a single girl and had beat off with suntan lotion about three times. Zero phone numbers or email addresses and zero chance of getting skin cancer on his junk.

He cleared his throat. "Mom? Dad?"

Not panicked yet. His parents were here, so nothing could be too amiss, could it? If not awake, they at least didn't appear hurt. The room thing was weird, but hardly perilous unless a tacky carpet was somehow fatal.

REINCARNAGE: MAXIMUM CARNAGE

Adam used the edge of the bed to pull himself up. He waited for vertigo to pass. A tableside lamp offered weak light. There'd be a Bible in the drawer. He thought his mom had to be one of the only people in the world who would take it out and actually read it. Kind of surprising she didn't bring her own from home, a heavily self-annotated book which usually factored into his lessons at some point. It was always good to get away from the house and home schooling in general.

Why was it so dark if he slept through the night? Adam stumbled over to the window, aware of an absence of crashing waves in the distance. They had been a constant in Malcasa Point, like rolling static, but here it was dead silent. He flipped the curtain aside. He may as well have stared into a black hole. He framed his hands over his eyes to block out the weak glare and peered outside.

Nothing.

His sluggishness vanished altogether. Adam hurried back to the bed. "Mom! Dad! Wake up!" He shook them both.

His dad stirred, opened his eyes in slits. "What? What time is it?"

"I don't know. Something's wrong." He patted the pocket of his shorts for his cell phone—something his parents provided him more for the convenience of tracking him than the benefit of his meager social life—and didn't find it. It was nowhere in the room.

No bags, he realized. There was a tall armoire and a dresser with an ancient-looking TV. He'd only seen its equal in the junk room at his friend Kevin's house. They covertly hooked it up to watch some prehistoric porno videos (relics from Kevin's father) on something called a "Betamax."

Adam pulled open both doors. A few wire hangers rattled around, carrying nothing.

His mother stirred. "Ed? What's going on?" She

already sounded panicked, but that was normal for her. "Where are we?"

Adam's stomach did an elevator dive. *They don't know how we got here either.*

His dad swung his legs to the floor and massaged his forehead. "Everyone calm down." He sounded annoyed, like they awoke him early on a day off.

Adam shared a frightened look with his mother. Her brow furrowed after a moment. "Why are you wearing those shorts with that shirt?"

He pulled the shirt down a little, as if to cover the shorts. "I didn't put these on."

Did she think he'd end up on the news, interviewed in clashing colors for the world to condemn?

His father looked around. "Where the hell are we?"

"This isn't the Coral Beach Inn."

"Thanks for the news flash, Pamela." His dad smoothed his rumpled shirt and frowned. The buttons were out of alignment. He undid a few and put them through their proper slots. It was a white shirt over yellow pants Adam wouldn't have worn in a million years. Like something from the special Douche line of golf wear. It wasn't the shirt his dad usually wore with them, a much darker shade of Douche.

Adam's mom wore a white shirt with orange capris, something she at least might have chosen on her own.

Why do we all look like we're shooting a Tide commercial?

"Adam, check if we're locked in." He said it without concern, as though asking for a socket wrench.

Adam swallowed. He considered checking earlier, but was too scared to find out they were indeed trapped. He'd hoped a simple explanation would present itself first.

He looked back to see his dad lift the receiver from a blocky-looking telephone on the nightstand. The handset had a red bulb for message alerts. He listened, tapped the prongs a few times, then slammed it down as if to punish it for defying him.

"Hell." He still didn't sound worried, only greatly inconvenienced.

Adam tried to imagine what they could say if it worked. *We're at a hotel we don't remember checking into . . . please send a SWAT team!*

He hurried the last steps to the door and checked the peephole before his father asked why he was gawking. He expected the blackness of the window but there was light and an empty hallway. He turned the knob. It clicked as the lock disengaged, and he pulled the door all the way open.

"It's unlocked," he said, suddenly lightheaded again. He slipped the chain through the crack so it wouldn't shut completely. Just in case.

"Thank God," his mom said. She pushed herself up from the bed as Adam turned back to them. "Maybe we can find someone who knows what's going on here."

His dad gave the phone the evil eye. "We'll find someone, all right. Someone needs their ass sued six ways from Sunday over this."

His mom winced. She didn't like that kind of language.

"I don't think we're at the beach anymore," Adam said. "You can't hear the ocean. You can't even see anything out the window."

His dad scowled and crossed over to the window, ear angled toward the glass as if to listen for a coin he'd tossed into the black hole. He pushed at the sill. It didn't budge. Adam thought of the blackness beyond and had the crazy thought they were in outer space and would be sucked right into the vacuum if his dad opened it.

That's stupid. What'd they do, strap a rocket to the hotel and blast us off?

His dream came back to him at that moment, unbidden, the buxom woman with no face. *Don't miss the shuttle, Adam. You know what day it is, don't you?*

Actually, he didn't know.

His mom walked over to where he stood and flipped on the light of the bathroom to his left. She peered in and checked a couple of drawers. All empty. What they wore was apparently all they kept of their belongings. He mourned the loss of his iPod. He'd had the complete discography of Busta Kapp, which Kevin downloaded from a torrent for him, in addition to four hundred other songs.

His dad thumped the window sill with the flat of his hand, as if it had conspired with the telephone. He turned away from it with a look of disgust.

"Did you see anything?" Adam asked.

"I think it was painted over."

He felt irrational relief over that—*not orbiting the planet after all*—but it was quickly tempered by unease over why someone would have blackened the window in the first place.

"Hey!"

Adam flinched. Someone was out in the hallway.

II.

ADAM'S DAD TOOK the lead outside. The voice belonged to a broad-shouldered man in loud green chinos with a look of bewilderment to mirror their own.

"Sorry, didn't mean to startle you," he said. "I'm Nathan, and I have no idea how the hell I got here. I'm guessing it's the same for you three."

He extended a hand and shook with Adam's dad. It struck Adam as funny that such social etiquette continued even in circumstances like these.

"Ed Kirshoff. This is my wife Pamela and son Adam."

Nathan nodded at them. "This is the craziest thing I ever heard of. Where are we?"

"No idea. Were you at the beach?"

Nathan cocked an eyebrow. "No, I'm afraid I don't get out to the beaches of St. Louis very often."

"*St. Louis?*"

"Yeah, I was on business."

Adam's mom couldn't take her eyes off Nathan's pants, as if to say, *You were trying to do business in* those? "We were on vacation in Malcasa Point," she said.

Another door clicked open a few rooms past Nathan and the head of a tall black man craned around the edge, as if to assess their threat potential. He muttered something back toward the room and held the door as a woman joined him. She had a much lighter shade of skin, but also looked to be African American. The man wore long green athletic pants of a flashy material and a lime T, a colorful complement to her lavender shirt and cream slacks.

"Stop me if you've heard this one," Nathan said. "You woke up in a hotel room with no idea how you got there—"

"Stop."

Nathan nodded. "Same here."

"I'm Marcus." The fabric of his pants hissed as he joined the group. "This is Suzanne."

Suzanne offered a little wave.

They were probably closer to Adam's age than his parents', but not by much.

"We also figured out we're from different places," Adam added.

Nathan looked annoyed, as if he should be the one to dispense all the known facts, but said nothing.

"Y'all ain't from Memphis?"

"We were vacationing in California," his dad said.

"St. Louis," Nathan said. "What's the last thing you remember? Any of you."

"We were in our room watching TV," his mom said. "Next thing we knew, we were here."

"Yeah, pretty much the same thing for me."

"We weren't at a hotel," Suzanne said. "We were driving to my parents'. We stopped to pick up a cake for my dad's birthday. I don't think we got there."

"Nah," Marcus said. "Cuz I don't remember any of that passive-aggressive bullshit we usually hear from your moms."

Adam's mom tensed, as if profanity was new to him and would instantly corrupt him. He heard worse just last night while his parents watched the regrettable movie of some Nicholas Sparks book, because Adam poked in an ear bud from his iPod and jammed Busta Kapp's "Bitchez Don't Be Knowin'." He didn't need subtitles to know the paramour dude always died at the end. Maybe the predictability of the movie put them all into a coma, allowing their transport.

"I'm not even sure what day it is," Nathan said. "When's the last one you remember?"

"Tuesday," Adam said immediately. He'd seen some hot blonde twins rollerblading and thought about saying, "Hey, is this Two for Tuesday?" But it was more like Mute for Tuesday because he never opened his mouth.

"Yeah, had tickets to the Grizzlies and Celtics and got to go to a birthday party instead." Marcus rolled his eyes.

"I told you three weeks ago," Suzanne said.

"I know. I just bet there wasn't nobody at the game who vanished. Except maybe Rajon Rondo."

Adam's mom cringed at this breach of contract with proper grammar. If there was one thing she wanted to instill in his studies besides a greater role of religion, it was a respect for the proper use of language. He wasn't sure what would offend her most about "Bitchez Don't Be Knowin'" between the profanity and grammar.

Nathan ignored the exchange. "Okay, so it's probably Wednesday. No cell phones, right?"

His dad shook his head. "No. All gone, and the room phone is dead."

"Ours too," Marcus said.

"Did you see anything out your window?" Adam's father asked.

Marcus and Suzanne shook their heads.

"Nothing," Nathan said. "It looked painted over."

Eels squirmed in Adam's guts. The blackened windows again. What was going on?

"We can break one if we have to, but no need to announce we're up just yet if no one's watching. Let's look around. We're not learning anything just standing here."

"Are you sure it's safe?" his mom asked.

"Why not? We weren't locked in and we're not hurt, are

we? What about you, Aaron? Didn't wake up with a burning asshole, did you?"

"Wh—" The words died in Adam's mouth. He barely noticed being called by the wrong name. His mom turned white as a sheet beside him. Marcus glared expectantly, though Adam wasn't sure if the question irritated him or he just really wanted to know the answer. He finally mumbled, "No."

"Good, then we're doing this," Nathan said. "Follow me."

His dad seemed to regain some of his earlier resolve. "There's a lawsuit in this, I guarantee it."

It earned him a funny look from Marcus, who shared it with Suzanne. They both shrugged.

Adam's mother took his hand and they followed his dad and Nathan. It was a bit embarrassing, picturing Marcus and Suzanne sharing another look and shrug behind him, but he knew it made her feel a little better and it wasn't all bad for him either, even if sixteen was a bit old to cling to his mommy. They spent a lot more time together than most mothers and sons because of the home schooling. Whatever occasional grievances he had about that situation, at least he was safe. Kevin told him last semester some kid got jumped in the bathroom and taken out on a stretcher with blood running from his ear.

He narc'd on Jordy O'Bannon for having brass knuckles. Found out real fast that Jordy didn't need 'em to put someone on Front Street, though. No bullshit.

Dad, of course, said the parents should sue the school's ass. He probably wished Adam went there so he'd be at risk of the sort of random violence that could put Ed Kirshoff on Easy Street with that lucrative lawsuit that was always just over the rainbow.

The doors were shut on both sides of the hallway. A few had DO NOT DISTURB placards, but knocks went unanswered and no one else emerged from any rooms.

REINCARNAGE: MAXIMUM CARNAGE

They found an elevator, though nothing happened when they pushed the up and down buttons. The corridor ended in a metal door with an EXIT sign and a sliver of a window with an encased grid of chicken wire. Nathan angled to see through the pane without putting his face up to it, momentarily obstructing an arrow painted on the wall to indicate the door, its triangular tip poking out behind him just below shoulder level. Satisfied of no threat, he at last pushed the bar. Adam expected it to be locked, but it opened on the stairwell.

They received an instant education in how woefully unprepared they were for anything as they froze stiff at the sound of approaching footsteps from above, too many to be one person. Two women paused on the landing one flight up. One was in her thirties, a blonde with ponytailed hair. She stood a head taller than her companion, a slightly older woman in a bright red pantsuit. The blonde relaxed somewhat at the sight of Adam. The other stared wildly at the group like they were supernatural manifestations. She clutched the blonde's arm either for support or to launch her as a projectile at the awful ghost people.

"Did you see anything upstairs?" Nathan asked.

The calmer one answered. "It was just us. Do you know where we—"

Marcus cut her off. "None of us know what the hell's going on."

"Do you two . . . know each other?" Nathan said this with only the slightest pause. Adam wondered the same thing.

"What? No." She indicated the woman in the red pantsuit. "I heard her wandering in the hallway for help. Her name's Annette. I'm Eliza."

Nathan only introduced himself, leaving Adam's dad to (correctly) identify the family. He showed no reaction to "Adam" instead of "Aaron." Marcus and Suzanne offered their names, which Eliza and Annette evidently took as their cue to descend the last steps and join them. Annette relinquished Eliza's arm but kept a pincer grip on the sleeve of Eliza's lime green shirt. This struck Adam as lame until his mom squeezed his hand and he remembered his own situation.

Eliza somehow managed to wear gray jogging pants, which seemed positively subdued compared to the primary color wheel everyone else represented. She came from the northeast, in Bridgeport. "It must have happened when I was out running," she explained. "But I don't remember."

Adam couldn't help noticing how well she filled out her lime shirt, even in all his anxiety.

I wouldn't mind seeing her out for a jog.

"I was shopping," Annette offered. "I think. Or picking up my prescription. No. No, I never got it. Oh God. I don't know. I don't know."

She didn't mention where she lived and no one asked. Adam wasn't sure she'd know that either. Up close he figured she must be in her mid-forties, a thin woman with chestnut hair, right around the age of Nathan and his parents. She dropped Eliza's sleeve when she talked and started fidgeting. She reminded him of a bird bouncing through grass, head in a perpetual swivel. His mom would have warned his head would pop off if he kept doing that. Her pantsuit seemed to be her choice rather than the sort of fashion tragedy which befell Adam.

"Are there any more floors up there?" Nathan asked.

"No." Eliza gestured up the stairs. "Ours was the top."

"Okay. Well, let's see what we can find downstairs."

They trudged down to the next landing, Adam more self-conscious about holding his mom's hand as their numbers grew. He assumed they would go straight to ground level, but Nathan held them up on the second floor.

"I think I heard something."

They listened when all their shuffling ceased, and sure enough, they heard faint voices through the door.

"Could be others like us," Adam's dad said, barely above a whisper.

"Yeah, and could be those mystery motherfuckers who brought us here," Marcus said.

Adam's mom made a strained sound in her throat which Marcus probably mistook for the prospect of a confrontation.

"I doubt they'd bring us here and let us get the jump on them," Nathan pointed out.

"Who says we'll even know when we see 'em? There could be a mole. We don't know what kinda game they're playing with us."

This brought them all up short. Suspicious glances spread. Adam took the opportunity to peer through the small pane of glass. He saw three more people, nobody seemingly armed.

"They look like us," he reported. "I bet they don't know how they got here either."

"Shit," Marcus said, making it at least two syllables. "How they gonna steal this many people with no one noticing?"

"They're not armed," Adam added.

"I ain't either, but I wouldn't tell nobody they was safe around me."

"We're going," Nathan announced in a normal voice and shouldered open the door.

The three people—two men and a woman— whirled around at the noise. Adam had a nightmare flash of someone hoisting a gun after all and shredding them, but they were empty handed.

Nathan held up his arms. "Sorry for the dramatic entrance, but I'm guessing we all have something in common."

Adam noticed Marcus fixing Nathan with his intense stare, perhaps less than thrilled with the haphazard way he decided a course of action without debate and risked all their lives. Nathan's recklessness didn't seem like the hallmark of someone who could keep his head in a crisis.

Nathan went through their roster for the new people, managing to get Adam's name right this time. He had to be corrected when he introduced Suzanne as Susan.

The first of the three was a beefy guy with a widow's peak named Lawrence, the only one among them to wear fairly restrained colors, a pink shirt but gray slacks. He had a film of sweat on his brow, though the temperature in here seemed neutral to Adam. Not potential "mole" material, but maybe that was the point. He fit into the age demographic of Marcus and Suzanne.

The other man seemed a much better possibility as a double agent. His name (he claimed) was Patrick. Probably around forty with a receding hairline, but still had most of his brown hair, rather neatly parted for a guy supposedly abducted. He had a stare sharp enough to blind anyone who made eye contact. He wasn't saying much. He showed more personality in his navy blue shoes. Khaki pants and a white shirt completed the ensemble.

Lastly there was Gin, a dark-haired woman of Asian descent. Not stacked like Eliza, but she was gorgeous. Adam saw some pretty girls at the beach this week, but Gin made them look like flaming dogshit stomped out on somebody's porch. She was younger, too. Not his age, but definitely early twenties.

With my luck, she's the mole and she'll slit my throat while I'm sleeping.

It was stupid to think of her like that anyway in this situation, but what he wouldn't give to know more about her. She looked to be a victim of the fashion assassin as well, in a yellow top with red jeans.

"What is *up* with these clothes?" Marcus said.

"I think they brought us here to shoot a Tide commercial," Adam said, hoping to get a laugh from Gin. No dice from her, or anyone else for that matter.

Oh right. We're all terrified.

Marcus inspected his green pants. "I didn't even know I still had these. Ain't worn them since high school and sure as hell didn't pack them for her parents'."

"Yeah, I didn't choose mine either," Adam quickly chimed in, lest Gin think him an idiot.

"Hey, what happened down there?" Suzanne pointed past the group to the opposite end of the hallway.

"We hadn't made it down there yet," Gin said.

They walked down en masse, awkwardly clustered together for strength in numbers. The lights on either side of the hall had burned out down here, offering only the faintest hint of what Suzanne spotted.

Nathan reached it first. It seemed to Adam like he hurried to do it. "There's a break in the wall."

"A break? It looks like Arnold Schwarzenegger smashed through it," Lawrence said, sounding mildly out of breath even from just the short stroll. Adam doubted they grabbed him while he was out jogging.

The hole was indeed the height and size of a very large man, with lots of broken plaster scattered along the floor and inside the room beyond the wall. A hint of light pushed through the opening. It was room 237.

"Want to check it out?" Eliza asked.

"Might as well," Adam's dad said. "We've been safe so far."

Yeah, Adam thought. *Until we're not.*

Nathan crouched and leaned through the hole. "Yeah, this is really weird."

Three people said some kind of variation of "What is it?" at the same time.

Nathan didn't answer, just stepped through. Adam saw what he meant soon enough. Someone had "broken" into the room because the door was barricaded. The armoire was tipped over and pushed in front of it, with the dresser shoved behind that as well.

Adam looked back at the special Hulk-smash entrance. *For all the good it did them.*

"Someone came and took them," Annette said, eyes ever moving, door, wall, hole, floor, ceiling, repeat.

"Maybe," Nathan said.

"Maybe?" Marcus echoed. "You think security kicked through the wall and threw 'em out for not paying the bill?"

"We need more light," Eliza said and flipped on the bathroom switch. It seemed like Annette started screaming even before the end of the *thock* sound.

The bathroom walls looked practically painted with dried blood.

III.

LAWRENCE WATCHED THEIR reactions with thinly veiled bemusement.

Eliza recoiled in horror, hand raised to her mouth as she sucked air in a bizarre parody of a gasp. Annette screamed. Suzanne broke a long silence with "*Marcussss*" and predictably he took the spotlight and ran with it. "Yo, man, this is messed *up*." Not exactly the macho "look how badass I am, fool" statement Lawrence expected of him. Annette screamed. Ed ordered his wife and son not to look. Annette screamed. Nathan took two quick steps in his stylish black and white brogues and clasped a hand over her mouth. *Nathan: man of action! Huzzah!*

Lawrence watched them through the hole, taking it all in, assessing, surveying, deducing, theorizing.

Annette angrily shoved free, but it was clear who decided to break the contact. She straightened her gaudy red pantsuit as if he left her disheveled. "Brute."

"Keep it together," Action Man stage whispered, so everyone could acknowledge the arrival of their born leader.

Annette opened her mouth, then opted to fume silently.

Three of the four vanity bulbs remained intact. Two still worked but only one had steady light, the flickering bulb providing a horrific strobe-like effect. Lawrence almost laughed—the all-too-perfect set-up like the first

17

scare in a haunted house, designed not to overwhelm so much as set the stage for the inevitable escalation of terror. The German word *demontage* came to mind, as someone had been dismantled; maybe several someones. Lawrence imagined them rag-dolled about the room stamping bloody depressions into drywall, shattering the vanity mirror, knocking shelves off the wall.

"Someone got their ass *wrecked* in here," Marcus sagely observed.

Or at least someone (Loonatik411, maybe?) wanted them to think so. Take a gallon of syrup, Hyacinth punch mix, chunks of rubber or foam, and spread liberally—voila! Instant murder scene. No body needed, just pieces that could have once been a body with a little imagination and dodgy lighting. The room smelled of mildew and stale air and mothballs, but not death or rotting flesh or even blood. Granted, he stood in the hall outside, but wouldn't decay have permeated the hallway, too?

Not real, you rubes! Let's move on to the next stage so we can get the hell out of here.

Lawrence seemed to be the only one in on the joke. Well, maybe the shifty looking Patrick knew the deal. He reminded Lawrence of the painting in a cartoon haunted house where the eyes moved, because otherwise his face gave up nothing. He sized him up as the chief competition if this were a game of wits. Judging by the Tide joke, Adam seemed to have his shit together, too—or he was showing off for Eliza the buxom jogger. Jury still out on that one.

Patrick and the Japanese chick also stayed in the hallway. Ed pointed/pushed his family toward the "exit," and Lawrence nearly bumped Patrick as he backed away to give them room. Mr. Personality deftly avoided contact by sliding to the left. His bright white T-shirt didn't blend into the shadows as well as his intentions.

"Watch your head, mom." Adam came through the wall first with his mother literally in tow; she would not relinquish the boy's hand. If she did, Lawrence figured it would only be to gather the fallen pieces of wood and drywall to build them a makeshift shelter.

"You a gamer?" Lawrence whispered to Adam.

Adam looked at his mom as if deferring to her for an answer, an answer in itself: no violent games for this kid. *No, you cannot play Mario Kart! There are bombs in that game!*

"What did you say?" Pamela's voice trembled.

"Nothing." Lawrence quickly stepped away to make Patrick a buffer between himself and mother hen.

As soon as everyone filed back into the hallway, Nathan cut through the mumbling and disparate conversations with an elevated, stern voice. "We need to keep it together." He had the air of an upper management type who took his authority for granted. He held both hands aloft with palms outward as he spoke, moving them forward slightly as if pushing his ideas outward to the others.

Or delivering the Sermon on the Mount. Is that #3 in 101 *Power Gestures for the Aspiring Alpha Dog?*

"Last thing we need is everyone running in different directions," Nathan continued, though nobody seemed to be in a hurry to go anywhere except his pocket.

"Or screaming to let everyone know where we all at."

Annette stared at Marcus with a slack expression like she'd heard him speak but hadn't comprehended a word of it. Lawrence's first impression of her still held: a few Xanax short of a full pill bottle.

"It's okay," Eliza assured Annette. "We're all scared."

"I want to go home. Can we?"

Adam's father said, "Someone is going to pay for this misunderstanding. I'm talking epic lawsuit."

Lawrence wasn't sure what kind of "misunderstanding" would land eleven strangers in an old hotel with no memory of it, but whatevs.

He'd yet to spot any cameras. Well-placed, strategically hidden, no doubt providing a running chronicle of their exploits in this crazed little motel hell. Who would do something like this and not film it? This was high entertainment for someone, possibly live-streaming on the net for uber-rich clientele with a taste for macabre theatrics. The only question was how far they would take it.

This many people? There's a limit for sure.

The best-case scenario involved everyone giving their consent beforehand and agreeing to some type of roofie. Latrunculin A could wipe memories in rodents, but that was a lawsuit waiting to happen if something went wrong here. He didn't need Ed to tell him that. Lawrence also couldn't see mother hen allowing Adam's participation without the kind of padded suit worn by attack dog trainers. More importantly, he'd never agree to this himself, much less a basket case like Annette.

There had to be a plant in the group, someone with a portable hidden camera. That ruled out the couple and the family; why set more than 10% of the group as double agents? Nathan? Too active. Patrick? Too obvious; he'd be a fool to keep himself so remote. The Asian wallflower would be too bizarre; a literal and figurative Manchurian candidate. Annette? Too theatrical. Eliza? She stayed in the thick of the action with the best vantage point. She flipped the bathroom light switch and put her back to the wall. Reaction shot? Her baggy gray jogging pants had black arrows alternating up and down; any one of them could have a camera peeking.

"We need to get downstairs and figure out our location and a course of action," Nathan said.

Let's all go to the lobby, let's all go to the lobby . . .

"Shouldn't we figure out what we got in common and who's doin' this shit?" Marcus asked.

You do just that, Flava Flav. Who be fuckin' with us, boyee!

Nathan hooked a thumb over his shoulder. "Whoever did that won't wait for us to get our bearings, Marcus. We don't have the element of surprise until we take it."

Lawrence imagined Nathan practicing this line in a mirror, to help take charge when the time came : " . . . *until* we take it . . . until we *take* it . . . " Experimenting with pounding a fist into his palm for effect [Power Gesture #15].

Lawrence snickered.

"You have something to add?" Nathan asked.

Pamela glared at Lawrence with the patented Mother's Evil Eye, a human shield for Adam.

"N-no," Lawrence stammered. "Good here."

"You think this is funny?" Eliza demanded. "This *isn't* funny."

Oh, it's okay for your girl Annette to scream like a banshee and give us away, but laughing is a clear and present danger. Got it.

"If you got something on your mind, maybe you should share it with the group," Suzanne said.

"Yeah, man," Marcus chimed, and others muttered similar tidings while it was safe to kick the scapegoat.

"What's your story, Larry?" Nathan asked. "If you know something, out with it."

Larry?

"He doesn't have a leg to stand on," Suzanne concluded. "Look at him sweating. He's just as scared as the rest of us."

Marcus pushed the air dismissively. "Fool don't know shit."

Lawrence saw his only out and seized it. "N-nothing. I-I have T-Tourette's, you fu-fu-fucks. Sorry. *Fuckers*! Hmmmmm."

Deception level: Expert.

He had his theory, but once voiced it could be poked at, its veracity questioned, its probability reduced by the chorus of dissenting opinions even if they had nothing constructive of their own to offer. Lawrence wanted to hold onto his explanation for now, keep it his, have a good laugh at the end and say he knew all along.

Such optimism felt misplaced. The bloody walls flashed through his mind.

"Need to keep your punk ass mouth shut then," Marcus said.

"Does Tourette's really cause that kind of stuttering?" Eliza asked.

Nathan thankfully cut off the inquisition. "Okay then. First floor it is."

He led the way followed by the Chinese girl, Marcus and Suzanne, Eliza and Annette, Ed, Pamela, and Adam, and Patrick and Lawrence last. He looked for cameras or nooks where they might be hidden, but in a stairwell with dim emergency lighting he saw nothing of note but the lighting itself. Were they to believe the only things replaced since the 1980s were the light bulbs?

Sloppy.

An unknown group had kidnapped and drugged them—their diversity and various points of origin throughout the continental US hinted at a large organization with broad interstate reach. They were deposited into a situation with no ideas and no clues. Possible ends: Mental experiment? Social experiment?

Internet vendetta?

Im going to find you and fuck you world, you little troll. Peter Griefin my ass, your real name will be mine and then YOULL be mine, you fukc!

In light of the situation, Loonatik411's (ungrammatical) words now seemed more than an idle threat.

Lolz, Goonatik. When you see my vid on the interwebz immortalizing the various and sundry ways I made you my bitch make sure you give me a thumbs down. Let's me know the wounds ain't healed. Lolz!

REINCARNAGE: MAXIMUM CARNAGE

Lawrence was a Griefer. He learned a game and/or found its hacks, entered multiplayer servers and proceeded to fuck with people and record the ensuing chaos for his and his fans' amusement. He'd done it for years and been called more names in more languages than the Devil. Loonatik411 was just another player Lawrence trolled under the cloak of anonymity.

Until two (?) nights ago.

While Lawrence injected fun into an otherwise successful (and *boring*) military campaign by unleashing Rocket Propelled Grenade chaos tempered with some random nutsack sniping, Loonatik411 appeared.

Hey there, Lawrence. Or can I call you Larry?

Nathan called him Larry. Coincidence? Maybe.

Gonna fuck you up, Larry. Dead meat. I know . . . Where. You. Live. LOLZ.

He found "Larry's" name and address a couple days before Lawrence wound up drugged in a weird hotel room.

Coincidence? Only if it was the most epic one ever. And if not Loonadick, a host of others who would gladly do this if he leaked Lawrence's identity to the right people.

But who did these other people here piss off? None seemed the online type except maybe the kid if he snuck games at a friend's house. Or Marcus—with his ample aggression, Lawrence could see him on a perpetual killing spree with a virtual machine gun. *Get some, you punk-ass bitches!*

There was daylight ahead. The lobby windows were not blackened. Nathan was first to the lobby and abruptly stopped, hand aloft to signal the rest of the crew to halt.

Marcus probably had a history of ignoring the Man and wasn't about to start obeying now. He charged ahead, glass crunching beneath his shoes.

I bet he'd call them kicks.

"Oh, shit!" Marcus turned back to Suzanne, his face warped by a grimace. "You don't wanna see this, baby."

IV.

JUST BEYOND THE carport was a traffic island where someone had staked five human heads on poles. It looked like a macabre group picture: The Headeys' family vacation. Lawrence identified three men and one woman with one unknown because the skull was too mashed. Gender X had been crushed in a vise or the wall-breaker's hands before mounting and slid halfway down its pole like a flag lowered to half-staff. The lack of symmetry, the lack of aesthetic neatness (the middle pole canted to the left), and the stringy stalactite hanging from male #2 stood grim testimony against Lawrence's theory of scare tactics.

"You've gotta be kidding me," Ed said. "This can't be real."

Nathan held up his hands again for calm.

Let's not panic, minions, for I have a different plan to proclaim unto you.

He didn't push his hands this time or his luck, though. Stock in calm wasn't a hot commodity as prayers, moans, and cries traveled down the line. Lawrence joined in this time. Flies buzzing around the head menagerie suggested something beyond slightly sophisticated shock effects. A prosthetic head tended to look like merely that in a movie if the camera lingered. He had no doubt these would hold up to scrutiny and macabre experimentation.

Most of the group turned away, a few gagging and

sobbing. Probably a good thing they found the bloody room to prepare them somewhat for something this horrific, although he had a little catching up to do in trauma as the Doubting Lawrence.

Annette seemed the most likely to melt down, but she took off for the front desk before panic consumed them. Nathan gave up any pretense of motivational speaking and crossed the lobby after her.

Only jagged edges remained in the frames of the windows. Something blew them out with explosive force, scattering glass throughout the lobby and pavement beneath the carport. Some panes were knocked inward and others outward. A bloody path trailed through the shards and out the front door.

"It doesn't work!" Annette slammed the phone on its cradle at the desk. She gave Nathan an imploring stare, perhaps convinced by the Power Gestures it was his responsibility to free them from this nightmare. He walked past her like she wasn't there and tried the phone himself, then slammed it down even harder.

"Did you try dialing nine?" Ed asked.

Nathan shook his head as he walked back. "No dice."

"What'd you expect?" Marcus asked. "They'd bring us here and let us call for help?"

Lawrence moved on shaky legs toward the windows with the growing dread of recognition, glass and broken tiles crackling.

A white Volkswagen Beetle of '70s vintage sat in the parking lot beside a rusted Ford pickup of similar age, an old Volvo, and a little farther away a burned-out Humvee, all with flat tires.

At the entrance to the lot, Lawrence saw another traffic island with six more heads. On the left side, more were staked in an overgrown picnic area. He added up nineteen decapitations, trying not to think of it as a "head count."

Then he saw the thing at the far end of the lot that

ended any notion this was a game. The fluorescent orange kiosk which like the Humvee seemed an anachronism, a futuristic device dropped into a place otherwise unsullied by technologies of the last thirty years. This had to be . . .

"The Morgan Falls Lodge!" Eliza practically screamed it.

Silence fell over the lobby. Pamela looked puzzled but also did not speak. No one moved, the revelation demanding mute reflection. It lasted several seconds before Lawrence heard the sound. Something low and eerie, discomfiting and *close*. Like a cat in heat, only long, sustained.

"Are you okay?" Adam asked.

Lawrence caught his sightline and tracked it to Annette who stood rigid, teeth bared, eyes vacant, a guttural moan rattling in her throat like glass. She'd turned down the volume on a scream and left it idling.

"*Damn,* bitch," Marcus said. "You need us to put a muzzle on you?"

Eliza rushed to the counter, threw her arms around Annette and whispered something. The vocal cord grinding immediately leveled off. In a strange way, her fit calmed them somewhat. They at least recognized the need to conduct themselves far more collectedly than she seemed prepared to do.

Pamela sensed Q&A was finally permitted. "Wait, what's Morgan Falls?"

"It's where Agent Orange is, Mom."

And there it is, the name said aloud. Richard Dunbar, the crazy Vietnam vet who went apeshit and slaughtered a bunch of people in the early 1980s. AKA The Morgan Murderer, the Sandalwood Slayer.

Lawrence waited for it to feel ridiculous. It didn't.

"We're not in Morgan," Ed said. "We can't be."

Not the voice of reason. It was a man asking his doctor to run the tests again. He didn't have stage IV cancer. No way.

"The hell we ain't," Marcus said. "That orange phone booth out there is a Chicken Exit. Someone's dropped our asses into Agent Orange's Kill Zone. If we don't get out of here five minutes ago, we're *fucked!*"

"We're only *effed* if we panic, Marcus," Nathan said. "Let's look at our options."

Run, hide, or die should just about cover it.

"Why would someone do this to us?" Eliza asked.

Ed curled protective arms around Pamela and Adam. "The government has Morgan and the surrounding area walled off and patrolled by the US Army. There's no way someone rolled us past them to stash us in the lodge."

"Man, there's ways in," Marcus said. "Dudes sneak in and out all the time."

"But they're doing it of their own free will," Nathan said.

"It's the government," Suzanne said. "Nobody else could get all eleven of us in here."

"But why would they do that, baby?"

"Why would they conduct the Tuskegee syphilis experiments or create HIV, *baby*? Because they can."

The Taiwanese girl followed the conversation like a tennis match, pausing only to watch Patrick inspect a light fixture mounted on the wall. Who changed out the bulbs in the Morgan Falls Lodge? Why would it have electricity at all? Maybe Patrick could figure it out with his patented Deep Gaze™.

"Well, we've got, what did you call it? A Chicken Exit? The bright orange phone booth over there, right?" Nathan asked. "I say we give it a try."

It wasn't a phone booth, more like one of those old open air "dial anywhere in the US for 50 cents a minute" phones Lawrence used to see. As the eleventh fastest person in the group, he wasn't eager to increase their chances of an encounter with the famed maniac by venturing outside.

"Doesn't mean the phone's gonna work," Marcus said.

"If it doesn't, we're no worse off," Nathan said. "But it should. Those things were put here for people like us."

Oh, people like us, who don't remember how the hell they wound up in Morgan?

Lawrence had seen the movies, played one of the games, watched the survivor stories on *Dateline NBC* and similar programs, read harrowing tales in magazines and newspapers, and read some of the hundreds of books on the subject, so if people were ever abducted and transferred here, he'd have heard about it. They were pioneers, or worse—and more likely—this happened before and no one lived to tell.

The bulk of Richard Dunbar's victims came from killing sprees in the 1980s when he repeatedly butchered Morgan Falls campers and town folk, and/or those in nearby Sandalwood in semi-annual campaigns of terror. It always ended with Dunbar's temporary death, but somehow he always returned to kill again. Miraculous? Supernatural? Impossible? All of the above. Theories as to how and why were as common as the "experts" who made the rounds on news and talk shows. Theories ranged from his exposure to experimental Agent Orange in 'Nam to dying on a cursed Native American burial ground at the end of the first spree. In reality, no one knew.

The government built huge walls around the abandoned Morgan town and lake to contain him. There were rumored to have been classified containment experiments including imprisonment, cryogenics, and an expensive rocket launch attempt, but it was like murder was the only thing that sustained him, and without it, he popped right back up in the Kill Zone. With him free to wander his hunting grounds with impunity, the massacres stopped for a while and the victim class changed from unsuspecting innocents to those who willingly challenged the walls. It replaced Aokigahara as the destination du jour for Japanese suicides, and daredevils added to the death toll while outside the wall the Agent Orange tourist trade boomed in Sandalwood.

The walls held until 1996 when Agent Orange broke through and painted snow-covered Sandalwood red just in time for Christmas. The town emptied faster than Pripyat after the Chernobyl disaster and more walls were erected, swallowing Sandalwood along with the Morgan Memorial, the Agent Orange Museum (since relocated to Marshallville), and a military barracks. Lawrence remembered the internet scandal of '97 when memorabilia scavenged from the Kill Zone—including still-wrapped gifts left beneath Christmas trees during the rushed Sandalwood evacuation—showed up on online auction sites. People known as Stalkers could get curiosity-seekers in and (sometimes) out unharmed for black market collectibles, a cutthroat market on both sides of the walls.

"But if we test the phone, we'll be in the open," Eliza said.

"If we're really in Morgan Falls," Ed said, "it's huge—"

"Over seventy thousand acres," Adam said. "Three towns."

Westing was blocked in a 2004 expansion, making it the third and most recent town abandoned, but hardly anyone lived there by then.

"Three towns. So the chances of him being close would be like lotto odds if we're really in Morgan . . . which we're *not*."

Suzanne laughed. "If you wake up in some field during a storm with an iron bar glued to your hand, obviously someone wants you to be a lightning rod."

Marcus stood by his lady. "Yeah, fuck your lottery odds, man. You know what they say . . . someone's gotta win."

Nathan pounded a palm in his fist again, chiseling the stone tablet of his commandments. "We need to get an evac chopper while we still have daylight and we're better off sticking together as a group. Are you with me, folks?"

Mumbles. This time he had no immediate takers except Adam's family, hostages to Ed's straw-clutching denial of reality. Adam flashed a pleading look at the Vietnamese chick and she followed, too. The moment caught Lawrence off guard. Did Adam have some sort of personal stake in the girl?

Ugh, don't think about stakes with all those heads outside.

Patrick started after them, too. The man of mystery's endorsement made this seem like less of a suicide run.

Before Nathan stepped through the front door, he said, "For those staying behind, please do us a solid and scream really loud if he shows up."

Eliza gave him the finger, thus being the first to invoke Power Gesture #1.

Nathan smirked at her. "Careful if you follow through the glass. You'll cut yourself." He ducked through.

"I don't want to go out there," Suzanne whispered. "But I don't want to stay here either."

Marcus rolled his eyes. "Got fucking Barbara from *Night of the Living Dead* up in here with Rain Man. Let's go."

How am I Rain Man?

Lawrence followed Patrick. Fitting through the mostly empty glass pane wasn't an option so he shouldered open the door. The ensuing squeak raised Nathan's shoulders and he whipped his head around angrily to stare him down, like Lawrence blew the platoon's position in a rice paddy.

This isn't the Vietnam War, you dickhole, Lawrence thought, face burning.

More glass crunched. Marcus, Suzanne, Eliza, and Annette gave up the hotel vigil. Eliza helped Annette shield her eyes from the heads.

"Just ignore them," Eliza said.

"And keep your spastic ass quiet, like our lives depended on it," Marcus said.

"Ignore him too," Eliza added.

Annette looked on the verge of catatonia. If Agent Orange came after them maybe she would lock up, buying Lawrence a chance to beat a hasty exit—well, as hasty an exit as he could.

Her psychodrama is probably as real as my Tourette's. First sign of trouble and she'll throw up a dust cloud like the Road Runner.

Ed, Pamela, Adam, and the Mongolian girl followed Nathan. Marcus had Suzanne. Eliza and Annette had a weird mother-daughter thing going. It made Patrick and Lawrence the odd men out, but Patrick obviously preferred it that way. Lawrence had to ingratiate himself with them or he'd be flat-out left behind when the shit hit the fan. Did he have anything to leverage? He'd seen a lot of the Agent Orange movies—who hadn't?—but the most recent video game could be his ticket. It was based on actual town layouts with a virtual replica of the landscape. He knew how to get to the lake from Morgan Falls Lodge.

The object of the game was to sneak into the Kill Zone and retrieve the key to a safe deposit box from a house in Sandalwood. The player had to break into the Sandalwood Savings and Loan to claim an unknown treasure while evading Agent Orange and random military patrols. The game hadn't been Lawrence's cup of tea and he only spent five hours playing, but no one had to know. He'd watched the walkthrough on YouTube . . . okay, he'd watched the walkthrough of the last five minutes of the game because he wanted to know what was in the safe deposit box, and it turned out to be nothing more than a riff on the briefcase in *Pulp Fiction*.

It was quiet out here, with a light breeze. Lawrence saw a deer amble onto the pavement at the other end of the parking lot. He pointed. Eliza looked at it and then looked at him in a way that said, "So?" His smile faltered.

The Chicken Exit was so named for the idiots who got themselves in here and then had second thoughts about sticking around. The CE enabled a quick call to the US Army which had a chopper on standby for such emergencies. A stiff fine, community service, and public ridicule probably seemed a small price to pay when you spotted your first head ornament.

"—called Lakewood," the Filipino girl said to Adam. Yeah, a town in Washington and she studied nursing at Clover Park Technical College. Lawrence had asked her where she was from, meaning in Asia, and she gave him the same answer. In perfect English. Adam clung to every word, his parents momentarily forgotten.

Poor Pamela. She'd lost her son's hand and would probably lose her head next.

The kiosk was mounted on a small concrete slab in a traffic island. The overgrown grass and weeds swayed in the breeze. No staked heads here, thank God. The kiosk had a huge dent and leaned to the left but the phone still hung on the cradle, with instructions beside it in twenty different languages. Stay calm, pick up the phone, press the red button, state the location when asked (this was number 15), answer any questions, stay calm.

Nathan fist-pumped. "All right, gang, let's get the fuck out of here." He hurried the final steps to the phone as if it would fly away on them.

Lawrence turned to watch the deer, comforted by the thought it could not occupy the same area as an inhuman killer. Eliza had missed the point.

The pop of a loud firecracker snapped Lawrence's attention back to the group.

Nathan grunted and fell sideways, knocking the phone loose. Wisps of smoke rose from the ground, but there wasn't a visible hole. He rolled, clutching his right foot.

Gobs of blood dripped from the shoe, seeping through his fingers. The top of his brogue had opened from the inside out.

"What the hell, man?" Marcus said. He and Suzanne backed away to the cracked asphalt. "Was it a mine?"

"Toe popper," Patrick said. "A buried shell that goes off under enough pressure. Careful . . . there could be more."

Ed pushed his family back. Annette broke out of her shock and clawed for the dangling phone, consequences be damned. "This doesn't work either!"

While Ed and the Thai girl tended Nathan, Lawrence made sure the deer was still there.

Don't go anywhere, Bambi.

Spooked, it stared at the group of humans huddled around the fallen man.

A distant wail slowly rose into a frightening crescendo.

The deer ran into the woods.

"What's that?" Eliza asked.

This time it wasn't Annette. The sound grew louder, a sonic wave crashing toward them like the tide. A civil defense siren.

To Lawrence, it sounded like the end of the world.

They stood rooted to the spot. Even Nathan momentarily ceased his writhing. A shared look of horror passed through everyone who met Lawrence's eyes, in doomed solidarity. He looked toward the Morgan Falls Lodge, thought of trying to barricade a door against Agent Orange. It might hold him off five seconds, if room 237 was any indication.

Annette went back to her swiveling head trick, on a perpetual word find only she could see.

Nathan cried out again, still plain as day over the siren, pained profanity which ended in vowels as if he lost half his tongue with half the toes of his foot.

Hate it for you, mastermind, but I'm not sorry to move up on the group speed chart.

"Come on, man, damn," Marcus said, looking around. "We can't just stand here holding our dicks."

Adam peered at the phone booth partition. "Hey, there's a directory for other Chicken Exits."

"*Adam, get away from that!*" Pamela yanked him back. "There could be more traps!"

Marcus halted immediately in his path to the phone. After pondering a moment, he said, "Hey, Nathan, can you see that directory?"

Suzanne shook her head at him, corner of her mouth curled.

"What? He's over there anyway."

"Marcus is right. We can't stay here." This came from Patrick, and Lawrence felt the corner of his own mouth curl into disapproval at the rapt attention he commanded. Finally opened his mouth to offer more than his name and they clung to every word like edicts from the burning bush. Lawrence said one little thing and he was "Rain Man."

"There may be three towns in this quarantine zone, but they put us in this one, and I doubt it was to give us a chance in . . . whatever this is."

Ooh, nice dramatic pause.

Nathan might have read the *Alpha Dog* guide, but Patrick probably wrote it.

"If they put us here, we need to be somewhere else. Somewhere we can arm ourselves."

"Sorry," Lawrence said, "but I think we're fresh out of guide books to Morgan Falls."

"I thought you had Tourette's," Patrick said, not missing a beat.

Lawrence felt the unwanted scrutiny of the group turn to him. The siren blared as if to alert everyone to his deceit.

"He sounded fine when he asked where I was from earlier," Gin said.

Cover blown. "It comes and goes, fu-fuckmou-mouth. Hmmmm."

"We ain't got time for this shit, Sling Blade," Marcus said.

Patrick gestured to the road adjacent to the Chicken Exit. "We don't have many options. Right or left."

"Or into the woods," Adam said.

"The woods?" Marcus echoed. "Man, why didn't I think of that? Oh right, cuz I don't want my head to end up on no damn stake."

"Not a good idea," Patrick said more diplomatically. "Could be more traps, too."

Adam blushed slightly, but didn't give it up. "They might not expect it."

"Yeah, they might not expect us to jump in front of a speeding train, either, but that shit'll still kill us dead, boy."

"The lake is that way." Lawrence said. He pointed to their left. They all looked back at him. "Bi-bitchlicks."

"Is that from the guide book you don't have?" Gin asked.

Adam laughed harder than the comment warranted.

Got yellow fever, Romeo?

"Morgan Falls Massacre. It's a game with a virtual recreation of this whole c-c-cocksucking town. Hmmmmm."

Pamela blanched at that word in particular, looked like she wanted to cover her little boy's precious ears. Lawrence wished he'd never thrown out the Tourette's excuse, but with all the petty vulgarities he saw online every day, he thought it had the most convincing shot.

i cornhold your moms asshatch cuz you aint shit, bitch u mad bro? and other such patented bon mots from the likes of Bustakapp187fool and sundry.

"Why do we care about the lake?" Marcus said. "Is there a tire swing?"

Suzanne smacked his arm lightly. "There might be a boat."

"Probably not," Patrick said, "but there were houses out there, right?"

Lawrence nodded. "The army has to patrol the water, too. Ti-tits and a-ass."

A lake patrol took him down in the game, matter of fact, and when he tried to continue the game put him on the other side of Morgan Lake. Between cheap shit like that and stingy save points, he gave up. He found the Army and Agent Orange a billion times. It made all of this seem less real, an urban legend like yellow dye five shrinking your penis.

"What about Nathan?" Eliza asked.

"I can make it! Fuuuuuuuuuuuuuuuuuuuuuh . . . I'm okay." He hoisted himself up with the help of the Chicken Exit booth, rather unconcerned another toe popper might give him a matching pair of shoes. His fingers left bloody smears on the partition.

"You're sure you can walk on that?" Patrick asked.

"Never better." He tried to test his weight on the wounded foot and groaned immediately. "Ah, Christ, that hurts, God, fuuuuuuuuuuuuuuuuuuuuuuuuuuuuh!"

Marcus made a "hurry up" gesture at Patrick and pointed to a nonexistent watch on his wrist.

"We're going to the lake," Nathan said, breathing ruggedly. He pointed the wrong way. He hadn't listened to Lawrence. Too busy cradling a shoe where he didn't have to worry so much about toe room any more.

"We'll hide there and figure out our next move," he continued. "Lawrence will help me."

"Lawrence will *what*, fuckass?" He hadn't tried to affect a Tourette's façade that time; it came from the heart.

"You're a bigger guy and you'll be slower anyway," Eliza said. "We can't leave him behind."

"Yeah, we can't leave him behind," Annette repeated, all the while scanning the woods in the word find for *cowardice, panic, opportunist.*

"That'll work," Marcus said.

Lawrence smirked. They'd all done the math on an

ambush and concluded that two easy targets substantially increased their own odds of survival. Well, at least he'd have a potential human shield and could let the man with a plan try Power Gestures on a crazed mass murderer.

The guy could be off in Sandalwood right now for all they knew. The lake was half a mile away, bicycled on the game in a minute.

Lawrence carefully went to Nathan and extended a hand, expecting Nathan to vanish in a cloud of bloody red mist from another trap, but he stayed in one piece. He consulted the Chicken Exit directory as he waited for Nathan to stabilize. It reminded him of the display in shopping malls, right down to a red dot which helpfully informed him "YOU ARE HERE," a feature which struck him as morbidly cynical.

Been awhile since some buffoon was on TV for a Chicken Exit evac, he thought uneasily.

The news stories excited the imagination for awhile, but it all became less interesting once people understood this place could coexist in the world as they knew it and they'd still have to wait in lines at the grocery store and post office and die of the usual things like cancer and heart disease, bored and deeply unhappy as ever. Hopefully diminished interest accounted for this dearth in media coverage.

The nearest Chicken Exit looked to be a long walk in the opposite direction of the lake. Good. Maybe Orange staked out those locales before ultimately staking the heads.

"Okay, I'm good," Nathan announced, neither looking nor sounding so. He clapped Lawrence twice on the shoulder. "Slow and steady wins the race."

Lawrence almost shrugged him away and booked, the unreality of all of this threatening to overwhelm him. He envied the bemused version of himself from twenty minutes ago. *Nothing amiss here, guys. Just mind games by some butthurt video gamer or rich degenerates scaring us for yucks, that's all.*

The group set off in a loose cluster with the expected alliances of Ed, Pam, and Adam, Marcus and Suzanne, Eliza and Annette, and that hot new power duo Lawrence and Nathan. Gin and Patrick gravitated to one another as well. Adam kept looking over at Gin like someone in a barber chair trying to see the TV in the corner until a stern glance from his mom snapped him forward again. Lucky for the boy everyone lost all their stuff or Gin might have Maced him.

The siren thankfully stopped. Heavy silence filled its wake minus Nathan's latest vowel-uble grunt (*Shiiiiiiiiiiii oh gahhhhhhhhhhhh*). For all the debate, Lawrence estimated only three minutes passed since the toe-popper.

"What did it mean?" Annette asked. "I bet it's bad. Oh God, why am I here? I can't be here. I'm not a bad person."

"And the rest of us are?" Marcus asked. He pointed at Adam. "You think that boy deserves to be here? I bet he ain't killed nobody or robbed a bank."

Annette resumed her ponderings, but at a more subconscious volume.

The open road ahead appeared perfectly nonthreatening, minus the woods flanking either side. There was tentative bird song in the trees, one bashful bird looking for any takers. Another answered and soon chatter grew more animated, as though in discussion of theories for the siren.

"It might have been on a timer," Lawrence said. He needed to stake a claim on some of the group esteem. His current portion of the pie wouldn't feed a goldfish.

A few looked back, Patrick and Gin included. They had an alarming lead already. He tried to pick up the pace a little, much to Nathan's *fuuuuuuuuuuuuuh*'d chagrin.

"The siren," he explained between breaths. "It didn't last very long and . . . nothing seemed to happen. Maybe it was just . . . just on a timer."

"Yeah, Sling Blade, and maybe they were ringing the dinner bell for that freak," Marcus said.

"It was bad," Annette mumbled. "Whatever it was, it was bad."

Eliza patted her shoulder. "We're going to get out of this. Hang in there." She actually sounded like she believed it. Maybe she and Annette were sharing psych meds.

Their feet shuffled on the pavement except for Nathan's. He dragged his blasted foot like a mummy. Lawrence's shoulder throbbed. They hadn't reached a quarter of the way yet. He was about to request a volunteer to give him a rest when Patrick's head tilted up sharply.

Lawrence didn't hear anything, but he felt something; a tightening in his guts.

Why did the birds go quiet?

Then it was like an avalanche in his senses with a light scattering of rocks before an entire ridge broke off and cascaded down the base of his spine, gooseflesh rippling across his arms and back with the revelation—*Agent Orange is here.*

Time seemed to slow to a complete crawl, and Lawrence fancied he could hear Patrick's lids slipping across the orbs of his eyeballs as terror sprang them wide open. His lips parted and he shouted one word that sent everybody off like a flock of birds from a treetop: *"GO!"*

Lawrence didn't think it through at all. He whirled away from Nathan as though trying to yank his arm from a coat sleeve.

It was enough to see a glimpse of the Minotaur, the god of the labyrinth. Fifty yards away, stationary for the moment as he pulled the drawstring of a black bow. Lawrence swore he heard it tighten. His stomach dropped as though the ground opened and he'd plunged a hundred feet into the earth.

His face, he thought.

There wasn't one. It was a mask, perhaps a hood with eyes like goggles.

The arrow was halfway there before Lawrence completed his turn and staggered forward into a run. Fear atrophied his muscles and he expected his legs to collapse in a rubbery pile, but he stayed upright and lumbered forward as fast as he could, anything to make the fifty yards more like fifty miles. He moved faster than he would have believed, but so did the rest of the group, as though borne on a whirlwind of their own screaming. Annette unsurprisingly laid claim to loudest, but second place went to a more masculine claxon that might be Marcus or Ed.

The grisly sound of punctured flesh provoked another outcry from Nathan with at last a completed oath (*"Oh, fuuuuuuuuuuuuuuuuuuuuuuuuuck!"*). Lawrence heard him hit the deck.

Don't look, don't look, Lawrence warned himself, even as he did; he had to.

The arrow jutted from Nathan's shoulder, the force strong enough to punch it through the other side. He stumbled into an upright position and limped a couple yards before his wounded foot crippled the effort and put him face down on the road. He extended a hand as if Lawrence could somehow pull Nathan twenty yards to him, twenty-five, thirty.

Sorry, Nathan, but this bird's gonna fly.

And he'd take wing while Agent Orange tore at Nathan like a beast of prey on a fallen elk.

Lawrence caught sight of a blur just before he faced forward again, and his arms and legs pumped with renewed vigor. He swayed in a lackadaisical zigzag pattern to discourage another arrow attack, knowing the difficulty would still be no greater for Orange than hitting a dead elephant.

Orange is running for all he's worth.

He could *hear* it, too, boot falls on the asphalt, like war drums, way too fast to simply stop and savor Nathan's agony before the obligatory dismemberment. It's what Lawrence naturally assumed—had *counted on*—to give him any prayer of escape. And why? Because that's how it happened in all the movies with the horny teenagers?

It was at that moment he realized the second place screamer was himself. He transformed it into actual words: *"Help! Please help!"* A petition for the very thing he never would have given Nathan because one man's mutilation is another's escape.

The others were way ahead of him. A few glanced back for an instant, but nobody slowed. It was like a relay race where everyone forgot they needed Lawrence to hand them the baton, or they were willing to do another lap to catch up with him eventually, but no hurry on that.

"You chickenshit bastards!" he screamed, his throat raw and stinging. *"Get back here and fight! He can't take all of us!"*

Of course he didn't believe that for a second, but he had to try. A rational remnant of his mind complimented him for staying in character with Tourette's down to the bitter end.

The war drums caught up, like the pounding of his own blood in his ears. Lawrence looked back, saw the crazed eyes in the goggled hood and a small orb over the mouth like the spout of a garden hose. He would have looked like a scarecrow without the goggles and mouth tube. It hadn't occurred to Lawrence to wonder why the chase at all from a man with a bow, but it made sense when he saw the machete.

For years he'd heard of mothers lifting cars off their kids and other superhero acts of adrenaline he now knew to be as suspect as the yellow dye five deception, because Lawrence would die if he couldn't outrun Agent Orange and he wasn't getting much of a fight-or-flight rocket boost. Shitting himself seemed far more likely than the saving grace of warp speed.

Lawrence heard a distinct *whoosh,* the unmistakable slice of the machete through the air. He waited for the *thunk* of metal to free his head from his neck or hack deeply into his brain.

It didn't.

He did see the flash of the blade from the corner of his eye, but at a much lower arc than expected. It puzzled him an instant figuratively before it completed the job literally. Heat exploded beneath the knee of his right leg and spread to the left.

Jesus Christ, he cut off my . . .

Then came the dropping sensation as he adjusted to the abrupt loss of sixteen inches in height in the span of one second. He didn't stop running despite his resignation to the execution, propelled forward on his now uneven limbs. All of his weight came down on the crooked stump of his right leg in a shocking detonation of pain. Then a sickening lurch as his unevenly distributed weight twisted upon gristle and carried him onto the left stump. He struggled to find footing in the absence of actual feet, impossibly close to the ground without kneeling. He pitched forward to the left, screaming far beyond the previously charted potential of his vocal cords. Lawrence struck the street and rolled, sliding to a halt on his back like an upended tortoise shell with stubby legs to match.

His legs and feet lay a couple of yards behind him at the end of a trail of bright red blood. Still wrapped in his pants, pieces of a human jigsaw that wanted to fit back together. He vomited down the front of his shirt at the sight of his blood jubilantly hemorrhaging from a tangle of arteries, like wires spooling from a fuse box.

Agent Orange stood over him. Lawrence maintained eye contact for about one and a half seconds. If he expected anything, it was an expressionless psychosis befitting the man's military background, but what he glimpsed was ecstasy. This was his surrogate orgasm, something as pleasurable the five hundredth time as the first, perhaps infinitely better. The wardrobe was combat appropriate with the black boots, camouflage fatigues of khaki, gray, and black, and the gas hood he couldn't face again. He would have been distracted anyway by the necklace, its length clogged with shriveled ears, trophies he'd taken from many heads in his illustrious homicidal career. Lawrence dry heaved and saw the blurry length of the machete held to Orange's side, pointed at the ground, then twisting and rising like a metal erection.

Lawrence cinched his eyes shut, not wanting to see it coming, but eager for a release from the awful agony. He uttered the strange new vowels of Nathan's language in his suffering.

"Uhhhhhhh . . . gahhhhhhhhhh . . . fuuuuuuuuuuuu uuuu . . ."

The thump of rubber receded.

The hell?

Lawrence dared to open his eyes, thinking Orange would wait for him to do that before the death blow, but the camouflaged figure had turned back to Nathan.

"Get back here!" He couldn't manage much beyond a groan. He sounded drunk to his own ears. "You can't leave me like this you . . . you . . . fuck!"

When had it gotten so cold?

Nathan managed to get to all fours, but not much else. Orange closed the distance with the sort of leisurely march Lawrence could have really used about thirty seconds ago. He thought bitterly of the others, all the time in the world to flee with Nathan and Lawrence as distractions, all of them still with their fucking feet.

Orange would find them, though. They were all going to die. Lawrence just got the message a little faster.

Orange stooped to pick up something in the grass beside the road. It was his bow, evidently cast aside to make it easier to run down his prey, although Orange could have chased him in a one-man band outfit with a tuba and a bass drum and still caught up with Lawrence inside of a minute.

Nathan held his hands out as though to supplicate his executioner, Powerless Gesture #6. Orange slashed in a quick arc. A pile of loose fingers broke off from Nathan's wave. He shrieked.

Orange sheathed and stepped around Nathan. He slipped the bow string over Nathan's throat with the bow a black grin behind him and hauled it back. Lawrence was close enough to appreciate the oddity of a man missing half his fingers trying to get his hands under a bow string to stave off strangulation. Only nubs left, half his toes blown apart, and stuck like a pinned butterfly, but still trying to live. Fascinating and awful.

Orange yanked Nathan up until he floated above the ground, legs bicycling, flap of his brogue waving with Orange at least six and a half feet tall behind him. Blood from the missing fingers painted his face an ugly shade of crimson to complement the suffocation. Orange relinquished the bow and cinched his hands around the cord to pull it taut.

Lawrence cringed at the strangled gasping, the world's longest death rattle.

Suddenly the bow cord chewed through Nathan's neck with a wet snap. His head dropped, somersaulting through the air and rolling away from his body, which slumped to the ground like a mail sack. A red pool sputtered from the stump of the neck, forming tributaries to join the blood lakes from Lawrence's legs.

Lawrence looked down with no little surprise to see he'd begun to haul himself away. "Crab walking" would be inaccurate given the absence of legs (and walking), but some kind of survival mode kicked in.

The effort made his arms rubbery and he fell onto his back again, having moved himself approximately five inches toward safety.

REINCARNAGE: MAXIMUM CARNAGE

Orange shook his bow to clear blood from the string. He mounted it on his back and gathered Nathan's head on the way back to Lawrence, clutching it by the hair. He crossed half the distance in two seconds, though Lawrence suspected he blacked out for a moment. This close he saw droplets of blood spatter the street from the viscera of Nathan's neck.

Another time warp and Agent Orange stood over him again, the metal erection of the machete rising.

He licked his lips. He couldn't let the guy snuff him without some kind of parting wisdom.

"Hey," he muttered.

Orange cocked his head.

"If you were such a . . . such a bad-ass in combat . . . why'd we lose in . . . in Vi . . . Vietnam . . . bitch?"

Yeah. That's how you went out. Not chump-style, gagging like Nathan.

Orange kicked his boot into the meat of Lawrence's nearest stump. He'd been on the verge of slipping away, but the lightning bolt of pain shocked him right back into his body like a defibrillator. He screamed, then abruptly sucked in air as Orange booted the other stump. He converted this into his finest scream yet when it all gathered in his lungs.

Orange put his bloodied boot on Lawrence's chest and pinned him. From down here, the machete looked like some kind of alien spacecraft in the sky, which whipped down to earth in a blur right at his eyes. The blade slammed into his face to form a line like half of an X shape. It ran from his left jaw line to his right eye. Lawrence convulsed. Something that looked like a cloud of black flies unspooled in his good eye. Not flies after all, but the black boot of his executioner eclipsing the sky before it stomped the back of the blade.

It drove the machete all the way through Lawrence's skull, bisecting his face.

V.

MARCUS WOULD HAVE reached the lake houses first if not for Suzanne. She kept up when they first broke off into a sprint, but he had to practically carry her the last bit. Not a good sign.

"Come on, baby," he urged. "You not hear that screaming back there? That's us if we don't *move.*"

The screaming lasted forever. Sling Blade went out like a bitch. Marcus didn't know him and wouldn't mourn him, but it sounded awful as hell. Marcus could outrun Agent Orange forever if he avoided the traps, but he couldn't bolt and leave Suzanne. Hopefully Annette would make a good enough distraction to give them a head-start. Dude could have her and Eliza both. They'd acted straight up stupid so far. He heard Annette's whining now like a homing device while Eliza comforted her with patience she didn't deserve. Crazy white bitches too dumb to know there was a fear that could keep you alive and a fear that could get you dead, and they were buying up the latter like a sale at Costco or wherever crazy white bitches bought shit.

Everyone was afraid, but at least Suzanne didn't express it with a lot of screaming and hollering, sending up smoke signals for that psycho to find them.

Most of these people were liabilities. Maybe not Patrick, but the others? Walking corpses. They almost followed that punk-ass Nathan to their graves. If he'd stopped crying long enough at the Chicken Exit to tell them a UFO would beam them to safety, half these fools would still be watching the skies.

It was funny to think of someone taking Marcus *out* of Memphis to endanger his life. They didn't cut a brother's head off in Memphis, though. They might blast it, like that deaf girl who got her brains blown out when he was still in high school, but they didn't stick your dome on a stake.

"Look!" Gin called up ahead. "We're almost there!"

A sign with a diagonal arrow read MORGAN LAKE where a side road branched into the woods. They were barely half a mile from where Agent Orange could be making lampshades from Lawrence's fat ass this minute. Marcus didn't like the idea of stopping now when they knew he wasn't off in Westing or Sandalwood. They'd better hope there was a choice cache of artillery in one of these houses, but since this was Sling Blade's idea, they'd probably be lucky to find a slingshot.

Gin beckoned to them from the road sign, Patrick right behind her.

Like we don't know to hurry.

If this plan wasn't agreed upon in advance, their one group might have splintered into three or four, scattering every which way.

Maybe we'd be one he didn't chase.

Suzanne hunched to her left, wincing with a hand to her side. She'd slacked on her swimming for awhile. Marcus pulled her down the lake road. The whitebread family, Eliza and Annette stumbled behind them. They didn't have to go far before they saw houses and the lake.

Gin and Patrick slowed at the first house in line, but something caught Marcus's eye. "There's a boat!" He dropped Suzanne's hand and sprinted with a burst of new adrenaline. He blew past five houses on both sides to the end of the road, pulled up, bent over, and wheezed.

He now had a full view of their salvation. It was a houseboat which the owner named *The Great*

Hammerhead. Now past some overgrown shrubbery, he could see it was partially sunken.

More like The Great Disappointment, Marcus thought.

Footsteps slowed behind him. He turned around sharply. Just Patrick. His impeccably sculpted hair had unfurled, but otherwise no sign of inconvenience from their race for survival. He looked at the lake stoically.

"What do you know," he said. "They had a tire swing out here after all."

Marcus at last noticed a rope hanging from a thick branch several yards away. The tire dangled in the weeds.

"Let's check out some houses," Patrick said. "Maybe they have a boat at one. We need to get out of sight anyway."

Marcus walked back with him. The rest of the group caught up in the meantime, all accounted for minus Sling Blade and Nathan. They met him and Patrick halfway. Suzanne looked at him expectantly. He shook his head. "There's a boat, but it's sinking."

Everyone's face fell at this announcement.

Marcus took stock of how the group fared in their flight. Eliza looked close to recovered. Patrick, Gin, and Adam seemed all right. Ed still huffed, but he'd need to go another couple blocks to be in the sorry state of Annette and Pam. Suzanne wasn't much better, and he'd dragged her half the way.

We might have to try the woods if he shows up again, traps or not. I can't pull her faster than most of these chumps can run.

"What did he do to them back there?" Annette asked. "I can't stop hearing it."

Patrick ignored her. "Come on, let's try a house close to the lake. We need to hurry."

He abruptly turned and jogged to a two story which seemed to have way too many windows, but the other houses on the street looked to be a product of the same architect. No point living by the lake if you couldn't be reminded of it from every room in the house, apparently.

"Those screams," Annette droned. "I can't get them out of my mind." As usual, Eliza gave her validation instead of telling her to shut the hell up, they all heard the damn screams.

The neighborhood looked like one of those empty Detroit suburbs or a web slideshow of "Top Ten Abandoned Places" that could double as a post-apocalyptic movie set: *28 Years Later*. People planted hedges against a house, not trees. You'd have to mow the lawn with a bulldozer or, in keeping with the general whacked-out Vietnam vet theme, use napalm and start over next year.

They gathered where Patrick waited for them, the spot with the least amount of weeds on the lawn. "Let's try the back," he said. From Nathan, it might have seemed a challenge (*We're trying the back, no debate, go now, bitch!*), but with Patrick it merely seemed the logistics of survival.

"Watch for traps. Try to step where the concrete is visible." Patrick led by example, stepping from one exposed section to another as he traversed what used to be a driveway.

Marcus hadn't needed the warning. Sling Blade's death would have been a solo act if Nathan hadn't blown a hole in his foot.

Alongside the house where the trees and bushes prevailed, Patrick took care not to break the small branches jutting in their way. He carefully handed off the limbs he couldn't avoid rather than let them snap back and shed leaves. AO could probably spot the white of a freshly broken branch a football field away. Good thing Sling Blade wasn't around to do the damage of his namesake.

Patrick paused at a wooden stairwell, assessing for traps or sturdiness. Or maybe to decide which way to go. A short flight led to the upper deck with a longer stairwell below. There was probably a walkout basement in the rear.

"Why aren't we moving?" Annette asked.

"There might be a trap," Ed whispered back.

Annette issued a high-pitched nasal drone.

"Turn off the dog whistle!" Suzanne snapped.

Eliza put a comforting hand on Annette's shoulder. "She can't help that she's scared!"

Marcus leaned in conspiratorially. "I'm about to give her some help."

Annette stopped.

Patrick at last opted for the upper deck. He alternated each footstep toward the stringers rather than the middle of the treads. He skipped the third step altogether, noting it for Gin, who pointed Marcus to it.

"Watch this third step," he whispered to the others.

It looked no more rotten than the other steps and he wondered what he wasn't seeing. Several of them groaned under his weight.

Sling Blade would have wound up at the basement no matter which way he went.

It sounded worse on the actual deck. The boards creaked like a boat at sea, buried beneath years of dirt and fallen leaves as though part of the forest's reclamation project with the overgrown bushes and trees and the thick bed of ivy plastered to the walls.

Marcus wondered how many people the deck could support before disaster.

What do we even hope to find here?

Weapons, yeah, but why? AO supposedly had the fortitude of a maniac high on bath salts with the added stubbornness of not staying dead if you managed to kill him, so what the hell would anything short of a bazooka do? They might scrounge some kitchen knives, but Marcus wouldn't trust any of these chumps to have his back even with a far better arsenal than that. He and Suzanne should have tried to swim to the other side of the lake. Maybe she couldn't run well, but she'd have no problem reversing the speed disparity in the water. She went to college on a swimming scholarship, which he hadn't realized anybody did.

Coulda been halfway to the other side by now.

He looked at his stupid-ass pants and imagined them waterlogged.

Okay, maybe she *coulda been halfway to the other side by now.*

The enormous green-hued window overlooking the deck at one time would have provided a hell of a view of the lake. All the new trees made it hard to see anything but glimpses now. For the best view you had to go to the far corner to see over the tops of the shorter trees. He tested the rail and leaned against it for a better look out.

The other side of the lake had a marina with a network of boat slips. Three boats roughly the size of *The Great Hammerhead* showed only their upper decks, the rest of them submerged. The fourth looked to have been steered on a suicide mission to take out the main building of the marina, now permanently wedged into the structure. Hundreds of yards from the marina toward the center of the lake another house boat seemed intact, probably anchored. Marcus was willing to bet the paint spill down the side of the hull wasn't actually paint at all.

This psycho swims, too? Fuckin' A.

A private dock extended from the deck below them but he couldn't tell if it continued unbroken to the lake since the woods engulfed it. He followed the shoreline and saw a similar dock a short distance away that originated from the house next to them. A canoe hung on a rack by the edge of the water. Not far from there was *The Great Hammerhead.*

Suzanne approached him. "Marcus?"

"Canoe down there." Marcus lifted his eyes from Suzanne to Ed to Pamela to Eliza to . . . Annette was the only one who had seen his momentary excitement. Her eyes lingered on Marcus as if she'd heard something, but she went back to her freaky white bitch nod.

Marcus acting strange . . . does not compute, he thought to himself in a robot voice.

The others filed into the house. Suzanne and Marcus were the last two into the den. Ed played doorman and closed it after them.

"Can't believe it was unlocked," Pamela told her son, still whispering. "Thank God for small miracles."

Yeah, a miracle they found an unlocked door they'd have kicked down anyway. Several times he'd seen Pamela with her eyes closed, muttering prayers for deliverance. Marcus knew the type; the smallest good found in the eye of the shitstorm was a sign of divine intervention. If Marcus had a direct line to God, he'd ask for more than an unlocked door. Screw that. Where's the soldiers roaring in to rescue them on speed boats? That's some shit you could believe in. Hey God, where's the chopper?

"Where's the phone?" asked Annette.

"Damn, she's got a steep learning curve," Marcus whispered to Suzanne.

"Don't lock the door," Patrick said.

"Huh?" Ed asked, having done just that.

"He'll know we're here."

Ed smirked and left the lock engaged. "You think he remembers which houses are locked?"

"Yes, I do. We should leave everything as we find it."

"Maybe we should lock it in case you're wrong," Ed said.

Patrick's stare said they weren't moving another step until Ed gave in.

"Shit, just unlock it," Marcus snapped. "Won't stop him anyway. You saw that hotel room."

There were a lot of houses and they would be easier for Orange to sweep if he only had to try the knobs. Maybe he'd try this one and move on—provided they left no tell-tale signs. They hadn't bushwhacked their way in so maybe they were golden.

Ed sighed and popped the lock.

An olive-colored couch with a herringbone pattern sat against the back wall of the room where people once relaxed and watched the television beneath the large window. The TV was one of those '70s jobs with oak veneer and probably weighed a ton. Put it in front of the door and that sucker wasn't opening, but Orange had three hundred windows for an alternative.

Great place to hide.

"This place isn't any safer than the lodge," Eliza said.

The couch was flanked by two more impossibly ugly chairs, the one nearest the hallway stained dark with blood. Someone came in here with a hell of a wound and bled out. Pam, Eliza, Adam, and Annette stared at the matted carpet in front of the chair.

Patrick sidestepped the blood trail and headed to the kitchen, followed by Gin. Marcus paused for Adam to fall in behind Gin but his mom cockblocked him.

"Adam, wait." He stopped in his tracks like they were playing Red Light/Green Light.

Marcus went around him, shaking his head. Kids were sexing it up younger than ever these days, but not this boy. They should get him a promise ring so at least it seemed like a choice.

To get to the kitchen they passed through an intersection with a dining room on their left. The dinner table had been flipped and two of its legs broken off. The six chairs were in a state of disarray, two knocked on their sides, one crushed into pieces beneath several holes punched into the wall, the other three chairs stashed in a corner. The hallway to the right ended at a door.

The blood trail led straight to the place of mauling. Someone had tried the drawers for a weapon and found a surprise instead. One of the cabinet doors had blown across the room along with someone's leg, amputated below the knee. AO may have taken the body, but not the leg. What remained of it still wore an old Converse All-Star beneath the kitchen table. It had dried out and didn't even stink anymore. Holes of varying sizes peppered the wall behind it, almost indistinguishable from the long-dried blood spatters.

"Sawed-off shotgun," Patrick said from his squatted position near the sink, peering into the open cabinet.

"Can you get it out?" Marcus asked.

"Not without tools. The recoil loosened the harness, but the wood is still screwed into the stock." He stared directly at Marcus and it wasn't like the looks from Nathan or Ed or Lawrence—Patrick knew when the shit hit the fan that Marcus was the most important guy to have around. Marcus wasn't sure how he felt about someone not named Suzanne depending on him. His stomach shrunk like Patrick had his hand in there squeezing. *You're gonna help us, right? Right, Marcus? Get in there and take one for the team, son! Don't tell me you don't have the guts!* Nuh-uh, screw that shit.

"Probably only had one shell anyway," Gin said.

Patrick looked at the other drawers and the closed cabinets but didn't touch anything. Gin seemed to be taking her cues from Patrick and also left them alone.

If the drawers were rigged, they'd probably all been emptied, too. No great loss. Knives in most of the hands here would be about as lethal as snow cones.

"I think we need to look for a boat," Ed announced.

"You go do that." Patrick squatted in front of the refrigerator and put his finger on a piece of metal on the floor. "Anyone with him?"

People looked at each other, at Ed, at Patrick.

"If that's your plan, you need to leave now. I don't want you drawing attention to the rest of us."

"Hey, you think Nathan died and made you the leader or something?"

Marcus smiled. Shit was about to get real. Suzanne tightened her grip on his arm; she had the same look she got when Marcus and her father argued Grizzlies versus Tigers. Pops thought it was crazy to pay grown men to play games but was down with colleges making bank off the backs of "student athletes." A pissing match between Ed and Patrick was a much bigger deal; no one's fate hung in the balance with ballin'. Marcus reluctantly found himself agreeing with Ed: a boat was the best move. Not necessarily one big enough for nine people, either.

Patrick seemed more interested in a spoon he'd found, rotating and examining it carefully. Could it be the key to everything? Fuck no, but you wouldn't know that to watch him.

Maybe this ain't the best guy to follow.

"Well?" Ed asked, throwing his arms wide.

"If you want to leave, leave." Patrick stood with the spoon in hand. So much for leaving things as they found them.

Adam moved further into the kitchen, closer to the cabinets.

"Don't open any drawers," Pamela warned.

"Nah, sure don't wanna bust a cap," Adam responded and had a look of instant regret as if he'd pulled the trigger on a sure-fire winner only to have it blow up in his face—cue blush. Shit was too serious for corny-ass jokes.

He turned away sheepishly when he saw Marcus looking at him. He was saved by the bell, or at least the civil defense sirens as they shattered the lake house hush. They were muffled in here, but loud enough to make them jump. Maybe they were on a timer like Sling Blade said. Everyone remembered what followed the last eruption.

Annette covered her ears and moaned.

"What's your plan, then?" Ed nodded toward the kitchen cabinets. "Since we won't be making our final stand with butter knives after all."

"This isn't very productive," Eliza said.

Pamela jumped to Ed's defense. "Is there something else we should be doing? We need to find one of those chicken phones. The directory said there's a bunch on the other side of the lake."

Yahtzee, baby.

"There's a reason Patrick thinks it's a bad plan," Suzanne said. "Why?"

Patrick looked at Suzanne and Marcus again and this time there was something else there, something Marcus couldn't place. Did the guy have a reason he didn't want to reveal? If so, why the hell not? They were all in the same boat, or *not* since it was apparently a bad idea.

"Did you see a boat?" Patrick asked Ed.

"Uh . . . no, but this is a lakeside community and—"

"While we're looking for a big enough boat for nine people, we're in the open. He's less than a mile away. Say we find a boat, say it miraculously has oars and we row it out of arrow range by the time he spots us . . . he could be halfway around the lake by the time we make land. And how much time will we have to find shelter before nightfall?"

With that, Patrick crossed the kitchen to a partially open door at the other side of the room. He nudged it the rest of the way with the handle of the spoon, leaning away if he had to promptly bail. Nothing happened.

"Basement." He looked at Gin. "The door at the end of the hall goes to the garage."

"So, uh, what? We hang out here and wait for him to show up?" Ed asked. "I want to be gone by nightfall, not looking for shelter. The sooner we leave this nonsense behind—"

"We won't be gone by nightfall."

"That's comforting," Ed said.

"Maybe we should follow a road out of town?" Eliza suggested. "All roads end at a military checkpoint, don't they?"

Annette pointed to Eliza. "Yeah, that."

"Why would the people who put us here rescue us?" Patrick asked.

"We don't know anything about the people who put us here," Ed said.

Patrick abruptly changed tact. "Adam, the last group they brought here . . . how did they get out?"

"I . . . uh . . . I've never heard of it happening."

"So are we the first group tossed in here as human prey, or has this already happened a hundred times before?"

"Why?" Annette asked. Her voice cracked. "Why would they want us to die?"

"Why would they want us to die, Adam?"

"Because it keeps Agent Orange from breaking through the walls to find victims?"

"Sounds like a winning theory to me," Patrick said.

"That's enough," Ed said. "You're spooking everyone."

"Nathan and Lawrence getting their asses slaughtered already had me spooked," Marcus said. "But what makes you so sure that's what's goin' down?"

Suzanne jumped in. "The lodge had electricity, Marcus. Who's around to pay the bills and change the bulbs? Who's in charge of maintaining the walls that keep *him* in?"

The government. Suzanne believed they'd drive a bus full of kindergarteners in here if it was for the greater good. Two busloads if they were inner city kids.

"I believe we're on the same page, Suzanne," Patrick said.

"Not even in the same book, sir." Ed shook his head, ran a hand over his face. "The government isn't in the business of killing its own citizens to appease some madman. How could they manage the logistics of gathering and transporting us here when they can't even run the Postal Service at a profit?"

"The people who took us have interstate reach and direct

access to the heart of this Kill Zone. Who are they if not some agency within the labyrinthine, bloated bureaucratic nightmare we call the US Government? If the only way to appease an unstoppable killer is to wall the place off and throw him some chum when he gets unruly, you can bet an agency is taking care of it. It's the pragmatic thing to do."

"That's crazy," Ed said. He threw up his hands for the benefit of the others and repeated, "Crazy."

"We've lost our lead. We need to dig in now and find something for defense."

"We never should have followed you here."

Patrick shrugged at Ed, nonplussed. "You don't have to stay."

"But he could be anywhere now."

"So the arguing bought us exactly nothing," Eliza said.

Marcus breathed a sigh of relief. Patrick convinced him, but he and Suzanne would have had to go too if Ed's family left on a boat hunt.

Patrick moved on, case closed. "Gin, would you try to find us some dark clothes, please? These bright colors will make excellent targets if we have to run, which I'm sure was the point. Full moon tonight."

"I can't be here at night!" Annette said. "God, this is a nightmare. I have a full slate of showings Saturday. There's so much to do."

And so much Xanax to take.

"I'll go with Gin," Adam volunteered.

"You're staying right here with us, young man," his mother snapped.

Adam gave his father a pleading look.

"He won't be going far, hon."

"There are traps!"

"Pam, keep it down. Adam, be careful."

Da-amn, son. Marcus thought Suzanne had a deathglare. Pamela looked fit to snatch Patrick's spoon and stab her husband repeatedly in the neck and face.

REINCARNAGE: MAXIMUM CARNAGE

Adam and Gin rushed off before his mom found something sharp. Instead of giving his mom a smug *in your face!* look before he exited stage left Adam tried to appear contrite. Tried.

"We need someone watching upstairs so we see him before he sees us," Patrick said. "We'll plan accordingly depending on how thoroughly he searches the houses, but above all, we've got to keep it down in here." He made it a point to look at Annette and Pamela.

"I've got to pee," Eliza said.

"Find a bathroom upstairs. Nine people pissing in a toilet that won't flush is the first thing he'll smell if we do it down here." Patrick looked from person to person. "If you have to go you do it upstairs."

Marcus wouldn't be able to put off taking a piss much longer and he knew Suzanne was long past due; she had a bladder the size of a walnut.

"Isn't anyone going to check the phone at least?" Annette blurted, as if they had overlooked the most obvious thing. She hurried across the room to a wall-mounted dark green phone with matching cord that dangled to the floor.

Suzanne rolled her eyes. "Order us a pizza."

Ed, Eliza, and Pamela followed Patrick, unconcerned they would miss Annette's surprise announcement of a dial tone. Eliza didn't wait for her pal? Maybe she was getting tired of Annette's craziness, too.

"Are you okay?" Pamela called.

So much for keeping it down. Damn, these people.

"Fine, mom," Adam answered from a rear bedroom.

"Why isn't there a dial tone?" Annette whined. The long cord swayed after she hung up.

Suzanne pretended shock. "For real? It doesn't work?"

Marcus laughed. "Maybe there's something on the news about that. Go try the TV."

Annette scowled. Like many certifiable idiots, she

reserved the right to act like one but didn't want to be treated like one. With a grumble, she went after the main group and left Suzanne and Marcus alone in the kitchen.

"So what about the canoe?" Suzanne whispered.

"Next house over on a rack at the dock. Maybe it ain't seaworthy if nobody's used it." He nodded at the severed leg. "Obviously motherfuckers been runnin' for their lives before us."

"Maybe it's locked down. But what good is getting to the other side by ourselves? What if they stick together and find a Chicken Exit and get rescued? We'll be screwed."

Marcus took a few steps to verify no one was within earshot.

Suzanne snapped her fingers. "Hey, hey, conversation over here." She snapped again. She knew he hated it; they'd argued over it many times.

How much time have we wasted arguing about meaningless shit?

He didn't let it faze him now. If time was short, it would be a waste of what they had left. The storm was coming.

"Too late to go." He nodded toward the front of the house. "He's out there somewhere."

"And now we don't know where." Her eyes widened. "If he breaks in, if we get separated, go for the canoe. These people'll leave you like we left Lawrence and Nathan. You don't owe them anything. Don't try some heroic shit."

Marcus smiled. "Don't worry none about that. Your parents would like it too much."

Her parents were civil to him, but only just. If he and Suzanne were never seen again, they'd believe he dragged her down with him, even though they didn't know shit. They thought he was some kind of thug for his "vulgar language" (her dad's term) and grammar that worked just fine at his own parents' house. Most of the people he knew talked like that and their biggest crime was just smoking some chronic. If her dad knew he did that at his boy

Dewan's, his stuck-up ass would petition to have Marcus sent to the electric chair. Missing Grizzlies for that chump's birthday was some bullshit. He'd never been to jail and had a perfectly legit job installing cabinets.

Maybe somehow this really was his fault, though. He kept it real. He could have set off the wrong person. Maybe they all did. Adam didn't fit, but he might be a package deal with his parents. Nathan, Lawrence, and Annette, no doubt they'd pissed some people off.

Suzanne would disagree, but to Marcus the group was several blacks and Mexicans shy for this to be a government plot.

Paint chips dropped on Marcus's head. Suzanne nodded at the cracked kitchen ceiling. "Should we be with them?"

Before he could answer, footsteps pounded down the stairs. Patrick returned first, followed by Ed. Gin and Adam also returned from the bedrooms with armfuls of dark clothing, now wearing black shirts.

"Pamela, Eliza, and Annette are watching the windows, Marcus," Patrick said. "They'll give us a heads up if they spot him."

"Okay."

"XL? Thank you." Patrick took a black shirt from Gin. He pulled the new shirt over top of the white one. "Pam and Eliza will need shirts. The black sweatpants might be a tight fit, Ed, but give these a try. The Man with the Yellow Hat wants his pants back."

"These are my lucky golf pants."

"Unlucky for everyone else."

Ed put on a dark shirt provided by Adam with the word "Foghat" written in bold white letters on the front, but it wouldn't draw any more attention than the long white sleeves of what was now a button-up undershirt. He expected to see a big cartoon bird on Ed's back, but then remembered that was Foghorn Leghorn.

What the hell's a Foghat? Must be a white thing.

"Thanks, son," Ed said, ruffling Adam's hair.

Suzanne squeezed Marcus's hand. "I've got to go."

"I can't hold it, either," Gin said.

"Uh, me neither." Adam.

That bathroom would smell hella good by the time Marcus got in there. Ammonia Central.

When everyone else but Patrick and Marcus left the room, Ed whispered, "Did you really have to tell everyone it's the government? Maybe it is, but . . . killing hope? What good is that going to do?"

"It gets seven people to drop the idea of looking for disabled Chicken Exits."

The sirens ground to a stop and the conversation with it. Nathan wasn't screaming to mark their position and they were sheltered from view this time, but the house still felt more like a trap than a fortress. Orange could either get them in here or intercept them if they tried to leave.

A board cracked upstairs.

At last Ed swallowed audibly and asked, "How do you know the Chicken Exits won't work?" He got out of his kicks and pulled the sweatpants over his lucky golf pants.

"Call it an educated guess. I wouldn't drop eleven people in here and give them a way out. If we—"

"You're basing a plan of action on guesses. Until we know the Chicken Exits don't work this is just a theory."

"But what if he's right?" Marcus threw in. "What's the plan of action if there's no help comin'?"

"We help ourselves," Patrick said. "Find weapons. At the least we need to hurt that bastard. Even if he can come back from the dead later he can be killed temporarily."

"Then what?"

"We have time to find our way out. You look ludicrous in those sweatpants. Aren't they too tight over your other pants? I don't see how you can even run."

"I don't need to go faster than my wife anyway."

"Suit yourself."

Marcus cut in. "Why are we here, though? You got a guess?"

Patrick indicated the basement stairwell. "Let's talk as we go." He took the first step cautiously. "Wouldn't a flashlight be great?"

Yeah, if it was tied to a missile launcher.

Patrick went down the creaking stairwell slowly, probably testing for tripwires or loose boards. In a few minutes he reached the bottom and they could see him motion for them in the hazy light. The solid black T-shirt made a hell of a difference. "We've got light, fellas."

Marcus and Ed descended and found Patrick in a huge, nautically-themed den cum game room that smelled of leather, cedar, and stale piss. Someone hadn't bothered looking for a bathroom down here and unleashed his spray on one of the ancient throw rugs. Or maybe Orange marked his turf.

"So why were we chosen?" Ed asked.

The dual windows, each as large as the one in the TV room, were partially obscured by curtains. Shafts of light came through at odd angles. Dust floated through the rays.

"Each of us probably fit a host of criteria which, unfortunately, intersected with our availability at the time of the round-up," Patrick said.

Even if the place had electricity the light above the pool table wouldn't work anymore. It had been suspended on either end by chains, but one side had snapped and the thing had swung down. Marcus ran his hand along the furrows it ripped in the felt surface of the table. Dangling cobweb streamers slowly fluttered.

"You were on vacation with your family. It could be a week before your absence is noticed." Patrick pointed to Marcus. "You mentioned you were traveling?"

"Just to see her parents. We're talking Friday night, get the hell out ASAP Saturday."

"How far?"

"Memphis to Nashville, three hours by car. That's the last thing I remember. We was gonna stop for a cake. They probably reported us missin' by now."

Floorboard creaks and moans drew his attention overhead. Every movement seemed to strain the house as if years of emptiness left it incapable to cope with the influx of humanity. For whatever reason, maybe termites, it didn't seem to be as structurally solid when listening down here.

"And there's three hours of interstate to search," Patrick said. Disobeying his own orders he peeled back the curtains to let more light into the room. One of the rods fell, bringing down the curtains of the left window. It set a billion dust particles free.

Patrick opened the other curtain. The second window was a sliding glass door. On the deck outside Marcus saw a toppled charcoal grill beside a picnic table turned on its side. This would be the lower deck that ran along the rear of the house, the path not taken at the fork in the stairwell.

"Dusty," Patrick mumbled. "But we have light."

Across from the sliding door, a pub-style counter jutted from the wall. There were a couple of pictures Marcus couldn't make out behind the bar. To the left of the bar was a pool cue rack and a long shuffle board. In the center of the wall adjacent to the stairwell, a doorway opened near the opposite corner and in the middle there was a mounted wooden ship wheel surrounded by various fishing rods. But the real showpieces of the room were on the opposite wall. Two large fishing hooks were port and starboard of several mounted fish, the largest a swordfish, all surrounding the large centerpiece: a harpoon gun with a two-pronged tip. The spear had a ring on the underside threaded with thin rope from a spool which hung from the wooden forestock. Cobwebs adorned everything—they were a part of the décor in every room.

Patrick crossed the room to the couch below the harpoon gun, a tornado of motes swirling behind him. "Might want to flip that shirt inside out."

Ed looked at the front of his shirt and then peeled it over his head. "Not all of us were on vacation."

"Accessibility is only one of the criteria," Patrick said. "Gin had a stalker, so guess where an investigation into her disappearance will focus?"

Marcus couldn't resist. "Adam?"

"Hey."

"Just pullin' your leg, man."

"He's home schooled. He doesn't get to interact with girls much."

"Home schooled?" Patrick laughed softly. He removed the couch cushions, probably checking for a trap rather than loose change.

"What's that supposed to mean?" Ed stood in front of the wall-mounted pool cue rack, which held no actual cues. Only three balls remained.

"That put you on the radar, too."

Dust from the disturbed couch and fallen curtains tickled Marcus's nose and throat.

"Because he won't be missed in class?"

"Something like that," Patrick answered. Satisfied he wouldn't get a nasty surprise, he returned the cushions and stepped onto the couch to reach the harpoon gun. Instead of grabbing it, he tilted his head and examined the wall around it. "The police will focus on Gin's aggressive lothario."

"Isn't Annette in real estate? She'll have houses to show."

"Shit, I wouldn't report her missing," Marcus said. "But Eliza was jogging. How's that fit? They just pull up and drag her into a van?"

"Does seem less . . . professional," Ed added.

Patrick shrugged. "Eliza will get a lot of press but a

police investigation won't lead anywhere. How many women go for a jog and never return?"

Marcus remembered a story about an owl attacking joggers in Highpoint, but the only thing that disappeared in those attacks was an iPod taken by that fucking bird. When Eliza didn't turn up, people would think she was raped, murdered, and buried somewhere—or captive in some nutcase's dungeon.

"Brilliant move to take some of us while we were far from home. We probably aren't officially missing yet and once we are the trail will be cold. Law enforcement from multiple jurisdictions will slow walk until something definitive turns up to prove we were taken from their turf."

"Where were you?" Ed asked.

"Vacation in Mexico." Patrick twisted small wires at each end of the weapon and lifted it from the rack.

"Damn, these people got some reach."

"What do you do?"

"Trader with Universal Exports." Patrick aimed the harpoon gun at the couch but didn't pull the trigger.

Ed said, "Think I've heard of them."

The name meant nothing to Marcus. The extent of his stock market involvement was a 401(k) on auto-pilot with allocations currently in the "aggressive" category. Chances of dying before the big cash-out? Also aggressive.

Patrick put the harpoon gun on the pool table and walked to the bar. Marcus wondered if he or Ed should be checking closets and other rooms, but they'd probably find a trap instead of anything useful.

Patrick ducked out of sight behind the bar. "Yesss!"

"What is it?"

"Find a gun?" Marcus asked.

Bottles clinked together and things fell over. Patrick slid an object across a shelf and Marcus felt something he thought he never would again: elation. Patrick had probably found a shotgun. It was big whatever it was.

When Patrick put a white beer cooler on top of the counter Marcus's smile slipped.

"What's in it?"

With a grin, Patrick pulled out thin canisters with dark rims. "Koozies." He immediately set about pulling the plastic rings off the tops. The koozies were emblazoned with different beer logos. Schlitz, Pabst Blue Ribbon, Miller, Duff, Viper. One by one he let the rings drop to the floor behind the counter. Ed and Marcus looked at each other to confirm this shouldn't be a big deal.

Suzanne, Gin and Adam clumped down the stairs. Adam carried a large metal gas can with liquid sloshing inside it.

"Half-full," Gin said. "It was in the garage. No boat."

Adam set the can on the floor. It was dented on top. Marcus found Suzanne's eyes, wondering if she was as in the dark as he was. She shrugged. Gin and now Adam seemed to be on a different wavelength with Patrick, like there was a clique and some of the others hadn't been asked to join—hadn't even known of its existence. Marcus had been paying attention to everything but he didn't remember Patrick requesting a garage search for gasoline.

"Excellent. Marcus, could you and Suzanne empty these bottles into a sink, please?" He pulled some large whiskey bottles from behind the bar.

"Why are we emptying bottles?" Suzanne asked. Marcus recognized the pissed look, like she was about to spit hot fire, before she whispered to him, "And why the *fuck* did you take off?"

"A Styrofoam and gasoline mixture is poor man's napalm. We'll light that bastard up like he was born on the Fourth of July." Patrick smiled wryly.

"Sorry," Marcus whispered.

She pointedly ignored him. To Gin, she said, "Was there a car in the garage?"

"Yeah, but I think all the tires were flat."

Always quick to dash hopes, Patrick said, "It won't run anyway. That battery probably died before half of us were born."

The stale piss scent suddenly overwhelmed as if someone had stepped in it and stirred it up.

"Found another bathroom," Adam announced, pushing open the door by the corner.

"Great, empty these in the sink. Please. Check for old soap. We can use it in the napalm."

Suzanne grabbed the bottles and handed one to Marcus before pushing him toward the bathroom.

"Don't you ever wander off like that again."

"We just went to the basement. We didn't go next door."

"Shut up while you're ahead."

Marcus had to strain to get the first cap to twist. He emptied the bottle into the sink, checking past Suzanne. The partially open door and Suzanne with hands on hips blocked everyone's view. If he couldn't piss in the toilet, he could go in the sink.

"Stay there for a minute," he whispered. He held a bottle between his goods and the doorway just in case Suzanne bailed and threw open the door in mid stream. He sighed with relief.

It was short-lived. Suzanne shook her head. "What the hell were you thinking?"

"I wasn't. Should have yelled upstairs and told you where we was headed."

"Don't do it again. We stick together. "

After shaking off, Marcus washed it down with some vintage whiskey and pushed the door open the rest of the way with his foot. A nip from what remained in the first bottle was pretty good. Bourbon.

Nothing left in the soap dish but the dried crust of an old bar of soap so he stepped out of the bathroom. Gin and Adam sat on the floor between the pool table and fallen curtains where they crushed Styrofoam and dropped it into a punch bowl. Large pieces were torn from the cooler and the koozies were gone. The bowl had plenty of crushed, torn Styrofoam.

Patrick took the bottles from Marcus and set them atop the bar. He'd been tearing the extra shirt into strips. For whatever reason, Patrick decided the T-shirt was better for his Molotov cocktails than the curtains.

"Did you see a funnel in the garage?" he asked.

"We couldn't see much of anything," Gin said. "Those bushes blocked the window and most of the light. Should we go back and see if our eyes adjust?"

"No, we'll be careful when we pour."

Suzanne nodded toward the stairwell. Her angry look was gone, so Marcus felt it was safe to move in that direction.

Patrick swirled the contents of the gasoline can. The metal cap squeaked when he unscrewed it.

At the stairwell, Suzanne whispered, "This doesn't feel right. We should be moving."

"Moving where? There's nowhere to go if he's right."

"I've seen those idiots who get evacuated on news and talk shows. People *do* get out of here. We can call from a Chicken Exit. Say our guide got killed in a trap, we're sorry, now please hurry the hell up and get our asses out of here."

They heard thumping upstairs. It was someone coming down the stairs from the second floor.

"How's he going to light his napalm? Did he find matches?"

"He didn't say."

"There's a *lot* he doesn't say.

"Oh gawd, *they left us.*" The unmistakable whine belonged to Annette.

"Down here!" Suzanne called in a harsh whisper. "Just wanna ring that bitch's neck. Rubs me the wrong way twice."

"He's coming for us." Annette nearly stumbled down the stairwell.

"You see him?" Marcus asked.

"Slow down," Eliza warned behind her.

Annette hurried past Suzanne and Marcus as if she were the one who had to make the announcement to everyone. The town crier, with an emphasis on crying. The others were already well aware of the crisis and gathered at the stairwell.

"He's here, he's here!" Annette pointed frantically. "What do we do?"

"Where's my wife?" Ed asked.

"She's watching him from the window," Eliza said.

"Okay, okay, just stay down here. I'll have a look," Patrick said. He called out to Gin and Adam, "Keep mixing."

Marcus wondered if splitting up was the best strategy, but decided it beat all of them stampeding up the stairs at once.

He and Suzanne followed Ed up the stairwell with Patrick close behind them. "Stay back from the windows," Patrick whispered. "No talking."

With only the swish of his pants to mark his sudden burst of movement from the stairwell, Marcus light-stepped toward the hallway. He didn't want to go upstairs and risk the only route of escape being a second floor window. The first room on the right faced the street outside.

Despite Patrick's warning, Marcus raced to the nearest window and lightly parted the wisp-thin white curtains. Not knowing where the guy was seemed just as dangerous as trusting the ones upstairs to warn everyone in time to scoot out the back door.

Marcus doubted Agent Orange could see him because he couldn't see much of the street through this window.

Suzanne put a hand on his back.

"See him?" she whispered.

He shook his head. Someone might just be jumping at shadows. He felt like Orange couldn't really be there unless he confirmed it for himself.

Then he saw him cross the street with what looked like a burlap bag over his head—a bag with eerie goggles sewed into it.

Marcus wished for the sirens now for a sonic buffer. Each footfall in the house seemed thunderous, like the pounding hearts of everyone hidden inside. More creaking floorboards. He wanted to scream, *WHO THE FUCK IS MOVING AROUND?*

Overgrowth obstructed Orange for a moment. Marcus saw a shape move behind the fluttering leaves. He was angled toward the house beside theirs, as though going door to door to inquire about beliefs in an afterlife—or at least speed people along to find out if they were right.

This hide and wait plan suddenly seemed like the stupidest thing ever. He and Suzanne could jet, but would Orange spot them through a window of the other house? Until he was on the opposite side of the street, it would be insane to make a run for it.

He needed the bathroom again.

Minutes passed in the silence. No sign of him. Apparently he didn't just jiggle doorknobs and move on. It'd be a lot more than a quick piss inspection when he dropped by here; probably like cops with a search warrant, but a greater chance of someone ending up dead.

A little *greater, anyway.*

Marcus shut his burning eyes for a moment to rest them. He half-expected that goggle-eyed mask to slip into the space between the window and the tree outside when he opened them again.

He thought of Dewan and more specifically his python, Sir Jinx. Dewan liked to hit a blunt and blow the smoke in Sir Jinx's face, usually ending up in a coughing fit as he broke out laughing.

I'm gonna end up making him docile and shit, but I can't help it. It's too damn funny.

Except showtime with the snake didn't always mean high times.

Check this shit, son. This is so dope.

Then they'd watch a formerly lethargic Sir Jinx delight in wrapping up a mouse and squeezing the life out that bitch with excruciating relish. Suzanne eventually refused to go over to Dewan's, and truthfully Marcus preferred to meet up with him far away from that creepy-ass snake, too.

And now they were holed up in here, getting the life and hope slowly squeezed out of them.

The unmistakable—and loud—breaking of a board cracked the silence. Suzanne jumped. Her grip on his shoulder tightened as she whispered, "Shit!"

He'd turned around to track the noise, which didn't repeat. When he faced the window again, he saw Agent Orange, though thankfully not inches away. He stood out on the street, unmoving.

"I think he heard it," Suzanne whispered.

It was better when she couldn't see him; Marcus didn't want her freaked out, too.

He finally unfroze and trudged toward the house across the street. The zigzag pattern would bring him this way afterward.

"We can't stay here," Marcus said. "He's coming here next."

"If we leave, he'll see us."

"Not if we head out the back door."

"Through the woods? He'll hear us."

He suddenly deviated from his path, turning down the street and away from the houses. Had he called it off? Marcus continued to watch, unbelieving. Why would he leave the last two houses unsearched?

"He's leaving?"

Orange dropped out of sight. Marcus stared at the

vanishing point, waiting for him to reappear like the retreat was a joke.

Thought I'd let you live after all? Psych!

Eventually he heard movement upstairs and ambient chatter.

We're saved! Let's find some more loud shit to break at a crucial moment!

He wanted to find the moron who'd snapped a board and snap their spine over his knee.

"Who the hell was moving around?" Suzanne asked. "Some of these idiots don't even want to live, I'm telling you. The further from them we get the—"

Someone screamed. A short, startling burst.

"Seriously? Seriously?"

Bad news for the group. They were in enough danger without Suzanne getting hotheaded.

Marcus eased back from the window to stand. His body protested from the strain of staying crouched so long. Suzanne rushed into the hallway, frantically motioning for Marcus to follow her up the stairs. His knees popped.

He saw Pamela first, but Patrick was close behind.

"Who screamed?" Suzanne asked.

Annette, who should have stayed downstairs like Patrick told her, said, "I saw a mouse."

"Oh? Did it have a machete? *He* does."

"We should move to the house he just checked before he comes back," Patrick said. More thumps as he pushed past Marcus and Suzanne and down the stairs once more.

"We should follow a road to the wall," Eliza said, right behind. "There's a military checkpoint. We should have done that in the first place and stayed ahead of him!"

Ed pounded down the stairs with Pamela, his needle reliably entrenched in a groove of the broken record about finding one of those emergency phones across the lake.

I'm starting to think this shit is sponsored by the makers of the Chicken Exit, Marcus thought. Pamela wasn't warming up to the idea, though, and good thing—he'd feel marginally bad waving to them after he and Suzanne commandeered that canoe and paddled away while they watched dumbfounded from the dock.

"If we stay here he's going to find us," Annette whimpered.

The first thing you said that ain't stupid as hell. Congratulations.

Everyone trailed downstairs after Patrick in the unspoken game of Follow the Leader, but Suzanne grabbed him and held him fast. From where he stood he could see the front door and the back door. Orange could knock either one of them down any minute.

He waited forever for the others to get down the stairs and well out of earshot, and still kept his voice to a whisper. "Okay, what?" While he wasn't sure he wanted to go next door or try for the boat, he didn't want to stand around with no input on what the group would do. They had napalm (maybe) and a harpoon gun, so why stick around? There were probably enough votes to override him if the group didn't like whatever Patrick had planned, but would anyone really want to separate from the guy who'd engineered the discovery of their only two weapons? Maybe they could make Annette the tie-breaker, as in Marcus and Suzanne would do the opposite of whatever she chose.

"We're running out of time to get to the other side of the lake." Suzanne squeezed his arm for emphasis. "He's going to convince them to go next door."

"Maybe we should go with it, see how it plays out. Orange already cleared it. He won't go back."

"And maybe he didn't finish the first time."

"What? You think he ran home 'cause he left the stove on?"

"I don't know what that was about, but I do know he can chase everyone if we all stick together. He can't be everywhere at once. He's gotta make a choice if we split up."

"Yeah, that's a great point . . . unless he chooses us."

"Marcus, who do you think he'll find first? Two people together or seven?"

"But baby, who has the better chance if he does find them? Two people with tree branches or the seven people with napalm? They could melt that motherfucker down to his boots. We'll be lucky to give him poison ivy."

They stared at each other for a long moment, a hidden conversation he suspected meant a lot more than his points about sticking with the group. Her body released the tension of the moment as she relented, though he knew she was far from convinced.

"Just don't forget who makes up those seven people you're counting on," Suzanne said, a finger jabbed in his face.

"Uh uh. It's 'cause of them we'll still be able to get away on our own if we have to." He grabbed her hand. "Come on, before they leave us behind."

Downstairs, Patrick, Gin, and Adam filled bottles with the napalm concoction. The gasoline smell overpowered the stale piss and dust downstairs. Orange would know they'd been here even if he had a mask over his snout.

"I think we should look for more weapons next door," Patrick said. "This was a decent haul, but—"

"One of us needs to go for a Chicken Exit," Ed said. "Maybe two. Is anyone with me?"

The sirens started anew.

"Fuck! This again?" Marcus threw up his arms. He meant Ed as much as the sirens. That dude was hooked on his Chicken Exit strategy.

Patrick stuffed the second bottle with a rag.

"What about you?" Ed looked at Eliza. "Will you go with me? Two sets of eyes are better than one. You're a runner. If he shows up, you could get away, no problem."

Eliza shook her head.

Good thing for you, Ed. She and Annette are a package deal.

"What was he wearing?" Gin asked. "A gas mask?"

Patrick answered, "Yes, a Macpherson gas mask. Useful invention for soldiers who didn't want to breathe through a handkerchief soaked in urine."

Of course he would know that.

Pam said, "Ed, don't be like this. You'd get lost or run into him just as soon as you'd find one of those phones."

Patrick picked up the bottles. "I've already got it on my hands," he said to Gin.

Marcus had worked his way to the sliding glass door, Suzanne right behind him. He glanced outside where the boards were covered in layers of old fallen leaves just like the upper deck. With a light tug Marcus tried to slide the door to see if it was unlocked. It came loose with a loud groan.

The various conversations ceased and everyone looked his way in horror.

"My bad," Marcus said.

"Better close the curtain over that, Marcus," Patrick said. "If he—"

Annette screamed.

The glass pane screeched along the old rails. Marcus felt himself tugged by Suzanne and he lurched sideways off balance and fell, taking Suzanne down with him. He looked over his shoulder in time to see Agent Orange step through the doorway not two feet away.

FUUUUUUUUUUUUUUUUUUUUUUUUUU

Orange moved away from the sliding door, leaving them a sliver of hope. Marcus scrambled to his feet, only playing hero to Suzanne. He jerked her up and pushed her through the doorway, leaves crunching under the pounding steps as they broke into a run.

Even before he glimpsed the bow propped against the

outside wall, Marcus knew Orange had come from the right side of the house. He would have seen his approach otherwise. Marcus swept up the bow as he and Suzanne ran toward an opening in the deck. He jumped and turned sideways, slamming himself between bushes and the wall.

"Go, go, go," Suzanne said.

Marcus broke through the soft bushes and headed straight toward the water. He looked over his shoulder, saw Suzanne, saw no one else. Maybe Orange would worry with those in the house long enough to give them a good head start on the lake. It seemed like too much to hope for, but the guy came out of nowhere and bypassed them for other targets, so they had some luck on their side. Marcus would take that shit . . . *and* the bow.

Try launching arrows at our asses without this, you Macpherson-faced fuck!

In an adrenaline-fueled, bow-flinging freak-out, Marcus slung the thing toward the lake as hard as he could. His right foot caught something on the ground and he pitched forward, convinced he was about to plant his face into a bed of spikes. He struck the ground as the bow splashed into the lake twenty or thirty yards out.

"Marcus!"

Suzanne had hoisted herself onto the deck.

"Go, I'm okay." He waved her on as he looked back. Still no Agent Orange. Through the trees he could see one person, then a second, hauling ass on the street. Between the brush and the trees, he couldn't tell who it might be.

By the time he'd jumped atop the deck Suzanne had dislodged the canoe, which struck the dock with a hollow thump.

Did she even check it for a trap?

Nothing happened, though. He lifted the deceptively heavy thing. The shoulder he'd messed up in a wreck with Dewan didn't care much for the effort. He hurried to the end of the dock. The left side curved toward the water and didn't look stable.

"No oars," Suzanne reported.

He'd paddle with his hands if he had to. Marcus stopped just before the dock started its lean and slid the boat over the edge. The prow hit the water and almost dipped beneath the surface as he let the rest of it slide over and jumped into the water beside it. His weight thrust his feet deep into the mud, like the ground wanted to suck him down below the lake. He pushed it back toward Suzanne so she could ease herself inside it from the shaky dock.

Marcus tried to free his feet from the mud. For a moment he had a horrifying image of himself anchored to this spot like he was encased in concrete while Agent Orange approached. He pulled against the hull of the canoe to give himself leverage. The suction of the mud dislodged his right shoe but he got his foot loose. His water-logged pants seemed to add an extra fifteen pounds to each leg.

"Come on, come on," Suzanne urged. Her horrified eyes seemed a few notches below the terror they should hold if Orange appeared, so he didn't need to look back.

The lake seemed to have a gradual slope, but with the water at chest-level he knew he was already too deep to climb into the canoe without tipping it. Lack of an oar was the least of their problems since he was so nautically challenged he hadn't even known how to set sail in the first place. He'd been moving parallel to the dock and finally cleared it. His legs were tired already from straining against the mud and the weight of his pants.

"Get in," Suzanne said, scooting toward the front of the canoe to give him a hand.

No good. Whenever he tried to pull himself up the thing tipped toward the water, threatening to capsize or dislodge Suzanne. Maybe Patrick had been right all along— better to keep nine fools who had no business around boats from seeking one as an escape method.

"Oh *shit*! Get in the boat! He's coming!"

Marcus heard the thumping on the dock. He rolled to his back in the water, clasped the top of the canoe and paddled with his feet as hard as he could. They were only a few yards from the end of the dock and Marcus felt like he was kicking through a thick stew of molasses. The shoeless foot seemed to have slightly less resistance and now he wished he'd lost them both.

Orange ignored the tilt of the dock, keeping himself toward the high end in a careful stride that seemed practiced, as if he'd walked to the dock's edge a thousand times in rehearsal for a kill that may materialize someday. He didn't need the bow to strike at them from a distance. He had the harpoon gun.

"Aim for the sunken boat!" Suzanne screamed. He heard her splashing in the water, paddling with a hand or both hands. It didn't seem to add to the thrust but it did make the canoe buck in his fists.

"Left, left! Get it between us!"

Marcus couldn't take his eyes off Orange, who took up a firing stance with the tip of his right boot hanging off the edge of the dock, left leg planted behind him. He had a cat-like agility, like a big fucking lion in his preserve where an obstacle for others—a dangerously tilting dock—became his advantage. It was clearly more durable than Marcus assumed and he couldn't help but think things might be different if he'd carried the canoe to the edge and put it in further from shore. With a distance of only six or seven yards separating Marcus from Orange, the guy couldn't miss. All Marcus could do was kick, kick, kick, as he propelled the canoe.

The harpoon snapped and the projectile closed the distance with the attached tether line unspooling from the roller. In a flash it punched Marcus in the gut.

"Marcus!"

Suzanne's movement jerked the hull from his right

hand—his left hand was already grabbing at the spear. His legs sank as he tilted upward. The pain bloomed like a bag of hot water burst inside him, heat washing in all directions at once, a searing pain that intensified when the projectile slid through his grip. Agent Orange wound the spool to get his harpoon back. Marcus could see it snaking through a cloud of blood just beneath the surface of the water, like an eel. The withdrawal of the spear left him with a lingering sense of being tugged, like he'd momentarily bonded with it and now its absence radiated shockwaves; phantom limb syndrome. On his tiptoes, head just above the surface, Marcus gasped for air and heard Suzanne calling his name.

"Go! Just go! I'll catch up!" he screamed.

Sure I won't.

The feedback sent to his brain from his hands didn't make sense or maybe his brain had to deal with too much sensory input at once. It was like some small creature with tentacles had latched on to his wound to drain the cavity, creating a horrible stretching. Then the realization struck him—he was squeezing his intestines as the slippery entrails uncoiled and slipped through his fingers.

Marcus screamed.

The harpoon rose from the rippling lake surface a couple yards away, its tip fastened to what looked like a deflated purple snake. Both ends of the snake extended below the surface of the water as Orange reeled in more and more of the creature. In this case, the creature was Marcus.

He heard a splash behind him. Arms on his shoulders, hands pulling him in the opposite direction as Orange wound the harpoon back. Marcus felt faint . . .

"Marcus! Damn it, come on!"

His eyes opened wide and he saw the trail of intestines slithering through the water, buffeted by ripples, like the ropes sectioning off an Olympic swimming event. He grabbed and squeezed, tried to keep it from slipping away, but the amount of pressure he applied seemed directly proportional to his faintness. The harder he fought, the more it blurred all other sensory input.

And it occurred to him Suzanne may get herself killed playing hero by trying to save him.

She can still make it.

The thought was a white hot flash in his mind to match the one in his guts. He was doomed; she didn't have to be.

"Go!" He shrugged her off and moved toward the dock lest he completely unravel.

Something shifted inside him, a painful re-sorting of his inner workings (*re-organ-ization,* he thought somewhere behind the pain) that filled his eyes with tears. On weak legs he shuffled forward, struggling to keep his head above water even as the excruciating pain tempted him to bend forward and suck a mouthful of water into his lungs because that couldn't be as bad as this. *Nothing* could be as bad as this. Burning coals had replaced his intestines.

Orange had the harpoon back. Suzanne must have finally realized what happened to Marcus for she unleashed a scream so horrific it chilled him. Or maybe the chill was from something else. The water hadn't been this cold a minute ago.

Rather than reload, Orange raised the harpoon and slammed it on the deck, lodging it between two boards. His intestines momentarily stretched taut, flinging water to the lake below, but Marcus tensed and more gushed through his fingers, slippery, increasing the slack.

"Go!" he yelled, his voice hoarse and without much power.

Agent Orange stepped from the dock and dropped into the water. Every move looked practiced.

Suzanne hit the water beside him and started to streak past to meet Orange head on. Marcus grabbed her ankle and jerked her back. The tensing of his abdomen strained more of the viscera in his other hand.

"Get to the other side or he will . . . *kill* . . . you," Marcus warned. "You gotta go . . . now. I'm done." He huffed. " . . . I'm done."

Alongside Suzanne now, he shoved her back toward the boat. Her red eyes showed more fear than anger. On some level he knew this was the last look they would share. She had to get away to make this right, even if he never knew.

Marcus shuffled toward Orange, but he had a hard time feeling his legs and wanting to move didn't make it happen. In fact, he wasn't moving at all. Orange had no such trouble. He waded through the water with his arms in the air and for a split-second Marcus's mind filled in the blank with the iconic imagery of a soldier wading through a Vietnamese swamp with his M-16 above his head. But it fell apart with a quickness. The M-16 became a machete, the camouflage-painted face a goggle-eyed, hose-mouthed motherfucker who'd turned him into William Wallace. He'd gladly yell "Mercy" if he could yell anything.

Marcus's stomach heaved and he vomited into the water. The nausea didn't abate. His mouth was full of blood. He spat.

In the splashing struggle to stay afloat, Marcus's face dipped toward the water. Only the struggle wasn't his—he wasn't moving, he was just sinking. So the splashing was Suzanne. Somewhere Suzanne was still alive, escaping.

Marcus opened his eyes and he was in the lake house, staring through the window into the goggles of Agent Orange. Only . . . the killer was right here, right now. For a moment, Marcus saw his own eyes reflected in the goggles, but then, like the shifting of a lenticular image, he saw the eyes of Agent Orange.

Holy . . . oh, holy shit.

Through the lenses were the windows to this man's soul where Marcus glimpsed the ultimate truth. Hell wouldn't take this guy and that's why he always came back; why he always would.

Orange's left arm burst through the surface of the water, the machete glinting in the sunlight.

In the distance, the purple snake slapped against the dock.

Buy her time.

Marcus stumbled back, tried to whirl around. It was like slow motion in his sodden clothes. A gloved hand hauled a gastric coil across Marcus's neck, looped it around a second time for good measure, and pulled it tight.

He thought of those mice at Dewan's, squeezed to their deaths by . . . what was that snake's name?

Marcus stumbled back against Orange, who yanked him back by the hair until he faced skyward. The machete appeared from his left, nudging the bottom of his throat like the tap of a fencing saber, followed by a sound like a heavy tree branch cracking as the blade punched through his skull.

VI.

SUZANNE COULDN'T LOOK BACK. As long as she didn't, Marcus wasn't truly dead. Any minute now, he'd tell her to return to the dock.

It's over, baby . . . we won.

Maybe he already did and she missed it underwater.

Maybe, but I'm not going to look.

Ideally she would swim beneath the surface with Orange not sure where she was until she had a comfortable lead, but her tortured breath—like each one gathered only for a new scream—sent her up sputtering. She heard a thump behind her from the canoe.

Marcus, of course, because he's as dead as Nathan, Lawrence, and all those people outside the lodge with their heads on those poles. His blood was like a dye tab filling up the lake. Soon he'll put Marcus's head with the rest. And mine—

Suzanne glanced back, not looking directly at the dock. Orange had worked his way to the canoe and clambered onto it. Now he was crouched in the boat that promised her and Marcus transport across the lake to freedom. In her mind she saw the stark image of the leg blown off in the lake house, and realized the paddles for the canoe probably *had* been there once upon a time, perhaps laid down near the dock. And someone probably got blown out of their shoes like some cartoon character when he picked it up. She and Marcus were insane to take the risk on the canoe,

84

though to say they were "lucky" half their limbs weren't floating up in an asteroid belt was a bit of a stretch.

She whipped her head forward and launched into a freestyle stroke. It wouldn't keep her underwater, but he couldn't run her down in a boat without paddles anyway. She could also breathe with this technique. It didn't take her long to find her rhythm, though she hadn't swum at all since last year. She found it very easy to hang up after college, and a lot of people at the rehab center played racquetball anyway. She rarely got the chance and usually didn't take it when she did.

Suzanne swung her arms through the lake as though pulling herself along an invisible rope, stealing deep lungfuls of air when her face lifted from the water. She lost her shoes as she pumped her arms and knifed her legs.

Breathe.

The bank on the opposite side seemed as far away as the horizon, three hundred yards at least, but she just needed to get enough of a lead on Orange to—

Something splashed in front of her face. She stopped her stroke on reflex, even though she understood the whole point of this was to distract her. It didn't matter. She sucked in water and choked, but somehow still managed to scream. She didn't need to look back at the dock to see what became of Marcus now. His head bobbed on the surface and tilted over to expose a stare that seemed accusatory to her even as it suggested a horror so profound as to be indescribable; something Orange pointed Marcus's eyes to see, and something they would always see. She saw the jagged underside of his neck, the tangled viscera of arteries and veins and a knob of clipped bone.

She launched herself to the right, prepared to swim laterally for a mile to get around it if she had to. She couldn't look at it another second, seized by the cold certainty she would go absolutely insane if she were to touch it. She'd been with Marcus eight years since assisting in the rehab of his shoulder following a car wreck, and she believed she'd always be with him (much to the chagrin of her mother and father). To see the eyes which had shown her such longing now communicating only the despair of eternal horror, she felt the temptation to view all of this as an impossibly lucid dream, but she knew Marcus would have mocked her for even trying.

We're here and it's real, he'd said at the lodge, when they thought they were alone in this. *The worst things don't make no sense, but they don't have to. They'll happen to you while you're sittin' there askin' yourself how they could, doing nothin' about it, and you may as well already be dead then.*

No, not dead then, but he was now. She thought she may have screamed again, but everything was one great cacophony; the thrashing of her arms and feet, her hoarse gasps for air, the pounding of blood in her temples. Even the ache of her burning lungs seemed to have its own sound. She angled herself across the lake once more, confident she was past the thing she needed to forget and must not touch.

There was a pneumatic burst behind her that canceled all other sound. The harpoon gun. She tensed, expecting the impact of the spear through her back, but it never came. She allowed herself a peek and saw Orange in a tug-of-war with the harpoon, hauling it back to the boat.

He missed me.

Not only missed, but apparently didn't have enough rope to reach her in the first place because she was out of range. If he wanted her now, he'd have to dive in.

I don't care if you've come back from the dead a hundred and forty-seven times, let's see how fast you can swim 50 yards wearing those big-ass boots, you psychotic piece of shit. You can't catch me now.

Thank God Marcus tossed that bow into the lake. He'd given her a chance.

Her eyes burned and everything blurred. She pushed the thought aside, hauled herself down that unseen rope one handful at a time. She didn't know what she would do when she reached the bank, but hopefully a military patrol would cruise by soon enough. She'd hide as long as she had to. She didn't believe he'd swim all the way out to trap the woods over there, but right now she didn't care. She'd be lucky if she could crawl ten feet once she made it, but he'd have to be one racist bastard to keep coming with so many others still scattered on the mainland any—

The pneumatic burst came again.

Unless you pulled the drain stopper on this lake with that harpoon, I don't know why you'd even waste—

The calf of her right leg exploded in pain. Her first thought was *cramp*. She'd been too far away for the harpoon before, had gotten even farther away, and his canoe was about as mobile as a beached whale.

She rolled over on her back and slipped under the surface. Her scream instantly went flat and watery as the heaviness of the lake crashed into her ears. A dark red cloud flowered beside her leg, not quite enough to obscure the object lodged there. The harpoon, of course. He'd cut the rope on the spear and taken one last shot to stop her.

She maneuvered herself above the surface again with the kick of her left leg and a crippled backstroke. The sky loomed above her, indifferent. Orange stepped off the canoe, apparently not bothered by the prospect of swimming with such heavy clothing and bootwear. Nor had he reason to be. Suzanne couldn't beat him to the other bank now and probably couldn't make it halfway anyway.

She screamed for help toward the houses, the instinct insuppressible despite knowing how much consideration they'd given the same plea from Lawrence an hour ago.

Can't nobody do nothin' for Sling Blade now, Marcus puffed in the sprint.

She thought it sounded like a warning, in case she had ridiculous designs about turning back.

I didn't hear anything, she'd said.

Hell no we didn't.

And they'd run that much faster and still hadn't heard it when the screaming began in earnest a minute later and didn't stop for several minutes that brought goosebumps all up and down her arms and tightened her scalp until she swore she felt every individual strand of hair. The same way nobody could hear her now.

It occurred to her she'd never heard an explosion back at the house. Patrick's napalm solution must have been as devastating as a carpet burn. Maybe AO finished off everybody in the house, though she didn't think he could have gotten them all so soon. He'd prioritized her and Marcus either because he thought they were going to get away for good or he was *really* pissed off about Marcus stealing his bow. Either way, they should have taken their chances in the woods, traps or not.

She kept up the backstroke, but couldn't involve her right leg for fear she'd kick the arrow with the left. A half-sunken boat was her nearest option, maybe thirty yards, a bit further from the shore than whichever one Marcus originally spotted from the lake road. It offered nothing beyond the hope she would find something to defend herself, maybe her own speargun.

His hooded mask bobbed above the water as he approached. However unstoppable he might seem in his pursuit, she was correct about his poor mobility with all the equipment. She would have easily beat him to the other side.

If there was a weapon, she was going to do her damnedest to hurt him bad.

The boat grew bigger as she closed the distance. It was a houseboat, and in a minor stroke of luck she was on the partially sunken side. She pushed toward a brass railing which disappeared underwater, spinning over like a seal to cross the last few yards with a faster paddle. She instinctively kicked with the right leg and regretted it. Pain ignited her calf, but her hands clamped the brass. The blood in her arms had been replaced with lead. It was a significant victory to move along the rail a few feet where she had more space to embark, but she still had to haul herself up with about five hundred pounds of wet clothes and a useless leg.

She knew how to get motivated, though. She checked on Orange, who'd gained a lot of ground, as though she'd seen him in a passenger rearview mirror before and finally turned to see him with her own eyes. Twenty yards away, a shark in camouflage, much faster than when he first plunged in.

She took a deep breath, imagined Marcus shouting at her: *Suzanne, if you don't get up on that boat right now, he's got you!*

His paddling sounded only a few yards behind. She boosted herself, left hand on the bottom bar to snatch the higher bar with her right. Her wet fingers nearly slipped as she hauled her left leg up from the lake and planted it on the boat. She breathed out as she rose with all her weight on the foot, could practically feel cogs grinding in her knee to propel her weight. She kept the right foot away from the boat as she lifted.

Suzanne was surprised her knee didn't give out. She was able to drag herself onto the deck of the houseboat. She gingerly set the right foot down when she found an angle that wouldn't knock the harpoon against the rail. Somewhere Marcus shook his head at all the time squandered. She kept her hands clawed around the rail because the sunken angle of the boat wanted to pitch her back into the water. She didn't need to look back to know he had almost caught her. He could probably splash water onto the deck now. She knew she would never manage to lift both her legs over the top bar, so she hugged herself to the bars and slipped her left leg through the opening as though climbing through a barbed wire fence. This allowed the right leg to dangle over the water, and she was certain Orange would snatch her ankle like a monster under the bed.

Hurry! Marcus's voice and maybe her own fear in harmony with it.

Once the left foot felt stable enough to hold her weight, she crouched and slid her upper body all the way through. Now water *was* splashing on the deck from Orange as he closed the gap. He appeared in the corner of her eye with her pierced leg still hovering overboard. She let herself fall backward and guided her right foot through the gap as she did. Orange's machete hacked into the boat where her foot hung a second before. The spear bumped the bottom bar on her way down. The blade dug through more meat in her calf before it settled back into its original groove. Suzanne shrieked with the shock of pain. She struck the deck in cruciform, careful to keep her head lifted up from the deck—any brush with unconsciousness would surely become permanent—and her right leg raised. The original pain became an awful throb, but this new slice felt hot and urgent.

Orange snatched her left ankle, his grip an immediate vise; something she sensed could smash and crumble the bones beneath like a package of ramen noodles. It felt like a spear shot into that side too.

"Spear," she whispered, seeing it in her leg.

Go, now! Marcus urged in her thoughts. *You know what you have to do.*

She knew.

She bent her right knee to her chest, calf ablaze as if to tease the new pain about to spark her nerve endings. She ripped the harpoon out with much more strength than it required, knowing she would only get one chance. Fresh blood spilled from the cuff of her pants. She leaned forward to plunge the harpoon like a knife. She screamed from both her agony and a summons of courage. She lost some of the velocity to angle the spear through the brass bars, but it stabbed into Orange's forearm with plenty of power. Although she was not rewarded with any wounded cries, he released her ankle instantly.

She didn't let go of the weapon, kept her fingers curled around it and yanked it from his arm as she tried to scuttle back from the edge of the houseboat. The impulse was to strike again, but he had lifted his machete up and she didn't doubt he could disarm her in the literal sense before she stuck the spear into his throat. Her foot slid on the deck and slipped right back to the edge. The back of her head struck the deck and a black swarm threatened to block out her vision, offering an escape from the pain in her body and mind alike. She shook her head to clear it. She planted her foot against the rail and shoved herself backwards, out of his reach. She slid on the sloped angle, turned face-down and got to her elbows and knees.

She tried to crawl on her forearms back up to the cabin of the houseboat. She had the weapon, but it still seemed like a slingshot versus a stealth bomber. Ideally she'd find something better in the cabin. Another speargun. One of those fisherman hooks. A bazooka.

He didn't even make a sound when I stabbed him, Marcus.

Orange could be killed, at least temporarily, so he wasn't invincible. What did it take to put him down, though?

She only heard her scramble up the slight incline. Orange had vanished. No splashing now. She swiveled her head in all directions as she dragged herself to the cabin door. He didn't reemerge.

It was not an elaborate ship, not much more than thirty feet, but something she and Marcus would be thrilled to have. It was probably nice once upon a time. The cabin was small, intended more for a bachelor than a family. *The studio apartment of houseboats.* She just knew it would be locked, but the door wasn't even shut. She pushed it open and braced herself with the handle to stand upright. She tested her weight on her right foot; too much and she'd drop over like a bowling pin.

She grew lightheaded at the sight of her own trail of blood. As if drawn to it, Orange burst up from the lake near the sunken edge, already halfway on the boat. Suzanne threw the door shut and fumbled for the lock, but quickly discovered its best days were long past. It jutted from the door like a loose tooth. Darkness descended upon her as tangibly as the sun vanishing behind clouds. The lock scarcely mattered since he could smash through it anyway, but it was ominous to see others had adopted this path and their footprints simply vanished in the middle of the survival trail.

Probably not their heads, though.

The cabin consisted of only two rooms connected by a hallway which also doubled as kitchen. The helm was here and past it she saw Orange stand to full height through the window. He stared back, as motionless as a reflection, and then his boots clomped on the deck as he went for the cabin. Not running now, but hurrying.

Suzanne hobbled to the kitchen/hallway, still clinging to the spear. She'd hoped for a huge carving knife on the counter, but it was empty. The sink offered nothing but dusty glasses. She noticed black smears on the wall behind her and thought better of yanking open a drawer. She hopped into the bedroom at the same time she heard the loud crash of the cabin door.

He's in. Find something!

The bedroom was wrecked, like the boat capsized then somehow righted itself. The mattress had upended, knocking over two chairs. She set the spear against one of them, grabbed the other and slung it down the hall. A weak stalling tactic, but she also needed extra room. The bedroom didn't have a true door, merely a flimsy wooden sheet that folded in like an accordion. She slid it over to close off the doorway and buy herself maybe half a second.

Marcus again: *There's gotta be something in here you can use!*

She could stake him with broken fragments of wood, but that was like giving up a knife for a can opener compared to her spear. Several drawers dipped from a dresser with nothing more formidable than sweater vests and socks.

She limped around the mattress and lifted it upright until it pitched against the doorway. Not a moment too soon as Orange demolished the accordion door with a boot.

She jumped against the mattress, hoping to catch him off guard as he burrowed through the splintered door. She didn't bounce back, so it must have worked with help from the incline. She'd barely stepped back when the mattress suddenly grew a machete. She ducked her head to the left, enough to save herself but not avoid harm altogether. Her right ear caught fire and blood rushed down the back of the ear to her shoulder, much warmer than the clinging dampness of the lake. Her knee buckled and she struck a tin box which had been covered by the mattress.

She cupped a hand to her ear, which filled with blood immediately. Nausea rolled through her guts. Where her fingers normally would have brushed her auricle, there was a gap. He'd sliced off nearly a quarter of her ear. A nub of soft cartilage dangled.

She felt like she hadn't stopped screaming for the past ten minutes.

Orange pulled the machete through the mattress. She braced her left leg against the bed, though he probably only had to lean to bring it down on top of her. The tip of the machete harmlessly punched through the mattress far from her foot. It disappeared as soon as it appeared and then returned in another spot as if he were testing for her location.

She stretched to retrieve the spear from beside the chair and quickly turned back to the mystery box. She nudged the arrow of the harpoon beneath the lid of the tin box and pushed it as far away as she could, knowing she'd still probably end up with charred Wile E. Coyote chic if he'd rigged it.

Good, long as it blows us both sky high and I get his ass back.

The blade slammed through again, this time in a downward arc which would have impaled her through the breast bone if she stood upright.

She held her breath and knocked the lid open, face turned away with her eyes squeezed shut. No explosion. She looked back, expecting to see a bounty hardly worth the risk she'd taken; surgical tape, a Band-Aid, maybe a pair of tweezers to help keep her from passing through death's door.

There was an orange gun in the box with a black grip.

Her eyes could have burst from the sockets. The retreating machete hardly registered. She barely felt the blood pour down her cheek and the slope of her neck.

A million questions exploded in her mind all at once: *Did he trap the gun instead of the box? If not, why not? Is it loaded?* Perhaps biggest of all: *Will it even work?*

She had never used a flare gun before, but had done target shooting at Marcus's insistence. She pulled the box closer and heard something roll around inside—cartridges for the gun.

Load one and shoot him in the face! Marcus ordered.

Suzanne fumbled with the gun to pull it open. The last inches of the machete slid away from the mattress. His leg burst through the center of the mattress with an explosion of feathers, which floated to the ground with all the time in the world. She twisted and buried the spear into the soft flesh above his knee. Once again no scream, but he pulled the leg back as quickly as if he'd set it down in a campfire.

She lost the harpoon this time; it vanished with him. She was committed to the flare gun now. She rushed to the box, fed a cartridge into the slot, brushed a feather away, and snapped the gun back together. She righted the fallen chair and used it to boost herself back up. The mattress jumped at her face as Orange threw himself into it like a tackling dummy. She involuntarily held up her hands to block it. It knocked the gun from her fingers and sent her close behind. She struck the box springs in the corner and rolled over, her eyes seeking the bright orange through a blizzard of white feathers. The gun bounced off the box springs and rattled in the corner, a yard away. She scrambled for it.

Orange trampled the bent mattress, the machete sheathed. The spear jutted from his leg. If it hurt him, it sure as hell didn't slow him down much. Suzanne clasped the orange barrel and tried to find a proper grip as she raised it in a sweeping arc back in his direction. She got her head around in time to see him launch himself across the five feet which separated them. He caught her wrist, slamming it against the box springs. His full weight crashed down, flattening her to the bed. It knocked the wind from her. She focused on the gun even though her lungs felt pancaked behind her ribs.

She couldn't move her wrist off the bed, but she still had the gun. She just needed to get the barrel turned up.

Orange deftly used her momentum to swing the gun in an arc so sudden she didn't realize it until the barrel came back around like a floating eye to her stare her in the face. He'd bent her arm into a wing. She managed to curl her trigger finger out, but his grip kept the gun tight in both their hands. He pushed her elbow with his free hand. The barrel punched her lips against her teeth. She tasted blood.

She twisted her head away from him, face to the box springs. The barrel bounced off her cheek.

He relinquished her elbow and pinched the piece of ear he almost cleaved from her a moment ago. She braced herself, but it was no matter. She somehow found the air to scream as he ripped the remaining strand of skin. He guided the gun to fill her mouth. She followed it with her face to keep it from punching out several of her teeth. He forced her index finger back through the trigger guard.

She found his eyes for an instant. She saw no trace of anger from the man (or whatever he could be considered now) she had stabbed twice, only a nearly palpable excitement; a child prodigy with a new chemistry set. His finger tightened over hers.

Maybe it won't even work, Marcus.

Marcus didn't answer.

Suzanne's finger depressed the trigger, and her world vanished in a rushing ball of flame.

VII.

FATHER, DELIVER US *from this unholy place.*

It was a talent Pamela had possessed since junior high, this ability to pray in one part of her mind while she continued to interact with the world around her. Perhaps the conventional wisdom suggested you should do it alone in a quiet place, but she always thought she needed the lifeline to God especially when she had to face everybody else. So much uncertainty, duplicity, and unpleasantness. And terror.

"We need to get to a damned phone," Ed said, as if reminded by the useless one in the kitchen as they marched past to the basement. The "useless" aspect of it reminded her of that plan too.

Protect us all in our time of need.

"It's not safe," she whispered to his ear. They led the way down the steps.

Watch over our family and all of these poor souls with us.

"You think we're safe here?" Ed didn't care if they were overheard on the stairs and didn't whisper back.

"We can't risk Adam's life on a maybe." She took his arm to guide him away from the group when they reached the bottom. "You heard what Patrick said; they might not even come for us."

Patrick unequivocally said there wouldn't be any rescue, but she didn't want to rile her husband any further. It would be horrible if the majority opted for "Chicken Exit suicide by committee" with Ed standing in for Jim Jones. He put the "Ed" in hardhead*ed* when he felt pushed. If Nathan hadn't fallen so quickly, they would have inevitably clashed.

Accept Nathan into Your shining kingdom, and may he have eternal peace with You.

"How would he know? Do you realize the reckless endangerment lawsuit they'd have on their hands if they didn't provide an efficient means of egress?"

Ed had never sued anyone but talked about it the way her brother claimed to be writing a novel for the past seventeen years, with the same net result.

"But he's out there right now, Ed. A hundred working phones won't do us any good if we aren't alive to use them."

Please let there be working phones and working us.

Adam looked up from the bottles on the floor to acknowledge her. "You saw him?"

"Not close up. He turned away." She suppressed mother impulses to provide a more positive spin on it but channeled them into leading Ed away before he tried to enlist Adam in his crusade. "You be careful with those, too," she warned, pointing at the bottles.

"Okay, mom," he said. The more genuine version of assurance pleased her. Sometimes he made "Okay, mom," sound like "Yeah, whatever."

She steered Ed toward the far wall. Who on earth would mount a swordfish in their basement? Tackiest thing she'd seen since the carpet in the lodge.

"Why are you taking his side?" Ed nodded sharply in Patrick's direction, where he crouched to evaluate Adam and Gin's progress. Ed had filled her in on the strategy. Was "poor man's napalm" really a thing?

Please let poor man's napalm be a thing.

She didn't like Adam helping, but it couldn't be much more dangerous than trooping through the house with that girl.

She tried to sound neutral, but her jaw clenched. "I'm not! I'm on *Adam's* side."

Wrong thing to say, of course. Knew it and said it anyway.

"Adam's the one I'm thinking about!" swore the man who let him roam around a potentially dangerous house. "Why would he trap the phone if it didn't work?"

Because people like you would be foolish enough to try it anyway.

Not a prayer that time.

"We're not even here because of Patrick," Ed said, a little louder as if he wanted Patrick to overhear him, but not truly loud enough. "It was that idiot Lawrence's idea to go this way, remember?"

She actually didn't until he said that, but yes, they came on Lawrence's say-so.

Please watch over Lawrence's soul if it be Your will. Even though he asked Adam, "Are you gay?" at the lodge so I wouldn't hear him (but You let me) and even though he used that awful C.S. word and a bunch of other bad ones too. It is not mine to judge, as it is between You and he. May he find redemption for his vulgarity and likely sodomy.

She rubbed her arms, suddenly cold. An ambient hum in the room tried to twist itself into Lawrence's screams. A friend of hers who'd seen Muslims decapitate a soldier on a viral video said it was the screams which made it so hard to watch and impossible to forget. A nauseous Pamela carefully avoided her for the next six weeks.

The others filed around the basement, thankfully not getting too close. Where were Marcus and Suzanne?

"Patrick said they got him in Mexico," Ed said. "What was he doing there, watching the donkey show?"

"What's . . . what's a donkey show?"

"You don't want to know. I'm just saying, it makes no sense to bring someone here all the way from Mexico. What if he's in on all this?"

"The guy mixing together napalm for us?"

"That's what he *says*. It'll blow up because he's using gas. Any idiot could figure that out. That doesn't make it 'napalm.' Even if it was, why would he know something like that? Think about it. They probably caught him whacking off to *The Turner Diaries* somewhere in South Dakota."

Please don't let Ed do anything stupid, Father. He means well.

"He's got Adam drinking the Kool-Aid. Look at him over there. He looks retarded."

She frowned. This was Ed in manipulation mode, a common theme at home. Things not going his way? Then invoke Adam's name and charge forward again behind a spearhead of spotty rationale.

"Come on, you don't want Adam tagging along with a guy who can make napalm, do you?" Ed said, right on cue. "He could blow us all to hell playing MacGuyver. Napalm is his opening move. What's plan B? Split an atom?"

Please don't let me do anything stupid to Ed, like try to strangle him.

"You just said the napalm might not really be napalm."

"Look, I'm sure you've noticed a bigger problem here. It's that girl. You know, if Adam got her pregnant she could sue him for child support and garnish his wages when he started working. Of course it's statutory rape if she crosses the line with him, and we'll have her ass in court faster than you can say Ho Chi Minh, but I'm just saying, she's in with Patrick, and Adam's ready to follow her right off a cliff."

Adam nodded enthusiastically at something Gin (who was Korean, not Vietnamese) said, head bouncing like a puppet on a string.

Lord, please please please don't let Adam get careless here over some silly crush.

Home schooling hadn't blunted the edge of hormones. Sometimes his sheets could practically be folded into a box. She didn't need an angelic messenger to tell her he was shaming himself in God's eyes. She'd avoided the whole topic out of embarrassment but it was high time she schooled him on the story of Onan.

Let us have the chance soon, with all this awfulness behind us. I'll welcome the embarrassment.

"You're worried Adam might be distracted? You're the one talking about lawsuits and trying to drag us all out of cover for a phone that might not work to call someone who might not help!"

"You're trying to twist my words! Why do you always do that?"

Please don't let that vein explode in his forehead.

Marcus and Suzanne finally trailed down the stairs. What took them so long?

Ed grabbed tufts of hair on either side of his head, as though to keep his brain from exploding. "And that's crazy! How can you buy into that idiot's paranoia? We're not a bunch of anarchists. We pay taxes and we vote. There's no rhyme or reason to dragging us here, and why would they bring a *child* into something like this on top of it?"

Pamela watched as the eyes of her "child" lingered on Gin's chest while she handed another bottle to Patrick. His knee bumped into a bottle and almost knocked it over. His hands flew to it just in time.

"The phones will still be there when he gives up looking for us here, Ed."

Take him away to another town, far from us. May we never so much as see him again.

Ed shook his head. "No way. Screw that." He turned back to the group.

"I think we should look for more weapons next door," Patrick said. "This was a decent haul, but—"

"One of us needs to go for a Chicken Exit," Ed said. "Maybe two. Is anyone with me?"

Outside, the sirens renewed.

"Fuck! This again?" Marcus said.

Thank you, Lord.

Language aside, the strong opposition to Ed's idiotic plan comforted her. Ed tried to petition Eliza, also to no avail. For all his bluster, she didn't believe he would dare go it alone. One more push and hopefully the whole matter would rest. When she got the opening, she said, "Ed, don't be like this. You'd get lost or run into him just as soon as you'd find one of those phones."

She wasn't big on it either, but ditching this house for another was the sounder of the strategies. She had no feeling one way or the other as to whether the government brought them here because she refused to think about it long enough. What mattered was staying close to her family and far from danger.

Guide us to freedom and safety, and thank You for keeping us all safe so far, other than Lawrence and Nathan, for whom You had a different plan.

Patrick said something to Gin she didn't hear.

Everyone looked over sharply at the sound of the sliding door. The air in Pamela's lungs whooshed out painfully as Marcus apologized. She couldn't take much more of this. Had the sound carried outside?

"Better close the curtain over that, Marcus," Patrick said. "If he—"

The spill of sunlight through the door suddenly darkened. *Marcus's shadow*, she told herself, and even when Annette screamed, she didn't abandon the theory— Annette had screamed more in Agent Orange's absence than his presence. But then the door flew aside, clattering in its track, and he stepped through, never breaking stride.

Marcus and Suzanne burst through the opening an instant without hesitation, never looked back. Either he wasn't too concerned or his peripheral vision in that hood left much to be desired.

He caught Patrick stacking the bottles on the bar. The harpoon gun was on the other side of the counter. Patrick jumped across its length to snatch the gun and aim it at the mask. Orange slapped it aside. The spear angled off into the far left corner where Eliza and Annette backed up. One of them shrieked—Pamela could guess who without looking—as they tackled each other to the safety of the ground and crawled into the bathroom. The spear stuck in the wall, its rope effectively cordoning off one side of the room.

Pamela looked at the easy route out of the basement, surprisingly unmarked by some kind of dust cloud lingering in the air from Marcus and Suzanne's hasty retreat, but she couldn't leave Adam's safety to chance. Ed stationed himself between her and Agent Orange, pushing her to the side of the couch. He was about as formidable as a sheet of wet paper as shields went, but she was grateful to have him and seized one of his hands. He squeezed back, then loosened his grip to step up on the couch and pry at one of the fish hooks from the display above her. She never thought to try for the other one, fixated on Adam.

The nightmare continued. Orange snatched hold of the speargun. Patrick tried to pull it back with both hands, but it barely shook in Orange's grasp, and he shoved Patrick with his free hand. He crested over the edge of the bar like a bowling ball toward a set of pins, the pins in this case unfortunately comprised of the napalm bottles painstakingly poured just a moment ago. Pamela's heart leapt into her throat. Glass shattered behind the bar, lots of homemade napalm seeking new life as highly flammable carpet cleaner.

Gin elbowed aside Adam and managed to yank away one of the bottles before Patrick cleared the others off the bar top.

"Lighter!" Gin shouted, a palm extended to Patrick.

Agent Orange stopped at her voice. He tilted his head as if puzzled, but there was no mistaking who captured his attention so completely. The speargun hung by his side, forgotten.

Patrick's brow knotted at this bizarre diversion, but only an instant. He turned back to Gin. "We'd incinerate ourselves in here! Stairs!"

Patrick pushed Adam through the doorway and bolted past him. Adam tried to look back, his eyes seeking his mother's. She thought she heard a "Mom!" over Patrick urging "*Gogogogogo!*" Gin slipped out right behind them, gone like a wisp of smoke.

Pamela tensed, waited for the staggering horror of the killer choosing to pursue a group with her child. Orange didn't go after them, though. His head swung back to Pamela and Ed.

"Ed," she said, surprised she could get the word out.

"Shit," Ed muttered. "Come on, you bastard!" He meant the fish hook, but Orange appeared to take it as a personal challenge. He ripped the spear back from the wall without turning around.

Eliza and Annette remained on all fours in the wake of the spear shot, as though to avoid smoke inhalation in a burning house. They crawled toward Pamela's side of the room after Orange reclaimed the spear, provided additional cover by the pool table. They had weighed their chances of getting past him to the stairs and apparently found them wanting, particularly with the speargun soon to be reloaded. They nearly had their heads taken off by a wild shot and probably didn't want to press their luck in a tight space against the guy who managed to hit Nathan from fifty yards out. There may have been a look of regret and apology on Eliza's face, but she didn't meet Pamela's gaze for more than a second. She grabbed Annette's wrist and dragged her out the sliding door.

And then there were three.

"Got it!" Ed cried. He turned to face Agent Orange with the hook.

The hooded face did not stray from Pamela and Ed as Orange angled the spear back onto the gun. Eternities had passed since he entered, but Pamela logically knew it might have been only twenty seconds. Hysteria almost consumed her at the thought she might have seen Adam for the last time, yet she could not move to defend herself; could only stand there like a tree to be felled.

What in the name of God . . . ?

His necklace, like a lei made of withered human ears, bounced from one side to another as he crossed the room to them.

Father, give me strength. Give Ed strength.

Ed reared back and Pamela found the fortitude to move; the arc of the hook came within an inch of blackening her eye. Ed shouted as he swung it at the gasmask, a primal sound millennia removed from the legally conscious threats for which he was infamous to his family. Like something ancient unleashed from his brain to strike its claim for survival.

Orange caught his wrist and drove both Ed and Pamela against the wall. He dropped the speargun to wrest away the hook with his other hand. Pamela sank to the ground, both to get away from the struggle and because her knees could not support her another moment. Orange pinned Ed's head against the wall, a gloved hand clamped over his mouth. Ed gnawed at the hand, grunting unintelligibly; something all too easy to imagine as the promise of a lawsuit if he was not unhanded immediately. Orange let him push off the wall, then pounded his head against it again, hard. Two times. Three times. Streaks of blood spilled down the panel, thicker with each heavy thud, and wood splintered. Ed stopped trying to bite, stopped struggling at all. The panic vacated his eyes. He looked like someone sedated, about to go under the blade.

Orange struck with the hook. The tip of the blade sank into Ed's eyeball, which burst like a cherry tomato, erupting down his cheek with a nauseating, almost sexual sound. He worked the blade deeper through the meat of

Ed's skull. Pamela watched from the ground, face a pallid shade of shock. Bracing Ed to the wall, he navigated the point of the hook back through Ed's face. Bone cracked and the hook burst free, a wide gap gouged between Ed's eyes as it hewed through nasal bone. Blood soaked his nose and mouth, cascading in a crimson waterfall from the newly created cavern in his skull.

It stunned Pamela to find the speargun in her hands, but they somehow claimed it while the rest of her bore silent witness to the horror. She tried to scream, but nothing happened when she opened her mouth.

Orange stepped aside. Ed's knees struck the ground first before he pitched over, arms limp at his sides, and fell directly onto his face with a wet slap. Bony fragments scattered as blood bloomed beneath.

He found her training the speargun at him when he at last turned back. She'd never fired any sort of gun before, but at this distance it would be harder not to hit him. She squeezed the trigger and the spear hissed from the gun. It stuck just below his heart, within "earshot" of his necklace. He dropped the hook, but other than that he barely reacted, like she'd bounced a paper wad off his chest. He didn't bother to pull it out as he knocked away her gun and grabbed a fistful of her hair. She didn't feel the strength to stand under her own power, but he had plenty to donate. It took only a moment before the roots of her shoulder length hair threatened to tear from her scalp. Only the toes of her shoes struck the carpet, too high to gain any purchase and alleviate the strain of her own weight.

Her vocal cords at last remembered their prime directive. She shrieked. She lifted both hands to pry at his fingers. The second hook was out of reach, and given how Ed struggled to free the other, Orange would scalp her first anyway. Her eyes rolled as if pinballed by the circuits of pain lighting up all through her scalp. They found the spear still lodged in his chest. She clutched and twisted it, felt the blade slice through muscle and hopefully vital organs. It had to be near a lung, but did he even breathe? He had blood around the rim of his wound, but not consistent with the damage it should have inflicted; more like a shaving cut. She tried to wrench the harpoon free to bury it a little higher, where his heart would (should) be, but it was stuck.

The machete.

He still had it in the sheath on his belt, ignored for new and better toys. She caught hold of the grip and freed it. He let her drop. She fell hard onto her ass as if her legs were made of old springs. Terrible pain pounded up her tailbone.

Orange regarded her from what seemed like a mountaintop as she squirmed. There were tufts of hair floating to the ground, and no sooner had she noted this than blood trickled down the back of her neck. She tried to scoot back, her tailbone still tingling. He knelt down and picked up the hook again, yet always watching her. It just seemed to be there when he opened his hand, like Thor's hammer in that movie she'd watched with Adam.

Adam.

Orange moved in quickly. She panicked and swung the blade at him wildly, but only sliced a hole in one of his pants legs. He swung the hook like someone pitching a softball underhanded. The hook disappeared under her chin. She pushed herself backward, but not far enough. The hook ripped through the soft flesh of her throat and the bottom of her mouth, the agony excruciating. She screamed again, her tongue momentarily pinned to the roof of her mouth by the point of the blade. She didn't dare shut her mouth, though it felt like the scream would never stop anyway. Her backward momentum instantly reversed, hauled forward by her head as he tugged on the hook. Blood filled the back of her throat, pooled over her bottom lip and through the corners of her mouth.

He yanked her up and over her feet. She planted her

palms on the floor to brace herself so the hook couldn't shred any more of her mouth. It nearly arced back out of her mouth now. Her upper teeth clicked on its curve. She could only crawl helplessly along the floor, a steady spatter of blood trailing her like juices from a burst Hefty bag. She was pulled over Ed's prone body, bleeding her way across his back. She managed not to touch him with her hands, but couldn't help her knees pounding him.

She maintained a steady groan/scream now in an *"Uhhhhhhhhhhhhhhhh"* sound. She couldn't look up to see him now beyond the black boots. He had stepped in blood—Ed's, undoubtedly—and left deep red prints on the floor which smeared as she pawed across them.

Suddenly the tugging stopped. A small puddle of blood formed below her face. The fire reignited as Orange wrenched the blade back through her mouth and throat. Warm wetness filled her mouth as she finally closed it. The hook clanked as he tossed it away.

She didn't want to know why and didn't want to look up at the face that had passed beyond life and death, a journey which had clearly driven him mad; a wrong turn from the path to salvation. She stared at the floor instead and the growing pool of hemorrhaging blood. The pain was still awful, but muted now by the shock of the trauma. She clamped her eyes shut as he crouched down.

Lord, deliver me to Your holy kingdom, far from this pain. Please watch over Adam.. He's so young, and there's so much he doesn't know . . . so much I didn't get to tell him. Watch over and guide him.

His hands clenched tight to either side of her head like vise grips and lifted her up until she hovered above the ground. He charged forward with her in tow, a sensation for her like flying backwards.

What is he doing with me? she wondered, but found an answer in a photograph snapped by her mind moments earlier.

REINCARNAGE: MAXIMUM CARNAGE

The swordfish. Mounted to the wall with the saber of its face measuring nearly two feet in length.

He gripped her head like a basketball and pumped his arms back as if about to slam dunk. Pamela tried to look everywhere but his face. She fixed on some point behind him, nominated that to be her escape in a moment when no longer confined by her body. The stare transitioned from defiant to glassy in one eye an instant later as the sharp point of the mounted swordfish drove through the back of her head and spitted her other eye at the tip. She was gone before it broke away from the wall mount to send them both to the floor.

VIII.

A DAM RAN. He followed Patrick's shape, everything blurry from the film over his eyes, their pounding steps like gunfire from trench warfare. The stairwell looked too narrow, squeezing them in, a world seen through the wrong end of binoculars.

Gin was behind him. She would be the first in line for Agent Orange if he came for them. He should have let her ahead, but he did well enough to remember how to put one foot in front of the other when Patrick dragged him through the doorway. His movements were unsteady, like the first time he rode his bike without training wheels. His dad took them off and both his parents cheered him on.

And he'd left them behind to save his own ass. Of course it was his best option. Adam had no delusions about his formidability after his first up-close look at the infamous slayer.

Might as well try to fight a tornado.

He had been frightened before this, but however logically he understood the danger of their predicament, he didn't believe it. Of course he was going to be okay; he and his parents, Gin, all of them. Lawrence and Nathan might have thought the same thing, but Lawrence was too out of shape and Nathan too careless. They would hide, flag down a boat patrol sooner than later, and get the hell out of here safe and sound, leaving Adam with quite a tale for Kevin.

Heads were staked everywhere, dude. And that Agent

REINCARNAGE: MAXIMUM CARNAGE

Orange thing . . . *I saw him. He was sizing all of us for more stakes. He was wearing a bunch of shriveled ears around his neck. I'm practically a hero now because of all this, but be glad it wasn't you. No bullshit.*

And of course he'd have a lifelong bond with Gin, which he would somehow parlay into a serious (and ideally sexual) relationship.

He was far less optimistic now, though.

Thing was, he didn't see what happened to Lawrence and Nathan. He heard it and it sounded pants-shittingly horrifying, but again, Lawrence never missed a meal and probably polished off some of the ones others had left and Nathan would stick his head down a cannon if he thought it offered a way out. They'd all seen Agent Orange, but he remained phantom-like; it was only for a couple seconds before they left him in the dust posthaste. That was the kind of advantage available to you when you didn't take up two seats on an airplane or step on a small explosive at the Chicken Exit.

To see him right there in the basement, though, that was the difference between watching surveillance footage of a robbery on the news and actually being in the convenience store when someone barged in with a ski mask and a shotgun. Much like room 237 at the hotel, Agent Orange smashed through the barrier of phantom status in Adam's mind to flesh, blood, and indomitable bloodlust. Wherever they hid, he'd find them. Whatever they did to him, he'd survive it. There would be an Agent Orange story with Kevin, all right, but it would probably go more like this: *Yeah, I knew that kid from here who got slaughtered in Morgan. He used to spend the night all the time. They found his head on a pole. The heads of his parents, too. No bullshit.*

Adam wiped his eyes. *Please let them be okay.* He didn't get a good last look at them, just a shaky glimpse like a shot from *Cloverfield*.

Patrick's image sharpened as he reached the top of the stairs. Adam thought they'd run for the deck where they knew it was safe, but realized they would end up at the back of the house where they could be easily intercepted. Duh. He followed Patrick to the front of the house, Gin close behind.

Patrick paused in the living room.

"He didn't follow," Gin said. "Do we stay?"

Patrick shook his head. "He probably has something trapped up here like the front door. If we don't trip it, he'll come after us." He looked around and pointed past Adam. "Will you grab that lamp?"

Adam followed Patrick's finger to a small table beside the couch with a wide-based lamp. The base had the pottery appearance of something molded rather than the brass kind favored by Adam's mom.

Mom, dad, please tell me you went out the door.

Adam folded an arm around the lamp to cradle it and lifted until the extension cord pulled taut. He ripped it out of the wall, and only then wondered if it was safe to pick up anything in this room.

Is that why Patrick asked me to get it?

No, that was silly. Patrick still held the napalm bottle, and Adam happened to be closer anyway. Besides, why would Agent Orange trap a lamp in a town with no power? Annette was the only one stupid enough to believe it could work. He wouldn't waste supplies on such a remote chance. The front door made the most sense as a trap.

They heard a loud shout from downstairs. Adam's heart felt crushed within a tight fist. There were still people in the basement. Maybe his parents.

He turned back to Patrick, who indicated the huge picture window above the couch. "Toss it through there. We'll get out without having to open anything ourselves."

Adam nodded, took a couple steps back for a running start, and launched it at the window. The lamp burst through. The surrounding panes of glass collapsed as if too tired to stay upright. It didn't completely clear out the window, but the right side opened enough to get through without too much danger from hanging shards.

Patrick snatched up a pillow to knock out the rest of the glass. "Okay, let's move." He gave Gin a little push to go first. He looked pensive as she maneuvered her slim body through the gap. Adam wondered if he was thinking about the strange scene from the basement. Difficult to say without truly being able to see Agent Orange's face, but Adam thought he'd seen longing there, with something more obsessive and deadly. Maybe he didn't follow them because of a trap, but Adam bet there was an element of savoring involved; he could look forward to killing Gin.

Adam bounded up the couch a little recklessly, trying to escape before he heard screams from downstairs that he might recognize as his parents'. He emerged on the porch, glass fragments grinding and sprinkling. Patrick held the napalm bottle through the window to Gin, then stepped through from the couch. Gasoline was sharp in Adam's nostrils, even outside. They probably all had it on their hands. Trying to light one of those bottles might have ended the whole thing for all of them.

He didn't see anybody out front. Adam had the sinking elevator feeling in his stomach again. He'd hoped against hope to see his parents round the corner and join them, Agent Orange too busy chopping Annette and Eliza into a body pile to come look for them. Cruel to think, but he didn't give a shit what happened to either one of them, especially if it meant his parents' survival.

Gin read his face. "They could have run like Marcus and Suzanne."

He steeled himself not to burst into tears in front of her and nodded, his lips a tight thin line. At that moment there was a very loud, feminine shriek. Adam's body temperature dropped about twenty degrees.

He was certain it was his mom, then half a second later just as certain it wasn't. He'd never heard anyone make a sound like that.

Patrick took back the bottle from Gin. "We can't stay here." He said it to all of them, but only looked at Adam.

Adam didn't trust himself to speak and did the tight-lipped nod again. They began the run up the lake road which brought them here barely forty-five minutes ago. Adam looked back with prayers buzzing through his head, like flies trapped in a jar. They were mostly of the bargain variety, such as a vow to adopt a sexless life of servitude if he just saw his mom and dad racing to catch up. But there was no one. Just another bloodcurdling scream behind the house at an octave level close to only canine perception.

They had an abundance of tree cover along the road, but still plenty of sun to bleed through the leaves and branches. It looked like late afternoon sunlight. In another hour or two, they would have the dubious pleasure of playing hide and seek with Agent Orange in the dark.

He wondered why they didn't follow his original suggestion of getting the hell off the road and into the woods, traps or no. There were a million places to hide in there, and they had dark clothes now thanks to him and Gin. They'd had napalm and wound up running in the opposite direction of Orange. That didn't inspire much confidence.

He tried to focus on Gin a few steps ahead of him. Crazy as it was, half an hour ago he'd felt elated. His days were usually boring and brooding with a faceless disappointment he didn't understand. *Angst,* his mom once derisively called it. Like some kind of radio signal to which he had been blissfully unaware until a couple years ago, but now beamed in loud and clear. It was waiting for him when his latest optimism proved unfounded, like going to the beach to have one of those "summer flings" he'd seen in a lot of raunchy comedies (at Kevin's, never his own house), certain he would score because it was time, and that's just the way things happened. It had only served to demonstrate that wherever you had to be to take that next step, he didn't know the way.

stream of talk while staying cognizant of the potential dangers. There was silence when there had to be, and when there didn't have to be, it was easy to keep up the conversation. They had common ground, that being a *stalking* ground. They were both terrified, but hopeful for some kind of rescue. They both wanted to slap Annette across the face. Best of all, Gin didn't have a boyfriend.

Even now, Adam felt at least a twinge of accomplishment for finding out. He'd been real smooth.

Your family must be worried back home . . . and your boyfriend. Perhaps he almost turned it into a question with the last inflection, but he didn't think so.

My parents would if they know I'm gone, but I don't have a boyfriend. Use that umbrella over there to push the closet open. You don't want to get your face blown off.

Check that—she didn't have a boyfriend *and* she didn't want him to get his face blown off.

She'd noticed his face.

It seemed like a good opportunity to mention the nonexistent Duke recruiters and his college hopes, where he could hardly be blamed if she interpreted that to mean he was eighteen, but he understood this to be the wrong move. Anything that brought age into the equation at all was to be avoided. He matured substantially in five minutes.

Then they found the darker clothes and changed. She stayed in the closet while he used the bedroom, but there was a handy mirror at the right angle to give Adam a glimpse inside. She had her back turned and he saw a leopard skin pattern from her bra. He wanted to see everything, of course, but it was still more than he'd seen in person before (his mom wouldn't dare emerge from behind a room until she finished dressing), and he hoped the steam blowing from his ears disappeared before she knew what he'd seen.

The time with Gin was intoxicating. Not because anything came of it, but because it didn't feel like he ruined it. He'd expected to. It made him feel like he could do anything, at least until half an hour later when he saw Agent Orange two yards away.

He couldn't believe it when Patrick turned left at the fork in the road. Adam knew it was wise to save his breath because it wasn't like he would mutiny (not if Gin didn't, anyway), but his father's reluctance to follow Patrick's program made more sense now. It had been embarrassing to listen to Dad harp on the Chicken Exits and see everyone's pained expressions, but what brilliant ideas had Patrick contributed? Napalm? Adam knew they had a weapon with the gas can. Adding Styrofoam to it didn't make you the new Napoleon of military strategy. It just meant you'd bookmarked YouTube.

Gin didn't let it pass without comment. "Why are we going back to the lodge?"

"Three reasons," Patrick said, breath whooshing. It took him awhile to get all the words out. "One, we know this stretch of road is safe. Two, I'm hoping he doesn't expect it. And three, there's a lot of room in the parking lot to use this if we have to." He held the bottle of gasoline and Styrofoam up.

Please, God, don't let him drop that, Adam thought.

It didn't seem like they'd run far when they left Lawrence and Nathan behind, but it took longer to get back than Adam would have guessed. Their fear made for a good adrenaline rush. He was surprised it hadn't helped Lawrence any to escape.

He'd hoped Agent Orange took them off the road somewhere, but of course this wasn't a populated city where a killer had to be conscientious about covering his tracks; it was a ghost town with a booming population of ghosts. Lawrence and Nathan were left in pools of blood. Adam clamped a hand over his mouth at the sight of Lawrence's legs far from the rest of him, puking an insistent suggestion at the back of his throat. The thick coppery odor of blood didn't help.

Both their heads were staked on the side of the road like mile markers, the ears removed. Flies clamored from one to the other, not sure where to start. Lawrence's cleaved-open face seemed a pretty popular destination, part of his head uneven. The stake was the only thing that held it together. The huge gap separating the imprecise halves gave the semblance of Pac-Man jaws.

Adam thought of maggots hatching in the eyes, and the reward of a helicopter rescue couldn't have stopped the flood from his guts, like a toilet flushing in reverse. He ran to the other side of the road as bile spewed through his fingers.

"Keep it off the road," Patrick admonished. "Maybe it'll dry up before he comes this way." He sounded disappointed, like Adam did it at an inopportune time; wedding vows or something.

Go find some more Styrofoam, asshole. Don't drop a speck of it anywhere, though, or he'll track us.

He kept it off the road, however, believing it might screw them even before Patrick pointed it out. Once it got going, more wasn't to be denied, and he heaved again. He felt Gin's eyes on his back and groaned. He looked weak. Hopefully she just thought he was sensitive. Girls were okay with that sometimes. He wiped his mouth off and used his shirt to wipe his eyes. At least he had an excuse for the tears in them now. He took a deep breath to gather himself and nearly spewed again from the blood stench. When he knew he wouldn't be sick again, he pulled his shirt up over his nose and mouth and breathed deeply before he faced Gin and Patrick again.

Patrick had a hand tented over his eyes, looking back the way they came. "Still looks clear," he said quietly. "Let's keep moving, though. He could cut through the woods."

"Why aren't we doing that?" Adam asked.

Patrick shook his head. "Too risky. If we get lost, we'll be stuck in it overnight. We'd be lucky to spot traps in daylight, and in the dark? Not a good idea."

Gin said, "He won't think to look for us in the only place around here with electricity?"

Patrick shook the bottle with the napalm, sloshing it around. "Let him. When he shows up, I'll have an eye out."

Adam found Gin's eyes, her back turned to the macabre scene by the road side. She stood hunched over, hands on her knees, trying to catch her breath. He was able to focus on her to the exclusion of the blurry shapes behind her. He gave her a conspiratorial shake of his head, a *What the hell are we doing?* gesture. He held back a fist pump when she shrugged in reply.

We're practically telepathic now.

Adam gave Gin a very thin smile which probably looked like a grimace, but he got one in return.

Kevin would be jealous if Adam ever relayed all this to him. He claimed to have screwed five girls, but Adam suspected the likelihood of that was the exact opposite of the "no bullshit" trademark Kevin tagged on all his stories.

They have that concession stand closed up but I gots the key. I go, "Let's ditch third period," and Cindy's like, "Okay, sure, but where can we go?" And I jingled the keys, and her eyes got real big and I knew she was thinking about cramming my whole ball sac in her mouth. You just know when it's gonna happen, man. No bullshit.

Patrick glanced over at him. "All done?"

"Never better," Adam said. His head was killing him. He needed something to drink. Agent Orange wouldn't have to kill him if he passed out in front of Gin; he'd simply die of embarrassment.

The road curved out of sight before the turn off to the lake houses, but a good stretch was visible. His parents weren't bravely staggering along to catch up to him. It was empty.

Adam and Gin fell into step as they walked away from the remains of Lawrence's detruncated corpse and the heads. Patrick brought up the rear. They didn't feel like they had to run with the lodge in sight. Nathan's body came up on the right, severed fingers scattered in front of the stump of his neck as if his head had been a firework that exploded before it could be tossed away.

"Hope we can find water soon," Gin said.

"Maybe in the lodge. There's light, so why not water?"

"Light. Very sporting of those assholes who brought us here."

"Yeah," Adam said. "Those assholes."

"I bet you they got the hell out of here as quick as they could."

"Oh, yeah, you know they did. Those . . . assholes."

"I just wish we knew why us."

They hadn't had much time to speculate. Government was the popular theory with most people not named Ed Kirshoff. Adam didn't think it mattered much whether they were selected by a computer algorithm or some covert op snatched random people. He didn't care if he never knew or if they kept doing it to other people. Just show the rest of them a way out of here now.

Come on, Mom and Dad. Be okay.

Adam shrugged. "Maybe it was just some secret lottery. It figures I'd win the one with no cash prize."

She didn't laugh. She only said, "Maybe."

Tough crowd, Adam thought.

They held a brisk walking pace and soon the menagerie of heads greeted them at the hotel parking lot. Patrick overtook Adam and Gin. He kept an eye behind them for pursuit or survivors, but their luck held so far. He barely paid the Chicken Exit a second glance. The little pool of blood where Nathan tripped the toe-popper seemed laughable compared to what they just saw. A papercut.

Patrick stopped suddenly at the entrance to the lodge, on red alert. Adam and Gin tensed, prepared to run back the way they came. They both saw what startled Patrick.

"Is that . . . ?" Adam trailed off.

A man in a white shirt and bright red slacks stood at the mouth of the lodge. If he'd worn some platform shoes, he could have stepped out of a time machine from the 1970s. He seemed to do the same gradual identification of their group, then broke into an ungraceful run toward them. He waved one hand madly overhead.

"Hey!" he called.

"Could he have been left behind from before?" Adam asked.

"Before when?" Gin muttered. "The Watergate scandal?"

Patrick shook his head as they watched him stumble over. "With all these heads around, he'd have to be an idiot to run to us without knowing the score."

He looks like an idiot anyway, Adam thought, then remembered his own original wardrobe.

His black hair was damp with sweat. It stuck to his forehead despite the white sweatband that ringed his head. He was Gin's age, in good physical shape. Adam noticed tiny spatters of blood on his shirt, but the guy was whole and unharmed. If there were near misses, they hadn't exhausted him. In fact, he seemed jittery, like he'd barely tapped his energy potential. He had to wonder if this guy's presence would cost him a fighting chance—with Gin *and* Agent Orange. He looked away for a distraction.

One of us needs to go for a Chicken Exit, maybe two. Is anyone with me?

At the time Adam considered it a stupid idea. He'd been embarrassed for his dad; embarrassed *of* him. If he hadn't wanted to stay with Gin, would he have jumped at the idea? Would they have been somewhere on the lake front by the time Agent Orange found the others in the house? Maybe Patrick was right, maybe the phones didn't work, but it wouldn't matter because at least they wouldn't have been at the house when Orange showed up. They'd be alive. Together. Meanwhile, Patrick's full-on napalm offensive would be falling apart as always destined.

"How many of you were there?" asked the stranger. Yes, he knew what was what in this place. He hadn't been left behind, he'd been left alive. He'd managed it wearing a bright white shirt and matching headband, which shat all over Patrick's theory about white shirts as the Kill Zone equivalent of red shirts on *Star Trek.*

Gin looked from the stranger to Patrick. Beautiful Gin. Hadn't taken much for Adam to turn his back on his parents. What must they have thought when he left them behind?

"Nine," Patrick answered, "but he's killed two of us. We scattered."

Adam kept his face turned from the others. He felt a stinging sensation in his sinuses. Stopping the tears this time might not be possible. Patrick had left the kill count at two, likely for Adam's benefit. But Adam knew.

A brief interlude prefaced the continued Q&A where Patrick introduced himself, Gin, and Adam and the stranger introduced himself as Lee. Adam mustered a weak "Hi" before he turned his back to them. His feelings began to plummet to the depths of despair. His parents were dead and he was in a war zone with Agent Orange. If he'd been depressed to the point of crying over his so-called "miserable" life in the past, what would happen when the magnitude of his loss set in?

Lee said, "I woke up in a motel in downtown Morgan, couple miles that way."

"What was the name?" Patrick asked.

"The Morgan Manor."

Adam knew the location from a map he'd bought off Kevin for ten bucks, a well-used supplement to the *Agent Orange: Thirty Years of Terror Summer Special*. Kevin had three duplicate maps but couldn't part with such a valuable treasure for less than ten bucks (only three dollars less than the summer special itself). Adam forked over the cash, angry he couldn't get a cheaper copy of the map *and* the summer special off eBay because his mother wouldn't let him use the internet without supervision. And he dare not ask anything concerning Agent Orange, a topic that would fall under capital "O" for Occult.

When the police investigation found Adam's stash of Agent Orange magazines, an old book by Charles Berlitz, a map of the Kill Zone, and photocopied articles, would they make a connection to his fate?

Lee's group of eight met under similar circumstances at the crack of dawn. Patrick estimated this happened roughly eight hours before their second group. Adam wondered if that meant there would be a third group to lend new meaning to "graveyard shift." Fifteen minutes ago he would have said it. Now . . . every joke seemed DOA.

"You speak English?" Lee asked Gin. Adam cringed.

"No, but keep talking and I'll try my best to follow along."

"Ha, sorry, there were, like, five Hispanics in our group. Only one could speak English well enough for us to understand. I thought you might be an undocumented worker—it's racist to think all undocumenteds are from south of the border, right?"

"How you say 'swam here last week?'"

"Yeah, yeah, I get it, sorry."

"Let's take this indoors," Patrick said. He sounded as perturbed as Adam felt.

"Uh, sure, but this was a pit stop for me, man," Lee answered. "I'm headed for the nearest military checkpoint to get my ass out of here. My band's on tour and we could parlay this crazy shit into some major publicity—if they're not getting chopped up in here somewhere."

"We should compare notes first, if you don't mind me picking your brain. Did the motel have electricity?" Patrick asked.

The question seemed odd but Adam couldn't focus on why Patrick would ask or why it should matter. All his efforts went into keeping tears at bay. He'd bawled like a baby when his cat Piper died last year and he hadn't shed a single tear for his parents. Did this mean he was in shock? Denial?

"Nah, there's no power in any of these joints," Lee said. "You know where we are, right?"

"Yes, the Chicken Exit was a helpful clue," Gin said. "My accent too thick?"

"Oh, snap; I see what you did there."

Adam wanted to throw up again. Were Gin and this guy flirting? It was the same light, playful tone she used with him back at the lake house.

"Wait, you said there's no electricity *here*?"

"Nah, man, I was in there looking for a weapon, catching a breather. The Chicken Exit over there doesn't work either. I've tried three phones and they're all dead."

Aside from slipping into depression, Adam felt he was slipping into irrelevance. "It had power when we woke up," he said.

Lee glanced at him briefly as if to say, "Oh, you still here, little brah?" but Patrick and Gin didn't even acknowledge him. The hell? He'd just lost his parents and it was like he didn't even exist. It wasn't like he needed coddling or anything, but she could at least treat him like he hadn't—

Gin turned to him, eyes full of concern. "You okay?" she asked.

The validation he'd hoped for opened a trap door

beneath his feet and his stomach fell through. Adam managed to show indifference with a shrug but feared such a response might not assuage Gin so he nodded and tried on his best smile. He wished for anonymity again. It wouldn't take much prodding for him to totally lose it like last night's supper. With Rock Star Lee on the scene, he didn't want to give her any more reasons to question his maturity.

"Wait, you started here and came back?" Lee asked. " . . . Aaaaahhhh, you don't think *he* thinks you'll come back."

"How did you get here if you didn't see the bodies?" Patrick asked.

"Through the woods. Me and Earnes escaped after the last attack, but there's traps all over this bitch. Earnes died on pointy stakes. Messed up way to go."

The distance separating Adam from the others became feet, became yards. Despite the gravity of the situation and the new revelations from Lee, Adam couldn't focus on anything but his mother and father. A reel of the Kirshoff family's greatest moments played through his mind, stripped of the frustrations and petty animosities that often made him feel an inchoate hostility toward his parents and life in general. He was suddenly possessed of a more profound understanding of his parents and how their love for him influenced every decision. He saw his mom outside the role of an overbearing mother hen, as a woman who never had time for herself because she spent all her time educating and preparing her son, whose development was too precious to leave in the hands of others.

Thank God the others paid no attention to Adam as he wiped his damp eyes, quickly turning away as a pretext to search the road for Orange or the others. He dabbed his eyes with his shirt. His heart jumped at movement in the distance until the blurred figures came into focus.

Eliza and Annette had not only survived, they made it

all the way back here. Seven of them had escaped the lake house. Agent Orange going 0 for 9 in the basement was impossible.

By now Ed and Pamela Kirshoff's heads were on stakes.

"Fucker!" Adam shouted. He felt clarity of purpose, a new course of action that made more sense than anything anyone else had to offer.

"Adam?"

He marched back toward the lake house. Patrick wasn't fooling anybody—none of them would make it out of this alive. They weren't put here to take out Agent Orange or escape him or even to give him much sport. This was like throwing lambs into a coliseum with lions. He'd left his parents behind once and he couldn't fix that, but he could turn the lake house into a bonfire and give his parents some semblance of a proper burial. They wouldn't be trophies.

Gin jogged after him. "Where are you going?"

"He's not putting their heads on sticks."

"If you go back he'll kill you."

Adam shrugged. "So?"

The two groups approached each other at the edge of the parking lot with Eliza looking from Gin to Adam quizzically. Annette appeared a changed woman, as if she'd stared death in the face and seen the afterlife that awaited her—probably hell, given the anger twisting her face.

During the approach Annette had kept her left hand planted upon her lips, but she took away the hand and opened her mouth. "Too late," she said almost wistfully. "Agent Orange fucked them up good."

"Hey!" Gin snapped.

"*Annette!*" Eliza's eyes nearly popped from their sockets.

This only confirmed what Adam already knew but it was like a kick to the abdomen. At least now he could feel free to hate Annette without being bothered by that whole Christian conscience thing.

"Where are you going?" Eliza asked. "He's probably right behind us."

"Let them go," Annette said, with a kind of cavalier demeanor previously not in evidence today between the shrieking and handwringing. "They'll buy us time. Lawrence doesn't know shit."

"Huh? What's wrong with you?"

Adam hoped Gin would peel away and stick with Eliza and Annette but she kept pace with him, trying to stay a step ahead so she could look at his face as they walked. Maybe she thought her appeals would get through if they made eye contact. He avoided looking at her, didn't want her to see the tears.

"I think she's on something, or maybe coming *off* something," Gin said. "But we've got to go back, even if she's there."

Nathan and Lawrence's bodies were ahead. Of course Lawrence "didn't know shit" now, unless you counted what lay on the other side of death. Adam felt the first chink in the armor of his resolve. If he couldn't see Nathan and Lawrence's bodies without puking, what hope did he have if he saw his parents like that or worse? He'd go out of his mind.

"Leaving them didn't change anything," Gin said.

"I abandoned them!"

Gin jumped in front of him and put her arms around him. His forward momentum ground to a halt; he let her hold him in place.

"Don't do this," she whispered. "Don't give yourself to him when we can still fight."

Adam's resolve short-circuited in Gin's embrace and he semi-collapsed against her, sobbing—just the thing he hadn't wanted her to see in the first place. What grief demanded composure could not thwart.

"Your parents wouldn't have left the basement until you were safe. You gave them a chance by leaving."

He sniffed. "It doesn't feel right."

"You did the only thing you could to live. Everything happened so fast, who had time to think?" She patted his back. "They gave you the chance to get away, so make it count. You can't throw it away rushing off like this, no matter how much it hurts. You're staying here with me."

Suddenly self-conscious of separating himself and Gin from the remnants of the group and even more worried about the danger this presented, Adam reluctantly broke contact with her. As he did so, he looked away and wiped his face. "We should get back," he mumbled.

Grabbing his hand, Gin said, "No kidding."

The hug and hand-holding would have put him over the moon thirty minutes ago, but there was only listless depression now. Nothing mattered. He and Gin would never be a thing just as he knew his life would be forever changed for the worst if he made it out of here. His only living relative was Uncle Vince, an author strangely lacking in output. Adam's father had joked he was the next Henry Darger, something Adam had always meant to look up.

Too late now.

It was stupid to play "what if." They were all going to die, like his parents.

"Over here," Gin said. She led him to the edge of the road where a stone balustrade had partially collapsed. A rushing creek passed beneath the road. They'd paid it little mind the first time with the siren, and on the way back, Patrick shook his head at Gin as if it wasn't safe to go down there—a sentiment Adam agreed with. This would be an ideal place for a trap as the first source of water by the motel.

"It may not be safe," he warned.

The mossy stone wing walls were in remarkably good shape, but the years hadn't been kind to the trees at the shorelines. Several trees crisscrossed the stream where they had fallen, their root systems undermined by erosion. If this wasn't a good place to run into a trap, it would be a great place to find a snake.

"I'll be careful. Watch for him."

"Gin."

"Good thing I'm wearing pants," she said as she waded through the weeds.

Adam looked back but he couldn't see around the bend to the stretch of road with Nathan and Lawrence. If he showed up, Agent Orange would be on top of them by the time Gin climbed back to the road.

This is not good . . . really not good.

Adam jumped at a snap, crack, and a loud whoosh. By the time he spun his head back to Gin, the spiked log had begun an upward arc toward her and neither he nor she had time to form a scream. Gin ducked and she got a half turn before the devastating impact threw splinters, bark, dirt, and vegetative debris through the air. Wood shrapnel pocked the flora and a chunk bounced off Adam's forehead.

"Holy shit," Gin said. The spiked log had buried itself in the side of a nearly uprooted tree which now leaned into the path of the trap. The twin ropes still vibrated as twigs and leaves shook from where it had been affixed in the boughs overhead. "Patrick's right again."

IX.

WE'LL GET OUT of this, write a memoir . . . it'll be a bestseller and we'll be set for life," Eliza said as she jogged. "Just you watch."

It was a cool, fair-weather day with temps in the low seventies but Annette felt like she'd taken a deep pull of Patrick's napalm concoction and chased it with a lit match. Breathing the cool air brought a short-lived relief until her lungs turned it to volcanic steam that scorched her mouth on the way out. This was only the latest hardship to overcome. Dizziness, nausea, body aches, eye twitches, trembling, cramps, fatigue, forgetfulness, and even traces of the dread malady that had started her problems so many long years ago—anxiety. This was like one extended stay in purgatory with all of her sins relentlessly dogging her in a loop of pain-shock-terror-pain.

"We should run. He'll come for us next," Eliza said, because this stuff came easy for her.

Annette looked at her arms, surprised they weren't beet red. Along with the interior conflagration came a drenching perspiration. All she needed was dehydration on top of all this. Where could she get water? Water . . . water . . . she remembered the lake and imagined being immersed in the placid waters, gentle ripples erupting across the surface and she remembered her last visit to a lake, a visit where she'd refrained from swimming because she hadn't thought to pack a flattering swimsuit and oh what she wouldn't give to have it to do all over again.

"Fine, we'll head this way." Eliza again, snapping Annette back from a happier place.

Annette looked around, but it was only her and Eliza. Oh shit, Eliza had been talking to her again. Why couldn't Annette pay attention? She'd probably missed something important. Deadly important. Someone was chasing them. Or maybe someone was chasing Eliza, but if this were the case Annette wasn't sure why she should care. Was Eliza important? She wasn't dressed like someone of any consequence. How embarrassing to forget such important details. Annette could be so scatter-brained. Sometimes she got lost inside her own head and didn't pay attention and it caused her no end of humiliation later. WHY CAN'T YOU JUST PAY ATTENTION?

Cracked asphalt road surrounded by an encroaching forest. Various small branches and twigs littered the pavement. The tableaux had a familiarity and she vaguely remembered coming through here yesterday (?), only she'd been traveling the other direction. They were at a fork in the road and the right-hand branch had a sign pointing to Morgan.

Morgan. You don't want to be there. You don't want to be here.

With a low, desperate hum she tried to imagine herself back at the lake where she'd decide to wear a swimsuit and her life would take a different direction . . . a trajectory that would prevent her from ever ending up here in the first place.

Eliza said, "Definitely want to head away from town."

Flustered by an inability to immerse herself in a fantasy of the lake, Annette focused on the moment at hand. In so doing she remembered the lodge with a nauseating shudder. This path would lead them back to the roach motel, a horrid place with a musty, mildew scent, vintage décor with an unkempt landscape replete with heads on stakes. And those horrible, snarky African Americans were there along with the grossly obese, stuttering pervert.

She clasped her head in her hands. The pressure within her skull grew by the second, an added discomfort when coupled with the inferno raging beneath her skin. She reached for the buttons of her pantsuit but they were already undone and she was exposed to her navel and couldn't even feel so much as a breeze against her skin. Why was she so hot? Why the hell couldn't she cool down?

Nnnnnnnnnnnnnnnnnnnn—

"Shhhhh," Eliza warned. "You're getting too loud again. Agent Orange, remember?"

Annette tried to remember. Too much hair on the back of her neck. She swept her hands to the back of her head to gather her hair and wrap it into a pony tail, but she didn't have enough hair to gather. She laughed absently. Yes, yes, of course, she'd cut her hair short years ago. Eliza's long hair must have confused her. God, wasn't she toasting under all that hair? Annette wanted to rip it off her head. Just seeing it made her own scalp bubble.

As Annette reached to snatch a hold of Eliza's head, she felt a burst of panic and froze with the sudden awareness she was doing something that wouldn't be in her best interest.

So she looked away from Eliza. Down. Around. Back. Up.

Nnnnnnnnnnnnnnnnnnnn—

The sky above glittered through the canopy of trees. It positively sparkled. Tilting her head back seemed to work for the pain so she kept looking up, up, up.

"Oh God, this is the way we came! Don't . . . don't look."

Annette saw the lumps in the road ahead, trails of crimson leading away from the burst bags of skin.

"Damn, it's too late to go back . . . we might run into

him if we double back now. That screaming had to be Marcus and Suzanne. We're next in line. The others got a bigger head start. Come on. Just don't look."

It was Eliza who shouldn't have looked. She bent over and gagged. Dry heaves. The worst kind.

Nathan and Lawrence stared at them from the side of the road.

The throbbing in Annette's head had subsided along with the intense heat. She remembered the fork in the road where Eliza chose the left branch. She looked back but couldn't see where the fateful decision was made. How had they covered so much ground in so little time?

Annette patted Eliza's back, thankful her own pain and discomfort were behind her. This was the best she'd felt all day, as if Eliza were pulling some kind of Christ-thing and taking on Annette's suffering.

"There, there," Annette said, leaving her hand atop Eliza's back just in case Eliza could drain Annette of her pain. "It'll pass." And it almost felt like the transference were real.

If she got out of this alive she could write a hell of a memoir; it would be a bestseller and she would be set for life. Weird, she'd had that thought before, hadn't she? The déjà vu passed. Encountering Agent Orange twice hadn't been the worst part of her ordeal. The cessation of so many different medications cold turkey was a roller coaster of emotional and biological activity the likes of which she hoped to never endure again. Worse, it had taken her years, fucking *years*, to get the balance of different meds right. It began with a two year struggle with anxiety and the various meds prescribed to her, all with their own side effects. Obviously the psychiatrists guessed about drugs and dosages so she did her own research and found new ones to offset the side effects of her official prescriptions. Depending on how long she was off her regimen here in this godforsaken place, her body would develop a resistance to their reintroduction. She may never get the balance right again. She sure wished she knew who'd screwed this up for her. Agent Orange was just a mindless automaton who only knew killing, it was nothing personal with him. The people who put her here? Now those were the bitches and bastards she would go after. And Ed would be right on board with her—he seemed to know a lot about law from what she remembered. He might be a lawyer. She abruptly remembered him cornered in the basement and realized Ed's legal advice was a thing of the past. Oh well, if she got out of here, she had connections. Probably better lawyers than Ed, anyway.

Annette looked at her hands. Rotated them. Took in the light breeze. Whoa! She felt . . . remarkably good! No headache, no burning, her joints didn't hurt and her internal cramping had subsided as well. She was through the withdrawal!

Thanks Eliza! You sucked the bad juju right out of me! Holy shit!

"Good for you," Eliza croaked.

Thank God it was over and she'd come out the other side. Other than an empty stomach she felt pretty damned good. In all actuality, the best she'd felt in years! She had such clarity of thought, too. Everything came back to her and, yeah, the situation kind of sucked, that couldn't be helped, but she felt so good it was hard to feel down.

Eliza moaned. "Ohthishurtssobad." Still, she managed to stand upright and take a couple of steps. The worst, it seemed, was over. Ah, she was much younger than Annette, she could handle it better.

The wind shifted and the smell of blood wafted their way. Eliza doubled over again.

Like a beacon, the smell drew Annette's attention to Lawrence's headless—and legless—body. There was a slight angle to the cuts of his stumps with one side visibly longer than the other, but the smoothness of the stubs was striking. Unlike Annette, who had foolishly used several types of saws to cut Bill English's body into manageable pieces for disposal, Agent Orange clearly knew his trade. Clean cuts. The amount of blood was the same, though. While she'd remembered to use plastic to keep the blood from soaking into the carpet, she punctured it several times with the saws. She carefully dismounted the liner with fresh booties in an effort to prevent bloody footprints only to find blood had seeped through the punctures and absolutely ruined the luxurious Fabrica carpet in her living room. What a nightmare *that* had been.

Out, damned spot, out, she remembered from reading the role of Lady Macbeth when Bill went out for Macbeth (and failed miserably, was lucky to be cast as "A Porter"). None of the damned spots came out of the Fabrica.

Bill, Bill, Bill, you poor stupid bastard.

Annette's eyes snapped to her hands again. The sight and smell of the blood triggered another déjà vu moment, so strong she expected to see her hands drenched with ex-lover.

It's me or your husband, your choice, but be forewarned—I don't play the part of the jilted lover very well.

As a third-rate actor, Bill hadn't played *any* parts particularly well, but he was pure method when it came to playing a corpse. Ambien put him down and a knife angled beneath the sternum into his heart kept him there. Sure, it took five or six insertions to get it right, but she eventually did and she hadn't Arias-ed the whole thing by leaving evidence that would lead back to her. She got away with what society would have called murder (to her it was self-defense; after all, Bill was going to totally jack up her life). Her marriage didn't last six months after Bill's "disappearance," but she sure didn't want the satisfaction of Reynolds finding out about an affair so he could justify his decision to cut ties—or get greedy during the arbitration.

"Help . . . help me . . . b-b-bitchlicks."

Annette glared at Lawrence. She pulled the bodice of her pantsuit together and buttoned it to deny the pervert his view of her brassiere.

"Let's go," Eliza whispered, her legs pumping as if she intended to outrun the next bout of vomiting.

"I'm with you, girl."

"Please! Just pull my legs and torso over here. Please!" Lawrence begged.

After verifying Eliza couldn't see her, Annette gave Lawrence the finger. He'd called her Barbara from *Night of the Living Dead*.

Ha! Maybe the ass-kicker from the remake, Porky! I don't see you among the living!

"I hope you're next, you cunt-stuffer! Sack-sucker! Fuck! Hmmmmmmm."

Annette laughed. What the hell was he even saying?

Eliza looked at Annette and smiled. "Yeah, I kind of lost it there. Feels like I've been kicked in the chest."

"You'll be next!" Lawrence screamed over and over until they were out of earshot. It got boring giving him the finger so Annette decided to ignore him, but his mantra felt like an incantation and she wondered if he actually could have some power over her fate. He was, after all, already dead—did that give him some sway over matters of mortality? Was he able to communicate directly with Agent Orange? Could he guide the Agent to her? Doubtful he would bother listening to Lawrence, but the seed of worry was planted and Annette knew how that little seed would germinate and blossom and . . . Shit.

No, no, no, you're fine. Nothing is wrong at all. Just keep your chin up, girl.

"Huh?" Eliza smiled. "Thanks, maybe I should try to stay positive."

Can you hear what I'm thinking?

Eliza laughed. "When you tell me."

Annette put a hand against her lips and tried to keep them still.

Can you hear me now?

Her lips hadn't moved, which was confirmed by her thoughts going unnoticed by Eliza.

With a sudden movement that startled Annette, Eliza began waving and pointing frantically. In a low, excited voice she said, "Look, the others. Someone's with them."

There were four people and it took Annette a few seconds of hard focus and concentration to figure out which one did not belong because she couldn't remember their names or faces. She relaxed a moment and they came to her: Patrick, Gin, and Adam. The fourth guy was a little hazy when viewed from this distance but he obviously didn't originate with their group because he wore a white shirt that looked like it had been soaked in bleach. Patrick was probably trying to get the guy to go shirtless.

Adam and Gin broke away from Patrick and the new guy.

"Oh, now they acknowledge us. They weren't too concerned when they left us in the basement," Annette said.

"We did the same thing to Ed and Pamela. Ah shit, Adam will ask about his parents. We can't tell him."

Why not? The little shit left his parents because he had the hots for Gin—that's what they called "yellow fever" and his case would be terminal. Tokyo Rose was smart enough to know a human shield when she saw one. As if it mattered. Annette remembered the way Agent Orange looked at Gin; it was the look of lust Lawrence got when he passed the dessert section at a buffet.

Pies and cakes and puh-puh-pussy-puh-puddings and tortes and cookies, I'll be buh-buh-buh-back for all of you, bitchlicks!

It lent credence to all the tales of Agent Orange as a Vietnam veteran; it was like the mere sight of her took him back to Pork Chop Hill and Guadalcanal. Hell, he might pack up and go home if he found Gin dead. Only problem being, this *was* his home. Shit on that little factoid there.

Adam looked out of sorts, alternately seeing and ignoring Annette and Eliza. Gin appeared desperate so this wasn't a warm welcome back to the group. No matter. Annette figured it was time to take her hand off her mouth and let her thoughts flow freely. The shit-asses ran off and left Annette in the basement hoping her death would buy them time. She hadn't been her best at those moments; she'd been hallucinating a little and if not for Eliza, she'd be dead.

"*Annette!*"

Annette somehow shocked everyone. Hand off the mouth and witness the magic. Oh well. Felt good. Felt great!

Adam and Gin power-walked out of the parking lot. Annette laughed at how silly they looked, but no sound came out.

"You shouldn't have said that," Eliza whispered.

"Why not? It's the truth." Or she assumed. Technically didn't remember.

"Where are they going? You don't think they're going to Morgan, do you?"

"They'll run into him before they get to the fork. Bet Agent Orange passes on that little Asian tart and shoves an arrow up the little douchebag's ass."

"That's dark, Annette. What the hell's gotten into you?"

Damn it, the cramps were returning. Out of nowhere it felt like she was passing a brick through her intestines. It was the dawn of a new bout with nausea, too. In the heat of the moment she let herself get too worked up and threw her biological equilibrium out of whack.

She grabbed Eliza's arm, but this pain didn't drain into the waiting vessel.

"Maybe the new guy knows something. Maybe there's a reason they came back here," Eliza said.

Annette didn't feel like talking—or thinking—she just nodded. If she leaned forward in an approximate one hundred and fifty degree angle it seemed to ease the pain in her bowels. Eliza gave her a look she didn't like, the insufferable "what the hell is this bitch doing now?" look that made Annette want to smack her across the face. Before this whole thing was over Annette would definitely smack the silly out of this girl. She had some facial swattage reserved for Gin, Adam, and know-it-all Patrick, too. And she'd like to knock Lawrence's head off the stake. Her to-do list in this accursed place grew by the minute. She'd trade it all for her pill box, though.

"Can't believe after all this we're back where we started."

Why don't you whine about it? Damn!

"Why are you snapping at *me*?"

The bad energy wasn't draining into Eliza anyway so Annette put her hand on her mouth.

"Nothing," she answered through her fingers.

They travelled a few yards further before a new burst of cramping nearly bent Annette over. An adjustment to a one hundred and forty degree angle eased the pain.

"We'd better hurry," she said and her tightly-pressed fingers obliterated the words.

Annette walked faster. The friction of her legs within her pantsuit renewed the body temperature problem. The inferno returned, worse than ever.

"Shhh!" Eliza warned. She put a hand on Annette's back, which only added to the discomfort by concentrating more heat between her shoulder blades. Like Eliza was transferring back the pain she took earlier.

She began unbuttoning the bodice of her one-piece pantsuit to give herself a head start.

"You okay?"

She burst into the lobby, looking for a restroom sign.

"That's Eliza coming through the door," Patrick said, "and this . . . "

Annette flew past him, elbowed him aside. The Gin and Adam dual power-walk suddenly seemed less funny as she pounded across the lobby. She smashed into the door to the men's room since it was the closer of the two, revealing a dim preview of the facilities. She bolted for the first stall. Darkness reclaimed the room as the door eased shut behind her.

" . . . that was Annette."

GIM WASN'T SURPRISED to find Annette sprawled on an old couch, tended to by Eliza, who lacked only a palm frond to fan her queen of social faux pas and survival sabotage. Lee watched them with both hands atop his head as if he wondered what the hell he'd stumbled into.

He noted her return and murmured, "FYI, avoid the men's room."

"Oh, thanks, I was totally on my way there right now," Gin said.

"Your funeral. Hella disaster in there, though."

They had righted the sofa and returned two of the three seat cushions to allow Annette to recline. In the gap where the missing cushion would have gone, Eliza sat cross-ways as she massaged the cramps in Annette's legs. Of course Annette couldn't keep the pain to herself. She moaned and squeaked, echoing through the cavernous lobby of the lodge. The intermittent air raid sirens at least blasted once again for camouflage. They still made her uneasy, but Orange's first appearance afterward had been coincidence. It had to be a timer.

Patrick walked over from elevator doors he had pried apart and wedged open with a chair. The shaft inside was oil slick black but for something which gleamed in the late afternoon sun.

"What the hell was that all about?" Patrick asked

Adam, truly ruffled for the first time. Adam opened his mouth to speak but couldn't find the words.

"He was—"

Patrick cut her off with a raised hand, glass crackling underfoot. "You know what, it doesn't matter. Don't run off like that again. We've enough worries without adding to them." He winced when Annette let out a sharp little scream.

Now that Patrick was close Gin could smell gasoline.

"They shut off the electricity while we were away," he explained. "It will be dark soon and the woods will be darker first. Our chances of cutting straight through them to Morgan with all our limbs intact are slim to none." He looked Gin up and down. "Although it looks like you've already been there."

Gin's jeans were muddy and still soaked from the creek. Water had never tasted so good. "Sorry," Adam said to Patrick. He cleared his throat. "For running off like that."

"It's done. Don't dwell on it. As an aside, both of you would do well to avoid the men's room."

"What gives?" Gin whispered.

Patrick looked pointedly toward the couch with Annette and Eliza. "Don't ask."

Lee held up a finger as he approached. "I already told them." *Rock Star Lee* as Adam had dubbed him, and it was hard for Gin not to laugh.

"Let's try to keep our distance from the front windows, too," Patrick added.

On the couch, Annette let out a loud moan. The tanning bed sheen of her skin had paled considerably from only twenty minutes ago. It was like this place peeled away several layers of her carefully crafted persona and she carried on like this unmasking was more of an existential crisis than Agent Orange.

Patrick kept his voice low, barely audible enough for

the three of them so it wouldn't carry to the couch. "I'm surprised she's lasted this long. She's coming off a dozen meds, most of which weren't officially prescribed to her. She rattled off shit I've never heard of. I'd say she'll become increasingly erratic—"

Gin opened her mouth to say something, but Patrick saved her the trouble. "Yes, even more so. She's cramping, which won't do her any favors if Agent Orange catches up. And there's a greater likelihood of that with her weird behavior making stealth a fifty-fifty prospect at best. She'll be a potential danger to the group."

Gin opened her mouth again.

"Yes, I know, she already was," Patrick said, "and our situation is admittedly not too dissimilar from before."

Gin thought it a little unfair to have this discussion without Eliza, who ran the biggest risk from Annette's antics, but even she appeared to be tiring of all her self-involved bullshit. Maybe she'd come around before it was too late.

Patrick's volume approached something more conversational. "The equipment in the shaft isn't the original lift system; it's defense contractor work designed for silent use. The car is a level below us, probably to block access to any lower levels they may have added to the building."

Adam's eyebrows jumped. "Can't we go into it through the ceiling?"

Patrick shook his head. "Try it and you won't need Agent Orange to kill you. The security here was designed to keep out something far more formidable than us. I shouldn't have even gambled on prying open the doors."

"Gotta jet, folks," Lee said. "Whoever's ready is ready. This waiting around shit is gonna get a mug straight up killed, you feel me?"

"Yes," Patrick answered, giving Gin a look she couldn't identify. "Lee, Eliza, and Annette intend to find a military checkpoint at the wall. Lee says there's a road from the rear lot that may take you there."

"Oh, it'll take you there. The wall wouldn't be more than a few miles away and it's mostly downhill," Lee said. "There's even a Chicken Exit on the way so I can order ahead for pizza."

Lee looked at Gin to gauge her reaction and when she didn't pass the test, she earned a sour look that seemed to say *fucking bitch doesn't like me, screw her.* She'd seen that one a lot when she hadn't let a guy have his way or refused to stroke an expectant ego.

Patrick looked at Adam. "Will the road take you to the wall?"

Adam nodded. "Yeah, that's about right according to the *Thirty Year* . . . uh, the map I saw. There could be patrols, too."

Lee laughed. "You need a little less video game in your reality, son. The military doesn't patrol with Humvees and boats and shit. Other than rescues, they only come in here when spotters have Orange in sight on the other end of the Kill Zone, and even then it's just for road clearing and routine maintenance. What can I say? I was into this shit. Once a boy outgrows trains and dinosaurs, then it's Agent Orange, cars, and quim." He winked at Adam. "That's British for 'girls'."

"No, it's Asshole for 'pussy'," Gin told Adam.

"It explains why the roads are clear of fallen trees," Patrick said. "They'd keep them like that for future operations."

He pointed out logs on the roadside during their trip from the lake house, but Gin hadn't understood the significance. So she'd seen the smooth cut of the log but hadn't actually identified it as anything out of the ordinary for a place which shouldn't have any public works upkeep. Maybe Patrick saw the trap at the creek, too. Gin usually picked up details, but this place was so out of her element she didn't know what to look for, much less know it when she saw it.

"But it's the law," Eliza said. "The military is supposed to patrol for trespassers and prevent suicidal people from getting in here."

Gin was a junior in high school when the son of a prominent Washington insider found himself deep within the Kill Zone with a bunch of friends looking for the thrill of a lifetime. It went from thrilling to killing with the swing of a machete when Orange found them. The outrage against the laissez-faire military policy reached its apex with the release of the young man's recorded Chicken Exit pleas for help. With bipartisan momentum, a law mandating greater military presence, increased patrolling, and more preventative measures passed through Congress and the Morgan Falls Protection Act was signed into law by a president eager to salvage a middling approval rating during a politically poisonous year.

"Yes," Patrick said, "true to their name, Congress passed a law that led to the opposite of progress for all but the bureaucracy. What no one noticed about the bill is that it took the Chicken Exit away from the 911 system and put it under the control of Homeland Security. The recorded calls and transcripts went from public records to privileged national security documents. Have you not noticed the decrease in news stories about these incidents?"

"But I've heard calls since then," Eliza said. "On the news. They rescued a teen last year."

"And your point?" Patrick asked. "They'll mollify the public with a story around the anniversary of Thomas Smith's death and give the media a reason to say 'MIFPA,' but they control the information, so meanwhile probably more people than ever are dying in here. Enter: us."

"If they really cared, they'd keep him cryogenically frozen or chained up somewhere," Gin said.

"Oh, they tried all that," Lee said. "They've probably

still got dude's head on a shelf with Walt Disney's, but soon as they froze him, his ass showed up here like a video game save point and you know what happened next." He mimed a stabbing motion several times.

"Then why don't they chain him here?" Eliza asked.

Lee shrugged. "You think a guy who's killed that many people can't do himself? Just swallow his own tongue and before you know it he's back in Morgan with a brand new body and an axe to grind; reincarnated, but more like *reincarnage*. So yeah, the military's about as successful with him as the actual Vietnam War. Sick burn from irony."

"But they're still supposed to help us," Eliza argued. "If we get to the—damn it, I *am* massaging, stop kicking me— if we get to the wall, they have to help."

"Obviously you've never heard of 'selective enforcement,'" Patrick said.

Lee sighed. "We finished with the civics lesson? We show up at the wall, the least they can do is open that shit up and let us out. Who's with me, 'cos the bus to Getdafuckouttahere is revving up."

Adam and Gin looked to Patrick, who said, "I'm staying behind. He may pass through here, and if he does, I'll lead him in the wrong direction."

"Let's go," Annette said. She swung her legs and dismounted the old sofa, much spryer than her earlier mewling indicated.

"She should stay with you," Annette added and Gin was surprised to find Annette pointing at her. "Yeah, you, Hanoi Gin. He wants you the most. You'll make a target of any group you're with, but he's saving you for last."

Patrick put a hand on Gin's shoulder but it didn't calm her any. "Hanoi Gin? I'm Korean, you fucking psychotic pillhead."

"Like anyone can tell. With those beady little goggles, you plenty VC to him."

"This is like playing Russian roulette watching *The*

View." Lee made for the exit and took a good look around before he eased through the doorway. "Talkingest bunch of people I ever did see. Fuck."

"If you're coming with us, keep your mouth to yourself," Eliza told Annette. She turned to Patrick and said, "Thanks. Good luck, you guys. If we're rescued we'll send help."

Undaunted, Annette continued, "He's saving her for last. He'll probably take a day to kill her. If she cared at all about the well-being of the group, she'd be the one sacrificing herself to lead him away." Before she followed Lee out the door, she turned back for a parting shot. "Also, she's not going to suck your dick, jailbait."

"Screw that bitch," Adam said, though waited for her to exit first. His face had turned a deep shade of crimson. "Don't let that stuff bother you."

"I don't," Gin lied. There were brass pillars for a circuit of velvet ropes by the front desk, and she ached to swing one upside Annette's crazy head.

"Place yourself in the middle of the pack," Patrick said to Adam. "You'll stand a better chance if we fail to draw him away."

We?

Gin looked at Patrick, who nodded. Adam's eyes followed the departing Eliza and Annette as they cleared the last window along the car port outside. Patrick took the distraction as an opportunity to mouth the words "Trust me."

She certainly didn't feel safe with Annette, but wasn't sure she felt any safer with Patrick if he planned on playing decoy. Maybe that wasn't his plan at all, which seemed cut throat and duplicitous with the life and death stakes. On this account alone she didn't want Adam involved in a ploy to buy her and Patrick time.

"Don't let them get too far ahead," Patrick said.

It wrenched her to think of the trio within the group

146

breaking apart. It didn't feel right. They had avoided catastrophe together, and maybe she was superstitious about disbanding a proven inner circle.

"I'm not leaving Gin behind."

She smiled at him until she realized this didn't mean they were any less screwed given the circumstances.

It could prove fatal to Adam to stick with them if they really did plan to serve as decoys. Patrick might be keeping her around only as a way to buy himself time if Agent Orange came for them.

Life or death stakes.

"You're not doing her or yourself any good staying here," Patrick said, but he apparently knew the futility of appealing to a teenager's better sense so he turned to Gin and quietly added, "You need to nip this in the bud. Don't lead him on."

Gin said, "What? I'm not—"

"Letting him think he has a shot is on you. This isn't the time or place for silly high school games with some kid."

Patrick's ultimatum made no sense. What purpose did it serve to send him off with rejection on top of the loss of his parents? Adam was the only person she truly trusted. He was smitten with her, for whatever reason. He seemed like a good kid, "kid" being very much the operative word. If they made it out of here alive she'd "nip it in the bud," but if he continued thinking Gin might be his girlfriend one day, what could it hurt? He needed to feel accepted now, not alone. Besides, he wasn't pushing his luck, obviously afraid to find out "what if" was more like "as if."

More importantly, why was Patrick so desperate to ditch Adam?

Patrick and Adam stared at her expectantly.

She grabbed Adam's arm. "He's with us." She could have made her point less dramatically, but Patrick brought this into the open anyway so what did it matter now? And it wasn't as if she'd flirted with Adam or actively led him on. What the hell was she supposed to do, qualify her statements with "Don't take this the wrong way, but I hope we make it out of here alive," or "Let's get some water from the creek; you know this isn't a date, right?"

If Patrick was pissed off, his face didn't show it, but he said, "Old habits die hard," which left little doubt he was upset with her.

"He's not Hoon and you don't know me," Gin snapped. *Asshole, let me deal with this my own way!*

Patrick was the first person Gin ran into, minutes before they found Lawrence. When none of them could figure out how or why they came to be here, Patrick asked two very interesting questions: *Who would want to hurt you?* and *If you disappeared, who would the police suspect?* Only Gin had a ready answer and his name was Hoon Kim (*Anni, anni, Kim Hoon or Hoon-ah or maybe . . . Oppa,* he would say). Introduced months ago by mutual friends, Hoon took such an obsessive interest in her that a restraining order hadn't breached his impertinence. Apparently Patrick's amateur psychological profile found parallels between her treatment of Adam and the creation of a stalker—more of the "you brought this on yourself" bullshit she'd heard from some of Hoon's friends. The threat to her life here didn't keep her from bristling any less over such an infuriating assertion.

"Sorry," Patrick said. "The three of us, then."

"Are we really creating a distraction for the others?" Adam said it in a low voice.

The sirens had stopped again and this was the second or third time Gin had not noticed until minutes after the fact. Had she grown so accustomed to the sounds of the Kill Zone?

"Distraction? Somewhat. Gin, could you keep watch for our homicidal host?" Patrick pointed to the desk and spoke to Adam. "And can you gather whatever flammable items are behind the counter, please?"

Patrick went to the ratty sofa and slid it across the floor toward the elevator. Gin cringed at the echo of the loud sliding through the lobby; this would definitely draw attention.

She looked for Agent Orange but the lot was empty other than his trophies. Their shadows stretched to funhouse mirror lengths in the weakening daylight. Only a couple hours remained at most. Her eyes tracked to the shell of the military truck. How could Agent Orange fight against soldiers? Did he have weapons more substantial than a bow and machete? If so, did he consider it merely unsportsmanlike to attack unarmed people with guns, kind of like the alien hunter in those *Predator* movies? Or maybe guns made the killing less personal? Yet, if that were true, why would he set up traps? It didn't get more impersonal than that.

He's saving her for last. He'll probably take a day to kill her.

He hesitated when he was close enough to grab her at the lake house. Could Annette be right? Could Gin expect an excruciating, lingering death?

With a shiver, she crossed her arms. She squatted in the doorway to make herself less of a target for his arrows if he spotted her first. From her new angle she could see the tops of the distant trees swaying in the wind. She couldn't help glancing at the shadowy faces on the stakes, but she quickly looked from the repugnant, dehumanizing sight to the woods again. Still . . . the heads remained in the foreground.

"Maybe check the bathroom for old toilet paper rolls if the light reaches," Patrick said. "They might keep spares near the front."

Adam hurried over and pushed in one of the doors, momentarily vanishing. He bounced back out a second later like the floor was on fire, gagging. "Oh, God!'

"I meant the ladies' room," Patrick said wryly. "Keep your head in the game."

She turned back to the parking lot. What would her parents think of her disappearance? Earlier with Adam she callously joked they wouldn't notice but they would, they definitely would, and she hated how Hoon had come between them. They loved him instantly, probably because he'd been in America for less than a year and it was their firm, non-negotiable desire she marry a Korean or a Korean with Korean parents (Korean adoptees of Caucasians ended up "too American," according to them). For them, it was all about culture. They hadn't understood why she rejected Hoon and refused to listen when she'd told them of his domineering side, which included a lot of wrist-grabbing like he thought he was the star of a K-Drama. The parents who'd never allowed her a serious boyfriend until giving their fickle approval were too obstinate to admit after years of careful deliberation they had made a bad choice. In their eyes the restraining order took things too far and suddenly everything she had ever done had been thrown in her face, including her use of the nickname "Gin" instead of her given name Ja-in—alas, to her parents "Gin" could be mistaken as Japanese (and apparently Vietnamese, too), something they found absolutely scandalous. Thanks to Hoon they'd barely spoken in the weeks leading up to her abduction.

Why me? Why couldn't they have chosen Hoon?

Despite the fact Hoon was a grade-A dickhead, she felt guilty for wishing him in here. This shouldn't be happening to anyone.

Her fingers were dirty so she wiped her eyes with the back of her hands and quickly parried the tears. At least her parents weren't in here. It was easy to play the level head with Adam, but she would have been prone to the same rash mistakes with her parents. And he'd have stopped her, too.

A loud clatter behind her made her jump. Patrick and Adam had inserted the sofa between the elevator doors, which knocked the chair into the shaft. The sofa had a plethora of flammable items on it, including an old phone book that would fetch hundreds of dollars for someone who managed to smuggle it out of the Kill Zone.

"Don't set me on fire," Patrick warned, and Gin instinctively looked for the bottle of napalm. It was several yards away.

When the phone book caught fire, Patrick shifted its angle so it spread upwards. "Back away," he told Adam. He knelt beside the sofa and used the flaming phone book to light one of the cushions. Gin could now smell the smoke from the burning paper. Gingerly, Patrick propped the burning phone book on the sofa where the missing seat cushion would have been. He pointed to the shattered coffee table. Adam fetched the scraps of wood.

Smoke rolled from the old sofa and rose to the ceiling. Patrick pushed the sofa halfway into the shaft and Adam tossed the kindling on top. The dark shaft now glowed with flickering red-orange light. Patrick crouched at the edge to observe its progress.

Adam joined Gin at the doorway. With a crooked smile, he proffered a cracked coffee mug with the words "Morgan Falls Lodge" written on the side. When Gin nodded toward the elevator shaft, he shrugged with no explanation for Patrick's act of vandalism.

The noxious smell of the smoke filled the lobby.

Patrick grabbed the bottle of napalm and hurried over to them. "That's what I like to call 'fucking with the contractors.'" He pointed across the parking lot to the forest. "Okay, one by one, five second intervals, we're going to take up station just inside the woods there."

"What if he's watching?" Adam asked.

"Why would he reconnoiter? He'd just come straight at us."

"Traps?" Gin asked.

"He can't have the entire woods trapped. Stay at the

edge. We'll get situated once we're all there. And don't drop that mug if you want water." Patrick tapped Adam's shoulder. "Go."

Adam ran for all he was worth. For a moment Gin worried this was all a ploy to separate from Adam. The fear escalated to horror as the seconds rolled on and nothing happened. Then she felt the tap and heard "Go!" and she was off. They hadn't seen Agent Orange since the lake house but Gin ran like he was on her heels.

Adam looked back at her several times to make sure she was behind him. Gin looked toward the lake road, half-expecting to see Orange materialize like some otherworldly specter. As Adam neared the woods, she was gripped by the fear she would hear the crack of a toe-popper or see him lifted into the air by a rope and swung against a tree trunk hard enough to shatter bones. None of this happened and he beckoned her from the spot. Gin hopped over the curb, through the tall weeds, nerves on edge that each step would put her on the ground like Nathan. In moments she joined Adam in the trees, panting. It took Patrick another eight seconds to reach them and as soon as he did she smelled the gasoline.

Wisps of smoke curled from the front of the lobby, but by now Gin expected to see it billowing. No flames were visible. The lobby seemed unbelievably dark, as if the trip from there had taken a half hour instead of a minute.

"So, what next?" Adam whispered, his breathing slowly returning to normal. He squatted so close to Gin the hair of his leg tickled the back of her hand.

"We stay put for a moment and make sure this works." He pointed to the hotel. "Next we go to Morgan to find a safe place to stay for the night."

"That's it?" Gin asked. *Stay* would not have been part of any plan she considered on her own.

"I didn't want to say this in there because they've probably got the place bugged," Patrick answered, "but there is no scenario where one of us escapes to tell the tale of some secret agency providing Agent Orange with kills. It's never happened and it won't happen. If we get rescued at the wall we're certain to meet with a nasty fate soon afterward." He shrugged. "Or we end up back in here, perhaps hobbled so we don't stand a chance of making it to the wall a second time."

If Adam made the connection Patrick tried to trade him to the other group and share their inevitable fate, he didn't let on. Patrick would probably have some clever way to justify it to Adam's satisfaction if confronted. It irritated Gin she had almost been a party to the separation. No, it flat-out pissed her off. Patrick had miscalculated her feelings. If Adam went with the others and Patrick imparted this "No Way Out" theory, she would have gone back for him.

"So we . . . have to fight Agent Orange?" Adam asked.

"What's it matter if we kill him?" Gin asked. "He comes back—or maybe he never dies in the first place. You're saying we die here or they'll kill us if we get out of here, but no matter what, we'll die?"

"I know this is upsetting but use your inside the KZ voice, please; that smoke should be the extent of the distraction we provide for the others." Patrick took his own voice to a whisper and added, "The powers that be gave us a death sentence, but we also have a certain amount of freedom. We just have to use our brains."

"But we're stuck here in the Kill Zone?" Gin asked.

"For a few weeks at least, yes."

"Why a few weeks?"

"By then they'll assume we're dead."

And we probably will be.

"What about surveillance?" Adam asked. "Can't they see us with satellites and high powered cameras?"

"Little known secret: electronic surveillance doesn't work very well with the Kill Zone. Bizarre variations in the electromagnetic spectrum around here cause distortions, which is about the only advantage we have," Patrick said.

"Advantage? With the government, maybe, but Orange is the more pressing matter, don't you think?" Gin sighed. "So what happens once two or three weeks have passed?"

"First, we have to find a safe exit that doesn't go through a military post. Those guys who sneak in and out of here . . . " Patrick paused to look at Adam.

"Stalkers?"

"Right, Stalkers."

How could a guy know top secret government information but not know the name for the men and women who stole Kill Zone artifacts for private collections and snuck people in on private tours? Even Gin knew that much. She also knew that contrary to popular belief, the name wasn't based on a video game series but a Russian movie. Patrick must have known but prompted Adam anyway. It seemed like a cheap way to make him feel part of the "team" again.

Patrick continued, "They have ways in and out that go around the military blockades. Those fuckers would be harder to track than Agent Orange but we'll manage."

"And then?" Gin prompted.

"I've got some offshore accounts. Nest eggs even the NSA doesn't know about. It's all up here." He tapped his skull.

"Does us a lot of good if something happens to you," Gin said with a light smirk so he wouldn't think she was too serious. In fact, she wasn't serious at all. Even if this wasn't a bunch of bullshit it was a long way from here to cashing in a secret stash of money that wouldn't get her any closer to reuniting with her family and living her old life again. NSA? It was getting real deep around here.

"I'll write down the information when we get to Morgan."

"What happens if you're killed before you can give us this retirement plan?"

"You're better off staying in here. You need resources for the outside. The spooks even found me in Chiapas. Your only chance would be to blow the lid off this and hope instant celebrity provides you with protection. But neither of you are the Julian Assange or Edward Snowden type so stick with the devil you know."

Adam gave Gin the kind of perplexed look that said he knew the devil, but not the other two, which underlined Patrick's point.

Addressing her somberly, Patrick said, "You'll want to talk to your parents, which will get you killed within one hour of the call. Them, too, if you mention what happened." He looked at Adam. "You'll be dead if you're with her. Do yourselves a favor: Stay here. Find a way to survive. Maybe you can even barter with the Stalkers—not everything of value has been looted. You trap, garden, live off the land."

Because she could smell the smoke she glanced at the lodge and now saw a faint, flickering glow in the lobby. Had it been Patrick's intention to burn the place down? She imagined his "secret agent men" would activate the sprinkler system to neutralize an inferno.

"How do we live long enough to harvest a head of cabbage when he's looking to chop off *our* heads?" Gin asked.

"I take it home schooling was strictly for the religious angle? Your parents didn't have a survivalist bent?"

Adam shook his head. "I do know gardening and canning, but . . . what she said. We won't have time to do anything but survive."

The glow in the lodge was much brighter now. The wall around the elevator doors was on fire. It would draw Orange soon.

"His death will provide a reset of sorts. You'll have anywhere from a few days to a few weeks. When he comes back he may not remember about us, though granted, that won't matter if he sees us again."

In their last encounter Agent Orange knocked Patrick silly and Gin had no reason to think the next time would be any different. None of them were armed well enough. Patrick increasingly appeared like a kid with big plans for the future, a kid who ultimately couldn't even get his lemonade stand up and running.

"How do we kill him without getting messed up?" Adam asked.

"We're very careful."

Elbows on knees, Gin grabbed her head with her hands and wanted to scream at all this unfair bullshit. *What did I do wrong? Why am I here? I never hurt anyone! I've been a good daughter and a super-awesome person to all of my friends! Why? Why? Why?*

A shriek echoed from the hollow behind the lodge. The long, plaintive wail pulled her back from a complete meltdown.

"Probably Annette." Patrick sighed.

Now there's a tragedy. She waited to feel bad for thinking it. She kept waiting.

"Either Orange found them or she's just being herself. Fuck it. Our work here is done. Let's pay Morgan a visit. We need a way to take him out and we'll find it there."

Patrick stood and led them from the woods toward what would probably be their deaths. Adam and Gin looked at each other and his "What the hell have we gotten ourselves into?" face was a mirror of her own feelings on the matter.

"We'll stop by the creek first to rehydrate. I assume that's where the mud on your jeans originated. Guess it wasn't trapped after all."

"We neutralized it," Gin said.

Adam smiled weakly.

Gin preferred to believe they would make it to Morgan, find a nice, safe place to hide for the night and maybe Patrick would formulate some brilliant plan to succeed where no one else had, but she'd begun to fear him another Nathan—a middle-aged guy unwilling to believe he'd passed his prime and well-read enough to think his knowledge gave him an edge against an unstoppable foe. He'd probably set off a trap playing Daniel Boone, his last thought *This wouldn't have happened to Liam Neeson!*

"Come on," Patrick said. "Eyes and ears open. We need to hurry. We're losing sunlight fast."

"We could get to Morgan through the woods if you're not worried about traps," Adam pointed out.

"Not all of us could."

Gin figured that was a shot at them. The great white hunter would walk between the raindrops while they fried in a lightning blitzkrieg.

"He's had *years* to trap his environment," Patrick said. "He was digging punji stick pits while you were still putting teeth under your pillow for the Tooth Fairy. Now everyone be quiet, please. I need to concentrate."

He walked in a crouch through the network of trees and bushes, head up, down, and around to ID any trip wires or log projectiles. Gin stepped right into his footprints when visible and gestured Adam to do the same behind her.

"Would have been better to stop by the creek before you set the lodge on fire," Gin said in her best inside-the-KZ quiet voice.

Patrick turned to look at her, obviously annoyed. He put a finger over his nose for silence and resumed his trap patrol, Elmer Fudd in wabbit season. It spared him from having to answer why he created a distraction and then marched them parallel to the road where Agent Orange could hear or see them if he came to investigate any smoke signals.

Long as you got to "fuck with the contractors," that's the important thing, right?

The cover of leaves made a prism of sun rays, and the

spots of light danced around them as a breeze ruffled the branches overhead. The magic hour was coming fast. They would never get to Morgan before dark. She'd scream if he proposed the lake house.

He'll never think to look for us there again! I'll write down all my Cayman Island bank account numbers on a scrap of paper. We can even stay upstairs so Adam doesn't see his parents stacked up like cord wood.

It took ten minutes of Patrick's maneuvers to get them to the creek. He spotted the tree trunk pincushion and shook his head at them. "That was really careless, guys. He's going to leave surprises near all the fresh water sources."

"He won't need them if we pass out from dehydration," Gin said. The blacksmith in her skull pounded away again despite the water earlier.

Patrick held up two fingers like a peace symbol and angled them toward his eyes. "You've got to *look,* at all times. There could be another trap, maybe two or three. This is what he does. He's not taking a break to watch *Silly Jackson* reruns. He doesn't sleep or eat. He traps and kills in an endless hunting season."

Gin waited for him to come even closer to quoting *The Terminator,* but he proffered a hand to Adam. "Cup?"

Adam passed him the mug.

"Me first since you had a trip to the buffet already. Firestarting is thirsty work." He stooped to the bank, still obsessively watching for anything amiss. She felt tense watching him despite drinking from the same place without incident (mostly), but nothing happened other than finding out Patrick was a bit of a slurper. He gulped down three cupfuls in rapid succession and poured a fourth on his face and head.

"That's damn good," he reported at almost normal volume, rather lax on the KZ voice protocol.

He held the cup to Gin and Adam. Adam predictably

beckoned Gin to go next, and she didn't disappoint his chivalry. She rinsed it in the water first before she'd drink after Patrick. She thought it tasted metallic, as if the blood of all kills in Morgan Falls overran it in a mini-Apocalypse, but it was cold and refreshing. The blacksmith in her skull decided to take five and the malaise lifted.

She passed the cup to Adam and found Patrick watching her when she looked his way again. He held her stare a moment, then swiveled back toward the road. It could have been nothing, but it didn't seem like nothing.

Trust me, he'd mouthed.

Oh, sure thing, guy. Tried to send a trusting Adam off on his own Bataan Death March to keep me with you, but no, nothing weird about that at all.

It would have been a relief if he merely fancied her, but it seemed more like a plan for survival where he alienated the group and kept her to use as a pawn. A basket case like Annette knew the score on Orange's special attraction to Gin, so a would-be strategist like Patrick had no doubt factored it into his blueprints probably before they left the lake house.

Adam tentatively scooted to the edge of the creek, though Patrick and Gin had already proved it safe.

"It's doubtful he'd put explosives right up on the water," Patrick said. "You don't want wet wiring if you can help it."

Adam didn't look back at him, only muttered, "There were a lot of monsoons in Vietnam."

And it's not like he's too concerned about keeping you alive.

She nearly gasped when she felt a hand on her shoulder. Patrick leaned in close to her, a whisper so faint she strained to hear it. Adam would miss it as he fussed with the mug along with the cover of rushing creek water.

"He's barely here with us. He's thinking about his parents more than his next step, and sooner or later that's going to be a problem for us."

Gin checked to make sure Adam was still preoccupied before replying, "Well, we can't just tie him to a tree and leave him."

She regretted it before the last word escaped her lips, expecting him to say that's exactly what they should do, right this minute. He merely gave her his patented look of survivalist disappointment (a special edition with a head shake) and turned his attention back to the road.

She spun in a slow circle. So many trees, layers of cover, a thick blanket of wood and foliage to disappear within. But Patrick had a point—a man (or whatever Orange was now) could accomplish a lot with dedicated trapping day by day for so many years.

Patrick was optimistic they could kill Orange for a reset, but he had a good track record the last several years. She remembered a news story when she was eight years old, Orange shredded in a hail of bullets at a wall checkpoint. There was optimism this time he was gone for good. He'd exhausted his nine lives and the scourge was banished (though he'd far surpassed nine by that point; Wikipedia lore put the total between twelve and seventeen times by that point, citations still needed). Ten days later they spotted him again, grainy surveillance footage as professional as a Bigfoot sighting, but nobody disbelieved it for a minute because deep down they all expected it. A radical outcry from hysterics suggested they evacuate the whole state and just nuke the fucker (the so-called Scorched Earth Exorcism Initiative), but that went over as well as New Coke. It was a grave new world, although "grave" was a rather vague concept for one of its citizens.

He'd been decapitated, blown apart by a grenade, shot, incinerated, impaled, and several combinations thereof, only to return to his killing fields a week or two later, arisen as a phoenix from the ashes to pick up where he left off. He bounced back from decapitation and cremation in a week. The grenade put him away for twelve days. No rhyme or reason. These had been experiments by the military, or at least the ones publicized. Some put the true figure of executions in the hundreds, even thousands. The new movement was to keep a drone on standby to patrol and destroy every time he showed up, but not many people (especially veterans) liked the idea of drones used on American soil, even if the target in question was a completely bugfuck psychopath. Plus maybe there were technical difficulties to consider if Patrick hadn't made up the electromagnetic weirdness.

Since that news story from her childhood, there might have been two, maybe three other confirmed "kills" of Agent Orange. If they had ever been initiated by anyone not affiliated with the military, there had been no reports. It didn't do much to inspire confidence in Patrick's "live off the land" plan; in fact, it made it sound like the sort of counterculture thing that might have been popular with people wearing bellbottoms back when Agent Orange was still a normal human being serving a tour in Vietnam.

Adam finished by baptizing himself with the mug like Patrick. She wondered if he did it to cover up tears. Men were funny when it came to such extreme emotion. Like it wasn't natural to fall apart when people you'd known all your life died so horribly, feeling like there was something you could have done to stop it.

She noticed a puzzled expression on Adam's face and followed his eyes to Patrick. He looked back in the direction of the lodge through the tree tops.

"I was hoping there'd be smoke."

There wasn't. No sign of an inferno at all. Nothing of note but the occasional ruffling of branches as a bird hopped around for a better spot. Patrick had to know the hidden security would have all manner of contingencies, be it an incursion by Agent Orange or a fire. Hurricane Rose tore through the area ten years ago and nothing happened. Orange stayed within the walls. They were prepared.

Gin's eyes drew once more to the trap in the creek. She watched the tree trunk as though it had some secret to part of the forest. She noticed Patrick looking too.

"You thinking what I'm thinking?" he said.

"Yes."

Adam came over to them. "What? What are you thinking?"

Gin answered, "We could set a trap of our own."

Patrick nodded beside her. "If we miss with the napalm, we're out of options. But if we catch him, we get a free shot."

Adam looked at them doubtfully. "Yeah, that'd be great, but with what? The napalm's our only weapon. We don't even have a knife. Unless you're MacGruber all of a sudden and you can turn a coffee mug into a land mine."

"MacGyver," Patrick corrected absently.

Gin wasn't so sure Adam wasn't right.

"It doesn't have to be elaborate. We can find enough materials in Morgan."

That's when they all heard the scream, way off in the distance from the direction where Lee left with Eliza and Annette.

"Sounds like the wrong group created a distraction," Patrick said. "Come on, we need to move fast."

XI.

LEE SEEMED LIKE a fun guy to be around, if you only had to deal with him for about 14 seconds, that is. Anything past that was torture.

"You girls would love my band," he assured them.

"Girls?" Eliza echoed.

Lee missed the implication entirely. "Yep. Been playing since I was in grade school. Fastest fingers you ever saw." He held up his hand and waved them. "Not just at playing music, either."

Eliza rolled her eyes.

She was interested in his experiences since waking up here, not his stupid band. It was called Jack in the Box, a sleazy pun of approximately zero surprise from a guy who used words like "quim." It was encouraging that such an idiot had survived this long, though.

Annette was out to lunch through this monologue, chewing the nails of one hand. She was lost in the latest crisis behind her eyes, thankfully a private one. Her eccentricities seemed much more embarrassing with someone who hadn't been around them all afternoon. Hopefully they'd get to the checkpoint before she started acting up again. Lee claimed they were close.

"I know that map like the back of my hand." He checked behind them. "I can't see the lodge now. We're making tracks, yo. They're probably still talking about what to do. In our group, someone came up with an idea and we jumped on it without a town hall meeting."

"You didn't last very long," Eliza pointed out.

Lee smiled at her. "I'm still here, though. Rock 'n roll destiny. Staying in one place when someone's after you, how stupid is that?"

Not half-bad if they don't know you're in that one place.

"We should keep a close eye around us and only talk when necessary," she said.

Lee mimed zipping up his lip and tossing away the tab. It made her want to hit him even more.

The path was wide open, a field of high grass bordered on both sides by tall trees. The horizon had few obstructions, offering a glorious view of the transformation of the sky to burnt amber as the sun slid past. She tried not to dwell on how this magic palette would soon be pitch black.

As if reading her mind, Lee said, "Yeah, we'll be at the checkpoint while it's still light out."

He led the way, and she was only too happy to let him. The grass grew wild over the years and no telling how many hidden things crept down in there. If one of them were to get bit, let it be Jack in the Box's lead guitarist. She felt tiny things scamper (or slither) over her shoes several times. A convoy of tiny bugs jumped ahead with each step as if to flee the judgment of the giants.

"You're sure they'll open up for us?" She didn't consider Patrick a fool, but he wasn't too far from wearing a funny hat with jangly bells. Captain Napalm turned into Usain Bolt back at the lake house without the slightest concern for those left behind. Adam too, ditched his parents like embarrassing chaperones.

Not that she couldn't commiserate on letting down family in a life or death situation.

"Positively positive," he said. "That's also the name of

one of our jams. They go crazy for that one live. But yeah, they'll open the gates. It's like the US Embassy."

"Patrick wasn't so sure."

Lee laughed. "Yeah, I'm sure he had a compelling argument not to find help. Tuned him out."

"He's a dead bitchlick." Annette paused in her nail chewing for a moment. "They all are."

Lee finally acknowledged her. "A dead what?"

"Long story," Eliza said.

Annette fortunately offered no follow-up comment, like someone roused from sleep slipping back into dreamland. A longer length of nail clacked as she snapped it between her teeth. Valerie used to do that.

Things got ugly at the motel, with Eliza in the unenviable position of defending her plus one at a party where Annette tried to microwave a pet parakeet. She went from scared to full-blown whacko mode (more shades of Valerie), but after sticking by her since the ordeal began, Eliza didn't want to concede they were right about her. Annette had her reasons. A bad situation and the added complication of no access to that laundry list of medications she reeled off to Patrick, of course she was in the Twilight Zone.

"All they can do us is send us back," Lee said. "Maybe they'll throw us a sandwich. I'm so hungry I could eat the ass-end out of a dead rhino." He glanced back at her, eyebrow raised. He rolled his eyes when she didn't burst out laughing.

Get your own material, asshole. I've seen Point Break.

Another clack from Annette. God, that would get annoying fast.

"We really need to be careful," Eliza said. "If he buried that bullet at the Chicken Exit, no telling what he'll rig near an actual checkpoint."

"Shit. Good point." He swiveled his head left and right and found something on the ground. He reached to pick it up.

"Careful," Eliza warned. She put an arm out to block Annette, who halted but continued to step in place the way Eliza jogged at red lights. She went through the rotation of her fingernails in rapid succession like corn on the cob. She didn't look at Eliza, focused on some distant point at the horizon.

Lee paused midway to look back. "He's not going to trap a random stick."

Eliza backed up anyway, nudging Annette with her arm.

Lee shook his head and snatched up a stick about as long as his arm. "See? Told you I'd *stick* around."

It was Eliza's turn to shake her head.

He continued to walk in front of them with the stick out, tapping the ground. She doubted it would be much of a buffer if he triggered an explosive, but better than nothing. It probably couldn't trip the toe popper thingies that would have assured Nathan a handicapped placard if he'd survived, but she didn't mention it.

Her stomach churned at the thought of Nathan in pieces, and right on cue she saw the poles fifty yards away to the left. She tapped Lee's shoulder and pointed, not wanting to alert Annette on the off chance they would penetrate her weirdo fugue state.

Lee squinted. "Not much of a welcoming committee."

There were at least ten, racked together like bowling pins. Her feet tingled, ready to run. She had the stamina to reach the wall. Ten miles would be easy. At least until the toe popper or land mine or whatever surprise he had for them, because there would undoubtedly be something. Callous though it was, her biggest concern about Lee dying in a trap was that he wouldn't be on point to catch the next one.

He continued to beat the grass before him. Eliza kept pace with Valerie, ten feet behind him. Discretion was the better part of—

She realized her mistake. Not Valerie, *Annette*. Annette walked beside her. Valerie wasn't. Valerie couldn't. She was buried with their mother and father back in Illinois, surprisingly without a coffin full of antibacterial soap.

I think I'm coming down with what mom had, El.

Jesus, you can't "come down" with pulmonary fibrosis. You're fine, Val. You always think you're sick, and it's always in your head, isn't it?

But it feels different this time!

It felt different last time too, and the time before that. Go to Dr. Ferguson if you're really that worried, but I'm telling you, you're fine.

Eliza assured her of the same two weeks later. The paranoia was bad enough before their mother died, but after that she was certain there must be a terminal illness with her name on it; a package that would show up at her door one day when they got it properly routed to her. Dr. Ferguson humored her as best she could. No telling how many times Valerie crashed her general practice with imaginary complaints since Eliza moved away. She'd been happy to leave her front row seat to the endless charade in exchange for the occasional cell phone update. She assumed there were multiple visits each time her sister reiterated her concern of "coming down" with pulmonary fibrosis.

It turned out Valerie didn't go to the doctor. She tried to buy Eliza's token assurances. After weeks of trying to believe it was all a delusion, she did go see Dr. Ferguson, who referred her to a pulmonary specialist. The diagnosis was idiopathic pulmonary fibrosis. Valerie was dead within eight months. Dr. Ferguson said an earlier doctor's visit might not have made much of a difference anyway.

Might not—meaning might have. Like if an apathetic sister hadn't assured her she imagined the whole thing and implied it was a waste of time to go to the doctor; implied also she would embarrass herself by going.

Valerie embarrassing herself wasn't the issue, though; it was the embarrassment by proxy to Eliza. It began as those sardonic smiles at school with her many absences, the students and gradually the teachers. *Oh, Valerie's sick again. Right, right. Of course she is.* It became Eliza's problem too. *Pulled yourself away from your sister's deathbed for the big algebra test, eh?* If she missed school, she always wondered if teachers joked that it might be a pattern they'd seen before from that MacColl family.

When it came time to choose a college, Eliza focused on the best possibilities out of state.

She watched Annette gnaw her fingers now. Not much like Valerie, really, but she latched on to the core element of comparison from the beginning. The way the rest of the group quickly took sides against her, annoyed and hostile, questioning her sanity. Things she knew she did to her sister. It was hard not to consider this a kind of karmic opportunity to get it right and redeem the guilt of failing Valerie.

But I'll still leave her behind if it's her or me . . . won't I?

She'd been with Valerie at the end and watched the awful decline, the regression of results with her incentive spirometer, the anguish that finally accompanied each breath. Her sister even seemed relieved to finally know what would get her after decades of wondering. Valerie never mentioned that Eliza told her she was fine. Eliza almost wished she had. It was worse to pretend it never happened, or that it didn't matter. She felt like she deserved to see the worst unfold, helpless to change it.

She became serious about running after that. Maybe she thought it would prevent the same thing from happening to her, or maybe she did it as a punishment because early on especially her lungs caught fire when she pushed herself.

Now she had Annette. No denying Annette needed

looking after or that nobody else really cared if she wound up drowning in a thimble of water. Annette should have been the one to suggest a pyrotechnic defense against Agent Orange, adept as she was at burning every bridge.

Eliza risked talking to her. "You holding up okay?"

Annette looked up sharply, still not breaking the rhythm of chewing. "Pies and cakes and puh-puh-pussy puddings."

"Yeah, she's coming up aces," Lee said.

Eliza resolved not to disturb her again. She focused on the sounds of their footsteps and the sea of grass sweeping their legs. Cicadas shrieked off in the trees, a sonic grinding that set her teeth on edge and seemed to fill up her skull.

Cicadas and Annette's fingernails.

The world around them remained still, other than wind through the tree branches. She doubted Marcus and Suzanne got away, but hoped they at least made him work for it. Even better, she hoped he still hunted for them back by the lake. The screams on their way out said otherwise, though.

"Hey, look," Lee said. "You see it?"

It was too far to be sure, but a couple minutes later, there could be little doubt.

"Told you so." Lee beamed at her over his shoulder. "A Chicken Exit on the way out. The checkpoint's probably a mile and a half away. We're real close."

"Why did they bother with one so close to the checkpoint?"

"If you thought you could get soldiers to drive in and get you, would you walk another foot by yourself? Breaking news, we're walking around with a *stick*. They've got machine guns and hand grenades and shit in that mug. Maybe even one of those rotating cannons on the jeep. Shit, it could be a tank for all I know, but point being—"

"Yeah, got it," Eliza said.

"It's probably dead, but we'll try it anyway."

"I don't know if that's a good idea."

"You're right, let's not worry about getting help. He'll probably run for the hills when we pull this stick on him anyway, the great equalizer."

"Oh, my *God*." Eliza held up her hands to the heavens. "Traps, remember?"

Lee shrugged without turning back. "That just seems too obvious, doesn't it?"

With his back to her, Eliza ran a full gauntlet of exasperated expressions. Her face had never felt so rubbery.

Lee was the sole survivor of his group. Really? He was either unbelievably lucky, or they were unbelievably stupid.

"If he knows someone will look, he's going to rig something, Lee. He'd be insane not to. I mean, insane in another way."

Lee shrugged again. "We'll be careful."

"We?" she echoed. "Do you speak French?"

Lee scowled back at her. "Let's stay on topic here, okay? You can hear my whole bio when we get past the wall."

A stretch of road ran horizontally through the grass in a straight line. The highway continued through a break in the trees to their left. The right showed only desolate road and bordering woods, a mirror of the one in front of the Morgan Falls Lodge. An abandoned gas station created a corner, and the Chicken Exit stood slightly apart from the tarmac. Tall weeds sprang up through the many cracks in the gas station lot. A lone number nine dangled from the sign overhead. Gas was well under a dollar a gallon when they evacuated the town.

They crossed the road. A mini-field of heads stood before the Chicken Exit, a *Who's Who?* of people who didn't want to walk another foot when they could call in the jeep with the huge turret gun. A few were little more than skulls by this point, albeit with clumps of long stringy hair. Most of the others showed signs of a long vigil with ragged skin worn from decay. Several mouths hung open in frozen screams.

The decomposition detonated in their nostrils almost instantly, finding Lee first.

"Oh, bro, that is *rank*."

At least she and Annette received fair warning.

One step the air was fresh, the next a sickening bouquet of rot. Eliza would have thrown up from this forty-five minutes ago had she not effectively purged herself over Nathan and Lawrence. Annette showed no reaction other than a more thoughtful look with her fingers to her lips.

Eliza jumped when a black bird cawed and streaked past them to light on one of the newer additions to the not-so-decorative garden. The crow buried its beak into the meat of the remaining eye in the head, tugged back and forth until it wrenched it from the socket, and flew away with the morsel as though worried it would draw a crowd. No scavengers went hungry here.

"I know that one," Lee said.

For a moment, Eliza thought he meant the bird.

"His name was . . . shit."

A man called Shit?

"I don't remember his name. He didn't last very long, though. It was like, 'Hola, mi nombre es . . . ' whatever, and then *thunk!* I knew where we were with a quickness, 'cause like I said, quim, cars, and Agent Orange. But it didn't matter. Forewarned was four dead in the blink of an eye, half of us gone with the motel still in sight."

"But you didn't come from this way," Eliza said. "And he's here."

"What the hell are you trying to say?"

"I just mean he must have brought the . . . the head all the way over here. Maybe that's where he came from when he got on our trail." She kept a neutral expression, but his defensiveness stunned her.

What was that all about?

"Well, let's hope he takes his time hanging up the decorations from your friends," Lee said. It tightened her jaw even though she hoped something similar a moment ago.

Lee crouched and used his stick to prod a stone out of the earth. Nothing happened. He picked it up. It was a misshapen triangle, bigger than his palm.

"We can toss this to set anything off, but if he went through all this trouble—" He gestured to the heads. "—I don't think he rigged it. Just seems like he's trying to scare us away."

There were four vertical rows to either side of a narrow path through the middle, enough of a divide to walk through. That seemed a little too convenient to Eliza.

"He put something in there, Lee."

"So I'll walk around."

"He might expect that."

"Well, Jesus, do you think he flew out with a jetpack? He had to leave room for himself! You're being paranoid."

And you're not being paranoid enough.

Lee faced the collection, stick in one hand, stone in the other. The stakes seemed to form a maze.

Annette returned from the void and resumed her rubbernecking. She noted Lee's staring contest with the head. "Make your play, bitchlick," she said.

Lee whirled around. "Hey, you want to try this?"

Eliza grabbed Annette's hand so she didn't take him up on it.

"That's what I thought." Lee turned back to the Chicken Exit and regarded his stick. He reached and tentatively poked a head in the front row, ready to jump back. It was a rare trophy without the frozen scream, but the push unhinged its jaw. A tiny ball of writhing maggots rolled off its partially eaten tongue to spill in a clump on the grass.

"Oh God." Eliza turned away, wondering if she would throw up after all. She breathed in through her mouth as her eyes teared. When she thought she had control again, she turned back around. The reek of putrefaction seemed worse now. She pulled her shirt up over her nose.

Annette had drawn even with Lee.

"I've got a plan," Lee announced.

"Let's just go to the checkpoint," she said through the fabric.

"I've seen three of these things and this is the only one blocked off. He brought one of our people's heads here to scare us off because it works!"

"If he didn't want anyone to use it, he'd just blow it up."

"He might not have explosives falling out his asshole, either. Just watch and learn." Lee reared back and kicked the nearest head. It stood in a row to the left side. The pole snapped and the projectile of the head struck the one behind it. It tilted over, uprooting from the soil as it hit the ground between the rows.

If Eliza's mouth were visible, they would have seen it open in shock. "What are . . . you can't do that!"

Lee looked back at her, the picture of cool. "Why not? Not like they'll hear me anyway. He took their ears."

"You're still *kicking* them."

"Have it your way."

He inched forward and this time pushed a stake in the front row with his free hand. It careened backward, took out two more behind it. He dropped his stick and rubbed his palms together vigorously, shuddering. "Mad nasty. There's some kind of ooze on it."

He sniffed at his hand and yanked it away instantly. "Damn, that's so rank. Don't touch any of them."

Eliza rolled her eyes. "Don't worry."

"No, I'm not," Annette said.

Lee crossed back to her, still rubbing his fingers. "Well, look who decided to join us."

"I'm *not* going to die," she said.

"Well, yeah, duh. That's what I've been saying all along if we just get—"

"You don't know shit."

Lee went from puzzled humor to looking like he wanted to tear her arms from the sockets.

"She's not talking to you," Eliza informed him. She pointed to the heads.

"We're still here," Annette told them.

Lee smirked. "I'm so glad we brought her with us. She's been a huge help."

He reclaimed the stick and stepped back into the phalanx, tapping it out in front of him like a cane. He drew close to another stake and kicked it in the center, but it snapped, dropped to the ground and did not knock over any others. He sighed, shrugged, and pushed the next candidate and the next. They fell like corn stalks. Now he had a full path to the phone through the throng.

"There might be one of those toe poppers," Eliza warned. "If it doesn't work, you'll be dragging your foot for over a mile. And if they won't open the gate—"

"*Okay,*" Lee said to shut her up. He hopped between the obstacles to get to his stone, grabbed it, and hurried back to his furthest point of entry. "Just keep watching for him."

Eliza did, though it was hard not to watch Lee in the home stretch. There were so many places in the woods for Orange to emerge. He might have kept pace with them in the trees through their whole exodus.

"He's not here," Annette assured her. "He's building his death temple. Blood will be the mortar. They say we'll be part of it, but I won't. You might and he might." She shrugged with what might have been apology. "I'll live."

"Thanks. Maybe tell Lee to radio ahead for some Valium."

Annette scowled. Perhaps she really had returned to the land of the here and now.

"Sorry," Eliza said and patted Annette on the back. "Just scared to death." She peeked over at Lee, who tapped the ground for the remaining five feet to the concrete. "Just humor me and watch with me anyway, okay?"

Annette gave that same shrug from a second ago. Not apology; apathy. "Oh, sure, they're just dead. What could they know?"

According to you, they don't know shit.

They heard a *thump* as Lee harmlessly bounced the stone on the ground in front of him. He took a long step to where it struck the ground and then another one to get to the stone platform of the Chicken Exit.

"Watch out for the phone itself," Eliza said.

"Sure. And hey, keep thinking of stuff. We don't want to get the hell away from here too fast. There's no sport in that." Nonetheless, he edged his way to the corner of the concrete base and crouched. He angled his stick between the phone and the handset and knocked the phone aside. It pleased Eliza that he turned his head when he did it (an instant before she did the same thing herself) to protect it from a potential blast of shrapnel.

The phone dropped to the end of its metallic coil, twisting and swinging. No trap. She'd expected something which would force them to move on without Lee. Maybe they could get help here after all.

"Hurry!" she said. "Try it!"

"Watch and weep." He seized the phone and brought it to his face. "We're about to blow this popsi—"

He screamed, a shrill sound Eliza might have expected from a female. Blood burst down his chin.

Poisoning? Eliza wondered. *Burning?*

He dropped the phone instantly, though she didn't understand how it toppled over but remained attached to his face. Then she saw his lower lip yanked halfway down his chin. Something stuck in the mouthpiece perforated his lip and anchored it. Wild eyed, Lee pinched with one hand

and pulled the phone with the other. He sank to his knees as red rivulets seeped through his fingers.

His anguished cry found form in a single word: "Shit!" Then two more: "Ah, fuck!"

"He'll hear you," Annette said mildly.

He took his palms away, caught the steady drip with one of them. "So what, twat?" He pulled his hands away from his clenched face and broke into a coughing fit. "*Rank*," he managed to choke out.

A moment passed.

"Well," Annette said, "did it work or not?"

"Did it work?" Lee said it in as childish a way possible to mock her. "I just had some needle from 1987 in my mouth! I've probably got hep C or fucking AIDS now!"

"You need to try it," Eliza said. "Be sure."

"Unbelievable." He took the phone again in a pincer grasp, inspected it closely, pushed the earpiece to his head and tapped the disconnect button several times after carefully examining that, too. He slung it back at the handset as hard as he could. "Fuck no it doesn't!"

He had the presence of mind to retrieve his stick before he jumped down from the Chicken Exit and stalked through the fallen columns.

"Be care—"

"I don't give a shit!"

She and Annette backed away from the heads. They both cringed as he goose-stepped on the stakes and whatever else came underfoot. There was a jagged tear in the flesh under his mouth, and blood continued to trickle.

"You should do something about—"

He grabbed Eliza's arm and pulled her with him.

"Hey!"

"We need to haul ass," he said. "We wasted too much time."

Eliza stumbled beside him. The shirt came down from over her nose. She yanked her arm away. His hand carried a death stench like bad cologne. "Come on, Annette, hurry."

Annette speed-walked to catch up to them and took hold of Eliza's hand.

"At least we'll be away from that awful smell," Eliza said. She glared at Lee. "Most of it, anyway."

They advanced more recklessly now. What Orange did to the Chicken Exit amounted to little more than a joy buzzer shock, if substantially more painful. Maybe he exhausted his trap supply on the staked victims. He could only linger near the checkpoint so long before the military opened fire. Maybe he wouldn't try to stop them this close.

She didn't feel safer, though. The shadows lengthened in the dying light, and the woods pushed in on them. The pounding in her head probably enforced that. She'd never been thirstier in her life. There were more noises in the trees now; maybe birds settling back, but maybe not.

It slowed her down, but she looked back periodically. Lee was right—they *(he)* squandered a lot of time for Orange to make up some ground.

It's all in your mind, she thought. She almost wanted to laugh. Just like Valerie.

He knew where they were. They could have scattered in ten different directions and he'd still know, like Jack looming over the hedge maze model in *The Shining*. This didn't ring false in her thoughts. Her feet carried her faster, now ahead of Lee, pulling Annette like a kite behind her. She wanted to drop Annette's hand and run, not stop until she hit the checkpoint. She'd pound her fists at the wall and shout for help until they let her through.

She forced herself to walk at a pace on the verge of jogging, and that's when the ground dropped out from underneath her.

XII.

IF THE KNOW-IT-ALL didn't have a death-grip on the crazy chick, it would have been curtains. Lee's first responsibility was to himself, naturally, so he didn't dare move in that direction at the first sign of trouble. In fact, he hit the deck in case the trap launched some sort of projectile. A retard from his group met the wrong end of one of those things. Lee couldn't remember the name of that sorry bastard either, but the trap swung some massive briar-looking deal into his knee caps hard enough to shatter them and wrecked the shit out of his legs. The idiot screamed blue murder in a world where silence was golden. A debate began about the best way to carry him, although Lee heard precious little of it because he opted for the best way, period, which was for him and Earnes to put a little buffer zone between themselves and the core group and leave those dipshits to face the slayer.

Good luck with your twig gurney or whatever, assholes . . . I'll find my own exit.

They could only blast him as a selfish coward if they actually made it back to the real world, and their altruistic suicide strategy didn't make that much of a threat.

The rigors of self-preservation now satisfied, he allowed himself to assess the predicament of his companions. He couldn't remember their names, but the one who gave him a shitty look for calling them "girls" (which he pretended to ignore, just to get her goat) was

178

halfway down a hole. The nutcase clearly broadcasting from radio station K-UNT held her around the hand and wrist.

Well, the know-it-all was right about the traps after all. The phone thing still pissed him off, but less so now that he hadn't tripped the more dangerous one. The honor of that booby trap went to the one with the boobies. Funny stuff. He was pretty sure that counted as irony.

"Lee, help us!"

He dusted the loose grass from his pants and adjusted his headband. He figured the crazy one had super strength and wouldn't drop her pal into the death pit. The friend was much hotter, but really, the groupie scene back home made them both look like crones. Even just playing local shows with a predominance of cover songs in the set list, those chicks in the audience were down to fuck. He'd been so astonished at the beginning of the sexual odyssey he actually asked a girl, "You realize we didn't write 'More Than a Feeling,' don't you?" She didn't answer. Couldn't get his throbbing gristle in her maw fast enough.

Lee scoped the surroundings real fast to make sure Major Maniac didn't run up their asses with a chainsaw. Still safe, but he'd feel better when the Chicken Exit wasn't a stone's throw away.

"Hang on, girl," he said.

"It's Eliza!" she snapped.

"My bad." Meaning, *So what?* He could know her name, birth date, and last four digits of her social, and he'd still boot her into hell's hole without a second thought if he needed to.

He put an arm around the schizo's waist, took Eliza's wrist with his other hand, and pulled backward. Eliza came up and out and they all fell in a pile, the nutcase's ass right on Lee's package. She took her time rolling off. He didn't mind. It took the sting from the pain in his mouth. Would that leave a scar?

Lee crawled to the edge of the hole when at last freed. Orange covered a trapdoor with tall grass indistinguishable from the rest of the field. Any weight sent someone eight feet below to a column of spikes. Eliza came a snatch hair away from a new career as a pincushion. Some of the points were sharpened stakes of wood, but he'd tied knives to a few.

That beats a stick any day of the week.

"I need your help, gir . . . ladies," he amended. "I can reach a knife if you two hold my legs."

They both grabbed a leg and he walked on his hands over the edge and down the length of the trapdoor. Lieutenant Lunatic dug out the hole to keep the door at an angle, assuring someone would bounce into the impaling grid—six rows of five stakes, approximately five feet high. He could drop between the rows, but had no room for a running start to jump back up. Maybe the women could haul him out, but he saw himself plunge back into the hole if someone lost their grip, stakes and blades punching through his major organs, dick included. J'nope.

"A little more," he said. Pressure grew against the walls of his skull. Droplets of blood coursed off his lip to patter his nose. One of them scored a direct hit down one of his nostrils. He pushed away his dread at the thought of an infected needle. Maybe not AIDS, but some kind of unpronounceable bacteria that would rot his face off, make him look Harvey Dent.

And the cocksucking phone didn't even work!

Not his finest moment.

He reached the nearest knife. It looked like Corporal Carnage tied it to the stake with boot laces. The bulging network of knotting resisted him at such a gnarly angle, but the black laces finally began to pull free from their hive. He didn't have to pull it completely apart. The grip of the knife became mobile, and then he worked it down a little and twisted so the serrated blade sliced through the ties.

REINCARNAGE: MAXIMUM CARNAGE

He sawed it free in seconds. John Rambo used a knife like this to slice up about eighty Vietcong in those movies. Versus Soldier Grue it may as well be a flyswatter, but it was something, and it could help Lee in other ways besides an unlikely showdown scenario.

"Got it," he called over his shoulder. "Pull me up."

He slid up the wall of the pit as they backed up with a foot and leg in each hand. With the ease of his rescue, he felt kind of chickenshit not going for more knives. Not enough to get back in the pit, though. Long as he got past the wall, the world would call him a hero. Jack in the Box would be signed faster than you could say "noble survivor." He thought the women were there before? It'd be like that carnival game where you aimed a water pistol at a clown head to fill up and burst a balloon, except the clown heads would be snatches and the water pistol would be his meat baton.

Eliza and Sybil collapsed simultaneously once they had him safely on the ground. Funny that it took him this long to make the Sybil connection. He only knew the reference from JITB's bass player, Murph, an older guy into King Crimson and ELP. He wrote a twelve minute song about her and all her personalities. It went over live about as well as the JFK assassination and they dropped it from the set list. They replaced it with more covers, including "Orange Mustangs."

"Good job," he said. He displayed the knife. "Came away with this. Couldn't get to the others without tearing open my sac. We should get moving."

Because of that MIFPA shit survivors of this place couldn't profit from the experience through books or movies but that didn't mean songs couldn't be written. Lee could feed Murph enough details about this adventure and faster than you could say "Neil Peart" they'd have their own "Red Sector A."

"We need water," Eliza said. She offered a hand to help Sybil to her feet.

"I know." Lee slid the knife into the belt of his red slacks, slightly dizzy as the blood drained from his head. "I haven't had a drop since I got here."

Total lie, of course. He practically drained half a creek when he ditched the dopes from Morgan Manor.

He wiped the blood on his nose with the headband and slid it back on. He'd lose the band the second they were safe. Lee wasn't too proud to keep the sweat from stinging his eyes for now, but he probably looked like Reed Rothchild in *Boogie Nights*. That absolutely could not happen when CNN, TMZ, and the rest showed up with the cameras. Hopefully the military guys had a change of clothes because he looked like a total geek in this get-up.

"With any luck," he said, "we've found the last of his tricks on the way to home base." *And if we haven't, let's hope you bitches wind up in those, too.*

"God," Eliza said shakily. "I came that close to dying."

"But you had me," Sybil said, "and I'm not going to die here. Stay close to me and you'll be safe. Screw those heads."

Lee rolled his eyes. She had a lot of confidence for someone who looked like she just pulled a train. It made him want to kill her himself, just to say, *Yeah, what up now?*

"Oh, snap," he said. "I think I see the wall." It was a faint impression, so far on the horizon it could fall off the edge of the earth, but it was there. He'd never seriously said *oh snap* before today, but it was such a disarming thing to say and felt like the right play back when the Asian twat was on her high horse. *Oh snap* made somebody sound like a mark.

"That's half the battle right there," he said, turning back to grin at them. The smile died on his face at the sight of a rushing blur on the opposite horizon.

"Shit!" That was all the warning he cared to give Sybil and Eliza. They'd get the picture. He threw the stick aside

and ran. The world bounced left and right, lingering vertigo from the pit, but he didn't let it slow him. The wall was all that mattered. Colonel Kill could only watch him escape. The army guys would light that mug up like the Tet Offensive if he got close. That was how it worked, that was the lore, legend was fact, had to be.

He ran like his ass was on fire, zero concern for traps. Dude wouldn't be gunning hell bent for leather if he thought he had something else to hold them up. The wall drew no closer as Lee pumped his hands and feet, though. He held the knife like a baton he would never pass to anybody else. The only relay to this race was the message: *Lee Gifford is getting the hell out of here, bitches. How you like me now?*

He could blame the vertigo on why it took him a moment to make sense of the figure in the corner of his eye.

The hell?

Eliza, her afterburners on full blast. He was impressed she had it in her, but also that she didn't let Sybil slow her down. Eliza would have wrenched her arm off if they were still holding hands. She left her in the dust instead.

"Come on, Annette!" she shouted, never looking back.

So Sybil was Annette. Good to know. It would make a more compelling story if he could provide the media a name, re: the tragic last leg of the escape. *If we just got there a few minutes sooner, Annette and Eliza might have . . .*

Eliza's ponytail bounced side to side across her shoulders. She was pulling away. Now he had to chance a backward glance to verify distance and pecking order, afraid Annette might overtake him too.

No, he still had at least fifteen yards on her. She clutched her side, teeth clenched in pain.

Guess the talking heads knew their shit after all.

General Genocide had a visible form now, blazing through the field, about to blow past the gas station. He took a step toward the Chicken Exit as though noting its desecration, then resumed his bullet trajectory. He held something with both hands that shifted back and forth even faster when he saw the fallen heads, like the crank of a handcar. Lee's eyes bugged.

Holy shit, that's a freaking axe, *son!*

Annette grunted as she stumbled over something in the high grass and plunged headlong. Lee didn't bother to hide a little smile as he turned his attention forward again. It slipped when he saw Eliza farther away from him now. Not good. Annette might have bought them enough time to reach the wall, but a second appetizer would seal the deal on a checkpoint arrival for the lead runner. Lee had to be the one in front.

He pushed himself hard until he closed the distance to Eliza, and launched himself at her feet. A huge risk, but fortunately he got a hand on her shoe and held it long enough to trip her. He scraped his elbow on the ground.

Move, move, move!

He didn't bother trying to pull up the leg of her pants, just grabbed her heel, set the blade on her calf and ripped it across as hard as he could.

Eliza screamed at ear-ringing velocity.

Lee winced at the cacophony. It was a guestimate whether he'd managed to slice her Achilles, but she sure as hell couldn't beat him to the wall now.

She clutched her leg and writhed as if she could seal the pain back inside. She saw him with the blade, knew he'd done it. Even within her agony, there was a tinge of bafflement.

"He has an axe," Lee said as he lurched to his feet. "You know how it is."

She shouted something incomprehensible. "Bastard" might have featured. He'd heard worse.

We now rejoin our regularly scheduled programming of Yeah, How You Like Me Now?

He meant to bolt right then—and slip around Eliza wide enough so she couldn't do something petty like reach out and trip him—but he heard something that made him turn back.

"Oh—" His mind blanked before he decided what he meant to say (but probably *shit*). The axe split the air as it whirled across the field like a helicopter blade. He saw its shadow before he spotted the curves of its splitting ends, headed right at his face. The maniac launched it all the way from where Annette sprawled, not even taking the time to treat her to a taste.

Lee didn't try to dive away, just dropped straight down like someone pulled a chair out from under him. Fire exploded across his scalp.

I didn't make it down in time, he realized. *But you still didn't take my head off, so suck on that, jarhead.*

Blood pooled down his head. Good thing he kept the sweatband or he'd be blind now. He tried to hold off the rising panic. Head wounds bled profusely and it didn't mean anything, but damn, this felt like a lot. He touched his fingers to his hair. They came back instantly wet, and more alarmingly, blood sluiced across the nails and knuckles in the second he dared to hold them there.

There was pressure on the back of his head too. He was scared to make sense of it, but it was hard to come up with theories while Eliza caterwauled a few feet away.

Damn, girl, I'm the one who got hit with an axe.

The realization struck. *Oh snap . . . mine now.*

Orange wouldn't let him get to the wall, and thanks to Lee's impromptu surgery with Eliza, he didn't have to. He had Annette right where he wanted her and Eliza wasn't going anywhere but into a state of shock.

Orange approached with an unhurried gait. Lee had to grab the axe and cripple him or they were all dead, himself most tragically.

He whirled around to find the best line of defense, and

frowned deeply at that sensation of pressure on the back of his head again. Maybe it was the John C. Reilly headband. He hooked in a finger to yank it off. The band caught on something and as he pulled it up, the something came with it.

He reached back and felt a large patch of his hair about six inches away from where it was supposed to be. He poked it. It slipped back onto his head unevenly. Frantic, he pawed it, aware of steady streams of blood seeping from places where his scalp no longer adhered to his skull. It was like someone crushed an egg and let the yolk ooze through his hair. His fingertips found something soft, too mushy to be skin.

That's my fucking brain!

"Christ Jesus!" He pushed the scalp back in place as best as he could without being able to see where the large flap of skin should go, and angled the headband to try to hold it in place.

He crawled to the axe, not trusting himself to walk. Hack one of those legs off and he could get away if he didn't pass out. Wet trickles raced down his ears in a steady rush. Ideally he'd waste the fucker outright, but as he wrapped his fingers around the handle, he told himself he only needed to injure one leg. Too bad so sad for Eliza, who might still be in a jam (and could vouch for the efficacy of one wounded limb), but what would he do to Lee? Crawl him down?

One swing, one leg, one escape.

Brigadier Bloodbath walked calmly and carried a big knife. Lee's axe was bigger, but quick mental calculus led to the conclusion an axe in his possession was far less deadly than a knife in the hands of Agent Orange. Could he incapacitate him before Commander Kill landed a fatal strike? Lee didn't like his odds.

Panicked, he turned around too quickly and blood sloshed from his scalp. A wave of nausea threatened his new plan, but he sucked it up and ran. He carried the axe in his right hand, the left atop his head to keep the scalp from flapping. It was like trying to keep a hat from blowing away. He misjudged the pressure and heard a bubbling squirt before a warm glob jumped the headband and raced down his forehead. He smeared it with the back of his hand before it dripped into his eye. His mouth throbbed like the bass at a rave but the top of his head was just a dull ache. That had to signify the wound wasn't so bad, right?

With Annette and Eliza in meltdown, Lee's mobility made him the snowball with the best chance in hell. If he made it to the wall it wouldn't guarantee immediate safety—the National Guard wasn't posted at every square inch. He might have to face his pursuer before he got within screaming distance of a checkpoint.

Daylight had ebbed unnoticed, as though Orange brought the darkness with him. Lee checked to make sure Field Marshal Mayhem busied himself with the defiant Eliza. He hoped the snooty little bitch put up a hell of a struggle and hampered the decapitation process like a champ.

What the fuck?

Lee jerked rigid when he saw Orange throw the knife, but not at him—he'd tossed it up where it rotated blade over hilt to fall into the palm of his waiting hand. He kept doing it as he approached, nary a glance at Eliza.

"You sexist prick!" Lee yelled.

Commodore Cliché was saving the girls for last.

He pushed on faster. The axe grew heavier and heavier, his arms rubbery. Oddly enough, he didn't have a splitting headache, but his body was slow and lethargic like the day's manic running had finally taken its toll. Had he really increased his speed? He seemed to be in slow motion while the world around him moved 2X. Not a good sign. His head felt lighter than air. Worse sign.

Gotta make a last stand, brah. Now.

Lee turned and hefted the axe with both hands. Sweat and blood glued the shirt uncomfortably to his back and seemed to restrict his movements. Still tossing the knife into the air, Private Pursuit closed the distance with the same nonchalant pace, ten yards away if Lee judged the distance correctly.

You can do this. Be a hero. Take this bastard out.

Lee reared back with the axe.

Wait for it, wait for it.

Within two yards, Orange caught the knife and readied it to strike. Lee swung the axe with a primal scream. Orange kicked faster and the bottom of the boot snagged the axe handle below the blade. The sudden stop nearly popped Lee's shoulders from their sockets. He didn't let go of the axe but involuntarily let go of an "Ugh!"

Orange slashed with the knife. The blade hit his face and his scream rose several octaves as his lower jaw dropped wide enough to fit a cantaloupe. Lee abruptly stopped screaming but couldn't close his mouth. His tongue tasted night air before hot liquid sprayed over the exposed muscle. The downward pressure of his jaw tugged his tongue and triggered his gag reflex.

Lee tried to swing the axe again, but his left shoulder struck his dangling chin, knocked it sideways, unleashed a pain so debilitating his legs went weak. He shuffled to his right and tripped over lumpy ground. He got a mouthful of weeds as he fell.

He had to face downward to breathe or blood would fill the back of his throat. Black droplets spattered across his hands as he pushed himself upright again. Vaguely aware this was his blood and he had little to spare before unconsciousness, Lee staggered forward several steps and looked over his shoulder, fully expecting to see the delivery of a death blow.

Orange held the axe above his head but was too far away to swing and hit Lee, who backpedaled for distance in case blood loss created an illusion of relative safety—*maniacs are closer than they appear.*

Lee underestimated how badly Orange wanted to nail him with an axe throw. He had no time to dodge. The blade slammed into his left shoulder, shattering the collar bone and knocking him off balance. The flap atop his head swung backward before he even hit the ground and folded under the base of his skull like a little pillow of skin. His unhinged jaw dropped against his neck and blood filled his mouth.

It felt like the axe blade pinned him to the earth. He tried to breathe but it wasn't air he desperately sucked into his lungs.

Lee heard the tinkling of a distant bell, a curious herald of the oncoming darkness.

XIII.

ELIZA STARED AT the outside world from the relative comfort of the stiff reclining chair. She had doubled back to the gas station in a hopping/crawling lurch, thanks to that bastard Lee. The pain in her leg had receded but any movement ignited it again. Not that it mattered. Orange knew exactly where she was. A bell above the door jingled at her entry, like he needed any manmade help to find her. She left a handy trail of blood, too.

Thanks, Lee, you prick.

Hell of a lot of good his chickenshit measure did him, too. He still died first, or she assumed so anyway. He wasn't the fastest runner and also had looked a little wobbly on his feet as she escaped.

Sitting here with the blood-covered shards of glass on the desk in front of her, she had a lot of questions for herself. Could she have done things differently? It didn't take long to rule out herself as a factor in Lee's attack. He'd have slashed her leg no matter what for self-preservation. He only caught her because she'd had nothing to eat or drink today.

Served me right for abandoning Annette.

No, no, no. No guilt. She stayed with Annette far longer than anyone else would have. She owed her nothing and sticking around wouldn't have helped anyway. The stress and drug withdrawal finally did its worst. Eliza assumed it was a seizure. She passed Annette amongst the weeds, foam and blood dribbling from her mouth, and if she wasn't dead, Eliza was in no shape to drag her to safety.

Why am I even here? Who did this to us? Why?

Questions she'd never have answered. Patrick thought it was the government. Maybe it was. If so, everyone simply lived an illusion outside the walls of this place anyway. If the government threw people in here as cannon fodder for some psycho, what kind of country had America become? She didn't want to live in that kind of place, although she knew she'd lived in "that kind of place" for a while now. In the name of increased security and safety, individuals gave up their privacy and a certain degree of liberty because a bunch of terrorists got lucky. Once a government started making decisions based on the "greater good" to maintain the public's safety, wasn't it bound to lead to an extreme like this? Maybe a few people had to be sacrificed for "the greater good" to keep Agent Orange contained. She would have never given any of this a second thought, kind of like you rarely give the starving kids in Africa or India or Haiti much thought when you're living your busy life—your busy, *safe* life—because the government supposedly kept the terrorists or Agent Orange at bay.

Most of the plate glass had been shattered like the lobby windows at the lodge. She noted a large chunk set at the bottom of the door, thinking she could have simply stepped through instead of bothering to open it, when someone wandered into view. Eliza squinted, not sure if she really saw them.

Valerie? Haunted though she had been by her sister for years, her presence still comforted her. Looking to lead her away forever.

Then the person swam into focus.

Annette.

Eliza managed only a hoarse whisper. "Run!"

Annette wandered around the lot just the other side of

the old-style pumps in a stupor, like she was looking for a gas station attendant or her missing car.

Eliza lost focus and her head tilted. She opened her eyes and saw words in another language. With concentration she understood the letters were backwards. Enough remained to make out *Al's Service Station* and hours of operation. There were dark spray patterns on the glass and inside wall. Someone died in here but the body was gone. The smell of blood was strong. Her blood.

Drip, drip, drip.

Pat, pat, pat.

Outside Annette slowly approached.

Why don't you run, dammit?

Too tired to voice a warning, Eliza watched her eyes close, a bystander within her own body.

A scream shocked them back open.

Annette's arms and legs flailed as she floated through the air toward the open window. How peculiar that Annette could fly.

Only she couldn't.

She dipped down and Agent Orange materialized behind her, his fingers laced through Annette's hair. He palmed her skull like a basketball and forced her throat against the remains of plate glass. Eliza saw the resistance and then the sudden downward thrust as the skin and tissue of the throat split with a crunch.

Eliza jerked her head toward a large round sign that blocked the entryway into the service bays. It said "Gulf."

Worse than the gurgling, Eliza heard sawing sounds as Orange raked Annette's throat back and forth across the glass. It squeaked like he was cleaning the windows. Back and forth, squeak-squeak-squeak. The glass snapped out of the frame. He pinned Annette's body against it and twisted her head. Once, twice, the neck snapped away from the torso with a moist crunch, but only let go after a final vigorous heave that snapped the relenting muscles. He tossed aside the body, a sickening thump that echoed under the gas station canopy.

Eliza watched him watching her through the shattered window.

Too late, asshole. I beat you to it. Thanks for Lee, though.

She wanted to raise a middle finger to him, but her arms were dead weights on either side of the chair, numb at the incisions she made along both wrists and forearms. All of her now numb, fading. She closed her eyes, faintly hearing the bell as he entered, and tumbled toward a lasting sleep.

XIV.

ADAM **FOUND THAT** the broken shop windows provided a backlight of sorts if he held items between himself and the scant light. It was the best opportunity to see—"seeing" in this case being the identification of objects by shape.

For whatever reason the shop owners left some stock behind, but the years took their toll on product placement; it was like someone ran through the aisles knocking boxes to the floor. The person may have been lucky enough to get past the tripwire at the entrance but his luck ran out if reduced to launching wing-tips at Agent Orange. Patrick identified the tripwire and told Adam and Gin to stay in the aisles and out of the stockroom. As if. Neither of them wanted to brave spider webs and the assorted things they heard scurrying in the shadows back there.

We need as many shoe strings as you can get. And new shoes, get yourselves some new shoes—preferably hiking boots—and socks if you can find them.

Gin found a bag of socks as soon as they entered. Ever since then they had been trying to find the shoes. Patrick needed a size ten and a half—"Wide, I have a fat foot"— to which Gin had replied, "Any particular brand?" He ignored the sarcasm.

"Yay," Gin said from the next aisle over. "Found my size. Just in time for my funeral."

REINCARNAGE: MAXIMUM CARNAGE

It was almost instinctual to say something positive, something like "You're not going to die" in the same way he might have responded "Those shoes look great on you" if she doubted her fashion sense. Yeah, "You're not going to die" would sound trite and stupid, the kind of thing he might have said to his mother when they were making their napalm salvation.

"What did he mean by the clothes not being right?" Adam asked as he unstrung the laces from another bad fit. Talking might alert Orange, but not talking let his attention wander back to his parents.

"Who knows?"

Adam heard the frictional whirr of a shoelace sliding through the last two eyelets. Gin had out-laced him three shoes to one by now *and* she'd already found a pair of shoes that fit her. If these were the type of skills that would ensure their survival she was on the fast track.

"We had a lead on Agent Orange and we're blowing it because MacGruber has no clue. All the laces in this place won't help him string together a plan."

Adam snickered. "You think he's stringing us along?"

"Doubt it's because he's into string theory."

"Or he wants to hamstring Orange."

"I'm a frayed knot."

The trip to Morgan had been quiet on the Agent Orange front even as Patrick grew increasingly erratic. He'd snapped at Adam when he made jokes—quiet jokes— but Patrick took to mumbling and didn't seem at all concerned when *he* broke the silence. Maybe Annette hadn't been in drug withdrawal but instead had some sort of weird virus and Patrick caught it. Maybe Patrick self-medicated, too. Took one to know one.

When they'd arrived at the outskirts of Morgan and passed the first set of staked heads Patrick sniffed all of them, shook his head, ran ahead to the next set of staked heads and smelled all of them, too. Afterwards he'd let out a resounding "Fuck!" to which Gin whispered, "Hey Orange, here we are in Morgan. RSVP."

The woods couldn't encroach with all of downtown Morgan's pavement as badly as it did on the houses at the outskirts of town. One and two story brick buildings with no space between lined both sides of the street for two blocks. Beyond that it looked like man-made structures gave way to forest again because Adam could see tree leaves catching moonlight. He guessed the Morgan Manor was on the other side of the town because they hadn't passed anything resembling a motel. It would have been hard to see regardless. Patrick had to point out several houses Adam and Gin had missed because the woods swallowed them.

It wasn't easy to see structures with only moonlight— harder still to find shoes without it. *Watch me end up with women's kicks.*

Agent Orange left three headless bodies in the streets, all within close proximity of the intersection that bisected the town. Not the best omen if they had made a final stand together. Patrick checked the bodies from several different angles, avoiding the blood spatter at first but eventually not caring as he made a good show of imitating a beleaguered coroner who didn't know where to start. His ultimate conclusion: *The clothes don't make sense.*

Adam couldn't see their clothes well enough to figure out what Patrick meant, but instead of sighing like Gin he at least made an effort to make sense of it. Gin had become more and more hostile to Patrick. If she'd once seen him as some sort of holy man who could lead them out of this wilderness, she'd lost her faith by the time they'd set things on fire at the lodge.

He's less than half an hour away, Patrick said before giving them instructions to find shoes and shoestrings. That was at least twenty minutes ago.

"Best use of a half hour *ever*," he said quietly, a little desperate that he wasn't holding up his end of the mission.

REINCARNAGE: MAXIMUM CARNAGE

He found a left shoe that fit but its mate got separated in the random pairs and boxes strewn everywhere. His size was nine so he'd found some for Patrick based on how loosely the shoes fit. It might not be the right size but the more time they spent in the shoe store the more Adam sensed impending doom just around the corner.

"I'm ready when you are," Gin said. "Probably have a dozen spider bites. Freaking webs all over the place."

He became careless about checking his own shoes for spiders five minutes ago.

He found a right shoe that fit and it wasn't until they reached the doorway that he realized he had two different styles and one had slightly more room than the other. According to Kevin you could get your ass kicked at school for such an oversight (no bullshit). It didn't matter here, though. They could come back in daytime.

If we live that long.

"If he doesn't have a good reason for this we're out of here," Gin whispered.

She took such a comically wide step over the tripwire he wondered if she was being sarcastic. That or she feared it was like a live wire that might arc and fry her.

"Be careful," she warned.

Like Adam she collected her shoestrings in a box, but hers was bigger and overflowed, the laces like multi-colored worms.

"You're coming with me if I ditch him, right?"

"Yeah," Adam said automatically, both thrilled and horrified. "We don't have to give up the laces, though, do we? They could be our best defense if Orange catches us."

Gin smiled at him. "We can throw the boxes at him."

"He'll go down in a tangle of shoestrings."

"The more he struggles the tighter they'll get."

"We'll string him up."

"He'll be fit to be tied."

It was funny how much comfort it gave him to share

these awful jokes with her. A lot funnier than the jokes themselves, though probably little wasn't.

If Patrick went anywhere during their shoestrings mission, he had since returned to the middle of the intersection, kicked off his shoes, removed a sock, and now held it in the air. A dark pile of clothing lay on the street near him.

"He's the alternate universe version of Mister Miyagi where 'wax on, wax off' was just a way to get his car detailed."

Adam chuckled like he knew what she was talking about.

"There's no method to his madness. Where should we go?" Gin asked. She pointed to the hardware store. "Bet Orange has that place rigged, probably more traps than the doorway, but you know . . . hardware store. Potential weapons."

"After all these years?" Adam asked.

The building had no windows and you could only tell what it used to be from the partial words ARDWAR STO still visible on the sign above the crooked awning. The place next to it might have been a post office; there was a blue collection box at the curb.

"Aren't all the useful things gone by now?" Adam asked.

"Psshht, they totally missed these deadly laces, didn't they?"

"This is true."

"We could find a yardstick or a leveler or even a bucket. You're such a downer, Kirshoff."

All trace of Gin's mirth vanished when she looked at Patrick. With her attention on Patrick, he could look at her. She was so beautiful. So cool. So sexy. He loved her, to which his mom would have surely said, "*You don't love her, Adam, you don't even know her.*" To which Adam could say, "*I'll never be proven wrong.*" He probably wouldn't live long enough.

Sadly, that also meant he wouldn't get to know her very well. She may not be his girlfriend, but she was his girl friend. ("Friend zoning" was one of the few things Kevin would proclaim to actually be bullshit, but Adam couldn't bring himself to care.)

Only a few of the businesses were boarded. Others had dark openings where boards either rotted away or someone (Stalkers and stalkees) removed them. Miraculously, there were windows here and there to reflect the moonlight. It looked so much brighter outdoors after the shoe store, but it was little comfort with Agent Orange on his way. They had to do something, go somewhere, but the potential traps were as dangerous as the hunter.

Patrick threw his sock to the street and removed his pants.

"Think he'd notice if we just walked away in our new kicks?" Gin whispered.

"He notices everything."

"Everything but nothing that matters."

Patrick stripped off his underwear and held it up to the moon, a cross between an escaped mental patient and a werewolf.

"Holy shit, he's really lost it," Gin whispered. She looked at the box of shoe laces as if it were a manifestation of his madness, suddenly unmasked, and they were fools to believe it could ever make sense.

Patrick pulled a dark piece of clothing from the pile which turned out to be pants. He pulled them on as they approached. And didn't bother hiding himself.

Awk-ward.

"You found the shoes," Patrick said as he mercifully zipped up. He took Gin's box of laces and sifted through them. "Great haul."

"So, uh, what's with the striptease?"

"Our clothes are embedded with small, trackable devices."

"I thought electromagnetics were sketchy in here."

He held up his underwear. "This is strictly short-range stuff."

"Good thing they aren't long johns?"

Patrick fixed her with a hard stare. "Be careful. There's a fine line between cynicism and healthy skepticism."

"Whatever, Patrick. We didn't follow you to Morgan to see your dong. Hey, maybe you don't even need us now that you have a lifetime supply of shoelaces."

"There will be a recovery team once this is over. We'll be tracked by our clothing."

"I'm not ditching my panties. Just not going to happen. We'll take our chances."

Come on Patrick, try harder, Adam thought. Patrick might be flying by the seat of his (new) pants but if his madness got Gin out of hers, it deserved a hearing. It wasn't like Adam had anything to look forward to that wasn't long, shiny, and sharp.

"Look, I can be . . . rather singular in my purpose. And I like to know what I'm saying is true because speculation can do more harm than good. If I've given you reason to doubt what I'm telling you—"

"You haven't given us a reason to believe *any*thing you've said. Gotta admit, I've been a little wary since you dropped the whole NSA and offshore accounts bomb, but sniffing those heads and now waving your underwear around? Agent Orange is on his way here and you've got us clothes shopping, so yeah, I'm starting to think you'd have a tinfoil hat if you found a grocery store."

"Which bone did you break? Arm or leg?" Patrick asked, not identifying which "you" he meant.

Gin answered "arm" the same time Adam said "leg."

After a surprised but cautious glance at Adam, Gin asked, "How did you know we had breaks?"

"The extraction team may not recover the head along with the rest of the body so we must have been selected because of secondary identifying characteristics. Annette will be the easiest since her breast implants have serial numbers."

Annette had implants? Adam figured he would have noticed something like that, but he hadn't given her much thought with Gin and Eliza around. Besides, she was older than his . . .

Wait, mom said she spent time in the hospital after the wreck.

"They took me because of a broken arm?"

"And a stalker, though I'm betting you wouldn't be here if you hadn't broken your arm."

"So now it's not Hoon, it's my arm?"

Patrick picked up his original pants.

"My mom broke her pelvis in a car accident," Adam whispered. "Dad had a replacement knee."

"*And* you're home schooled *and* you guys were on vacation when the time came for a round-up." Patrick shook his head. "Didn't stand a chance."

"This could be coincidence, Adam," Gin said. "So explain the head-sniffing weirdness."

"Did you notice some of the heads at the lodge were better preserved than others?"

"No."

"Who would, right? No one looks at them any longer than they have to." Patrick stuffed his underwear into a pocket of his old pants along with his previous socks. "The recovery team will come in here with more heads to replace the ones they remove."

"That makes no sense. They're out there killing people to replace the heads of the ones they let Agent Orange kill?"

Gin gave the bag of tube socks to Patrick, who tore into it eagerly. They were calf length with three colored bands near the top. Patrick sat in the street and pulled on the new decades-old socks.

"They don't need to kill anyone on the outside. There

are plenty of sources. People willingly donate their bodies to science when they die. Hell, the spooks can get heads from Mexican cartels." Patrick motioned to the nearest set of staked heads. "Orange doesn't collect heads so much as use them to terrorize. Get *in* our heads."

"He collects ears," Adam said. He handed the box of shoes to Patrick.

"Yeah, he's weird that way, but he doesn't look at these heads and wax nostalgic about Group A from last June. They decay and they're unrecognizable after a few days anyway. As long as it's on a stake, why would he think twice about it? Great fit on these boots. Thanks."

Patrick stood and hurried to the pile of clothing.

"Why extract our bodies?" Gin asked. "Why take the risk?"

"This many bodies can't suddenly appear after one of these heightened alert drills. Stalkers would see them and the National Guard *might* see them—the Guard won't have anything to do with this operation other than serving as gatekeepers. They probably have to fall back to a safe perimeter until the sirens stop.

"If today is any indication, a bunch of us were abducted for Kill Zone fodder. All these disappearances year after year would add up, so *some* of us have to be found again. And each year some of the dead here will be found elsewhere, closing out old missing persons cases."

"They couldn't figure out from the bodies it had something to do with Agent Orange?" Gin asked.

"How? They'll be found weeks, months, maybe years from now in faraway places, probably in rivers or woods, places terrible for the preservation of forensic evidence— or for the body staying in one piece."

Adam almost joked about Orange getting a "head start" with that, remembered his parents, and shut his mouth.

"They know what they're doing. The state of the bodies will dictate the array of possibilities for disposal. He'll never get the credit for killing us. Sure, it will obviously be murder, but the how, when, and why of it will remain a mystery that points everywhere but here."

"Think he's upset his official body count is way off?" Adam asked.

Patrick looked annoyed by the question. "Shush, the grown-ups are speaking."

Okay, then . . . dickhead. It stung, knowing Patrick obviously considered him dead weight.

"Even if every corpse is entered in ViCAP, Orange doesn't have a signature other than head and ear removal and even then he removes heads in different ways." Patrick shrugged. "I'm sure our abductors can deal with tool marks on the vertebrae."

Gin turned to Adam and said, "Violent Criminal Apprehension Program," making it one less acronym he would go to his grave not knowing. Actually, it was kind of impressive she knew what it meant, just another reminder she was far in advance of him. Once out of high school the experience gap increased exponentially. The years became a chasm.

"By now we're the final three," Patrick said as he handed Adam a couple pairs of jeans. "So we need to be thinking about what happens once we deal with Orange."

"We've got a glorified Molotov cocktail and shoestrings, and he knocked you on your ass the first time. You sure are taking the whole 'deal with him' thing for granted."

"Hold that thought." He abruptly set off in the direction of the Ardwar Sto.

Adam sorted through the pants. They were different sizes since Patrick didn't know what would fit.

"He's full of shit. Didn't offer to show us any of those mysterious tracking devices, did he? You're better off in those pants, though. Briars and poison ivy will tear you up in the woods."

Instead of the hardware store, Patrick went to the post office box. He circled it a couple of times.

"It kind of makes sense if you think about it," Adam said, checking tags. One of the pairs was his size. Did they really have tracking devices in their underwear? He couldn't see Patrick convincing Gin this so-called recovery team had a line on her unmentionables.

Adam continued, "They dressed us in our own clothes, but they picked the brightest or goofiest things we own. We thought they did it to make us more of a target, but what if they did it because they didn't want us to question the real motive?"

"We weren't naked when they took us," Gin said, "Why not sew the things into *those* clothes so we didn't question it at all?"

"Because they can't dump our bodies in clothes with those devices inside," Adam said. He kicked off a new shoe and removed a sock so he could hold it up to the moon. "A murder investigation would turn up anything out of the ordinary in our clothing."

"Yeah, I guess our consummate pros couldn't deal with just taking them off when they dump the bodies."

Adam couldn't find anything in his sock. He crumpled the fabric between his fingers in case he could feel what he couldn't see. No sign of any device and he felt foolish for supporting Patrick at the risk of Gin thinking less of him.

Meanwhile, Patrick crouched behind the postal box and opened the rear panel. Adam wanted him to succeed in something other than setting off a trap. If he was going to die anyway he'd rather spend his last hours alone with Gin, but there was a slim chance Patrick knew what he was talking about and could help them survive.

"You're turning into his mini-me."

Patrick looked both ways before entering the street, probably an old habit. He hurried to them.

"What if he's right?" Adam asked. Guilt tugged at him

as though he'd contributed to her doubt by poking fun at Patrick with her and laughing at her mockery. Still, he'd go with Gin if she insisted upon leaving.

"Unless he brings something besides dead letters and more crap, we're out of here."

In his left hand Patrick held a survival knife with a saw back blade and hand guard on the hilt; in his right hand he had a spiked ball and chain on a length of wood; on his face he had a smile for Gin.

"What. The. Hell?" Gin asked as she took the mace.

"It's a one ball flail, a medieval war mace, probably out of someone's private collection in Sandalwood. Truthfully not very practical if you aren't striking at someone who's using a shield. Maiming someone with this has to be on his bucket list."

"No, how did you know it was in the postal box?"

The knife blade was at least ten inches, maybe even a foot long. It wasn't a machete, but it was close.

"Got a whetstone, too—it's in my pocket. He'll have stashes like this all over the place. The mailbox is centrally located with easy access and who's going to look inside?"

"You, obviously."

"This is far less than I expected. He's had firefights with the military so there have to be firearms within reach," Patrick said. "Hoped it was there."

"A knife and a ball mace," Gin said. She handed the mace to Adam and it instantly seemed like an unwieldy weapon. And too loud when the links clinked against each other. Adam didn't want to take any weapon for granted but it seemed like the best idea would be to throw this thing to the highest branch of a tree so Orange would never get the opportunity to use it on someone—least of all someone who'd just tried to use it on him.

Gin was onboard the Patrick bandwagon again but Adam wasn't sure how much time he'd bought. He may have shown he wasn't completely full of shit, but he was still long on mumbling, extreme theories, odd busy work, and public nudity, and short on a solid plan of action.

"We'd better get out of sight." He took Adam's sock and stuffed it into his old pants. He grabbed the pile of clothes. "Come on, I found a place to ambush him. Bring everything."

Gin shrugged and followed Patrick. She had the bag of socks and her box of shoestrings. Adam slipped his bare right foot into his new shoe and followed with the mace, knife, his box of shoestrings, and the jeans in his size.

Patrick led them to a building on the corner of the intersection. There was no sign discernible above the boarded windows and the doorway was completely open, the door removed altogether. Adam could see a light from inside the building but once closer he noticed it was moonlight from a window along the side wall.

"He trapped the entrance so don't get gung ho and run past me here," Patrick said.

He stopped in front and checked down the street, the first time in a half hour he'd shown concern for Agent Orange.

"Look." He knelt to the pavement and pointed just inside where a thin wire ran parallel to the floor by three or four inches. "Just like the shoe shop so they all must be this way. Trip this and get a torso full of spikes. Same with the exit in the back. Let's get in here and turn it to our advantage."

They carefully entered and Patrick hurried ahead. From the aisle he chose you could see the building end-to-end, both entrance and rear exit, although the back of the store was far distant and in the blink of an eye someone could slip into the darkness either side of the doorway.

Adam heard the clothing hit the floor. A solitary button struck the metal of the shelves. It reminded him of jeans in a dryer, a metal snap or button intermittently striking the wall. Funny how the things he'd once hated to hear (*Adam, fold the clothes, please*) he would die to hear again.

Oh, you'll die all right. No worries there. Where are you going when you do?

The building had a musty smell kind of like the shoe store, but not nearly as concentrated; clearly the ventilation had helped. The boards came off two of the windows facing the adjacent street but the lower halves still had panels attached. They remained an unlikely entrance for Agent Orange. Nothing could stop him from kicking through the boards, but why would he? He knew about the door traps and would simply step over them.

"Knife?" Patrick asked and took it from Adam.

The floor was gritty beneath Adam's feet. After more than two decades of accumulation there were layers of glass, dust, plaster, dirt. He could be walking on crushed bones.

"Laces on the bottom shelf." Patrick squatted to the floor and took the first box. "Didn't have time to sweep the other aisles for traps so let's keep to this one for now. Gives us sightlines to both entrances. I'll watch the front, so you two have to watch the rear at all times."

In the available light it seemed to be a grocery store. Not only were the shelving units similar, the top shelf had four cans the size of canned vegetables. In the faint light he caught Gin looking at him. She shrugged. He shrugged. She looked down at the back of Patrick's head. And shrugged again.

"The fire must have bought us some time," Patrick said. "If the smoke didn't draw him to the lodge the smell may have. There's a good chance he'll think we doubled back to the lake. That could give us hours. Maybe too much time."

"Too much time?" Gin asked.

"Tie the laces together as tightly as you can. End to end. Think long rope." He held up an example in the moonlight. Tied end to end they looked like a mini version of the classic gym rope Adam (thankfully) never had to climb.

"Double knot because it's crucial these do not come apart," Patrick said. "Adam, have you seen *Full Metal Jacket*? No? Of course you haven't. Match our old socks and put one inside the other. Then drop a small can into each. Imagine swinging the can to bust Orange in the head. Got it?"

Adam cringed because it reminded him of a tale Kevin told him about a fat kid at summer camp, nicknamed Piggy. Several kids went into the woods to sneak a smoke and Piggy ratted them to the counselors, which meant a latrine duty punishment. *That night, after lights out, the counselors went to the mess hall to play cards, and we each put a bar of soap in a sock and took turns whacking Piggy in his bunk. It was brutal, man. No bullshit.*

"Yeah, yeah, got it."

Adam selected a new set of socks from the bag. Impossible to tell which color stripes he wound up with but the white glowed ethereally in the low light. He pushed them as far down his ankles as he could but they still shone against his darker sneakers.

Afterwards, his original ankle-cut socks hugged the can like a sheath and left no grip for swinging. Fail for that weapon. He fished Patrick's socks from his pants, threaded them one inside the other, and dropped a can into them. The fabric didn't stretch as much as he thought it would, but centrifugal force would stretch it taut if spun a few times. While the cans could pack a wallop on a normal person he couldn't imagine doing any degree of damage to Agent Orange. The chances of someone uttering the lines *"Yeah, took out his ass with a can in my sock! It was lights out, boddy!"* were a zillion to one.

Adam could imagine himself David before Agent Orange's Goliath. He could also imagine far different results. David was armored with the righteousness of God, confident of his success in the face of overwhelming odds. Adam? Not so much. Not at all. Armored only by the shame of impurity, he'd be lucky to get two spins of the sock before Orange dropped him like a bad habit.

"You can put those socks on the shelf there," Patrick told Adam. "Gin, he'll need yours."

"We're really going to beat him with cans?" Gin asked as she set aside her shoestring box.

"Hell no, you want to die? If we discard our clothes, the recovery team will wonder why. We want to be classified as missing and presumed dead. If they think we're alive and planning to sneak out they won't wait for us to try. Let's not give ourselves something else to worry about. So we tried to make our socks into weapons. Comprende?"

Adam knocked something on the shelf askew; it fell and rolled, a sound much too loud in the confines of the building.

"Careful," Patrick warned and Adam could have almost lip-synced it. Patrick's admonishments reminded him of his dad's. He thought of that face he'd never see again and squeezed his eyes shut against the building storm. He couldn't break down again now and remind everyone he was the weakest link. Gin almost ditched Patrick when he annoyed her; Adam didn't want to test how far he could go before he annoyed her to the same extreme.

Something struck him in the neck and his eyes flicked open. Gin's sock dropped to the floor at his feet. Her second one flew at his face. She seemed to smile, but he couldn't be certain.

"How did you know to look for tracking devices?" Gin asked. "How do you know so much about who *they* are and how they run things?"

Silence followed. Adam carefully filled Gin's socks and placed them on the shelf without a sound.

"Do you plead the Fifth?" Gin asked.

Patrick shuffled across the floor, crunching debris underfoot. He looked out the doorway left and right. Adam waited, not even daring to suck in a breath until the doorway vigil ended with a nod.

"What do I do next?" Adam whispered.

"Hold tight."

Patrick squatted at the wire for closer inspection. "He built the swing arm with a newel or baluster from a staircase. When the restraining mechanism is released, gravity will do its thing on this one." He squat-walked backward, releasing shoe string as he went. "One of the spikes is broken and another looks splintered. Used at least once."

"We're going to use his traps against him?"

"Newsflash, we're not making a jump rope. Mmm, sarcasm does make you feel smart, doesn't it? Anyway, the key is to wound him if we don't outright kill him with this. I don't know how the resurrection thing works. Does his body regenerate damaged cells? Is it an active process while he's alive with wounds healing unnaturally fast? These are things we'll need to know."

"But we're not going to worry about it now, right?" Gin asked. "We're going to kill him, not incapacitate him."

"We'll see when the moment comes."

"I don't like that answer, Patrick. I'll feel a whole lot better when he's dead."

"So you can start wondering when he'll reappear?"

"Aren't we doing that already?" Gin muttered.

"This string is long enough. It's on the shelf here, see it?" He pointed to the bottom shelf on Adam's left. "When he steps through the doorway one of us has to pull it. Wrap it around your fist and tug the fucker. No sissy shit or it won't work in time. *As he steps over the threshold*—don't forget that." Patrick brought his hands together to mimic a hard tug. "Sit right here and plant your eyes and ears on that doorway. Gin and I will set up the trap in the back."

"How long?"

The chain clinked on the ball mace. Patrick had picked it up to carry with him.

"Ten minutes. Stay sharp and wait until he steps through the doorway. Don't get any ideas with the napalm, though."

They headed to the rear of the building. Adam felt incredibly alone, like this was it—this was when they would sneak out the back.

Gin wouldn't leave me.

But he couldn't be certain. Patrick already tried to ditch him once; did he take Gin to the back to try to talk her into it again? *Hey, it's not like we left him without a weapon. He's got the trap, the napalm, and three socks full of beans.*

Only two people wouldn't have left him behind and they were dead. And he did to them just what he feared Gin and Patrick might do to him.

Adam felt for the string. His fingers found it on the dirty shelf. It triggered a sense memory of his mother's hands around his, teaching him to tie his shoes. Early home schooling.

And bedtime, before he was too "cool" and withdrawn.

Do you love me, mommy?

Only for always and forever.

He cried as soundlessly as he could, heart wrung in his chest. Try as he might, he couldn't keep it together. Grief was an unstoppable force demanding its due.

XV.

HAND OVER HER HEART, Gin stared at the doorway where a frightened cat just darted over the tripwire into the back lot.

"They've done studies on this ecosystem," Patrick said from the floor. "Feral descendants of domestic animals. Plenty of wild game. Deer, turkey, rabbit, squirrel. We'll be sick of the latter two by the time we learn to catch the others. Right now I could eat that damned cat. Bastard jumped right out at us."

Gin nodded in the darkness. She remembered a rock song from a few years ago called "Orange Mustangs," about the stable horses left behind in Agent Orange's stomping grounds. They escaped during one of his attacks and it apparently made a great topic for a deep, navel-gazing song.

Patrick tied Gin's string to the tripwire.

"You and Adam can add to the length. You'll want more than a yard's distance from this doorway. Not sure if you can see the trap but it's a two-piece device, one on each side of the door. Snaps like a pincher. That's why you two are back here; if one side fails, you still have the other. Better odds."

They might be able to set off the trap in time but Gin didn't have a good feeling it would be enough. A boogeyman wouldn't get ensnared in his own device; it was too easy to think he could.

A safety placebo.

"If we even neutralize him, where are we going to get food? Underwear?"

"Sandalwood. It's far enough into the Zone to not have any tunnels. The Stalkers probably don't even bother much with Morgan so whoever put us here doesn't have to worry about outsider interference. Sandalwood is a different story. It practically vacated overnight and they'll have some good stuff. Just don't expect a mall or even a Walmart."

"Shouldn't Adam hear this, too?"

"So tell him."

"I will, but . . . why don't you want him around?"

Patrick sighed. "He may be smart but he's only sixteen and he's reeling from a loss you can't fathom. You could hear it in the woods on the way to the creek. We were trying to step softly, keep the noise to a minimum. Adam was either distracted or incapable of the kind of stealth that will keep us alive."

The forest shuffle had been a test? Of course. There had been enough daylight to avoid traps and it gave Patrick the opportunity to test.

"I trust myself and I trust you not to do anything reckless or stupid, but Adam didn't have much to begin with and he's lost it all."

"Sounds like the perfect candidate for the hermetic life."

"That's not where the math led me. He'd be dead if you didn't stop him from going back to the lake house."

Patrick went to the doorway. He leaned out and looked both ways, then waved her over. As she approached he whispered, "Always know your escape route. Left takes you to the street. Took a quick look earlier and there aren't any traps between here and there. To the right? Anybody's guess."

Gin didn't like the exposure, but she joined him outside, minding the tripwire. Three trees had forced their way through the asphalt a long time ago, almost evenly spaced between the rear of the store and a neighboring building. Tall weeds grew everywhere, in any crack they could find. To her left it was a straight shot to the street—this must have been a dual-purpose delivery and parking lot, but any pavement markings were probably long gone.

Patrick said, "If something happens to me, get to Sandalwood on the other side of the lake. You don't want to be around when the recovery team arrives."

"If they arrive," she said. "You're guessing."

"Suit yourself, but by the time you see them they'll have seen you and it'll be too late. Just say I'm right. What if his body begins regenerating when it dies? What if there was a way to speed that recovery so he woke up during their clean-up?"

"How?"

"We embed something in his skull like one of his bodkin arrows, then yank it and get the hell out when they come for him. He's always incinerated just in case he runs out of do-overs. It's possible he could wake up on them."

"That sounds like a huge risk for a 'possiblity,'" Gin said. "He's always incinerated? You seem to know a lot."

"Just . . . speculating."

Is this what it would be like to live in here with Patrick, their lives forever dictated by his wild notions? Would he experiment with their lives without explanation, without consultation? If given half a chance he would probably try to capture Orange just to set him free on the agency.

Your little elevator fire. You were trying to point Orange in their direction somehow, weren't you?

"I don't want this, Patrick," Gin whispered. She felt like crying and did a little. Lingering effect of the cat scaring the shit out of her, maybe. She was tired and the emotions were spinning out of control. She thought about Adam and his lost parents and felt guilty for being so upset she may never see her own again. At least they were alive.

Alive and suffering. Her disappearance would burden them for the rest of their lives.

"Why would they do this?" She made tight, useless fists. "The government or your faceless agency or whatever? Why would they put us here?"

Patrick smiled. "Nietzsche said, 'He who cannot obey himself will be commanded. That is the nature of living creatures.' Americans have ceded their power to the government, creating a byzantine, amoral Leviathan that creates more power for itself with decreasing accountability. And hidden somewhere deep within is the agency that deals with the Agent Orange crisis by providing him human sacrifices to keep him away from all the consumers and voters and fine upstanding citizens."

"So breaking a bone and taking a trip or getting a stalker or homeschooling could mark us for death, but we're just getting what we deserve because we let government get too big?"

"You're so precious. Tens of millions of you seethe when you're TSA playthings but you don't question why airport security can't be more like Ben Gurion. Mass surveillance, warrantless wiretaps, growing civil forfeiture abuses, you get what you deserve when you're not paying attention. Not everything is as obviously sinister as The Reichstag Decree. If it's any consolation we were most likely selected by a computer. Nothing personal; it never is with Holocausts, Holodomors, Great Leaps, Cultural Revolutions, and the like."

Gin wiped her eyes with the back of a hand.

"Glad you're paying attention, otherwise you'd be in the same boat . . . oh, wait, you are."

He patted her arm. "Come on, smartass."

Once inside and safely past the trap Gin felt more at ease. A dark, abandoned building could be acceptable sanctuary from a killer. Necessity would lead to many compromises in the coming days. A sense of security?

Gone. Favorite foods? Gone. Warm showers? Gone. Welcome to your new, hungry, desperate, stinky life.

This would have been a store room/receiving area. The stingy moonlight didn't provide much beyond the area immediately around the doorway and Patrick had already warned her not to explore, which suited her just fine.

"There are three of us. One of you can be a go-between, but the other *must* man this trap at all times," Patrick said. "If I need something I'll whistle . . . only one of you comes. He could attack any time. Guard up. Listen. Don't fall asleep."

They weren't any more than eighty feet apart and all it would take was a shout, but maybe the point was to keep them from attempting to communicate at all. However, the last edict struck her as very unlikely.

"Fall asleep?"

"Fatigue will surprise you. Stay awake and keep vigilant. A few seconds separate you from life and death. You want Adam here? I can keep him with me if you like."

"Why the hell would I want to be alone?"

"We're not that far away. Thought he might be irritating you." He turned abruptly. "Be seeing you."

She couldn't see Patrick's face and couldn't formulate the question she wanted to ask, wasn't sure how she could ask it, wasn't sure if she *should* ask it. And then he was off, back to the other side of the building where she could see the shadow of Adam as he sat on the floor working with the string.

Patrick knew a lot about the place, maybe more than he'd let on. Had he known how Agent Orange would react to Gin all along? If he knew Orange would save her for last could he have used proximity to her as a talisman?

What about the clothes? Had he known as far back as the lake house the clothing might be trackable? Was the street performance just that? *Oh, I figured out we've got to change everything because they could track us . . . but not yet for you two.* Conveniently, Patrick was ready to hit the road, untraceable once the so-called recovery team came knocking. They were playing the waiting game now so why not take the opportunity to be ready?

Adam's feet crackled on the floor, the slight echo shifting from one room to the next. Patrick's footsteps had been half as loud, despite having twenty or thirty pounds on him.

"Friend or foe?" she whispered. "Answer or get the sticky end of a ball mace."

"It's me," Adam said, his tone flat like Patrick gave him a good admonishing before sending him off. *"Now you sit still and leave her alone, okay? She's had a rough day and doesn't need to hear more out of you."* It would take a few minutes for her to undo the Patrick Effect.

"Did he say anything about changing our clothes?" she whispered.

"No. I wondered about that, but didn't ask."

"Go back and get the jeans."

"All of them?"

"Yes. Tell him we need something to sit on. The floor is filthy. And walk quietly."

"Uh, sure."

Adam walked slowly, which didn't necessarily equal quietly, but he was trying. She listened to the crickets outside—some were in the room with her.

The shoe string was at her feet, but she didn't feel like an attack was imminent. Maybe she'd grown complacent after so long without seeing Orange, but it felt like the time for a siege had passed. He'd have to check the buildings one by one, but he had to guess they came to town in the first place.

While she waited she pulled her left arm inside her shirt, reached to her back, and unhooked her bra. If she had to take it off she might as well get it over with.

Privacy. Another relic of the civilized society they'd left

behind. She imagined bathing with Patrick or Adam keeping watch, probably peeping because she was the only female in their foreseeable future. The idea of Adam seeing her didn't bother her much (he'd probably worship her), but she had an unnerving feeling about Patrick. Maybe because he was older, had probably seen a lot of naked women, could compare her to them. He certainly hadn't been shy himself.

A screech outside.

She hurriedly pulled her bra through her sleeve and dropped to her knees beside the shoe laces.

Another screech followed by a low-pitched mewling as two cats squared off.

Her body quaked from the near miss. Anything out of the ordinary was a near miss—it could have been Orange coming for them.

Can I live my life this way every minute of the day?

XVI.

GIN SAT ACROSS from Adam in the dark where she worked on tying shoe strings together because *it gives me something to do.* Crates at their backs, they were eight feet from the doorway, legs outstretched, the soles of their shoes flat against each other. He wore jeans now, his shorts and underwear atop the crate behind him. They had changed right here in front of each other and Adam had never wished so hard for a flash of lightning in all his life. It wasn't to be; he had to be content knowing she wore nothing from the waist down as she tried on jeans until she found some that fit. Those few moments could have had a much higher rating, but he'd have to settle for a PG moment with "adult situations." At any rate, they were ready to disappear deep into the Kill Zone once this whole killing Agent Orange thing was concluded.

Yeah. This Patrick *killing Agent Orange thing.*

Meanwhile they waited and it was like watching the most boring movie ever. G-rated with utterly no plot. *Watching the Door.* But it could just as easily turn hard-R with a horrifying plot, *Guess Who's Coming to Skin Them?*

Adam stared into the dimness outside in a trancelike state after having told Gin a story from two years ago.

Honey, I've been to Kids in Mind, *it's a hard R. That word is used nineteen times. Maybe when he's fifteen he can—"*

He can watch Saving Private Ryan. *It's something he*

needs to see. He already learned that word from your brother, by the way

Nine of ten on the Violence and Gore scale. Nine out of ten! *Unacceptable.*

It's the context. He's not watching a horror film.

Nine of ten, Ed! To me, that is a horror film.

Dad won. He usually did in those arguments. The movie was awesome, the best he'd ever seen. Kevin had already seen it several times (of course). *Oh yeah, dog, all the best movies are R. The harder the better.*

"We're living a hard R life," Gin whispered.

It was so easy to tell her things. Some questions he knew he shouldn't ask her; relationship stuff. Otherwise he felt he could talk to her about anything.

"I wish I'd done more. Back home, I mean. Kevin was always into something."

Usually something not very Christian. Kevin isn't saved.

Lately Adam felt like he wasn't, either. Talk about apostasy.

"I figured I'd go away to college and it'd be . . . different." His fantasies made *Old School* seem as realistic as the Normandy invasion in *Saving Private Ryan*, probably more in line with Kevin's summary of *Cocksucking Co-Ed Cum Slutz* ("They cram for the big exam, no bullshit"—a movie that mysteriously never materialized when Adam spent the night). "Feels like I didn't do much and now . . . "

He trailed off with a shrug she couldn't see in the dark. It was hard to express all this without it sounding like a criticism of his parents, and thoughts of what his life hadn't been vividly reminded him of what it was and never would be again. Patrick and Gin needed him focused now, or there wouldn't be a later to indulge his grief.

"You have to decide to survive, Adam," Gin said. "I have. If I have to live in here, I'll live in here, but he isn't going to kill me and neither will they."

He thought he heard a smile as she said, "Besides, you're polite and well mannered. If I might be locked in this prison camp the rest of my life, you're the only sixteen-year-old guy I'd want to be with."

Adam laughed softly. He looked in her direction, surprised he didn't see the after image of the doorway burnt into his retinas like the image left on the television screen in the den back home.

Her right foot pressed against his. He pushed back gently.

"I'm not giving up," he said. "Doesn't feel like we have much of a say either way, though."

"Our lives were automatic out there, not about survival. Not like in here. This place will obey us and give us what we need to survive. If we can't kill Orange, we can avoid him."

"So now you don't think Patrick's full of crap?"

"We're screwed if we get out. I think he's right about that much." Her voice had been a whisper all along but she dropped it even lower to add, "And I don't trust him yet. We have to know how to survive on our own. We can't be dependent on him."

"He tells us to do things without telling us why."

"Screwing with our heads. Getting us in the habit of doing what he tells us because it might make sense later. He could have told us why we were gathering strings."

"Yeah. Still don't get the dash from the lodge to the woods."

"He throws so many crazy things at us, but just enough of them have an explanation that we don't question the rest."

"I thought I was bait. Or maybe no one would follow me."

"I wouldn't have let that happen."

But Adam wouldn't put it past Patrick to engineer a situation where it *would* happen. He was sly. If he didn't want Adam around, Adam wouldn't be around. *Hey, can you hand me that log over th—oh shit, sorry, didn't see those spikes. Well, I told him to be careful . . .*

"You know which one of you I'd choose," Gin said.

"Sometimes I feel like," Adam whispered and his heart accelerated because he knew he was going out on a limb even as he scooted himself along the precariously thin branch, "like I have a chance with you."

Gin scoffed, the sound a dagger in his heart worse than any deathblow Agent Orange could land. He cringed at his recklessness. He'd held back so many similarly rash statements only to unleash one in an unguarded moment, but he had to know. He wanted to recall the words, but all he could do was await the verbal smack down to come.

"We may live here now. A lot can happen."

"Like . . . what?"

"Let's wait and see."

Something punched Adam in the side of the neck and knocked him sideways. His right hand hit the floor and slid through the dust, gravel, and grit. Warmth spread from each side where it felt like pinchers had clamped him. He sucked in air and his lungs inflated without problem, but the pinched nerves in his neck were almost debilitating in their pain. He grabbed at his throbbing neck and found a thin shaft.

"*Adam*?" Gin whispered.

"I'm hit! Get behind the crate!"

How had Orange seen Adam? Outside Adam could only see the dark shape of a tree in the distance, nothing else, no movement.

Adam slid along the floor, keeping his head perfectly still. He traced the length of the shaft and found the fletching were only a few inches from his neck. On the right side, the arrow had torn a gash. The tip of the arrow was past his shoulder.

"Patrick!"

Instead of hiding, Gin had crossed over to him.

"Where are you hurt?"

"Go to the string," Adam said, surprised how his voice could sound so normal. So . . . calm. He attempted to swallow, but it hurt too much.

"Where are—"

Her hands moved along his arms to his shoulders and bumped each side of the arrow almost in unison.

"No!" It came out like an anguished whine. "Adam!"

"I think I'm okay."

Was that possible in this situation? No, he was probably completely messed up and in shock or something, but he wasn't swallowing gallons of blood, he could breathe, and he could feel and move his limbs. Somehow the arrow missed everything vital. It was a miracle, probably, but what good would it do him? There were no hospitals, no antibiotics.

Gin's hands felt along his neck, seemed to identify the exit wound on the right side was worse than the entry on the left. "Hold this against it."

Adam held the fabric against his wound. It felt wispy and thin, like a small handkerchief. Her panties. So it took a mortal wound to get a hold of those. Anything was possible after all.

"Hide. Grab the string," he said.

"Patrick!"

"Maybe he's already dead. Let me check."

"What?"

Adam pushed Gin aside gently. "Stay behind the crates. Watch for him."

Something he'd taken for granted: how many neck muscles the act of standing required. Pain exploded through him. He expected another arrow to hit him in the back as he cleared the top of the crate. When he stumbled to his left and frontward, though, nothing hit him.

"Stay here. I'll be back."

"Be careful."

His pain was really something, but it hurt worse to hear her cry.

Sideways through the door and then slowly, slowly toward Patrick's last known position. Right hand holding panties to staunch the flow of blood, one careful, deliberate step at a time. No outline of Patrick ahead, but a clear doorway. The trap had not triggered so either the trap jammed or Orange never came. It didn't matter. He had no weapon, but what he hoped to have was enough time to warn Gin that Orange was on this end so she could run for her life.

Please, dear Jesus, please, please, please let Gin live.

"Patrick?" Adam whispered.

The moonlight cast a rectangular gray box along the doorway. Patrick's old pants were a crumpled shape on the floor at the furthest reach of the light. Adam rotated to look Gin's way. He couldn't see her outline.

When he turned around he saw the dark shape in the doorway. No time to search for the napalm and lighter, Adam took several steps forward and dropped to his knees, grabbing for the unseen string Patrick left on the shelf. Orange stepped through the doorway, his boot high over the wire.

The trap clicked and swung downward with the metallic screech of a long-dormant hinge. Clumps of debris and a cloud of dust accompanied the crashing wallop as the wooden panel struck Agent Orange's left knee and outstretched left forearm. Patrick rose from the shadows of the next aisle and threw his body into the backside of the panel. The panel splintered and strained past its mooring. Orange reeled backward, hopping on his right leg. It looked like the measured retreat of a wounded warrior, positioning himself to parry the next blow or deal one of his own. Off the curb now, he put the right side of his body forward to face Patrick, who charged around the trap. He went at Orange head-on, but then feinted left.

Adam smelled the napalm. He quickly retrieved it and stuffed Gin's panties into his pocket so he could grab the lighter.

Outside Patrick ducked and dodged his way forward, to the side, in reverse, his left hand flashing toward Orange and then withdrawing. It was like watching a bantam weight boxer totally outclassed in size and weight, dancing around his opponent and landing light, quick jabs. Orange swung a machete with his right hand but Patrick ducked or hopped backwards, staying out of its range with ease. He was so much more than the basement showdown suggested—a giant slayer.

And the giant dropped to his left knee in a growing pool of blood. The Macpherson gas mask had been replaced with a different version, one adapted to accept very modern night vision goggles.

Adam edged around the trap and the lighter came to life on the first try. He held it to the stiff cloth wick and it caught instantly. Adam feared it might explode in his face.

"No!" Patrick yelled. He rushed at Adam and batted the bottle from his hand, which shattered a couple yards across old asphalt with a whoosh.

Orange seized the momentary distraction to swing the machete and Patrick blocked it with his smaller blade, but it knocked him off balance. Orange's left arm, which had hung limply at his side since the trap sprang on him, swung around with something smaller than the machete, but effective enough to dislodge the knife from Patrick's hand. The blade skittered across the pavement toward Adam, halted by a clump of weeds.

Adam wondered how he screwed anything up by attempting to set Orange ablaze. Sharp, burning pain lit his neck as he stooped for the knife. Would Patrick knock this from his hand too? Did Patrick feel there was room for only one hero?

Patrick ducked beneath a machete swing, then jumped

and hammered his fist onto Orange's goggles, knocking them askew. He rolled backwards beneath a reverse swing that would have taken off his head. It gave him time to return for his knife. He had his right hand tucked to his chest, dark with blood.

Adam lifted the knife and looked to see if Patrick approved, wondered if he blamed Adam for wasting the napalm though he couldn't have missed with a proper throw.

Patrick's eyes were vacant as if he'd checked into some other world. He didn't go for the knife. He put his foot against Adam's arm just below the shoulder and grabbed the arrow along the fletching. He braced with his foot, wrenched back on the shaft, and yanked it free as gracefully as a magician pulling the tablecloth from beneath a banquet spread.

Adam screamed, expecting to see fire shoot from both wounds. He tensed on reflex to stay upright and the explosion of pain dropped him to the street, the impact with the sidewalk a merciful distraction from his neck for about half a second until both pathways converged for a network of pulsing anguish.

"Don't move," Patrick ordered needlessly. He turned back to face Orange, whose crippling injury had slowed him enough for the extraction procedure. He still had a couple yards of clearance. Orange held the long blade at ear level.

The napalm fire turned the storefront into the neon of Las Vegas compared to a minute ago. Shadows swam through Adam's vision, shades he knew weren't really there. He rested his head on the curb to take pressure off his muscles, at a good angle for the Patrick/Orange showdown.

Patrick still had the arrow. He lunged with it and just as quickly snatched his arm back as Orange hacked at the limb. A distant part of Adam realized if Patrick fell, so would he.

I hope Gin took off, but if we somehow manage to kill Agent Orange, how will we find her again?

He buried the question deep. His head felt heavy enough without the dilemma, even as that same logical part of him laughed at the idea of "we." *Patrick* would be the one to stop him, with Adam's contribution solely voyeurism.

Always glad to be of service.

Patrick bounced back awkwardly as Orange slashed in a wide arc with a backhand motion. Patrick stuck him in the exposed rib cage.

Come on, Patrick, cut him up!

It couldn't have been too deep, however, as he withdrew the arrow without much effort. Orange went for a death blow, a high swipe of the blade at Patrick's head. He hit the deck and rolled away on concrete.

"Stay off the ground," Adam mumbled. He could barely hear himself.

Patrick sprang up. They moved uncomfortably close to Adam. He tried to call out a warning, but the world seemed too loud. It would be a cruel twist of fate for Patrick to fail because he tripped over Adam, though he wouldn't have to lament this for long before Orange permanently cured his nagging neck pain.

Patrick struck with the arrow again. Orange dodged it easily, but stumbled and went down on his injured knee.

Holy shit. Adam wasn't sure if he said it or only thought it, but regardless, it was amazing Patrick had brought the slayer to his knees. If they got out of this, he'd never question Patrick again.

Patrick raised his arm and in a flash drove it at the top of Orange's head. There was a loud cracking sound like a tree trunk splitting in half, and Orange slumped to the ground motionless. The fire light revealed the shape of the black arrow protruding from his head.

Patrick crouched low to reach for Orange's weapon.

Adam waited for him to spring to life and lop Patrick's head off as effortlessly as the fluff from a dandelion.

Movement from the corner of Adam's eye.

"Adam!"

Damn it, Gin . . . I ran out here like an idiot so you'd get away, and you never left the stupid store?

He couldn't have been more overjoyed to see her. Tears threatened, a combination of his pain, sorrow, relief.

She's still here. It really sucks that I'm probably going to bleed to death.

Patrick pulled the blade from Orange's hand like Excalibur. He flung it over in Adam's direction. It clattered a yard from his head. Another clatter followed, which he recognized from the mace as Gin set it down. She slipped an arm beneath Adam's and started to haul him upright.

"Careful," Adam warned. He meant the pain, but also not wanting to get his blood all over her. Not when they'd just traded out jeans.

She stayed for me, he thought. *She didn't leave. She* couldn't *leave.*

He could come up with a thousand reasons later why he was foolish to think this. He needed the hope to keep him in the here and now. He blinked several times, wincing as Gin dragged him to a seated position.

"Stay with me, Adam," Gin said.

Patrick stood to full height and backed away, not taking his eyes from his fallen opponent.

Fallen? That's a weak word. Patrick conquered *him.*

"Is he really . . . " Gin began. After a few seconds, she let herself finish. "Dead?"

"Is he ever?" Patrick asked, still not turning to them. "He hasn't moved. It's not a wise tactical move to fake his death and let us disarm him. He hardly needed the advantage of surprise."

"Didn't stop him from taking it anyway," Gin said. "Big man. Shot a child in the dark like a coward."

"A child who nearly napalmed him."

"Can we not . . . not call me that?" Adam said, his voice almost normal again. Gin's healing touch? "I'm old enough to have a driver's license."

He didn't, but he *was* old enough. It didn't do much for his flutter of joy to hear Gin refer to him as a child, either.

Guess I don't need to loot Sandalwood for an engagement ring.

Patrick bent down for a closer look. "Hope we don't need to cauterize that wound, Adam."

Adam began to feel like a passenger in a car where the driver kept looking at him as he talked instead of the road. He kept his head steered where he could see Orange, but if he'd moved, it was as imperceptible as the minute hand of a clock. Hopefully Gin watched too.

The thing that murdered his parents, still motionless.

Patrick tilted his head from side to side to examine Adam's neck. "Doesn't look like you've lost a scary amount of blood."

"It hurts," Adam said.

"You got lucky. A couple more inches either way and we might not be talking right now."

"Yeah. Lucky me." Although he did feel lucky with Gin's hands on his shoulders. She wasn't massaging or anything, but it was amazing compared to the inexperienced guy—*of legal driving age*—who woke up earlier today wearing such stupid clothes. With the starkness of black and white crime scene photos, he remembered how the presence of his parents at Morgan Falls Lodge had been his lone comfort in all that fear and uncertainty.

"I can't believe you killed him," Gin said, pulling him back from another meditation of grief.

"Just needed the advantage of the trap," Patrick said. "Aim for the brain and you can't go wrong."

"We should take his head off. To be safe."

When Patrick made no attempt to answer her, Adam asked the burning question: "What the hell was the deal with the napalm? I would have hit him. Why did you knock it away?"

Gin's voice sharpened. "What does he mean you knocked it away?"

Patrick sighed. "It's like we talked about in the back."

Irrational as it was, jealousy stirred somewhere in Adam's heart at their private exchange. His own with Patrick amounted to *Stay focused and try not to get us all killed*. Gin's was probably no different.

Probably.

Patrick continued. "Orange is no good to us burnt to a crisp. If he's dead for days or weeks, what does it do for us?"

"It keeps us from getting shot with arrows for days or weeks, for one!"

"You two still aren't seeing the bigger picture here."

"No, we understand perfectly that you want to play games with the recon soldiers or whatever. It doesn't help us. You can kill fifty of them and we'll still be stuck here."

"When you kill him you can decide what we do with the body," Patrick countered. "This is my call."

"It would have been my kill if you hadn't blocked it," Adam said, though he couldn't really buy into the idea he would have shut down the killer elite by his lonesome.

As if in agreement, the napalm flames tapered noticeably.

"Sometimes we might not get a choice," Patrick said, ignoring him. "We may have to overdo it. So be it. This time we've got a chance and we're going to take it."

He stood up, dusted off his backside, and hesitantly approached the body.

"I don't understand any of this," Adam said.

"That makes two of us." Gin scooted to sit beside him

on the curb. Metal slid over concrete as she dragged the mace with her.

"Why'd you stay?" he asked. He wondered if he could stretch and yawn as he slipped an arm around her. He decided the move would be more effective if it didn't result in covering her shoulders with his blood. It wasn't exactly like giving a girl your letterman jacket.

"The fire," she said. "I thought you guys hit him with the napalm. I had to see."

She has a really cryptic way of saying, I couldn't bear the thought of leaving you, Adam.

"I'm glad you stayed," he said.

"I'm glad you did, too."

It was probably the best he would get tonight, but he'd take it. He was still alive and a lot could happen from day to day. She'd pretty much said so herself.

Yeah, right before he shot me with that arrow. Way to ruin a moment, dickhead.

It was funny how there wasn't a way to go back to a moment that was barely five minutes old. It would feel too forced now, the vibe completely disrupted.

"You're right about cutting his head off," Adam said. "And I should get to do it."

"Well, he can't watch him forever," Gin said. "You might get your chance."

Playing Mr. Guillotine right now seemed like an awful idea with his injuries, but he'd do it. And if that wasn't satisfying enough, he'd probably get another crack at it in a week or so.

Patrick surveyed Orange like a golfer trying to line up a difficult putt.

"Paging Dr. Patrick," Gin said as they watched. "He thinks Agent Orange can regenerate fast from something like the arrow. He wants to turn him on those recon soldiers. You know, poke the bear. Great plan, huh?"

"So what, we'll tie some shoelaces to the arrow like the trip wires, then yank it out when they get close?"

Gin shrugged. "Yep. Like pulling away a coin from someone on the street."

"If that's the case, we're going to need a lot more shoestring."

Patrick gave Orange wide berth as he circled, craning his head. The black arrow stuck out of his head like some kind of toy accessory. Patrick stooped down, extended a hand and tapped the arrow, then jerked his hand back.

"It's in there deep," Patrick reported. "Didn't budge."

Adam made himself stand, just in case. Patrick seemed likely to go full scientific experiment here to prove Orange truly deceased. Maybe he intended to unmask him. The archives of Richard Dunbar were limited to some grainy newspaper pictures and a couple of snapshots from Vietnam, something that seemed unthinkable to Adam, who was used to people immortalizing every trivial moment of their lives on the internet now with digital cameras and phones. "Who is Richard Dunbar?" was the sort of thing missed on *Jeopardy!* because about as many people thought of him by that name as they did Terrell Wilson as Busta Kapp. Seeing his face would go a long ways toward humanizing him, though Adam didn't expect it to stay his hand too much when he chopped the fucker's head off. Might as well get his hits in while he could because Orange would probably pay him back one of these days.

Probably? Well, his newfound optimism was remarkable. It helped to see Orange—*Dick Dunbar*— dead right in front of him and know it could really happen. He didn't buy Patrick's theory of resurrection, but say it did happen . . . those recon soldiers would be trained to finish the job. The three of them were safe for a little while. Enough to find a place to hole up and trap in case Dunbar dropped by unannounced. A lot could happen with Gin in a week or so.

Patrick reared back and kicked at the body, hard. It didn't connect.

"Shit!" Patrick shouted. Orange—he was Orange again, as someone named Richard Dunbar would have died from that head wound—had caught his ankle. "He's still—"

Gin sprang to action beside him with a clattering of chain lengths. He grimaced as he followed her movement, the ball of the mace swinging beside her like a pendulum.

We should have taken his head while he was down, Adam thought miserably, but despite what Patrick said about faking, if there was some kind of regeneration, he'd just bought himself a few minutes to engage the ol' mutant healing factor. They never really had him vulnerable.

His neck pulsing as though needled by some medieval torture device, Adam staggered forward with the knife.

XVII.

GIM SHOUTED AS she surged forward to save Patrick's idiot life. The mace was cumbersome, but it only needed to strike one good time to leave that gas-masked asshole at their mercy—of which he'd find precious little.

Orange sat up and caught Patrick's leg with his back turned to her, the arrow still jammed between the straps of his gas mask. Patrick swung the long blade at the hand clenched around his ankle and Orange let it go. Patrick dropped backward and hit the lot.

Gin heard footsteps pound behind her. Adam. Brave but foolish. He could barely hold his head up. Her strike had to count. She let all of her momentum infuse the swing of the mace. The heaviness of the spiked ball did the rest of the work. The gas mask turned to her and he moved without taking any time to assess the threat. The ball lodged in the meat between his shoulder and neck.

That's for Adam, prick.

Behind him, Patrick stumbled to his feet. Orange eclipsed him as he stood. She tried to pull the mace back and perhaps deliver the death blow, but it stayed embedded, caught in bone. He knocked her hand away.

He was a bizarre sight in his gas mask, the arrow in his head, the heavy length of chain dangling. She couldn't see his eyes for the night vision goggles (perhaps a gift from a careless Stalker or a recon soldier), but just like in the rec room of the lake house she obviously transfixed him, paying no mind to Adam rushing up beside her with the knife or Patrick or even the mace.

Eyes only for her.

Adam reached him first, stuck the knife into the side of his head. Orange finally acknowledged the boy, turned and reached for him.

No playing possum now.

Gin took a protective step over to cut him off, in time to see Patrick charge with the long blade. He held it out like a spear. Orange saw him, held up a hand to ward it off. It slammed through the palm of his gloved hand, stopping inches from his mask.

"The mace!" she yelled to Patrick, hoping it might remind Orange to return to his special Gin vigil while Adam and Patrick finished him off. With two blades in his skull and none the worse for wear—so far not even a sound of inconvenience—Patrick probably needed to find a mail collection box with a hand grenade in the next four seconds.

He spun around with an outstretched arm, the blade stuck through his hand on a collision course with her face. She flailed backward, knocking Adam down and tripping over him. The blade missed by inches. Arteries of grass peeked through various cracks in the asphalt, but did little to smooth her fall. The rock scraped her arm as she hit on her side. She and Adam formed a broken V.

Gin scrambled up, stung from the abrasions of the parking lot. Adam would be in the most danger with his limited mobility and she needed to protect him somehow. Thankfully she saw Patrick reengage him and find another knife—the one Adam jammed into Orange's skull, which should have ended this whole nightmare in conjunction with the arrow.

She glanced over to see Adam on his hands and feet with his face down. Poor kid, in such pain he couldn't look up to assess his own safety. She didn't know what they could do for him if they survived the next five minutes. Her best weapon still stuck in Orange's shoulder, she wasn't sure what to do in the next five *seconds*.

Patrick crouched in a knife-fighting stance. Orange stood without pretense, examining the metal struck through his palm. He slipped it through the hole like a scabbard. Patrick struck before he pulled it out, a quick knife jab into Orange's throat. Blood cascaded from the puncture as if from a bloated sac, drenching the mace in ichor so dark it looked completely black in the weak glow of the flames. Orange fumbled his machete, and Gin had her best chance to arm herself. Patrick advanced, cutting in a wide swath, and Orange obliged him by retreating from the strike. It separated him an important step from the fallen blade, and then another.

Gin took her cue and ran to seize it. If she could get behind him again, plunging a bigger blade like this through the base of his skull might finally put him out of commission if he had any kind of nerve center. She began to circumnavigate, pacing around Patrick by ten yards. Orange noticed her, but he didn't fixate this time. Maybe he still wanted her last. Past them, Adam tried to steady himself, upright at last. Orange could probably knock him over by blowing in his direction, even through the gas mask.

Without the distraction of the long blade, Orange reached for the mace with his good hand. Patrick lunged and snatched the grip himself. He about-faced with the chain roped over his shoulder, like a man trying to haul a car. The mace detached.

Yes! They had him now. Give Adam the knife and they would all be armed. They could cut him down.

Patrick swung the mace like an Olympian, though Orange stood outside its arc and didn't need to budge. Gin tried to maneuver herself into his blind spot, a few yards away, mulling the best place to stick him. She needed something to wound him and create an opening for Patrick if Patrick didn't create an opening of his own in Orange's skull with that mace.

Patrick flipped the knife over to Adam, where it landed at his feet.

Gin gritted her teeth. *You son of a bitch!* Orange turned to see where the knife went and abruptly switched course. Easy prey, easy weapon. The man who wouldn't flambé Agent Orange because he wanted to bait the black ops soldiers didn't "accidentally" endanger a teenager; that was the whole point. Whether it worked out as the perfect distraction to use the mace or Adam wound up dead before he delivered a solid swing, Patrick would be content either way.

Gin ran, heedless of the danger, and hacked the blade across his vulnerable back from left shoulder to right flank, half of an X. He snapped upright in a shudder—was he beginning to feel the wounds the more they inflicted upon him?—and turned around. The mace hit him in the side of his mask with a satisfying *thunk*. It didn't do as much damage as hoped, but it rocked his head viciously to the left and knocked his mask askew.

"Hit him!" Patrick commanded, trying to set for another swing.

She swung in an X pattern, backing him off. Patrick struck again. Orange sidestepped it and in a fluid motion reached to retrieve the arrow jammed in his head. Then it was Patrick's turn to fend off an attack with the flat of his hand, too off balance to dodge it. He screamed as the arrow pierced it, stopping it right in front of his face.

Gin rushed, realizing Patrick's hand wasn't the only one they were about to lose; the upper hand was slipping fast too. She aimed to cripple Orange, remembering Patrick had a lot of success with the trap. The advantage hadn't held after his little "death" a moment ago (had he somehow regenerated like Patrick predicted?), but it slowed him once and it could do it again. She buried the blade in his hamstring, avoiding bone, and managed to pound it in all the way to the hilt. She hauled it back out, though not quick enough to avoid an intercepting fist to the face. He didn't turn to look, just lashed out blindly and struck gold with the back of his hand. The worst of Hoon's meltdowns stopped before this stage and she had never been punched before. It felt like she'd been hit with one of Adam's tube sock cans.

She lost the blade and her sense of up and down. When she claimed it again, she was on the ground. She saw Patrick flail the mace again, but much more weakly. The blow landed at Orange's face, but it barely slowed him. He seized the wrist of Patrick's perforated hand and the back of his head and violently thrust the arrow until Patrick's hand slapped his forehead as though to squash a mosquito, the arrow angled through his eye socket. The chain links of the mace slapped the ground, relinquished. There was a faint moan and a sickening crunch, like someone stepped on a Styrofoam cup. Blood spurted between his fingers. Patrick dropped to his knees and slumped over face first. The arrow protruded from the back of his skull, a piece of rubbery-looking tissue stuck to the point. If any arrow had remained on the other side of his hand, the ground pushed it through. A black puddle oozed beneath his skull.

Orange stepped on the back of Patrick's neck (more crunching, and the point of the arrow shifted slightly) as he took hold of the fallen mace. His left leg looked a bit shaky, although it neutralized the encouragement of the injury now that a dangerous madman had a crazy medieval weapon to use on her and Adam.

Adam.

She hunted for the machete, in time to see Adam claim it and move between her and Agent Orange.

"Adam, no!" she shouted. Her mouth was full of blood,

the taste bitter on her tongue. She pulled herself to a crouch and stood, face throbbing.

Adam swung the blade overhead with both hands, Conan style. It couldn't have been his full strength, but he buried it in the top of Orange's skull. It wedged into place, solid as an arrow at the archery range. Streams of blood poured from the fork of handle and blade, trickling down the front of his gas mask. It bisected the top of his head, the grip sticking out like the bill of a ball cap.

He stood motionless, as though in shock. He'd begun to seem like a crazy variation on a martyred saint, except he could use all the blades that pierced him.

Go down, you bastard!

Orange snatched his wrist. Adam yelped.

Gin retrieved a knife from the ground, the one Patrick tossed.

Adam stumbled away, freeing himself from the wrist lock. He looked back to see Orange midway through a launch of the mace.

Gin could only watch.

The spiked ball smashed into Adam's face with tremendous impact, easily wielded with one hand by Orange. The back of his head blew apart as the mace pounded all the way through his skull, detonating all the interceding meat into an explosion of wet chunks of bone and brain. An instant shower of glistening confetti exploded at Gin as if fed through a leaf shredder. She opened her mouth instinctively to scream, and found herself choking and spitting out the giblets of Adam's cranium.

Adam's body went slack and collapsed to its knees. The mace had rolled past his neck to his back. Orange hauled it back out like a fish from a stream to let the velocity decimate what remained of the head, leaving him with only a U shape on top of his neck. Orange cleared away fragments which adhered to his mask and flung them to the asphalt with the outstretched fingers of his glove.

The rest of Adam's body slumped over, still twitching.

Gin screamed. Orange's head snapped to attention. The machete seemed downright comical, stuck in his head. He finally seemed to remember it and slapped the top of the handle to bounce it from its trench. The position of his head never deviated, keeping her lined up in his sight.

And then there was one.

He was a blur through the tears in Gin's eyes. Pain tore through her soul. With Patrick, she lost a valuable resource, but someone who considered her a survival chess piece. Adam was a friend who'd died to protect her. She wiped her eyes, though the blur was preferable as a barrier between her and the world; it made it less real, more like a dream.

Orange made no move to collect the dislodged blade, as if daring her to take it. One on one for the final battle, Gin, just you and me.

Screw that.

Gin ran.

She returned to the store, thinking of the trap in the back and the slim chance he might have forgotten about it. She vaulted over the sprung panel of the front door, and realized it didn't matter if he'd forgotten because he'd get a nice reminder when he saw her jump the wire again. *Shit.*

She ran down the aisle to the back of the store, past the shelves where Adam made the blackjacks with socks and cans. Orange's steps were heavy behind her. He slowed down considerably to climb past the board of spikes he'd reconnected with earlier. She noticed every other step hit the ground harder. The stab through his leg gave her a great advantage, and hopefully he couldn't heal unless he stopped to rest. The downside was if he really had a regenerative process, everything they managed to do to him a moment ago would become null and void if she escaped.

It sure as hell beat the alternative, though, when she'd brought a knife to a tank fight.

She jumped the wire at the exit.

Always know your escape route. Left takes you to the street.

Patrick said the path was clear of traps. She raced past the back of the building, now officially out of "next moves." The reality truly set in that she was probably the last survivor. He had no more distractions, no one else to chase around while Patrick plotted silly pranks against his faceless government and sent her and Adam off on cryptic errands. She had only her own strategy and experience to help her now.

She considered doubling back to the store for a possible hiding place, but doubted she had enough distance to pull it off. Plus there was still the fire light and the complication of two entrances if she even reached a dark aisle without setting off a trap.

The *thump-THUMP* pounding renewed behind Gin, like her own frightened heartbeat trying to catch up to her. She kept to the middle of the street as she ran past the empty buildings. The moonlight was weaker now, offering only a faint cross-section upon Morgan's defunct downtown. Black squiggles spiraled through her vision from the transition of fire glow to deeper dark. The strip of deteriorating buildings suggested an alien landscape.

A loud scraping sound dared her to look back, like something dragged behind a car. She wouldn't turn her head, but decided it was probably the spiked ball on the street. He was letting it dip now, perhaps tiring a bit. Not nearly as much as someone should with a sliced leg, a morning star wound, and *a huge split in his effing dome,* but she was glad for it.

As if to level the playing field, she stumbled and nearly twisted her ankle.

Seriously? she thought, but she kept her feet beneath

her and her arms and legs pumping. The middle of the street should be the safest as far as traps, but the street itself was tenuous after decades of neglect. The asphalt was broken and crumbling under her shoes, and in daylight would have looked like patches of fish scales. The uneven surface could put her on her face.

So much for not being trapped.

The sliding sound of metal scraping rock seemed closer now, and a quick look back revealed a deeper swirl of ink in the darkness a couple of blocks back. Her survival sprint could only feed off adrenaline for so long. She already felt her lungs heating up like the burners of a stove, each breath heavier and harder to circulate the air. She was horrified when a distant voice in her mind suggested she just succumb and let the mace finish this whole nightmare. Her body rebelled against the impulse, powered by a new burst of speed.

Submission is for the weak.

If she didn't have the fight within her, she'd still be with Hoon. It didn't matter that it might have prevented all of this if she stayed with him, because that would have been no life at all. Here there was hope if she was willing to battle, and her will was inexhaustible.

She hooked to the right of the next intersection before she consciously formulated a plan. It looked to be a dead end, but not before a few branching streets offered her options. The two-story buildings formed a wall against the available moon light, which would have been nice if he couldn't see plain as day with his goggles. She liked the prospect of doubling back on him—it had been an effective temporary solution today after the lake house—so she hurried to the second alley on her right. She could only hope she didn't run face-first into a dumpster or bounce off garbage cans like a human pinball.

Or find one of his stupid traps.

Gin padded down the alley as quietly as she could, a

hand clamped over her mouth so she would breathe through her nose. Her lungs protested, but the sound was like a pin drop compared to all the gasping. After a moment she heard the faint pounding of his footsteps and the rattle of the chain, a weak echo. It wasn't getting closer.

He went left, the wrong direction.

She badly wanted to sprint back the way she came, but she had to maintain silence. She actually tiptoed for the first time in ages. It was a relief to reach the end of the alley and a new street.

She paused for an update. No footsteps now or the chain.

Of course not, he probably traded the mace for a bazooka—

And how would he do that? She could almost hear Patrick lead her with that question.

The same way he would have had the mace to begin with.

Her heart resumed its own sprint. She turned left at the corner and squinted. A dark shape excited her, but it wasn't what she wanted. It was a newspaper rack. Too dark to see inside it, but of course he wouldn't use one of those anyway. The object was to hide weapons, not stash them for emergency retrieval where anyone could see them.

She wished for the deafening sirens. Without their cover, her footsteps were like glass shattering. *Hey, the "Vietnamese" girl is over here if you want her!*

Gin checked behind her, knife at the ready to slice his balls off if he had any rape ideas. There was nothing random about her being the last. It was why he targeted Adam with the arrow instead of her. She was scared to death, but she wanted to hurt him—kill him—for what he did to Adam as much as for her own survival. The rest of them, too. Even Annette. More or less.

Morgan must have been a quaint town before the evacuation. Places like these nowadays eventually transformed into a kaleidoscope of strip malls and big chains to allow the convenience of city destinations without having to live in the city, until there was practically no difference.

Another intersection and she had to suppress the cry of joy. There it was—the bulky outline of a mail collection box, and hopefully a stockpile of weapons. She maintained the cautious gait, though she wanted to run and hug the damned thing. The ambient noise of the night seemed shrill in her ears as she crossed the remaining five yards. She expected him to pounce from a doorway, knowing her own plan before she did. Or he'd fixed a trap, a mail bomb to set her arm down about three blocks away.

Yeah, because it's so obvious he would stash weapons around like that.

Of course it wasn't, and that's why this was going to work.

She knelt beside the box, checked in all directions, tried to listen for anything beneath cicadas and the pressure in her head, like the sound of the world grinding along its axis. Wondering if Patrick's government boogeymen could see this through a live feed somewhere and cheered her on (yeah, maybe they'd shed a tear when they shot her execution style on a clean-up later).

Gin felt blindly along the surface of the box until her fingers found the outline of the retrieval door. She expected/dreaded it to be locked, but it came easily; he'd oiled the hinges. Up close the scent of the lubricant was strong and she breathed it through her mouth, hoping it would supplant the copper and sushi aftertaste of Adam's brain.

She sheathed the knife in her waistband, reached inside to play Mystery Box and frowned at the discouraging amount of space. Okay. It would have been nice if it had been so stocked full of weapons they poured out like coins from a slot machine, but there was *something,* at least, set down at the bottom and larger than her stupid knife, so an upgrade. She found the smooth wood of a handle and withdrew it.

There were two handles in a V pattern and she identified it easily enough when she pulled them apart and heard the *snick* of the blades.

Hedge clippers.

Her hope sank as if tied to an anvil.

Well, what did I expect?

Better; she'd expected something a hell of a lot better than this shitty thing. Something she didn't have to be practically dry humping him to use, for God's sake.

She tried to look on the bright side. She'd seen much smaller ones than these, which were at least two-handed. The blades were about a foot long, and there was no resistance to the scissoring motion when she worked the handles. He took good care of his toys, considering all the WD-40 must be dried up without them airlifting new cans into the Kill Zone (at least she hoped not, but she remembered the sarcastic YOU ARE HERE from the Chicken Exit map and felt less confident).

Realistically there were only so many viable weapons he could put there, but a gun would have been nice. She had a .38 at her apartment, something she'd taken to the range a few times when Hoon wouldn't leave her alone. Screw her earlier guilt about trading places with him; if she'd known his attention would plug her into an algorithm of ideal candidates for the Kill Zone, she'd have dropped him like a sack of laundry and hoped for a jury of abused women.

Well, she'd take the clippers for now and hope a gun was in the next one.

She would have to forage sometime in daylight when she could see all the mailboxes. Right now she just wanted to find a straw and hide underwater for about a week, but no way, couldn't risk getting any rust on her trusty clippers!

Wouldn't want to hedge my bets. That would be shear foolishness. I'd really be cutting it close.

She allowed herself a watery sigh. Adam would have enjoyed the terrible jokes. It had been a long time since someone had been so infatuated with her. Not obsessed like Hoon for selfish reasons of control, but someone who simply enjoyed her company. Pretty remarkable in these conditions.

She stayed crouched low and crossed to the other side of the street. If he followed the alleys leftward, he might be four of five streets over now. A little more and it might be safe to run. She wanted to hide for the night, and most importantly rest. Maybe she'd do something extreme like find a room at the Morgan Falls Lodge and sleep under one of the beds. Patrick might approve of that. Orange wouldn't expect her to take shelter in the place they'd tried to burn down, presuming he knew it was their handiwork. Best of all, there might be a new group in there eventually. Well, not so great for them, of course, but she could use the manpower.

Use . . . just like Patrick.

She tried to think of it more like time travel. A redo with different people, knowing a lot of things which would have helped her own group if they had such information upfront. Arm all of them with the bounty of the mailboxes—hedge clippers naturally bequeathed to the weakest link—and it would be twelve versus one to disarm Orange (literally). Chances were good they would prevail and cut him down like a paper doll.

I can make it through the night. This one and the next one and the next, however long it takes for reinforcements.

Long as she didn't have to do it with just these overgrown lawn scissors, she believed it.

The moon tracked her like a spotlight, now visible again through clouds, turning her sickly white. She noted a stop light overhead, swaying from its wire in the wind, creaking. A street sign informed Gin she stood at the corner of Irving and Wallace. She turned onto Wallace.

A shadow appeared to her left and she almost screamed—even opened her mouth. Something kept it prisoner in her throat. She bent over to wait for the faint feeling to pass.

It was a mannequin in the storefront window of a business which had retained only two characters of its sign: An E (more than likely the first letter) and an apostrophe. There were other humanoid forms, and the part of her that still wanted to panic envisioned lurid interpretations—heads replaced by Orange's trophies, limbless torsos that weren't actually mannequins, guts draped around the pale figures like garland around a Christmas tree. It had to be a clothing store.

She pushed the silver bar of the entrance. The door quietly rattled in its frame and did not budge. There were openings in the storefront glass, but nothing big enough. Snatch and grab ops by Stalkers, maybe, who wouldn't waste their time for a Members Only jacket. The prized artifacts truly suggested the essence of Morgan. This stuff was rummage sale fodder.

She wished she could pick the lock. Maybe she could connect with a Stalker one day who'd bring her the tools to do it. It wasn't a fortress or anything, but he might not suspect anyone could get in or think it important enough to trap. Keep up the ambiance of "disrepair chic" and it might be a good hideout. Plenty of Jordache to hang herself if she decided to give up one day, too.

Gin felt him before she saw him, an electricity in the air, something that made her scalp tingle and raised the tiny hairs on the back of her neck.

She didn't hear the arrow that struck Adam, but she heard this one. The snap of the bow line, the air slicing open in its trajectory and the thunk as it embedded in the knot of muscle on her left thigh. Her knee buckled and the hedge clippers hit the ground with her. The knife slid away.

The intensity of the pain seemed to illuminate the night. There were heavy footsteps now, still with the same hesitance every other step, and the light rattling of the mace. He ambled up Wallace a block away.

Gin gave the wound a cursory glance. A small arrow this time, not much more than a dart, but it couldn't have hurt worse if he set it on fire first. He had effectively slowed her as she did him. She could hobble away, but he'd easily catch up. He had something set on his shoulder, probably his crossbow. He'd pulled it from somewhere around here. Crossbow to his shoulder, spiked ball swinging in the other hand, all the time in the world to kill with a slow shuffle, twenty-five yards out.

Gin moaned as she retrieved the hedge clippers and pulled herself up. The mannequins watched her from the other side of the glass, offered no encouragement. She raised the clippers overhead, gripping a handle in each palm, and swung the blade against the glass of the door. It cracked slightly. Another swing and the fracture became a spider web.

A quick look behind. Twenty yards.

Come on, you bastard.

She jumped and threw all her weight behind the clippers. The pain pulsed through her leg, jolted as she landed, but the glass shattered into a cascade of pieces like a crumbling jigsaw puzzle. She crouched and hopped under the push bar, using her right leg for balance.

The darkness swallowed her. She didn't have long to hide. A wall stood immediately to the right, so she pushed forward and left. Racks of clothes brushed her as she scrambled past, like a red cape across a bull. She put as many of them between her and the door as she could. He'd be able to see her in seconds through the night vision. She had only a dim outline of the racks. She collided with something which crashed to the ground. She took a zigzag pattern away from the entrance to arrange enough obstructions to conceal herself, like a small animal fleeing a predator through underbrush.

As a child while out shopping with her mom she used to sneak in the middle of circular clothing racks. It was fun to be so hidden. It was the only thing she could think to do now. She found one and pushed her way inside it, managing to avoid a fingernails-on-chalkboard scraping from the hangers.

Gin fingered the tail of the arrow in her thigh. It was dry, so she probably hadn't leaked a trail he could follow. She clenched her eyes shut against the mounting pain and sat perfectly still in complete black, no hint of the moonlight underneath the jeans. An enclosure overhead hid her from all angles. She crouched with one knee down, blades open on her hedge trimmers, listening.

Shit . . . I never got the knife back.

Gin's eyes burned as sweat dripped into them. She tried to keep still and breathe through her nose. The air was stuffy and her eyes and nose twitched from all the dust, ready to trigger a sneeze to seal her fate. She bet some of the clothes would disintegrate if touched.

He made no effort to disguise his search. Footsteps clomped to the far corner on the right. She didn't hear him draw aside any clothes to look. Encouraging, although she didn't know if anything over there needed to be moved to see.

The steps got louder in her direction.

Shit, this is it, this is it, she thought, clenching the hedge clippers tight enough to hurt her fingers. The steps continued, but not a direct line to her spot. He might have seen the rack she knocked over.

The chain lengths clinked, closer now. He moved nothing for a better look.

Is he looking for blood?

She took one hand off the clippers to test her arrow again. Still dry. Touching it seemed to twist it deeper into her leg.

How the hell will I treat this?

It was a problem she really hoped she still had to figure out in the morning.

The clump of his boots trailed away again. He never passed close to her, though she still expected him to snatch a fistful of her hair and yank her out, then slam the mace so hard it caved in her face. She thought of Adam twitching on the ground like a cow on the killing floor. Had he been aware of his pain then?

Not now. Plenty of time tomorrow when I'm looting pharmacies for Band-Aids.

Orange's movements muffled noticeably. She dared to stick her face through the fabric. There was a rectangle of deeper black to the rear of the store, some kind of back room. She had no way to know how long it could occupy him, or she might have tried to create a fake blood trail to lead him outside (well, fake trail but real blood).

Gin looked to her left. Something she missed in her initial rush for a hiding place stood in the far corner, one of the better illuminated places in the room. Past the mannequins which startled her in the first place was a bone white spiral staircase. It carried its own risks, but she sure liked how it only had one entrance.

She slipped out of the rack quietly, wounded leg first to ensure nothing caught on the arrow to wrench out a scream. She continued to hear his faint steps in back, so she hobbled toward the staircase, crouching below the level of the racks. Too late to squeeze back through the entrance, but he might hear the glass crunch on her way out anyway.

So I'll just put all my hope in these ancient stairs not creaking on me. Way better.

She reached the staircase and craned her good leg up three steps, grabbed hold of the iron rail, and boosted herself up. No creak. She repeated the process up two more stairs, which brought her around the first bend of the spiral. She heard a little pop that sounded like a bottle rocket in the heavy silence.

She was halfway up and about to curve through the next spiral when he emerged from the back. He didn't rush out on red alert, so she set the hedge clippers on one step, planted her face on the stair above it and pressed her body to the stairs below. The shape of the staircase concealed most of her, although he would be able to see her head.

Which is all he wants anyway.

In the night vision, her black hair would just seem a shadow among shadows. She didn't dare turn her face to him.

He started to move, and of course it seemed like a purposeful march her way. It took everything not to stumble the rest of the way up the stairs in a panic. Her heart seemed to bounce off the stair wedged against her chest.

And now I die, halfway to what was probably a dead end anyway.

His steps were distant, though, and came no closer to her. She tilted her head up. Her hair continued to cover her face, but one eye could see through the strands. She barely made out his shape, momentarily confused when he vanished right into a wall. For an instant, the word *ghost* flickered like a subliminal message.

Another back room?

No, not a back room, she realized. A fitting room.

GO!

Her arm felt rubbery as she hauled herself back up. A wave of dizziness nearly put her back. She let it subside, then completed the ascent. He would come upstairs eventually. She just hoped for a better chance up here, either to defend herself or hide well enough he thought she escaped.

Better moonlight allowed a decent picture of the second floor. More mannequins, which made her think of old atomic test footage. Females modeling mostly knee-length dresses. She would have crouched under a billowy enough dress if Victorian had been the style in the '80s. It might have worked.

There were also more racks. She could slip into one of those again if she got desperate. Women's shoes dominated one corner, so there might be a stock room up here also.

There was a loud crash downstairs. Gin jumped.

What the hell was that?

Another one followed close behind, and this time she heard the chain. Gin's stomach knotted up. He was either randomly smashing things in frustration or he was breaking apart those enclosures over the circle racks to scare her out or search and destroy.

She scoured, desperate for some kind of plan or advantage. She almost ran into a spinning rack of sunglasses. There were racks of purses past that. A row of mannequin heads modeling hats. A spinning case on a countertop with watches, possibly Swatches in inventory. More clothes, more mannequins, more shoes, more absence of anything that made this move to the second floor anything but a delay of her own head modeling the latest in chic decay. She spun in her hopelessness, careless with stealth measures. Another crash below bought her some timely cover.

She still couldn't see everything. Like she didn't have enough odds stacked against her with the arrow wound and a dumb lawn care accessory versus a psycho who'd done nothing but kill hundreds of people in myriad ways for decades. Gin's biggest kill was a possum with her dad's Kia. It seemed horribly unfair not to have a full inventory of options, as if the moon a couple more inches to the left would reveal an anti-aircraft missile launcher next to the Maybelline make-up and perfume bottles.

She found the backroom but the light didn't carry far enough to reveal a place to hide or a better weapon alternative. An enclosure in the wall held a fire extinguisher but it would have dried up ages ago, its usefulness expired even as a distraction, and as a potential bludgeon—a guy who pulled blades and arrows out of his *brain* could handle a bump on the head.

She waited for another crash from below, which didn't come with the succession of the others. She frowned; it was like hearing eleven chimes at midnight. Finally there was another rack obliteration, but he must be running out. She had to commit to something.

Gin maneuvered around another mannequin and her heart jumped as she found a metal door with a crash bar. She could not quite read the letters above it with the available light, but it had to be an exit sign. There was a sticker on the wall, probably to admonish an alarm would sound if the door opened.

Not these days.

She quietly pushed until the bar clicked and the door eased open. Available light was sparse behind the building but enough to see a line of steps to the left. She had hoped for access to the roof like a ladder she could defend, but she was happy to get anything.

More racket downstairs. There wasn't much time.

Gin grabbed a blouse from the nearest rack and stepped outside the emergency exit. She wedged the hedge clippers in the doorway, stuffed as much of the blouse in her mouth as she could fit and took hold of the arrow.

God, this is going to suck.

She wrenched the arrow free, screaming into the blouse. Between his noise downstairs, the mostly closed door, and the shirt, she thought she would get away with it. She choked on dust, coughing into the fabric.

She needed a little longer. He would be thorough downstairs, but there were only so many viable hiding places.

She wrapped the blouse around her thigh and tied a tourniquet, then slipped back inside. She left the clippers wedged and hurried back to the spiral staircase with her accelerated hobble, arrow in hand. The chain sounded close to this corner of the shop. She shook the arrow at the floor as if sprinkling fairy dust. It left black drops in the moonlight. She retraced her steps, marking the way with blood spatters. Her throat felt closed up and she was scared she would burst out coughing.

Gin created a red trail all the way to and through the emergency exit after collecting the hedge trimmers. She tossed the arrow over the rail and eased the door shut.

She stuck the point of one of the blades into her pants leg above the knee until she could tear off the fabric. She kicked off her shoes and used the scrap of her jeans to wipe away blood which trickled down to her ankle. She cut at the knee of her pants on the other leg and tossed the severed pieces and her shoes inside one of the racks.

She pulled a black dress from the rack and slipped it over her head. She thought the tourniquet would keep the dress off the wound so blood didn't seep through, but best not to take the chance since so much depended on it. The black would cover it. The dress almost reached the floor. She staggered to the mannequin heads and selected a sunhat. The wide brim was what she needed, almost conical. She folded her hair up as much as she could and slipped on the hat. She started back to her place by the exit.

Wait . . . the hedge clippers.

Gin looked from side to side, hoping for some kind of shawl, but if there was anything of the sort, she couldn't find it. Thumps carried up the stairwell.

Oh God, here he comes.

She hurried back to the emergency exit, snatching up a heavy sweater from a table display. It was more than she wanted, but there was no time for anything else. His boots hit louder as he ascended, Death knocking at the door.

Gin picked up the hedge clippers by the door. It seemed like the best place for her to be when he arrived. He wouldn't be able to see her yet with so many racks and displays in the way. She made sure the blood trail went through an obstacle course to keep his eyes off her as long as possible.

She swaddled her weapon in the sweater and cradled it like an infant. She wanted to stand closer to the door but allowed five feet of clearance. The mannequin she'd passed before locating the exit now stood beside her, hopefully enough for her to fit with the décor. Her head seemed full of helium; maybe the hunger, the dehydration, or the terror. She didn't have to make any move and she still had time to hole up inside one of the racks, but she knew if she had a window of opportunity, she would take it.

The seconds ticked down.

Gin tilted her head toward the floor, enough where she would still be able to see him walk past and her face would be covered by the brim of her hat. The hedge clippers nestled in the crook of her arm, covered by the sweater, and she had a firm grip on one of the handles.

The mace rattled as his footsteps approached. The temptation to look for him was enormous, but she held the fixed position of her "still life" and tried to breathe as little as possible.

He emerged from the labyrinth of clothing racks as designed by the blood trail, clothes whispering like palm fronds as he brushed past. The spiked ball swung into eye line. She couldn't see very much of him at the angle—the chain, part of his leg, the gloved hand. The left foot seemed uncertain under his weight, still giving him problems.

Is he wondering why it's so bloody up here when it was dry downstairs?

As if cued by the thought, a blood trickle edged down her thigh from beneath the tourniquet and crested over the bone of her knee cap, down her shin. Her mouth opened into a startled oval and she sealed it shut. She stifled the impulse to pat it dry with the dress. She arranged the blood trail to keep him a couple feet away from her until he passed her, but he knew its destination by now. He was more purposeful in his stride, only interested in the door. He would pass within inches of her instead of a yard.

A tiny ball of tumbleweed rolled around in her throat, daring her to cough it away. Her nose became micro-sensitive to all the dust particles floating around the department store after years of deathlike silence, stirring her sinuses with the assurance of an easy way to clear it all out. Her eyes watered. She squeezed the handle tightly. If he was looking at her, he'd have seen her arm shake slightly.

If he bumps into me, he's going to know I'm not a mannequin.

Gin had to remind herself not to shy away from him. Had she seen more than the waist down, she might have flinched. With the moment arriving, all the compelling arguments for a surprise attack seemed foolish and suicidal. Let him walk outside and she'd keep still, lay low in here until sunrise and hoof back to the lodge.

As long as he doesn't wonder why the blood conveniently stops once he gets to the stai—.

He stopped barely a foot past her. She thought the sirens started back up, but it was only a screaming alarm in her head that the entirety of her existence would be reduced to the next few seconds. Her hand shook and the bundle stirred in her arms. He would have only heard wood or metal lightly brushing against fabric, but it triggered something; maybe an acquired sixth sense for stalking honed by decades of practice. He about-faced, already raring back with the mace, the chain rolling out to its full length.

In her panic she should have dropped her clippers and stood there staring blankly with a sweater draped over her arm until the ball decimated her skull and turned her into a mannequin as efficient as the one beside her. Somehow, she didn't. It seemed to happen as a scene she watched from outside herself. The sweater dropped away as she lifted the clippers with the right hand, the left automatically enclosing the other grip as she thrust, the blades a united shape with a triangle tip. She wrenched upward, the area of his throat the only semi-vulnerable place with the protection of his mask.

The point of her blades caught him under the chin and seemed to punch through it as easily as a square of butter, albeit with an abrupt crunching as it speared through bone. He backed up and fumbled the grip of the mace, which thumped and rolled behind him. He tried to pull the clippers from her by turning and stepping sideways. It may not have happened if she hadn't wounded that leg earlier, but his foot came down in spatters of blood and slid. He went down hard face first. Gin kept a hand on the clippers. Her grip kept his head pulled forward as he dropped. She went down with him. The floor met the bottom of the grips and pounded the blades deeper through his skull. More crunching, wetter now.

His hands flew to his throat, groping for her wrists. Gin wrested the blades side to side, mostly to avoid his grip rather than inflict more damage with the blades, but conveniently doing both. He fought his way to his knees, clawing himself upright for better momentum to fight. She knew he would win, too; petty things like a brain partially bisected with glorified scissors still wouldn't cost him his strength advantage.

Gin pulled the blades open.

They didn't give easily, even with all the additional divots she sheared through his gray matter, but she ripped both handles to either side, widening the arc of the blades in his cranium. She saw a hint of the blade poke through the right side of his head like a tiny horn. They cleaved through bone on both sides, within his head and jaw. He stopped moving instantly, dropped both hands to his sides. She heard a hard spattering sound, like rain water through a gutter. Blood sprayed her arms, surprisingly warm for a dead man. Clumps of mush dropped through the newly created divide as an exodus of brain tissue spilled to the floor with moist slapping sounds.

The hedge trimmers pulled from his head with the ease of car keys from an ignition. He settled back like a man who has committed seppuku, hollowed out. Gin didn't hesitate. She stepped around and pushed him on his face. The adrenaline mercifully muted the fire of her arrow wound and she acted while she had the reprieve. She settled on his back and opened the jaws of the blades, pushing them against the back of his neck. It was much slower going here as she shredded through tough muscle, opening deep gouges until the clippers met the block of spine; then an additional struggle to saw through that block of resistant bone, aware of seconds ticking as though in a countdown to defuse a bomb (which in a way, this was). She stood up and put her lower body into the effort as a dark pool seeped out beneath his face. With a final snap, the blades clasped shut and the head sheared away. She rolled it awkwardly, a little superstitiously. It didn't go far with the bulky mask, but she was satisfied.

She crawled away, still holding the clippers, not wanting to touch him another second. She admired the shadow of the blades in the weak light.

"I'm sorry I didn't trust you more," she said. "I couldn't have done this without you."

Gin imagined him talking to his weapons in Vietnam, and decided that was enough dialogue. She considered a look with the night vision behind the mask, but it seemed far too much effort at the moment. Weariness settled into her body with profound soreness in her arms and shoulders. She hurt all over as the shock of battle wore off.

It would be easy to let gravity do its work and drag her down into blissful sleep, but she remembered Patrick's theory of a recovery team.

The countdown wasn't over.

XVIII.

AS IT TURNED OUT, if they had tunnels they didn't use them for the "recovery" operation. In a post-adrenaline stupor she hobbled down the road out of Morgan when a sharp skid and crash broke through the dull monotony of the distant sirens. Gin lurched into the woods seconds before a convoy of four white box trucks led and followed by two black Humvees rounded the bend without headlights. They didn't slow down as they passed her on their way to downtown Morgan. She wondered if Patrick's tracking device paranoia had saved her life.

On the road again, she picked up her speed to make the most of the new adrenaline burst. The journey was more bearable with a makeshift crutch beneath her armpit; she'd cut the bristles from a push broom, wrapped the head with a sweatshirt, and lopped a few inches from the handle so it would be the right height. The clothing store yielded other treasures with the help of the night vision goggles: a change of clothing, a first-aid kit, a map, and brochures about local tourist destinations. Thirty-year old Wrigley's Doublemint gum practically dissolved in her mouth but when she spat it out it took the taste of Adam's skull with it. She procured a backpack for all of this (minus the gum) and used it to stow the crossbow bolts, knives, and the giant-slaying hedge trimmers. She wore the goggles.

The store had been an anomaly in Morgan, a place practically untouched. She found unsent letters (the stamps cost twenty-two cents) on an office desk and bagged them for potential Stalker commerce. They suggested how immediate the desertion of town had been along with the entire shelved and racked inventory locked in a strange state of suspended animation, forever stuck between one work day and the next.

A rustling in the woods spooked her and she halted, unslung the crossbow and aimed into the trees.

It's him. He's back already.

She didn't really believe that (she doubted she would hear him at all), but it was something sizable based on the snapping and swaying. After a moment she saw the ethereal glow of eyes staring back at her in a green haze. A deer attempted to rise but it was kept grounded by a broken foreleg and two rear legs that didn't work at all. She swept her head toward the road and saw skid marks with glass debris from broken headlights.

What a difference context made. Survival turned you from a gawker into an active agent in securing continued existence. Her hands went for her reclaimed knife before she realized it. She could take a shoulder or shank from a foreleg and cook it with a fire once she got to Sandalwood. Her first few meals were assured. The ones afterward were an unknown, along with what she could find for her wounds along with the first aid kit, but at least she had this.

The deer struggled when she grabbed its head from behind and slit its throat. It thrashed against her, knocked her down, but she held onto it as wet warmth seeped into her clothes. The scent of blood seemed omnipresent; life's precious commodity flowed freely here.

"I'm sorry," she whispered as concession to an act she'd have found appalling before today.

Gin held the animal as its life ebbed, two victims of the same machinery thrown together in the Kill Zone.

THE END OF REINCARNAGE

GIN BYUN WILL RETURN IN THE DUNBAR EFFECT

AGENT ORANGE WILL RETURN IN REINCURSION

EXTRA CUTS:

REINCARNAGE BONUS MATERIAL

NORA

I.

NORA WATCHED THE pavement support each one of her steps with something like amazement. She'd lived near a corner gas station that closed down a few years ago, and the lot crumbled away to allow patches of grass to shoot through the decay. That's how this whole downtown area looked, but that wasn't why she kept looking as she walked—it was because she fully expected to plunge through this impossible veneer. How could any of this be real?

She'd dismissed the possibility of a nightmare upfront, even though the yellow top she found herself wearing seemed like the sort of subconscious detritus that would take shape in a dream. She'd thought about the yellow shirt this week, and the vacation she last wore it. A four-day-weekend, a timeshare with other girlfriends. Higher caseloads and court appearances started running her into the ground after that, like everyone conspired to stress her within an inch of her life while she was away. So she had anxiety dreams, sure, but not on the order of this. Usually it was the day of The Big Court Case, but she hadn't prepared, didn't know her opening statement or witnesses or even the charges, and it was too late now, she would be fired from Thompson, Mihalka, and Maylam by lunchtime.

Watching her steps also kept her from looking at those severed heads on the lamppost up ahead.

When was that vacation, three years ago now? *That* seemed impossible too, just with the routine existential terror everyone knew as "real life," where years passed in a matter of months, with a collection of memories that only amounted to a few days. She'd gladly go back to that kind of terror. It was the white noise of existence, much like those crashing waves each morning at the timeshare.

She'd noticed the yellow shirt in her closet many times since, but it never felt like the right day for it, as if it now had to be associated with escape. She didn't have that now. She needed it in a way she never had before.

There were three heads on the lamppost, hung like Christmas wreaths. They all had long hair, which Agent Orange had knotted to tie them firmly in place. Screaming mouths of silent horror on all save the lowest, which had no jawbone at all. Maybe Orange tried to sculpt it to match the others and advanced rigor mortis snapped it right off in his hand. Or someone took it for an ID reward with V-R.I.P. They paid for the jawbones, which always struck Nora as morbid. She would want to know a loved one's fate here, but she'd hate knowing they were further desecrated beyond a killer's ministrations.

Would someone take her mandible out of here months from now? And would everyone know that Nora, who respected the law, would never risk her life and livelihood on such a pathological frolic? She'd always been level-headed, reliable. She showed up on time, she came prepared. No one would ever think to look for her here. Her vision blurred, the moment towered. It was happening.

She didn't know how she got here. The others didn't, either. They wandered out of Morgan Manor like people who hadn't seen the sun in years, waiting for something to anchor them back to reality. The explanation revealed in less than one block only left them further unmoored— blood, bodies, decomposition. Horror.

They filed down the cracked sidewalk now of a street whose name had been yanked from the sign, possibly sold back in the world Nora needed to return to. A place where these mementos could be collected as a substitute for raw experience, like a band shirt for a tour the collector never saw. Agent Orange created a totem pole from the sign, three more heads spitted on the post through their necks. Fresher specimens than the lamppost. Flies buzzed around stump viscera.

"Tzompantli." The word floated through a haze, disembodied, a piece of a sentence she wouldn't have understood anyway.

More heads watched from the other side of the street from atop the meter poles, enough of the cranial contents cored out to slip them over the meters like bulky gloves. Some strange detail about the trophies demanded she look, against her better judgment. Their shorter hair clued her in at last—they were missing their ears. Hear no evil. She'd already seen enough to fill a jury box, with alternates.

She stopped and put her hands on her knees, breathing in and out until the swarm of black dots disappeared from her eyes.

"Are you okay, Nora? It was Nora, right?"

She nodded, remaining hunched over, her view limited to a pair of loud orange parachute pants. Why did most of the group look that way, with the vibrant colors? Some of them didn't even match. They all denied selecting these wardrobes before the blank spot in their memories, though everything came from their respective closets. Only some of the Hispanics wore clothes from the secondary section of the color wheel.

She stood up and nodded. The parachute pants belonged to Ward, she remembered. A hospital admin who accompanied patients in the role of translator, fluent in three secondary languages including Spanish and Mandarin. She forgot the third, but the Spanish already proved invaluable because four in this group weren't comfortable with English. Two of them were brought here together, Ward translated, brother and sister, but the other two were strangers. Though the one called Ernez could communicate in English, the four of them stuck close outside Morgan Manor, exchanging quiet, rapid conversations as the scope of their predicament became apparent.

Nora figured Ward for the oldest of the group, past forty with graying hair and a soft middle. He had a kind face. She could see him thriving in a care role.

"We'd better keep moving," Ward said, a little apologetically. "In case he's close by."

"Why are we here?" Nora asked. "Why the hell would someone bring us here?"

A man in a baseball-styled shirt with red sleeves turned back to them. He wore a matching red and white Marlboro hat and smelled like they'd probably sent it to him as a loyal customer. She blanked on his name, couldn't remember him or the guy in the white headband, white shirt, and red pants a little further up tapping his foot like he had a bus to catch.

"Some fuckin' sicko, maybe," said the Marlboro Man.

Ward blinked at this crass diagnosis. "Be that as it may—"

"Dropped us in to watch and whack." He nodded sagely. "Ten gets you twenty."

"Thank you for that, Colton."

Colton, that was it. He may have provided an occupation, but he only impressed as a full-time idiot. Eight people pulled from all walks of life and domestic time zones, deposited in a secure area—these moves involved logistics beyond the wont of a pud-pulling degenerate. It spoke to power and answers she wouldn't like. It made her wonder about her caseload, and how far someone would go to take her off the reins of a murder defense. Why Ward, though, or Colton or any of the others? The plan was for all of them to die, obviously.

"Let's get back to the search, okay?" Ward said.

Of course she would sign off on that. She'd proposed it in the first place, after the initial shock wore off a little, because unless their bright colors terminally blinded Agent Orange, they would need some means of defense. Purpose helped in a crisis. Something to do besides wring your hands and hope everything magically resolved itself. They wouldn't have to worry about the why of all this if they didn't get through the now. Easier said than done, though.

Sirens began in the distance, miles away but loud enough to jolt them. They looked around in all directions, expecting the worst—*him*—but the only movement Nora noticed came from flies sifting around bloody remains and wisps of dead hair stirred by a breeze that would have been pleasant if not for the reek of putrefaction it carried.

"Are they gonna nuke us?" Colton asked. So much for ten getting her twenty on his sicko theory.

Ward spoke to Miguel and Juanita, the brother and sister. Both wore sensible blue jeans, a white shirt for him and light heather green for her. It's what they actually remembered wearing before the fugue. Same with Hernán's deliberate khaki pants and a blue shirt. Only Ernez got the snatch-and-switch treatment, yellow track pants and a lime green shirt. It almost hurt to look at him.

"They think it's Orange," Ward said after Miguel and Juanita returned to their discussion with Ernez and Hernán. "Maybe he's trying to get out."

That wouldn't be a bad thing, as long as the military stopped him at the wall. The world didn't need another Morgan or Sandalwood, but it could only be a good thing for Nora's group if he was miles off with no awareness of them.

"We can't take the chance," she said.

He nodded.

The guy in the headband continued tapping his foot, obviously ready to keep moving. She didn't remember his name. He seemed like a bit of a goof, the person you get thrown with in a group project and know you'll have to carry his ass.

Assured the sirens bore no immediate influence on their location, they forged on. The totem pole street sign waited as they neared the corner. Headband reached it first, leaning past the adjacent building to see down the street to his left, then right.

The sirens stopped.

"Clear," he reported.

No one followed close behind when he ventured past, waiting for some horrible shriek of pain, but eventually they felt safe enough to trail after him.

"Oh snap," Headband said. "Mailbox!"

He stumbled over loose asphalt in his zest to hurry to the collection box. "You know how much someone will pay for a letter from this place?"

"Lee, are you crazy?" Ward said. "Don't touch that."

Oh, right, Headband's name was Lee. She now remembered him saying something about playing live music. What was he, one of those DJs at a club or a wedding?

Lee looked back, frowning. "What?"

"That thing could blow your face off, man," Colton said.

"Jeez, okay. Chill."

Miguel pointed down the opposite stretch of road. "Hay un auto ahí abajo que deberíamos revisar. No hay forma de que aun funcione, pero podría tener algo de valor si logramos entrar."

Nora followed his finger to a car sandwiched in a small alley or side street. Hailstorms and other elements through the years had left it pockmarked and rusted.

"He says we should check that car," Ward said.

"Dude, I've had cars that wouldn't start after sitting

around two weeks," Headband said. "That thing's been here for more than two *decades*."

"He doesn't mean we're going to drive away in it. It might have something we can use for a weapon, like a tire iron."

Nora had never even changed a flat using a tire iron, so "optimism" scarcely began to describe the hope of felling Agent Orange with one. They had to start somewhere, though, and if they all had something formidable to fight with, could the maniac easily stop an eight-pronged attack? She had no doubt they could hurt him. He always came back, but he could be stopped at least for a little while. Long enough to get away and stay ahead.

They passed shop fronts flanking both sides of the road. While Agent Orange's decorations were less overzealous on the pillars and posts here compared to the last street, he'd turned one display into a grisly tableau. Bad wigs on a couple of mannequins turned out to be real scalps. Dried blood inked their fiberglass faces.

"Hey, here's a bar," Colton said a few shops down.

A sign above a window of smoky glass said RACKERS SPORT BAR. They couldn't see the interior because the treated glass kept the sun from spoiling the mood for anyone hoping for an afternoon happy hour. The lower half of the door beckoned, shattered and apparently swept up at some point over the years.

"You hoping to get Orange drunk?" Lee asked.

Colton ignored him, ducking inside the bar.

Ward squinted as if he would magically see through the glass. "Should someone go with him?"

Nobody made a move, other than Lee. He paced the sidewalk, wandering off toward the alley with the car.

Nora glanced back the way they'd come. She heard wind chimes somewhere, but in the prevalent quiet, they could have been three streets away. Everything felt so still, a world on pause. Fear seemed to fill all the empty spaces.

Ward took a breath to call out to Colton, then must have thought better of it. Faint sounds within seemed conclusive enough of his safety, with bar stool legs rattling and scraping the floor as Colton wove through them. Hopefully the regular drunks did a better job back when. A moment later he crouched and stepped back out on the sidewalk.

"Finders keepers," he said. He shook an aluminum baseball bat in his hand. Somebody had written PEACEMAKER with black marker down the barrel. "It was under the bar. The cigarette machine was cleaned out, though. The liquor too. Damn, I could really use a smoke."

Nora frowned. Would someone collect booze from an evacuated city? Who would even authenticate it?

She'd never bought into the fascination with the "Kill Zone." Whatever the government learned about life and death here, she doubted they would disclose anything profound anyway. It didn't bear thinking about. She had been twelve when Agent Orange laid siege to Sandalwood in 1996. The news reports disturbed her, but the threat seemed more or less contained after that, particularly when they added Westing to the walled-off territory. No news outlets would have reported much of anything about the place for years if not for the illegal cottage industries that sprang up around it, and the reckless people who risked life and limb to get in. She'd only expected its reality to intersect with hers through some criminal case down the line, one where she'd have to scrounge up the enthusiasm that came much more naturally to her when someone didn't plot around so many obstacles to willingly throw themselves in harm's way.

But now here she was herself, through no intent of her own.

"Good find," she said finally. "Let's see about this car."

They made their way down the block to the vehicle, a mostly red Oldsmobile.

"So he'll trap a mailbox but not this?" Lee said. He'd made it to the car ahead of the others, but now he eased back until he stood the farthest from it.

"He could," Nora said. "But you said yourself, a car won't run now."

"Someone still wanted to get inside," Ward said. Someone had already taken out the driver's side window. Once again, glass fragments were missing.

Something else about it bothered her in a "what's wrong with this picture?" fashion, though she didn't think it was anything necessarily insidious.

Lee backed up another step. "Or Orange broke it open with someone's head."

Nora shrugged. "What's the black market for a pine air freshener from Morgan? People seem to collect all this other morbid shit, so why not that?"

"Whoa, Miguel!" Ward took a step toward the car, where Miguel inserted himself through the window to pull the sun visor.

Lee scoffed. "Dude, that's movie shit, no one on planet Earth has ever hidden their keys in—"

Keys jingled as they dropped into Miguel's hand. He turned around with a big smile.

"Podemos abrir la cajuela."

Nora turned to Ward, who translated, "The trunk."

Hernán stood behind the car. He held his hands up and Miguel tossed the keys to him.

"Ten cuidado," Ward said. "Él podría haber dejado algún tipo de trampa ahí."

"Did he just call the girl a tramp?" Lee asked Colton.

"I said he could have trapped the trunk."

The loose semi-circle of the gathered stepped farther back until they joined Lee's cautious orbit.

Hernán shrugged. He sat on the street and stretched out so he would be lower than the bumper, then turned the key and rolled away. The trunk groaned open. Nothing exploded or popped out to impale him. He raised his head up to see over the lid, and the tension fled his posture.

"¡Hay un arco y flechas adentro!" he said.

Ward walked around the car. "A bow and arrows?"

"¡También hay otras armas!"

Nora followed. Sure enough, the trunk held a quiver of arrows with a bow, but more than that—a crowbar, a knife, and a mallet. More than they could have hoped for, unless they'd needed a spare tire.

That was the thing that seemed incongruous to her before, Nora realized. The car didn't need a spare tire. Shouldn't this thing be sitting on all four rims after so many years of disuse?

"Wow," Colton said. "We got real lucky here."

Nora refrained from pointing out how being kidnapped and dumped in the Kill Zone ran contrary to any notion of good luck. They could already arm most of the group, and they had something that could cut.

"I doubt someone was just driving around with all this stuff thirty years ago," Ward said. "Look at the mallet."

He reached inside and withdrew it. While it looked like a typical item for a garage, someone had hammered spikes into the flat sides of the head.

"It's a weapon stash. He probably has them all over the place."

Everything looked to be in pristine condition without traces of blood, but why else would someone alter a mallet like that? It gave Nora an ominous feeling to know Orange had stood right here and might have used these very tools on human beings. He had a reason to come back here.

"Dude must not know that sun visor trick has been in a thousand movies since he went apeshit," Lee said.

Nora glared at him. "I'm thinking he's probably not much of a movie buff, no."

"Hey, let me take the bow," Colton said. "Someone else can take the bat."

So much for finders keepers.

He elaborated. "I did archery club in high school. I could slice the ass off a fly at thirty yards. Probably."

Ward conferred with Miguel, Juanita, Ernez, and Hernán, presumably about their prowess at slicing off fly asses at thirty yards. None of them seemed to care who wound up playing Robin Hood. Hernán held a hand out to Colton, who gave him the bat. Colton took the quiver from the trunk and slipped the strap over his head.

"I'd like the crowbar, if no one has any objections," Ward said, then repeated it in Spanish.

"Were you in crowbar club in high school?" Lee asked. "Gonna go all Jason Todd on a bitch?"

Ward's benevolent caregiver affect slipped slightly as hints of agitation crept in. "Jason *who*?"

"Nothing, man," he said. "Take the crowbar, that's all you."

Miguel took the mallet for both him and his sister, and Nora grabbed the knife. That left Lee and Ernez as the odd men out, but Ernez's group-within-a-group had a couple of options they could share.

Lee shrugged. "My weapon of choice is my guitar, and that's back in Grand Rapids."

Nora remembered her impression about having to carry his ass in a group project. Sometimes she hated to be right about people.

She walked closer to the car, peering inside. Not much to see but trash on the floorboards and upholstery shredded over the years by vermin filching building supplies. As fastidious as Orange seemed to be about maintaining the health of his weapons, she didn't think he would sabotage one of his caches. She reached through the emptied passenger side window and pulled open the glove compartment.

"¿Hay una pistola?" Hernán asked.

She didn't need Ward to translate that one. She shook

her head. While not empty, the glove compartment didn't offer much more than an owner's manual and a 1985 complimentary cassette from Oldsmobile featuring songs like Cyndi Lauper's "Time After Time," Michael Jackson and "Billie Jean," "Almost Paradise" by Mike Reno and Ann Wilson, along with Julio Iglesias, Beethoven, Mozart, among others.

"I thought they were building the wall by 1985," she said.

"New year models launch the prior fall," Colton said.

"Dang, brah only got to enjoy his ride a month or two before they booted everyone's ass out. Talk about depreciation. Hey, any Police or Boston on that tape?" Lee asked.

She stuck it all back inside and shut the compartment. "I was looking for maps. We need to figure out which way to go."

"Aren't we going to hit the wall no matter what?" Colton asked. "The whole town's closed in."

"He won't go near the wall, either," Lee said.

"Right. We're home-free if we get there."

"Okay, how did he break out and invade Sandalwood if he stays away from the wall?" Nora countered.

"They have guards now," Colton said.

"They had guards then too."

Lee straightened his headband. "That was different." He didn't clarify how it was, and Nora knew he couldn't.

"I'm not arguing we need to get to the wall, but we want the fastest way that also gives us the best chance. Isn't there a lake or river around here?"

"Yes," Ward said. "By Morgan Falls."

"That means we could walk for hours just to find miles of water we can't get across, with the wall way on the other side. And even if we could get across, why would they post guards with such a natural obstacle? It's all for nothing if we can't find an outpost." She shook her head. "Christ, getting arrested might be the best case scenario here."

"We could call from a Chicken Exit," Lee said, swiveling his head as if they might have overlooked one of the gaudy stations. "They're supposed to be all over this mug."

"That's great, if they still work. We'll try one out. But we need a contingency if they don't. I bet we can find a map in one of these shops."

She waited for him to ask why the hell wouldn't the Chicken Exit phones work, but he said, "Hey, whatever. I'm all for anything where we don't stand around waiting for him to kill us. Let's find your map and go."

II.

SPLITTING UP NEVER worked out too well in movies with a killer on the loose, but with time of the essence, they paired off to check out the businesses on the street which offered an easy way in due to shattered doors and windows or prior forced entry from the vultures who looted the Kill Zone. The majority looked to be open to the public, even with the public long evacuated. They were to stay in sight of one another's prospects with a plan to be in and out of each store in no more than a minute or two, since what they sought would hopefully be hung on a wall or stuffed in a spinning rack.

"Watch for traps," Ward warned. "Cuidado con las trampas. Podrían estar en cualquier lugar."

Once Ward filled everybody in, Nora partnered with him, Lee with Colton, brother Miguel with sister Juanita, and Hernán with Ernez. Ward and Nora agreed to trade so one of them was always stationed to peek out front every few seconds to verify Agent Orange hadn't shown up. With each fruitless search, Nora's anxiety soared with the certainty they'd already been here too long, they were all going to die and it was her fault for not just flipping a coin and choosing a compass point.

Nora and Ward went into a framing shop where they found an empty spot for a painting advertising a local artist named Ginny Steel. It fit the idea of a lost place. Maybe she painted landscapes of Morgan from memory in the post-evac years.

A travel agency gave them hope, but the maps inside only proved continental.

They leap-frogged to the next empty spot each time,

hoping someone would announce success elsewhere. The possibility of the sirens portending an Agent Orange escape felt more remote as the minutes mounted. They'd not heard the crack of rifles or heavier artillery. Maybe it only signaled him back to the downtown area where their abductors wanted him to mop up the new guests.

"I hope we haven't been here too long already," Nora said. They bypassed a barbershop with Colton and Lee scoping out opposite walls. Across the street, Miguel and Juanita emerged from a tobacco store, shaking their heads.

"I know," Ward said. "There's a lot of square miles in the walls, though. He could be hours away."

"He was already hours away when I woke up yesterday. A couple *time zones* away. I liked that a lot better. Where were you?"

"Cleveland. They must have got me at work." He shook his head. "It's so weird not to remember it. Makes all this seem less real."

Nora thought of her usual response when someone asked her first memory: *I don't remember.* An absurd reply, but how could she say for sure in the jumble of images and moments she recalled from early childhood? Fleeting consciousness and sensations. Maybe that should make life feel less real, to get such a finite time and forget so much of it. Terror had a way of imprinting a time and place.

"Who do you have to get back to?" Ward asked.

"My mom. My cat. Friends. My life. You?"

"Most of my family passed years ago. I thought maybe that was why I was here. They'll definitely notice when I don't clock in for work, though."

They found themselves back in front of the shop where the mannequin scalps hung crookedly. Probably the only humanoid victims who kept their ears in Morgan. She couldn't conceive of taking the same knife she now held in her hand to remove those from a human being. How did someone ever cross that line?

Ward continued. "I haven't asked, but if some of Miguel's group just crossed the border, they could have been traveling light. Maybe that's why they don't have clothes like we do." He sighed despairingly over his parachute pants. "I think Ernez has been in the States awhile, but it'd be easy for those other three to disappear."

"I can think of one way it will be hard for us to disappear," Nora said. "These loud clothes they stuffed us in. Why else would they do that?"

Ward groaned. "I don't want to think about it."

She studied the sky before she ended up focused on the totem pole and lamppost again. Cirrus clouds shielded a hazy morning sun. On the other horizon, the jagged purple teeth of mountains in the distance.

"Five more minutes," she said, "then let's just choose a way and hope for the best. Maybe not west with those mountains. I doubt they'd put an outpost there. If the Stalkers haven't yanked up all the signs, we can figure out where the lake is and change course if we have to."

Ward smiled faintly. "I think they call them Prowlers now. They're not the ones who loot everything."

"Anybody who wants inside these walls seems ghoulish enough to me."

They crossed the street to a store called Best Buds. The front glass had been shattered, and the door pulled open when Ward tested it.

"It looks like they just sold flowers here," he said. "Why would someone break in?"

"Maybe someone got desperate on Mother's Day."

Somehow the store carried a faint scent of its former glory, although most of the inventory had withered to brown husks apart from plastic flowers arranged in vases. It seemed strange to her that husks would still be here after so many years. Nothing hung on the walls. She made her way behind the counter.

"Come on," she said. "If they did any deliveries, wouldn't they need a map?"

"You'd think." Ward leaned through the empty storefront to check up and down the street. "Still clear. Thumbs down from Hernán and Ernez."

She chewed her lip. "Maybe they only kept it in their van or . . . "

Nora could see the back corner case where she stood. The colors stood out with so much withered and rotted inside. She found herself drawn to it, stepping through the rubble of shattered pots. Clay shards crackled and broke under her shoes.

"What do you see?" Ward called.

"You won't believe it," she said.

"On my way. Be careful."

She wasn't, really, drifting down the aisle like a sleepwalker. She passed baskets and bouquets filled with remnants of withered decay. The floral scent seemed unlikely before, something she shrugged off because the store had been closed up for decades. Except Ward just leaned through the empty front, so how could it have preserved this olfactory stasis?

She told herself the flowers were fake like some of the others in the store, but she knew better. Roses and tulips thrived in the spotlight of the sun, red, yellow, purple, pink and fragrant through the broken glass of the case. They couldn't have been here all this time, could they? Anyone who broke in would have taken them. She didn't believe for a minute they had been cultivated by a certain morbid florist.

She flashed back to the Oldsmobile tires. Maybe someone inflated them recently, but she could think of no logical reason why they would. Were there such resistances to entropy hiding in all the nooks and crannies of this place largely unknown for any purpose but death?

"Oh, wow," Ward said. "How . . . "

"I have no idea."

"Do you think if you took them back home they'd . . . " He paused to consider a suitable word. "Keep?"

"I doubt it." She was tempted to find out, but they wouldn't be allowed to take anything out of here anyway. She'd rather it stay preserved in here, rather than turned over to military scientists prepared to kill something to isolate its magic. She preferred chrysanthemums anyway.

"Life and death are a little different around here," Ward said. "I've read a few things on the forums. I'm sure ninety-nine percent of it is lies or delusions, but even a single percent would be . . . life-altering." He laughed a little. "Maybe death-altering, too."

"Hey, guys!"

They both jumped as Colton rushed through the front with Lee on his heels. The bow hung off his shoulder.

"Check out what we found," he said. He held up a white square slip of paper.

Ward accepted it, frowned, and passed it to Nora. It was a business card. It read:

GARY'S GUNS & AMMO
GARY FOSTER, GUNSMITH
Gun repair, modifications, and special orders.
"We aim to please."

A phone number and address were printed in the lower right corner.

"Found it on the barbershop wall," Lee said.

"Okay," Nora said. "I'm failing to see the relevance."

"The rele—" Colton looked off as if for commiseration from an invisible audience when Lee didn't seem appropriately irate. "There's an arsenal somewhere nearby. I mean, your knife looks pretty sharp and all, but we need an equalizing force if we can get one, don't you think?"

"It'd probably take a nuke to be equal with him," Ward muttered.

Nora handed the business card back. "It sounds good

in theory, but we don't know where 331 Fraser Trail is."

"No, not yet." Colton pockcted the card. "The guy probably gets his hair cut in that shop, though. It could be half a mile away."

"If it is, it's probably cleaned out, maybe by Gary himself," Ward said. "And if there's anything left, what are the odds it still works?"

"I like them just fine." Colton nodded to the roses and tulips. "Those don't seem to be doing half-bad."

"I'm going back out," Lee announced. He narrowed his eyes suspiciously at the corner case. "Man, fuck those zombie flowers."

As he turned away, Miguel and Juanita ran across the street, waving their hands. The latter called, "¡Encontramos un mapa al otro lado de la calle, en el consultorio del doctor!"

"Please tell me it's good news," Nora said, hoping *mapa* meant what she thought it did and nothing to do with "Orange."

"Better. They found a map."

She looked back at the roses as they walked out. Maybe it meant nothing and she didn't believe in omens, but she'd take what she could get today, particularly life flourishing in the shadow of so much death.

III.

MIGUEL AND JUANITA led them to a building with the sign PROMPT CARE. No surprise someone smashed their way into there, if there was any chance of drugs on the premises. Nora had to credit Miguel and Juanita for persevering once they opened the door out of the waiting room. Not only did the hallway to the exam rooms become ominously dark with only hints of sunlight under the doors, but the air became rank. Nausea stirred in her belly, and it grew worse the closer they came to an open door toward the end of a curving corridor.

Ward coughed. "¿Qué es esa peste?"

"Es exactamente lo que crees que es," Miguel said. "Hay algo muerto ahí dentro. Piezas."

Nora pulled her shirt collar up over her nose.

"I think I liked it better when we didn't have a map," Colton said, gagging.

They stepped into an exam room. There was more than one map inside. Of most use to them was the one on the wall for the Morgan and Morgan Falls area, and part of Sandalwood. An odd decorative choice, but maybe someone decided it would be engaging in a more neutral way than laminated informational pages on the walls elsewhere about the dangers of smoking and the signs of diabetes and heart disease. Perhaps the other exam rooms offered such quaint touches.

The second map came in the form of an anatomical model in the corner. It presented a transparent view of half the anatomy of a human body, a rubber composite of muscles, arteries, veins, and organs encased in plastic. It seemed cartoonish after all the real displays of anatomy ornamenting the streets of downtown Morgan, but it wasn't all so artificial after all. That was the source of the stomach-churning reek. Agent Orange had popped open the plastic casing and where there had been sensible parts for the small and large intestines that neatly filled the spaces like building blocks, he had tossed them out and replaced them with someone's extricated bowels. The switch hadn't been recent, with the tubes taking on a more runny consistency, through which maggots writhed behind the plastic like an ant farm of putrefaction. Nora noticed a disposal bin within reach, and promptly flipped up the top and explosively hurled her own insides.

"That is so wrong," Lee said, muffled under his shirt.

Colton turned his back to it. "How could he even know someone would see that?"

"There's probably fifty of those for every one found," Ward said. "Same with the traps." He seemed to be handling the conditions better, perhaps well-served as a veteran of hospital employment.

"Let's take it," Nora said, her stomach still quivering. She held her breath as she reached for the frame of the map. Ward grabbed the other side and they walked it into the hallway. Someone mercifully closed the door behind them.

Nora led them back down the hallway until they were near the lobby door. She opened one of the first exam room doors and they went inside. The others filed in until the room filled up too much, and the rest watched from the doorway.

No map in here, but there were pictures of places from around town. The Morgan Lake Marina. An advertisement for the Morgan Falls campgrounds, featuring a collage of smiling camp counselors, kids at play, cabins, and a campfire gathering. An idyllic picture of boats drifting on a lake. A cascading waterfall, presumably *the* Morgan Falls. A smiling woman in a flowery dress and a wide-brimmed sunhat cutting a ribbon at the "gala" grand opening of the Owl Creek Department Store. The Morgan Falls Lodge where "You'll Lose Your Heart." The Morgan Water Park. Clearly, the Morgan Chamber of Commerce left no stone unturned in their effort to make this the area's top tourist destination. Another picture, this one the Morgan Gem Mine, so, literally, no stone unturned.

The rot hadn't permeated the air here, and she hoped they would have a little sound cover for what had to happen next.

"Okay, let it drop," she said. "Watch your feet."

The frame hit the floor and the glass shattered, sprinkling over the tiled floor. The whole thing didn't break apart, but enough broke away to tear the map from the frame. They spread it out on the exam table.

"Does anyone see an address for this place?" Nora asked.

Colton plucked a sheet of paper from a bin mounted to the door. "It says 1475 Gardner Lane."

Nora scanned the map.

"There." Ward pointed at the page.

"I knew it," Colton said, tapping another spot on the map. "There's Fraser. It's not even half a finger from Gardner." He tapped it again. "There could be a shitload of guns sitting there right now!"

Nora prepared to disappoint him, but to her surprise, the layout didn't undermine the possibility of dropping in. Its eastern trajectory led them away both from the mountains and the lake area too. Circumventing the lake would bring them toward Sandalwood and Westing, where they were only likely to find remnants of the original Morgan wall, forsaken since the prior expansions. East could take them to a currently monitored stretch of wall. With a little luck, they'd happen on one of the outposts and see about arranging evacuation.

The Army might have a lot of questions for them, but

that was okay. Nora had a lot of questions for the government, too. They'd probably disappoint each other.

"Okay," she said, tracing the route. "We take Gardner to Main, then branch off to Spring. We'll pick up Fraser there."

"Looks kind of remote," Ward said. "Smack dab in the woods."

"*Good,*" Colton said. "No one's busting in if they can't find it."

Ernez explained the plan to Miguel, Juanita, and Hernán. "We are all good," he said at last.

Nora exhaled and began folding the map. "Okay, let's get the hell out of here."

IV.

HER FATHER BELIEVED in winning. As an adult she realized he was an unapologetic frontrunner—his favorite team was whoever suddenly got good and won championships. The Lakers and Celtics in the Eighties, the Bulls and Cowboys in the Nineties, the Patriots and the Lakers again in the Aughts. He would proclaim his former favorites "sucked" when the pendulum swung back. "The next champion, that's my fave," he would joke. The way he saw it, if the players could defect to better situations, why couldn't he? He never offered the cliché about how it didn't matter if you won or lost, only how you played the game. In his mind, you lost the game because of how you played, and that was the bottom line.

She played basketball for one year in high school on a team that won twice more than it lost and took a first-round exit in the postseason to a team with two losses all season. She always wondered if her dad defaulted to privately supporting that other team, the established winners. He loved an underdog, sure . . . but only when said underdog won it all. Not when it held its own in a losing effort, which Nora's team really hadn't done anyway.

This preyed on her a little when she entered law, lingering after he passed away from an embolism. Compromise felt like agreeing to a tie, and she had a fierce desire to win. She knew it wasn't always possible, but Christ, OJ Simpson—practically caught red-handed—walked, so it always *seemed* possible. Trip up that one expert witness, decline the most fatal jury members, introduce that reasonable doubt. Win, repeat. This artificiality felt infinitely preferable to the pressure of life and death stakes, and the cosmic ramifications of every decision. Even the winning came with its sleepless nights—was that a would-be rapist or killer back on the street? She made her peace with it, then often had cause to reconsider.

The other night, she received word that someone serving prison time in a case she put in her "loss" category took a shiv to his left kidney five times. She rolled the dice on that one, rejected a plea because she thought she could win outright. Had he been innocent? Probably not. But was she herself? That plea might have put him in a lower security facility, away from the sort of people who punctured someone's organs in a lunch line. Yet, it paid off other times when she or a client turned down an offer. She didn't want to think about it, or the little voice that said this dark night of the soul probably wouldn't crack the top ten when all was said and done. It took a few glasses of wine before sleep to not feel like she sucked.

Now, life and death stakes again, this time for herself. It made ironic sense to wake up here, in her own prison with someone who could get pretty stabby himself. Successfully negotiating her way out of here wouldn't definitively prove anything to herself about if she'd previously made the right decisions, though.

It did not take the group long to depart downtown. A place like Morgan might have expanded its points of commerce like a lot of compact areas over the past couple decades, but at the time of Richard Dunbar's mayhem, a bustling metropolis it was not. Main Street cut through the middle for a couple blocks, then fed them to Spring Street. They soon left behind the concrete and brick buildings for rural territory.

They did see a Chicken Exit on Main, marked #9, but the excitement faded when they discovered the phone cord ripped out of the box.

"What a stupid design," Ward said. "He could disable all of these things."

Nora wasn't convinced Agent Orange did the sabotaging, but kept it to herself. Whoever dumped them here wouldn't want them calling for rescue if the comms people didn't know about the operation. Maybe that was a good sign, in a way.

Within ten minutes of leaving Prompt Care they passed a co-op, a lawnmower repair shop, and a fruit and vegetable market with the woods behind them encroaching on the lots, as if to swallow them

While their rural migration initially reduced the proliferation of carnage displays, they soon encountered staked heads on the roadside, and a couple of bodies cinched to telephone poles with barbed wire. The chest cavity of one briefly stirred until a buzzard squawked and tore something long and stretchy off the body. The expressions of both cadavers hinted at a glimpse of pure hell. Bloody divots in place of ears.

"Where do you think they came from?" Colton asked.

"Maybe someone brought them here like us," Nora said, "but people are crazy enough to come in here on their own."

"Wish they'd done us a solid and left a note on how they got in this bitch," Lee said.

Colton nodded. "For real."

"What good would that do us?" Nora asked.

"What do you mean, what? We'd blow this popsicle stand through their hidden entrances."

"I'm sure the people who arranged our little trip would just love that."

"Those people can eat me. We get out, we win."

"It's not that easy. Dumbasses break in here all the time. Agent Orange isn't getting bored, but they specifically brought us here to die anyway."

"You don't know that," Lee said. "I just play music, man, that's it. There's no reason for anyone to want me dead."

Nora didn't ask him to sing a couple bars just to make sure.

"I don't really want to think about it," Ward said quietly. "I just want to get out. If we do that and drop it, why should they care? None of us saw anything."

"I don't want to drop it," Nora said. "They're trying to kill us."

"You don't even know who *they* are. If we do see them, there's not going to be any story to tell. They'll shred us in about two seconds."

"Screw all this conspiracy shit," Colton said. "Ten gets you twenty, it's just dark web snuff TV. Rich old perverts."

Nora let it lie. They were miles from the possibility of escape, and she might as well be worrying about the check engine light on her car back home.

Colton took a test shot with the bow at a telephone pole. He missed to the left. "The sight's a little messed up," he said. "I can adjust for it."

He picked up that arrow and fired it a second time. True to his word, this one hit the pole. He gave them a satisfied look, the high school archery savant.

The sirens began within sight of the turn-off for Fraser, which had maintained its street sign. A dubious omen. Out here the sirens were louder, churning the hot ball of worry in Nora's guts. She could never quite forget the inhuman danger thanks to the extensive decorations he'd left behind, but the sirens weren't his doing, and they made him seem more imminent. How many more times would they hear it before it stopped being a drill?

"Are we sure about this?" Ward asked. "It's a gravel road."

Ernez said, "If only one gun, still worth it."

"If we cut through the woods off Fraser, we'll also get to the wall faster," Nora said. "We might as well try it."

Lee, Miguel, Juanita, Hernán, and Ernez were already trudging up the road, following its rightward curve. Juanita held the mallet now, maybe taking turns with her brother. Hernán choked up on the bat, which he'd held by his side before the sirens kicked up again. Colton nocked an arrow in his bow, studying the woods.

They hurried their pace noticeably on Fraser until the sirens quit again. After a moment, the birds returned to their activities in the trees and the urgency diminished. Nora kept her knife in hand, but relaxed the grip. Colton withdrew the arrow.

Fraser ran parallel to Spring Street after the curve smoothed out. The woods pushed in closer here, perhaps emphasizing why this was considered a "trail" rather than lane or street.

"Is there anything else on Fraser besides the guns?" Ward asked, when after five minutes they hadn't seen any break in all the trees and brush. No houses, no businesses. It felt creepy and isolated.

"Maybe not," Nora said. "I didn't see an outlet on the map."

This would usually result in a dead end sign, but Nora figured that had to be one of the most highly sought signs from the Kill Zone. Maximum irony.

Ward traded the crowbar to his left hand. "It can't be much farther, can it?"

At some point they would need to find water to help make their push to the wall. Nora already felt her shirt sticking to her back, despite a tempt somewhere in the fifties and plenty of shade on this road. A dehydration headache had begun to stir at her temples. Throwing up at the urgent care had started to take its toll.

"Hey!" Miguel suddenly said, pointing to the left. He stepped between two trees, arm outstretched.

"Oh snap," Lee said. "I see—"

Something else *snapped* almost in tandem, followed by a whoosh with respondent thumps and cracks. Miguel dropped to the ground, screaming, every bit as loud as the sirens. His sister ran to him. Red splotches appeared over the kneecaps and shins of Miguel's jeans. Something poked out in a couple of places. Nora thought it was bone at first.

When he plunged into the green, he'd tripped some kind of lever at shin level. A grid of pointy wooden daggers sprang out and hit him right in the knees. A couple went with him when he fell back, like embedded shark's teeth. They punctured his kneecaps, maybe his tibias too.

"What the hell happened?" Ward asked. "Why'd he leave the road?"

Lee pointed. "That tree."

Nora followed his fingertip to a beech tree with a notch in the trunk. "Is that a hatchet?"

"It looks like it," Colton said.

Juanita spoke urgently to her brother. Nora heard the word *silencio*. Miguel, tears streaming down his face and spittle flying, shouted a long stream of words including *puta* before lapsing back into his anguished cries.

"He's, uh, in a lot of pain," Ward translated.

Ernez sidestepped the spikes, pushing into the trees.

"Careful! There could be more traps."

"Brah's being way too loud," Lee said between Miguel's screams. "They can probably hear him in Westing."

On the verge of panicking herself at the volume, Nora snapped, "What do you want us to do, shoot him?"

Ernez picked up a twig and placed it between Miguel's teeth. The screaming transitioned to loud, but far more manageable grunts. Orange would have to be a lot closer to hear those.

Ernez gingerly made his way back to the beech tree. He reached inside and just as quickly yanked his hand back, waiting for something to snap shut on him. He turned back and shrugged, then grabbed again.

Had they won? Did they stop the screaming before it alerted Orange to their position? She wondered if her dad considered the killer the ultimate winner. Always coming back, adding to the body count in his endless game.

"A fake," Ernez reported as he returned to the gravel road. He handed the hatchet to Ward.

"Shit." Ward threw it to the ground. "Rubber. Looks like he spray painted the head silver."

Lee's mouth gaped. "A rubber hatchet? Did kids not have fucking GI Joe back then?"

"El hacha ni siquiera era real. Caíste por un juguete de goma," Ernez said to Miguel.

Miguel's grimace turned into atomic rage for a flash, and his teeth sank deeper into the twig. Pain took the reins back in a couple of seconds. He writhed on the ground, grabbing his sister's hand, causing her to grimace in a similar fashion.

"What do we do?" Nora asked.

"He can't walk," Ward said.

"And we can't stay here."

"¡No puedes abandonarnos!" Juanita cried.

"No vamos a abandonar a nadie," Ward said. "Lo prometo."

Ward said. Whatever it meant, Juanita looked calmer afterward. She worked her belt out of the loops on her jeans, cinching it around Miguel's thigh as a tourniquet for one leg.

"He could put arms around two persons and walk with them," Ernez said. He demonstrated a scarecrow pose or a ghost with palsy.

Ward nodded. "That could work."

Lee looked unhappy about it, probably anticipating he would be one of the first shoulders to lean on since he had no weapon. Not suited for group work yet again.

"Dude, crutches!" he said. "I saw some at the urgent care."

Nora said, "Ward, do you think he could get by on his own with those?"

"I mean, even draped on two people, he still has to walk a little."

"We can't do that all day. It'll take forever to get to the wall. And if *he* shows up, that's three people who aren't ready to fight. We need everyone with a weapon, or there's no chance."

"There was a wheelchair too," Lee added. "He could wheel himself if we stuck to the road. I bet they had pain pills and bandages and shit."

"Pain pills from the Eighties wouldn't help a paper cut. We need that other stuff, though."

"But what about the gunsmith?" Colton asked.

"We have to get Miguel help," Nora said. The headache had begun to throb, stress accelerating the discomfort of dehydration. "The urgent care is fifteen minutes away. The gunsmith might be another two miles."

"Couldn't we make something to carry him with sticks, and just go on to the gunsmith?" Colton said. "You know, like how you'd make a raft?"

"A twig gurney?" Lee said doubtfully.

"Like a stretcher."

Lee backed away as if Colton's suggestions were contagious.

A conversation between Ernez and Hernán further derailed the absurd line of inquiry, since Orange would have all their heads staked before they'd even gathered up enough sticks. Nora watched the new exchange with rapt attention, as if an intense enough focus could overcome the language barrier.

Ernez said, "Tú continúa por la carretera, ve qué puedes encontrar en la tienda de armas. Si eres lo suficientemente rápido, puedes reunirte con nosotros de nuevo antes de que lleguemos a la carretera principal. Tendremos que ir despacio por Miguel."

Hernán nodded. "Cuida tus espaldas. No confío en el de la bandana."

"Él dice que es músico . . . así que probablemente tengas razón." Ernez turned back to the others. "Hernán will go to the guns. He can bring back to clinic."

"Wait a minute," Colton said. "We can't send one little guy up there if there's all kinds of guns. I should go too."

"Jesus, Colton, how many guns do you think you'll need?" Nora asked.

"Every one I can get my hands on."

"Forget it. The whole place could be cleaned out, and if there's anything left, I'm sure Hernán can figure out how to bring enough back to us. We need you. We can't lose any more weapons."

"Maybe they got some souped-up wheelchair at the gunsmith that fires missiles and shit," Colton said. "And we're turning away from it."

"Come on, Earnes," Lee said, tugging at Ernez's wrist and drawing him away. "We'll take the point. You know what that is?"

Ernez went with no objection, not correcting Lee about his name, though he shared a look with Hernán Nora couldn't read.

Ward and Hernán went back and forth a couple times before Hernán nodded and started jogging up the road. He disappeared around the bend in seconds.

The fifteen minute walk to the clinic accounted for eight able-bodied people. The way things were now, Hernán might get back with Gary Foster's guns or confirmation of their absence before Nora's group reached their destination.

Colton stared unhappily at the empty road Hernán left behind. "Hey, what if he finds a stockpile and doesn't come back?"

"Why," Nora said, "is that what you'd do?"

"Of course not," Colton said. "But someone should have gone with him."

Ward sighed, watching Lee and Ernez wander away

from the group. "Well, I guess Lee volunteered *not* to help out with Miguel." He went over to where the siblings sat on the road.

Nora cursed the unfairness of the last two and a half minutes. The path to freedom grew more miles by the second with her intended shortcut through the woods now off the table. They'd have to stick to the roads. Even with a wheelchair for Miguel, how quickly could they travel to an outpost? This morning sun might be sinking behind the mountains by the time they made it to the wall. If they even did. She couldn't fathom the Kill Zone under the cover of darkness. No, not an option.

Escaping it, though, wouldn't that be like the ultimate win? She'd love to be able to tell her dad about that one. Whatever ills had befallen them thus far, an hour inside with no Orange called to mind the old saying about any landing you could walk away from being a good one.

On behalf of someone less able to walk away from any landing, Ward grunted as he and Juanita boosted Miguel to his feet, his arms draped around both their necks. He'd spit out the stick, now groaning miserably but not alarmingly loud. Ward held the crowbar like a cane as they pushed back the way they'd come. Juanita held the mallet in her left hand.

Ward must have caught the look on Nora's face. "I'll be ready if anything happens," he said.

"We all need to be ready to circle him and take him down," she said. "It will work."

It would of course have worked better with five armed people laying into him, even if Hernán just smashed his legs with that bat. If Orange could die, he could break.

"I can turn him into a porcupine before he's twenty yards away," Colton said. He carried the bow by the grip, twirling an arrow in the fingers of his other hand

"Just get his legs if you can," she said. "If he's like Miguel, he can't catch us."

For all she knew, he could just regrow snapped tendons and broken bones, but it wouldn't be instantaneously. Not even those silly *Kill Zone Bloodbath* movies or whatever they were called tried to perpetuate such a myth. Maybe that had changed, though. Weren't they trying to switch things up with the next one and throw him in a winter setting? What next? Outer space?

The Juanita, Miguel, and Ward threesome advanced lopsidedly, with Ward hunched a little to make up for a height disparity. He had about six inches on both the siblings. Miguel could set one of his feet down to help propel them forward, usually with hissing intakes of breath.

"Ward, please tell her if anything happens . . . just be ready." She didn't want him to say Juanita should drop her brother like a bad habit and heft the mallet, but she thought it, for sure. The quicker Juanita did that, the more likely she'd get the chance to pick him back up. Ward passed along some version of the message.

Fraser Trail ran crookedly, never allowing a long look down the road before it disappeared around a bend. Lee and Ernez were a good twenty yards ahead. Nora tried to wave them back, but Lee only returned the wave to signal everything was fine up ahead. She figured he did it on purpose.

Nora swallowed with a dry throat. She felt a bit leery about drinking water from Morgan now, but knew in another hour she wouldn't care if she had to scoop it up with an animal skull. The water was probably safer to drink here than back in her own state anyway, with no factories around for miles to dump their waste.

Colton's head shifted side to side, another arrow nocked in his bow. He kept it pointed at the ground. He and Nora tried to keep pace with the trio, though impatience inevitably put them a few steps ahead until they backed up or paused.

NORA

After a few minutes of walking in silence apart from Juanita and Ward encouraging Miguel, Ward said, "Nice of him not to set up all his heads on this road."

Nora and Colton mumbled their assent. She hadn't thought about it until he said it, but she didn't find it as reassuring. There might be several roads like this throughout the three towns, but she worried he did it to encourage people to seek it out. Maybe just for the trap that hit Miguel, but maybe something worse at the gunsmith. She couldn't help feeling like they'd seen the last of Hernán.

Within sight of the curve that would take them back to Spring Street, where Lee and Ernez had almost slipped past the bend and out of sight, Ward said, "I might need to rest."

A boulder sat by the road side here, bulky with a flat face better for leaning than sitting. He and Juanita maneuvered so they could lay Miguel against it. Ward leaned his crowbar against the side of the rock and did windmills with his arms. Juanita rubbed her shoulders.

Lee and Ernez had paused now that they'd looked back to find the caravan stalled. They didn't make any move to reunite.

"Those two really need to come back and take a shift," Ward grumbled.

Despair settled on Nora's shoulders. They were moving *so slow.* Cruel as it was to admit, they would have been better off if that trap hit Miguel in the chest. Whether the screams alerted Agent Orange or it slowed down a group enough for him to catch up later, it was win/win for him.

"Can you keep carrying him?" Nora asked. "Can she?"

Ward sighed. "I wouldn't say no if Colton wanted to switch out."

"Sorry, dude," Colton said, "but I need to be able to command the bow and be the MVP here."

The word "command" implied to Nora that he'd

prepared this excuse for the eventuality of being asked to help. "MVP" confirmed it.

Ward started to say, "Colton, at some point, you're going to have to—"

The sudden burst of sounds shut him up. Nora barely had time to form the hope that Hernán or Lee and Ernez were responsible. Branches snapped and rustled as something bulky strafed through the woods beside them. The size and intent were unmistakable, and a chill extinguished the warmth of their prior exertion.

"Colton, get ready!" Nora backpedaled from the roadside to get out of Colton's way and stand with the others.

Colton's arm trembled as he drew the bowstring.

"Take out his legs!" Nora said.

"¡Apunta a sus piernas!" Ward told Juanita. He held his crowbar like a ball bat.

Juanita and Nora raised their weapons.

"Circle him and hit him from all sides," Nora said, regurgitating the talking points of attack in her mind from the past hour, though the actual meaning of the words suddenly seemed nebulous.

Miguel slumped against the boulder, looking around frantically. He said something to Juanita that she replied to without turning back.

Agent Orange appeared in flashes, like something too horrifying to be allowed its true form at first—a hint of camouflage here, the rubber of a gasmask there, the black of a glove here, the withered flesh of severed ears there. He charged through the brush like a bull, snapping through limbs, his boots rapidly thudding as if synchronized with their heartbeats.

Colton fired into the brush when enough of a visible moving target presented itself. Whether he intended to go low or not, the arrow zipped past Orange's mask and out of sight, perhaps to slice off a fly's ass about twenty yards deeper in. He cursed and slipped out another arrow, awkwardly trying to line up the bow with the nock. He still had a shot at MVP, but it was looking more like Most Vulnerable Prey for the self-proclaimed archery expert.

Nora felt unexpected awe, like seeing a flying saucer at close range on a sunny afternoon, this massive artifact of something unknown and unknowable. Orange burst free from the woods, hulking and faceless but for the rubber and plate of a gas mask the necklace of ears bouncing off his chest. Larger than life, profounder than death, yet also its undead embodiment. A machete holster hung off his waist, but he carried nothing. Colton's second shot skipped off the gravel.

She glanced down Fraser Trail, hoping Lee and Ernez would be charging back to play cavalry, but instead she saw flashes of red, white, lime, and yellow as they disappeared into the embrace of the woods. Though they were unarmed, she felt a pang of disappointment at their abandonment. She, Ward, Colton, and Juanita were on their own.

"Get around him!" Nora said.

They spread out uncertainly, Nora and Juanita on one flank, Ward the other. Orange had no uncertainty, running straight at Colton in the middle of the line. Maybe he didn't like seeing someone else playing with his toy, or maybe he prioritized him for the sin of attacking him. Colton backpedaled, fumbling the bow, hands raised in placation. Miguel screamed behind him.

Ward seized the peak attack opportunity. He lunged with the crowbar like someone on a boat trying to spear a shark as Orange blew past. It would have drilled his kneecap if Orange didn't simply take the crowbar from Ward like a relay baton. In one fluid motion he jammed it into the soft flesh of Colton's throat past his chin. The crowbar speared Colton's head claw-first, bone crunching until the bar popped out antenna-like in a burst of blood and brain, lifting the Marlboro hat. Colton's arms dropped to his sides and his eyes rolled back. Orange cranked the hook end of the crowbar, driving the bar up through Colton's face on one side while the claw end reciprocally cleaved the back of his head until the whole thing popped free, laying a huge divot through the middle of his skull. The wedges of Colton's head flopped apart in an uneven V shape, and dislodged cranial contents slapped the gravel ground as he tipped over on his quiver.

Juanita abandoned the plan and swung the mallet at Orange's head, going for a kill shot that had as much of a chance of resurrecting Colton as it did putting down the killer. Nora ran at the backs of his legs, looking to cut him. He ducked the mallet and hacked at Juanita with the crowbar, letting it slide in his glove to find the right trajectory. Juanita's eyeball burst as the hook sank into her socket, and a yank on the bar ripped half her face from her skull by the zygomatic bone with a sharp crack. Juanita spun away from him, Miguel shrieking uselessly from the rock.

Orange vaulted at the boulder with Nora's blade inches from slicing his Achilles or the backs of his knees. He yanked Miguel off the rock and let him fall over on his face, Miguel's legs unable to support his weight. The crowbar swung back toward Nora, blood spattering her face. The hook passed beneath her chin and heat spread across her throat.

Ward scrambled to seize Juanita's mallet. Bones popped in his hand as Orange stomped it, and with his weight keeping the hand glued to the ground, Orange wrenched Ward's body up until the arm stretched to its full extent. The shoulder socket snapped and flesh ripped. A fan of blood erupted and the arm slumped to the ground, detached, fingers still wrapped around the mallet. Ward screamed.

Miguel crawled weakly toward his sister, and

something wet and warm coated Nora's palm as she clasped a hand over her throat.

Agent Orange pinned Ward to the ground with the crowbar, somehow possessing the strength to plant it through the flesh and bone of his sternum, then through gravel, and deep into the earth. Ward writhed around it like a pinned insect. The maniac grabbed the lost arm by the wrist and swung it overheard. It hammered against Ward's head in a barrage, cutting off his cries, a whip of bulky flesh and bone uncoiling and bludgeoning his face over and over as the pieces shattered beneath the force like a thin sheet of ice. Just like that, Nora wouldn't have recognized Ward if called to ID him, his cheekbones and maxillae collapsed into the fissure beaten into his face.

Nora sat down, lightheaded.

Orange tossed the severed arm away and returned to Miguel, who was almost within reach of his sister's body, sobbing. Orange grabbed him by the ankles, triggering a new outburst of screams as broken bones ground together. He swung Miguel up and overhead like a sack, slamming him on the boulder. Miguel's spine shattered instantly, an inverted L-shape with Miguel bent in half the wrong way.

A silence like a scream of its own filled Nora's ears. Blood soaked the front of her formerly yellow shirt. It squirted through the fingers locked over the groove the hook of the crowbar sliced into her flesh, as well as the throb of the severed artery against her thumb.

Orange turned to her, wiping spatters of blood off the plate of his gasmask. Somehow it reminded her of a man removing a condom after sex. He stooped to pick up the knife she hadn't known she'd lost, and came to her with the blade held forward, as if to ask if she dropped it.

She took her hand away to let her wound bleed unimpeded. She didn't want to be here for what happened next. He knelt beside her almost tenderly, though the touch of his sodden gloves in her hair felt blunt and impersonal.

The jagged teeth of the knife, so much like those mountains far from here to the west and beyond the wall, settled against the cartilage of Nora's ear. She tried to find the void that must be hovering nearby before he started cutting, wondering where he would place her in his menagerie.

HERNÁN

THE BAT ROSE and fell in Hernán Cortés's peripheral vision. He ran with a one-handed death grip on a purely defensive weapon. On the streets of Guatemala City the bat would give him confidence in most any fight, but on a gravel lane in the Kill Zone he might as well swing a stick at an approaching cyclone.

On the road ahead, a burnt-out military transport hinted at the fates of the better armed. The truck's front end had plunged into a trench dug into the gravel road, presumably hidden at the time and filled with a flammable substance set on fire by some mechanism if not Agent Orange himself. In blocking most of the road, it stood like a counterargument to Ward and Nora's strength in numbers theory. What chance did eight lightly armed people have against the man who could do this? Slower together? Yes. Safer together? No.

Hernán slowed to give the area around the decaying behemoth a good visual search. Miguel's fate still haunted his mind. It could happen in a blinding flash, his eyes on this and not the thing that could cripple him. Dividing his attention between the truck and the path ahead, he treaded cautiously.

Only the front end and cab were scorched. The military must have put out the fire or it burnt itself out before reaching the bed of the transport. All eight of the rear wheels were missing. The bare wheel hubs on the two axles showed signs of rust. This had been here awhile.

It took Miguel's unfortunate accident for the group to finally do something that made sense and send Hernán ahead. Hernán had a pretty good idea a search of the gun shop would yield no guns, but at least the entire slow-moving group wouldn't end up in a cul-de-sac with a lot of backtracking to do. Hernán didn't mind running ahead, in fact, he preferred being alone. He couldn't stand to see Miguel in his current state. The man already hated himself for what had happened to his sister during the dangerous trek from Honduras, but now Miguel had to wrestle with becoming a liability to Juanita's very survival. He couldn't walk on his own and Juanita would not abandon him.

Ward and Nora took charge of the group early. Hernán did not mind this so long as they made good decisions. Sticking around Morgan for a weapons search yielded results, but it also prolonged their time at ground zero. If someone dropped them in Morgan there had to be a reason. Hernán tried to voice his concern to Ward. Everyone thought the gun shop gambit was the smart thing to do. Now they had a crippled Miguel.

The can-do attitudes of Ward and Nora reminded him of the missionaries that came to the villages when Hernán was a child. Several times a year they arrived bearing gifts, building things, teaching their religion, but mostly carrying the pride of the place from which they'd come. They spread their philosophy of what works to a land where, for many reasons, things worked less well. Hernán was eleven when his friend Javier casually undercut the enthusiasm for an impending visit with, "You know the Americans want us to think like them, but they want us to stay where we are."

A short bypass lane carved into the forest allowed passage around the dead metal hulk and Hernán took this to continue his journey. He carefully watched his steps along the dirt path with only sparse gravel. Tire tracks were set in dried mud, the wide treads of a truck. Another print gave him pause, that of a boot. Hernán put his foot inside the massive footprint. It dwarfed his own.

Once on the road again he stayed at a brisk jog rather than a full-on run. Would he see changes in the gravel that might indicate a trap? He didn't know, but he kept a wary eye on the path ahead. He saw the same tire treads in the dust, but no other footprints and no sign of traps.

If Javier's comment planted the seed for missionary cynicism, Rosalynd fertilized the ground and made it bear fruit. A beautiful, blue-eyed blonde from a church in Iowa, Rosalynd came with her mission group in the fall of Hernán's eleventh year and he immediately took to her. Hernán proudly told her the story of his namesake, the great conquistador who vanquished the murderous Aztecs, ending their human sacrifices forever. Rosalynd recoiled. Cortés! *Mal hombre!* A killer! Cortés who danced across the ocean looking to plunder and rape. A song on her little Apple box helped prove her point. As they listened, each with one earbud, she would pause to translate and it saddened Hernán. If people wrote such songs was it not proof of her claim? That night Hernán quietly retreated from the campfire, hating the beautiful girl who'd so casually stripped him of the pride of his name. He didn't go back that week or ever again.

He passed a sign, one of the few he had seen. Ahead a vast open space with sporadic new growth trees signaled the end of the road. A parking lot, next to it a building constructed with conflicting materials of cinder block, multi-colored bricks, and logs. Bullet holes pockmarked the cinder block walls at the rear and side, some so clustered they had blasted chunks from the walls. A hodgepodge of shingles and metal sheeting atop the building looked like a hastily constructed repair job. Twin brick chimneys rose from the roof, one red brick, the other orange. Behind the building were stacks of orange bricks and a pile of creek rock.

The gravel road became a one-lane driveway and wound toward the woods to the left of the building. The drive ended where a larger structure, possibly a house, a garage, or the gun shop itself, had burnt to the ground. Here and there charred black pieces of wood or metal rose from the debris like scorched bones. Unlike the road to this place, weeds and saplings had overtaken the driveway.

Directly past the parking lot a mostly empty expanse stretched the length of several football fields. In the distance were several old targets, apparently part of a gun range. Midway through the field, three stakes with familiar bulbous decorations made Hernán recall the Aztecs. He once asked his mother why the Aztecs sacrificed so many people. She told him sometimes things happen that leaders don't understand or cannot control and in response, they often kill others as a means of hiding their own weakness. For the Aztecs the killings were sacrifices to the gods, for Nazis the genocides were sacrifices to genetic purity, for police in Guatemala City the executions of street children were sacrifices to the social good, and so it went, malignant pride so often leading to the deaths of others. Hernán had joked to his mother, that when leaders lose their heads, people lose theirs. His mother had laughed. God, he missed her.

Hernán headed for the building, wondering if Ward, Nora, and the other Americans understood the significance of their fates. If the U.S. government made offerings to Agent Orange, it did not surprise Hernán to find himself, Miguel, Juanita, and Ernez here. The four of them were not supposed to be in America. No one would know they were missing for quite some time, with the possible exception of Ernez, who had been here for a while already. They were easy sacrifices. What did it say that America also offered its own?

A strange wagon parked at the front of the building was a fusion of two different pickup truck beds atop a four-wheeled chassis. The axle closest to Hernán was fitted to a contraption hooked to a trailer tongue. The tongue rested on a cinderblock, some sort of harness attached to it. The gate of the front bed hung down. Pieces of wood of various size and length lay inside, but nothing that would make a better weapon than the ball bat. A tarp covered the other bed.

Hernán approached the wagon and recognized the tire treads. He tightened his grip on the bat and rethought this solo venture. Having the entire group along didn't seem like such a bad idea any longer.

At the rear of the wagon, Hernán took a cautious whiff of air. Not a trace of decay or rot. He dipped the bat beneath the tarp and tossed it backward as he beat a hasty retreat. The tarp didn't hide a trap. He approached the bed and looked inside. A huge single-barrel gun, around five to six feet in length, a chain gun usually mounted on a truck or a helicopter. Next to it a crate of huge shells, maybe 33 millimeter. He leaned into the bed and threw the tarp back further. Several old car batteries sat atop a piece of plywood behind the gun. Two spools of electrical wire were next to the plywood and some sort of gutted black control box.

Hernán propped the bat against the wagon and grabbed the barrel of the gun. It took a lot of effort to slide the thing. It easily weighed over a hundred pounds. Worse, it didn't have an obvious trigger mechanism.

Taking a deep breath, Hernán backed away from the wagon. He hadn't been here five minutes and found a military-grade chain gun with ammo. In his estimation, the odds of finding a useable gun just skyrocketed. Unfortunately, so did the odds of encountering Agent Orange. The wagon seemed to be his or, at least, his at one time. The wagon could be a relic of one of Orange's past lives, forgotten upon resurrection. In the 90s he'd figured out how to get past the walls, but hadn't done it since so maybe he forgot things after death.

Hernán swallowed. This could also be a thing from Agent Orange's *current* life.

If so . . . he looked at the bat—and knew he needed a better offensive weapon.

The entrance was on the left side of the wall facing the firing range. The solid wooden door and the large picture window next to it had no signs or stencils to indicate a shop of any kind, but the black iron security bars on the other side of the glass seemed to prove this was the gun shop.

Hernán put the side of his sweaty palm against the window. Inside were display cases. The outline of a cash register.

Bullet holes too numerous to count studded the walls all around the oddly unharmed window and door. When there were windows in Morgan still intact, they were cloudy with decades of dirt and filth. Not this one, clean and transparent. It reminded him of the tale of the live flowers found in Morgan. This was truly a place of strange and useless miracles.

His back to the wall, Hernán passed the bat to his left hand and took hold of the doorknob with his right. For the second time he whispered a little prayer to spare his right arm. Unlike opening the car trunk, this time he at least had a wall to hide behind. He twisted the knob. It turned. He took a deep breath. With a quick thrust, he pushed the door with the end cap of the bat and jerked his arm out of the way.

A bell rang.

He sucked a breath of air, but nothing happened. Angling his head, he looked at the top of the doorway and saw a shop bell. No traps.

Hernán looked through the doorway to a dimly lit room. He pushed the door wider with the tip of the bat. The security bars cast long, thin shadows along the floor, display cases, and wall. The doorway didn't have a tripwire so Hernán took a step inside. The shop felt warmer inside than out and it had a smell he couldn't place, a smell like something scorched, something sulfurous.

He scanned the display cases. Completely empty. The lack of useful miracles continued.

Hundreds of holes dotted the wooden wall behind the counter, a wall stripped of all signs, posters, pictures, calendars, or display weapons. The cash register had taken several bullet hits. There were no glass panels on the display cases, but neither were there shards of shattered glass anywhere. Someone had cleaned the debris. Maybe the shoot-out happened before the official closing of Morgan. Maybe the shop owner took steps to renovate for a reopening that never came. Cleaning did not seem like the work of the Kill Zone's resident decapitator.

The size of the room only accounted for a quarter of the building's size so Hernán crossed the shop to a doorway on the far right of the business counter. Maybe he could find something in the stockroom.

A wooden panel to bridge the counter to the opposite wall stood upright, opening access to the business area behind the counter. Directly ahead the closed door of the stockroom, another trap opportunity. Hernán found no tripwires when he stretched out and swept the bat along the floor, so continued to the stockroom door. He cast a glance to his left. Dark alcoves and drawers beneath the counter might have something useful, but sticking a hand into those dark spaces could wait until he exhausted all other possibilities.

Solid, free of holes, and of a color that didn't match the wall around it, the stockroom door hung thick and heavy. He turned the knob, pushed with the bat, and jumped behind the counter as the door swung into the dimly lit stockroom. Nothing came through the doorway except more heat and a stronger stench of sulfur. He imagined a long stairwell descending deep within the earth, the place Agent Orange emerged every time he returned from hell.

In the center of the large room, rectangular shafts of light descended through two cloudy skylights. Hernán slowly stepped into the room, letting his eyes adjust. Everything outside the direct light dissolved into increasingly darker shades of grey. He took baby steps, swinging the bat above the floor to test for wires, hoping he only tripped something out of range. Each step became a risk of life and limb.

Thick beams of timber spread haphazardly through the open floor space held up the roof. The illumination through the skylight revealed a tree trunk half a foot in diameter Ovals of shorn branches dotted the surface of the makeshift support.

Along the right wall thin slivers of outside light bled through the cracks in a set of double doors. Hernán took a few more cautious steps.

Slowly things outside the skylights took shape. Several tables were scattered throughout the large room. Scraps of metal strewn across the first table caught Hernán's eye. Among the pieces of iron and steel were old blades of varying length, most without handles, but nestled among them he saw the large grip of a substantial weapon. He pulled it from the pile. A machete with only a third of its blade, the rest lost in a clean break. He put it down and grabbed another hilt. The six-inch blade of a knife jutted at a thirty-degree angle, bent and dull to the touch. He found several more handles, all with broken or missing blades. Nothing on the table was of more use than the bat.

Hernán crept beneath the first skylight, shielding his eyes with his left hand to better see the contents of second and third tables. More scrap metal, including an iron gate.

About to move on, his eyes bulged at a familiar shape from hundreds of war movies. He grabbed the M-16, only belatedly giving any thought to a trap. He detached the magazine. Empty. Should he take it in case they came across ammunition later? Or maybe as a deterrent? With this in his possession, would Agent Orange think twice about attacking the group?

He held the rifle in the light. Near the flash suppressor, a bent barrel rendered it useless even as a scare tactic. Reluctant to give up this find, Hernán wedged the barrel against the concrete floor and put the weight of his foot against it. A futile gesture. He discarded the rifle.

Hernán could finally see the back of the room, albeit dimly. Two furnaces explained the scrap metal as well as the chimneys jutting from the roof. A thick stovepipe rose through the ceiling on the left and the one on the right had a flue of creek stone construction rising from the firebox. In front of the leftmost one, he recognized the shape of an anvil. From the ceiling hung tongs, long fire pokers, and flat objects of varying length and thickness, maybe blades. The pokers or blades might make good weapons if he couldn't find a gun.

As he neared the left forge, shadows took form in the dull light. A variety of tongs and hammers with heads of different shapes hung from metal rings embedded in the creek stone. One hammer rested next to the anvil atop a large, round rock. Hernán put his left hand on the anvil's cool surface and tried to move it, but it didn't budge. The blacksmith had anchored it to the boulder.

Heat radiated from the hearth. Hernán pushed the tip of the bat against the coal. He uncovered a glowing ember. Another push of the bat uncovered half a dozen more glows. A wave of heat struck his stunned face—someone recently used the forge!

Quickly withdrawing the bat, he backpedaled and bumped the anvil. The back of his head tapped something hanging from the ceiling. A grip-less machete blade dangled from a hook. As he reached for it, something moved to the left of the forge. A shadow low to the floor rose haltingly. Hernán froze, trying to make sense of this strange movement.

His hand tensed on the bat.

The shadow rose higher and higher. His mind made the connection only when the shadow became a hulking grey form—a god rising from the underworld.

Twin flashes of orange ember light flared in gasmask lenses like hellfire.

Hernán abandoned the machete and fled with an involuntary scream. He raced for the oblong rectangle of light on the other side of the room where the gun shop lobby beckoned. He took five strides toward the exit before a cacophony of shifting metal and screeching table legs made him duck. A table lurched into the light and slammed a support beam. Metal clattered across the floor. The timber shivered from the onslaught. Dust fell from the ceiling like the last sand through an hourglass.

His escape cut off and the heavy thud of boots closing behind him, he spun in a surprise attack. The ball bat in his right hand swung forward with all the force his whirling body could muster.

The shadowy figure lurched into the light with his own one-armed swing. A solid blow struck Hernán's right bicep and momentum sent the bat flying. Nerve endings screamed contradictory signals of frigid cold and sizzling heat. Strangely, the thing flying through the air separated into two pieces. The long, thin form of the bat struck the hanging chains and ricocheted with a metal rattle. The shorter, bulkier form landed with a crunch on the hearth, sending tiny embers swirling into the air. Panicked at the sudden realization he had lost his arm and must save it, Hernán lurched toward the hearth.

The shirtsleeve burst into flames. The fire engulfed the piece of Hernán like a burnt offering to an angry god.

In desperate motion toward the forge, Hernán felt a kick in his backside that sent him airborne. An audible crack at the bottom of his spine reverberated all the way to his cervical vertebrae, snapping his head backward. He smashed through the hanging metal and left it jangling in his wake like wind chimes. His outstretched left arm broke his fall as he struck the forge just short of his burning right arm. Bizarrely, incongruously, he reached for the flaming appendage with his stump before crashing to the floor.

He gasped for air. The noxious scent of burnt hair and bubbling flesh choked him.

Hernán scrambled to his feet, but lost control of his legs and fell to his knees. He threw his left hand atop the anvil to compensate for his faltering legs and tried to pull himself off the floor. Sharp needles jabbed his legs from hip to foot, or foot to hip, he couldn't tell, the reverberation bounced back and forth so rapidly.

He looked over his shoulder to gauge how much time he had left. Goggle lenses reflected the flames of Hernán's small sacrifice. A downward swing briefly eclipsed those twin flames. The hammer struck his hand hard enough to ping the anvil beneath. Blood and debris smacked Hernán in the face and sizzled across the hearth. The agony of a smashed hand somehow flared more brightly in his brain than the loss of an arm. He screamed. His hand flopped at the end of his wrist like a piece of rubber, split in half. His ring finger stayed on the anvil.

Another scream caught in his throat when Agent Orange grabbed him by the neck. Rising through the air, Hernán tried to kick the angry god, but landed only feeble blows. He had no idea how much blood he'd shed through the severed stump of his arm, only that he heard it dripping on the floor, little spatters he almost mistook for a leak in the roof.

Pain flared on both sides of Hernán's head when the killer hooked him to the ceiling chains. The hand at his throat went away. Gravity did its work and the weight of his body pushed the hooks into the flesh beneath his jaws.

Suspended in the air, Hernán rotated toward the forge, his lost arm a shriveled conflagration. Smoke billowed into the stovepipe. Left hand throbbing, legs tingling, right arm remnant aching, his head on fire at either side, Hernán kicked helplessly, but it only bounced him on the chains. The hooks sunk deeper. Orange tugged down on the waistband of his pants, and the hooks erupted through the back of Hernán's tongue. Air sucked through clenched teeth could not quench the inferno in his throat. He swallowed gouts of blood.

He rotated toward his executioner. The fire-lit gasmask shifted. Agent Orange became the dog-headed man, here to claim his sacrifice. Xoloti swung his blade. Every pain below the neck fell away. Hernán's head, shorn of the weight of his body, bobbed high into the air before chains arrested the inevitable fall.

The dog-headed man stood before him, statuesque, unmoving. Curiously, Hernán heard a crashing ocean wave, louder and louder and louder still, endlessly rising as the dog head faded into the bright, rectangular box of a distant doorway to somewhere safer, somewhere better, somewhere painless. His smiling mother beckoned.

Hernán found he could run again.

TYPHON MITIGATION EFFORT REPORT
2 APRIL 2014

After Action Summary Group B

Supervised Physical Distribution
Only—Sensitivity 10

Wyngarde, P
12-04-2014

TYPHON MITIGATION EFFORT REPORT 2 APRIL 2014

After Action Summary Group B

For reasons unknown, on Thirty March 2014 the Typhon Energy Signature (TES) began to spike to dangerous levels, which continued to increase in the days following. On Two April a mitigation effort was deemed necessary. All factors indicated a two-Group insertion of eight plus eleven the optimal remedial action. On Four April at 1203Q Group B activated in Morgan Falls Lodge while Typhon pursued the remnant of Group A near Morgan (see Typhon Mitigation Effort Report 1 April 2014: After Action Summary Group A). Weather conditions for the day were mostly clear with a temperature low of 65° at 0105Q and a high of 74° at 1340Q, with Electromagnetic Events ranging from a low of Grade 3 to a high of Grade 5. The Grade 4 escalation at 1655Q disrupted TES readings. The escalation to Grade 5 circa 2345Q disrupted verification of Typhon dormancy, reduced range of gastric trackers, nullified RFID signatures, and hampered surveillance flights (see Typhon Mitigation April 2014 Climate Conditions Report). Typhon encountered Group B beginning 1348Q in six unique engagements culminating with a circa 2300-2345Q engagement that led to the dormancy of Typhon, a prolonged Grade 5 Electromagnetic Event (EE) and an ongoing Level 5 Security Disruption (see Subject B040414-11 Security Disruption Report April 2014). Field agents McKern, L. and Nesbitt, D. oversaw Group B Post-operations (see Nesbitt, D. Fatal Accident Report, 06 April, 2014),

Group B Engagement 1

At 1348Q, Typhon engaged an intact Group B on the grounds of the Morgan Falls Lodge insertion hub and dispatched subjects B040414-01 and B040414-02 in the predicted order. Squad 2 recovered all six components and both gastric trackers by Five April, 0208Q. At this time, Squad 2 also recovered the discarded gastric tracker of subject B040414-05 at the Morgan Falls Lodge location.

Damage sustained to subjects B040414-01 and B040414-02 is rated severe with multiple amputations. Scavengers removed some parts from the scene prior to recovery operation. Both subjects have decapitations with auricle excisions.-Reintroduction options are under evaluation.

Group B Engagement 2

Following Engagement 1, the remaining subjects fled via Morgan Falls Lodge Drive to Morgan Lake Boulevard where Typhon engaged them at 3412 Morgan Lake Boulevard. The TES readings indicate Engagement 2 occurred circa 1723Q. The Exclusion Zone began experiencing a Grade 4 EE at 1655Q hampering efforts to pinpoint TES spikes and attempts at location tracking. Typhon dispatched subjects B040414-06 and B040414-08 outside the predicted order and beyond acceptable tolerance level. Squad 3 recovered all six components and both gastric trackers by Five April, 0517Q.

Group B subjects constructed incendiary devices in the lower level of 3412 Morgan Lake Boulevard. Remaining subjects used one incendiary device during Engagement 5.

Damage sustained to subjects B040414-06 and B040414-08 was within tolerance for the planned reintroduction scenario. Both subjects were reintroduced along with subject B040414-07 one mile from Malcasa Point, California on Five April, 2314T. Monitoring of local law enforcement indicates a successful reintroduction via simulated auto accident with fire.

McKern's opinion is the presence of subject B040414-10 introduced operational anomalies that disrupted the integrity of the operation (See Subject B040414-10 Operational Integrity Disruption Report April 2014). Manifestations of this disruption became apparent beginning with Engagement 2.

Anomaly 1: At 3412 Morgan Lake Boulevard location, subjects replaced insertion clothing beyond normal tolerance level. Squad 3 collected and incinerated the insertion clothing discarded at the 3412 Morgan Lake Boulevard location. Anomaly attributed to B040414-10.

Anomaly 2: Analysis at the scene indicates subjects B040414-03 andB040414-04 stayed with Group B longer than predicted, accounting for dispatch outside the predicted sequence. Anomaly reason unknown.

Anomaly 3: Deterioration of subject B040414-05 did not fall within expected parameters, accounting for dispatch outside the predicted sequence and the eventual discarding of the gastric tracker.

TYPHON MITIGATION EFFORT REPORT

Group B Engagement 3

With Engagement 2 Group B dispersed into three to four smaller clusters. Typhon dispatched subjects B040414-03 andB040414-04 in the Morgan Lake cove bordering the properties of 3412, 3414, and 3418 Morgan Lake Boulevard. Engagement 3 occurred at roughly 1750Q. Squad 3 recovered five components and both gastric trackers by Five April, 0227Q. Squad 1 recovered B040414-03 component 1 on Five April, 1840Q on the shore of Lake Morgan.

Damage sustained to B040414-03 andB040414-04 was within tolerance for the planned reintroduction scenario, with modifications. Both subjects were reintroduced outside of Knoxville, Tennessee on Seven April, 0320Q. Monitoring of Memphis and Knoxville law enforcement indicates a successful reintroduction via suspicious auto accident with fire. Interagency partnership has introduced the expected inefficiencies of process. Police agencies are pursuing the desired drug-related murder/revenge scenario. Monitoring is ongoing.

Group B Pre-Engagement 4 Activities

Surveillance at Morgan Falls Lodge indicates Group A subject A040414-08 arrived at the Morgan Falls Lodge at 1810Q. Upon departing at 1824Q, subject A040414-08 linked to subjects B040414-07, B040414-10, and B040414-11. At 1830Q subjects B040414-05 and B040414-09 arrived. Subject B040515-05 passed the gastric tracker unnoticed in a men's bathroom stall. At 1906Q subjects A040414-08, B040414-05, and B040414-09 departed Morgan Falls Lodge. Subjects B040414-07, B040414-10, and B040414-11 began a fire in the Lodge's elevator shaft that drew Typhon to the Lodge at 1936Q. Subjects B040414-07, B040414-10, and B040414-11 departed for Morgan at 1925Q.

Anomaly 4: Audio surveillance at the Morgan Falls Lodge insertion hub indicates subject B040414-10 knew about the active elevator system and its use in subject placement. B040414-10 set fire to furniture placed in the elevator shaft. It is McKern's opinion B040414-10 deduced the functionality of Morgan Falls Lodge based on situational awareness.

Anomaly 5: TES readings at 1147Q indicated Typhon probably encountered subject A040414-08 northwest of Morgan but did not dispatch. It is McKern's opinion Typhon entered Stalk mode, leading to the dispatch of A040414-08 outside predicted sequence.

TYPHON MITIGATION EFFORT REPORT

Group B Engagement 4

Typhon engaged subjects A040414-08, B040414-05, and B040414-09 near Morgan Falls Parkway circa 2030Q. Squad 2 recovered all nine components and two gastric trackers by Five April, 0418Q.

Damage sustained to subjects A040414-08 and B040414-05 are rated severe. Both subjects are decapitated with auricles removed.-Reintroduction options are under evaluation.
Damage sustained to subject B040414-09 was moderate, some of it self-sustained. Due to the subject's premature expiry, Typhon did not decapitate and left auricles intact. Subject was reintroduced to Bridgeport, Connecticut residence on Five April, 2340Q. Monitoring of local law enforcement indicates a successful reintroduction via home invasion/murder scenario upon discovery Six April, 1324Q. Monitoring is ongoing.

Group B Engagement 5

Typhon engaged subjects B040414-07, B040414-10, and B040414-11 at Kendall's Grocery in downtown Morgan, circa 2245Q. Items recovered at the scene in addition to a Typhon damage assessment indicate the subjects found a weapons cache. Additionally, the subjects utilized a rudimentary shoestring rope system to deploy doorway traps against Typhon. One trap deployed successfully. An incendiary device detonated prematurely or Typhon deflected it. Despite the multiple injuries sustained by Typhon in this encounter, Typhon dispatched subjects B040414-07 and B040414-10. Squad 1 recovered all six components and two gastric trackers by Five April, 0235Q. Squad 1 discovered the subject B040414-10 gastric tracker discarded in a toilet in the Morgan Hardware Store.

Damage sustained to subject B040414-07 was within tolerance for the planned reintroduction scenario. The subject was reintroduced along with subjects B040414-06 and B040414-08 one mile from Malcasa Point, California on Five April, 2314T. Monitoring of local law enforcement indicates a successful reintroduction via simulated auto accident with mutilation following vehicular ejection.

As per directives, subject B040414-10 was incinerated onsite.

Anomaly 6: Subjects B040414-07, B040414-10, and B040414-11 retained no insertion clothing. Black light examination led to recovery of insertion clothing left at the Engagement 5 scene. Squad 1 incinerated all insertion clothing.

Anomaly 7: Subject B040414-10 acquired a decades old bottle of magnesium citrate and used it to force the expulsion of the gastric tracker. McKern attributes the knowledge of the gastric tracker to situational awareness.

Anomaly 8: Squad 1 found a notepad with the identities of seven of the Group B subjects and some of their cities of origin in the pocket of subject B040414-10. This necessitated a door-to-door search of Morgan buildings where three such documents were recovered with the heading "April 2014 Dunbar Sacrifices." Precautionary door-to-door searches conducted throughout the Morgan Lake Boulevard area on Five April recovered two more documents in rooms of 3412 Morgan Lake Boulevard and a third in a corked bottle. A thorough search of Morgan Lake on Five and Six April found no bottled messages. One further message was discovered on the counter of the Morgan Falls Lodge.

Group B Engagement 6

Typhon engaged subject B040414-11 at the Owl Creek Department Store circa 2300-2345Q. Due to the damage sustained in Engagement 5, Typhon was unable to dispatch the subject. Subject B040414-11 decapitated Typhon and left the scene with a crossbow, with any weapons in Typhon's possession, and with his gasmask. Due to the absence of any tracking devices at the Owl Creek scene, Squad 1 did not discover the dormant Typhon until 0311Q. At 0318Q, Squad 1 recovered a crossbow bolt behind the store with the blood of B040414-11, indicating Typhon wounded the subject.

At 2345Q the TES dropped to zero and a Grade 5 EE began. Due to the onset of the Grade 5 EE, verification of the TES change took 36 minutes. The cleanup operation began on Five April, 0016Q.

Following a thorough examination, Squad 1 incinerated Typhon as per protocol.

Anomaly 9: Subject B040414-11 appears to have actively avoided discovery following the events of Four April. Given the actions of subject B040414-10, McKern believes B040414-11 carried out a pre-planned action based on directives from B04040414-10.

Subject B040414-11 Post-Engagement Summary

For the detailed report see Subject

TYPHON MITIGATION EFFORT REPORT

B040414-11 Security Disruption Report
April 2014.

Four April: Prior to Engagement 6 subject B040414-11 replaced entire insertion wardrobe, nullifying black light tracking. Grade 5 EE nullified local RFID tracking and reduced the detection range of the gastric tracker. Grade 5 EE delayed Squad 1 deployment, giving subject B040414-11 36 minutes to evacuate Morgan unmolested. At this time, non-dispatch of B040414-11 was unknown to Squad 1.

Five April: Squad 1's sporadic detection of the discarded subject B040414-10 gastric tracker was falsely presumed to be the presence of another dispatched subject, allowing B040414-11 more time to distance from Morgan. Confirmation of the non-dispatch of B040414-11 occurred when Squad 1 swept the Owl Creek scene at 0322Q.

The search for the messages seeded by subject B040414-10 diverted valuable resources from the search for B040414-11.

At 1500Q, the U.S. Army, unaware of ongoing operations, began pressure to reduce the Exclusion Zone status from red to yellow.

Six April: Nesbitt and Squad 2 recovered the discarded B04040414-11 gastric tracker a half-mile southwest of the Morgan Lake Marina at 0726Q, The Grade 5 EE continued to hamper field communication and it was misunderstood as recovery of the entirety of subject B0404014-11. The miscommunication went uncorrected until 0820Q when a Typhon IED destroyed the HMMWV used by Nesbitt, by which time the U.S. Army lowered the Exclusion Zone status to yellow and began standard Typhon dormancy operations.

At 1900Q, the U.S. Army agreed to Exclusion Zone status orange based on a terror threat narrative, but continued in-Zone operations. As a precaution, field agents were embedded. The escalation to orange status enabled the continued deployment of local law enforcement agencies on the Exclusion Zone exterior.

The Grade 5 EE slipped to a Grade 4 EE by 2030Q.

Seven April: At 0850Q, the U.S. Army agreed to Exclusion Zone status red based on a revised terror threat narrative with CIA and Department of Homeland Security support. However, the U.S. Army saw no reason to discontinue Typhon dormancy operations inside the Exclusion Zone.

Eight April: The final subject B040414-11 RFID readings occurred at 1940Q in downtown Sandalwood. The Grade 4 EE slipped to a Grade 3 EE by 2317Q.

Nine April: Expected expiration for subject B040414-11 occurred between 0115 and 0145Q and the Level 5 Security Disruption downgraded to Level 4. Recovery efforts continued through Twelve April but all components remain unaccounted. As a precaution, monitoring continues.

Related Reports

Nesbitt, D. Fatal Accident Report, 06 April, 2014 (Cargill, P.)

Subject B040414-10 Operational Integrity Disruption Report April 2014 (McKern, L.)

Subject B040414-11 Security Disruption Report April 2014 (McKern, L.)

Typhon Mitigation April 2014 Climate Conditions Report (Gordon, C.)

Typhon Mitigation April 2014 Subject Post-Dispatch Examinations (Morris, M.)

Typhon Mitigation April 2014 Subject Procurement Report (Cookson, G.)

Typhon Mitigation April 2014 Subject Reintroduction Analysis [Expected July 2014]

Typhon Mitigation Effort Report 1 April 2014: After Action Summary Group A (Lyons, J.)

[H]ACKNOWLEDGEMENTS

The authors wish to express their gratitude to their test readers for all the invaluable feedback—Kelly Robinson, James Carroll, and Pierce Zirnheld. Thank you to Jarod Barbee, Patrick C Harrison III, and Death's Head Press for this new re-incarnation, and Alex McVey for the morning star cover art.

Thank you to Jeff Burk and Deadite Press for the original version of this book in 2015.

Special recognition goes to Arkady and Boris Strugatsky (RIP), whose influence was vital to this novel. *Reincarnage* also could not exist without the slasher films of the '70s and '80s.

Ryan would like to thank Edward Lee, Lucas Mangum, Chandler Morrison, Kristopher Triana, John Wayne Comunale, Bryan Smith, Ann Laymon, Brian Keene, Christine Morgan, Regina Garza Mitchell, Geoff Cooper, Mike Bracken, Philip LoPresti, Jeremy Wagner, and Brent Zirnheld.

ABOUT THE AUTHORS

Ryan Harding is the three-time Splatterpunk Award-winning author of books like *Genital Grinder* and collaborations with Kristopher Triana *(The Night Stockers)*, Lucas Mangum *(Pandemonium)*, Jason Taverner *(Reincarnage and Reincursion)*, and Edward Lee *(Header 3)*. Upcoming projects include the collection *Transcendental Mutilation* from Death's Head Press, a novel with Bryan Smith, and a Splatter Western.

Jason Taverner is . . .